Beyond This Horizon

David Thompson

Published by Last Passage
www.lastpassage.com

Copyright © 2012 David Thompson

The right of David Thompson to be identified as the Author
of the Work has been asserted by him in accordance with
the Copyright, Designs and Patents Act 1988.

First Published in Great Britain in 2012 by
LAST PASSAGE
www.lastpassage.com

Apart from any use permitted in under UK copyright law, this publication may not be reproduced, stored, or transmitted, in any form, or by any means, without prior permission in writing of the publishers or, in the case of reprographic production, in accordance with the terms of licenses issued by the Copyright Licensing Agency.

Beyond This Horizon is a work of fiction.
Cataloguing in Publication Data is available from the British Library.

ISBN: 978-1-908956-00-2

Typeset in Times by Last Passage Studios, Nottingham UK.
Cover Design and Illustration by d3
www.d3-design.com.

Last Passage Publications,
Nottingham, UK.

GET THE EBOOK VERSION FREE!
SIMPLY EMAIL YOUR PAPERBACK RECEIPT TO
WWW.LASTPASSAGE.COM

Follow David Thompson on Twitter: @StoneSculpt
More information: www.stonesculpt.co.uk

For my brother Peter.

David Thompson

David Thompson is a professional sculptor born in 1939 and brought up in Kirkby Stephen. He attended Appleby Grammar School as a boarder with his two older brothers. He studied at Carlisle College of Art, specializing in sculpture, followed by three years as a postgraduate student at The Slade School of Fine Art, part of University College, London.

His career includes numerous solo and group exhibitions, public and private commissions, with eleven years of unbroken exhibiting activity in the Royal Academy Summer Exhibition. David became a full time tutor in the sculpture department at The Kent Institute of Art and Design in Canterbury in 1970 and took early retirement as a senior lecturer in 1989 in order to concentrate upon his own work. His chosen material is stone. Twelve years ago he moved to Nottinghamshire after living in and around Canterbury for almost 30 years. He is married to Rebecca, a primary school teacher, and they have two sons. David has three children from a previous marriage.

'Beyond This Horizon' is his first novel. A sequel to this book is planned which will take the central character, Thomas Arthur Taylor, to active service as an army captain, just in time to participate in the bloody battle for Hong Kong and suffer almost four years as a POW under the Japanese. Problems await him on his return to Cumbria. This book will be called, 'An Inherited Voice'.

BEYOND THIS HORIZON

Photograph by Lucinda Peranic

FROM OLD WESTMORLAND

How often has our common rural clay disclosed pure gold to glorify the day?

In this high limestone locality keen winds surge in to smudge crag tops with cloud, rains sluicing cold down heedless Pennine slopes to swell the stony Eden's early course.

A spartan landscape, bones close to the skin, its modest fell farms and their native stock cling fast to hard-won acres made fertile only through lifetimes spent in dogged toil.

From such exacting territory springs a stubborn crop of strong determined folk, reserved yet quietly articulate, their dialect an easy home-grown tune.

Sometimes transformed to richer melody by one whose singularly gifted voice vouchsafes a heartfelt poetry so true that all the wider waiting world responds.

How often has our common rural clay disclosed pure gold to glorify the day?

Brian Campbell

Contents

Chapter	Page
1 – Proof Of Gigantism	11
2 – A Turning Point	16
3 – The Plan	26
4 – The Playgrounds	37
5 – Tracking The Giant	43
6 – The Exam / & Gypsies Gather	48
7 – The Pursuit	54
8 – The Initiation	69
9 – Appleby Horse Fair	95
10 – War Is Declared	103
11 – A New Headmaster	110
12 – The Baritone's Future	122
13 – University College London	133
14 – The Homesick Chimp	139
15 – Meeting Artists	147
16 – Joining The Crowd	155
17 – The First Opera	165
18 – The Eigth Sitting	175
19 – Christmas Vacation	178
20 – Dick's Revelation	191
21 – Christmas Day	198
22 – The Sittings Continue	212
23 – A Surprise Outing	214
24 – An Artist With A Suitably Impressive Reputation	221
25 – The Seduction	228
26 – Shocking Naivety	235
27 – Tat's Injuries Heal	237

Contents (cont'd)

Chapter	Page
28 – An Unforseen Invitation	242
29 – Jazz At The Palladium	247
30 – At Last	256
31 – Calm After The Storm	259
32 – Exploring London	262
33 – Drawing The Band Leader	271
34 – Casting The Portrait	275
35 – The Unveiling	280
36 – An Unexpected Drama	285
37 – Jazz At The Morton Club	298
38 – Unpredicted Largesse	304
39 – Jane Visits Fell End	310
40 – A Chance Meeting At The R.A.	329
41 – Assisting Epstein	337
42 – A Shock For Olly	340
43 – Grief	347
44 – The Voice Finds It's Place	353
45 – The Letter	358
46 – The First Rehearsal	360
47 – A Subdued Christmas	362
48 – Discovering Treachery	369
49 – Revenge	373
50 – Welcome Encouragement	379
51 – The Final Rehearsal	383
52 – Good news From Fell End	388
53 – The finishing Touches	392
54 – The Visitors Arrive	394
Acknowledgements	403

PROOF OF GIGANTISM

Bill Fletcher had taken to tramping the lanes around Winton again early in the spring of 1910. It didn't take long for the news to spread that he was back in the neighbourhood. The huge, shambling man would be absent from the area for months on end, and then suddenly reappear. The children at Winton Primary School, twenty-two in number, always became excited when Bill Fletcher returned to their locality. This was hardly surprising as Bill's sheer size set him apart from other adults.

His clothing was bizarre, to say the least. He wore a battered trilby hat, which was tied with discoloured string under his enormous, bristly chin. No one had ever seen him without this. His tattered jacket and trousers were inevitably far too small for him. The sleeves of the former reached to just below his elbows, and the legs of the latter to the middle of his shins. In winter he sometimes wore a ragged overcoat secured around his waist with a length of fence wire. Although the state of the weather seemed to have little effect on Bill, when it was bitterly cold he sometimes wound lengths of old sacking around his lower legs and forearms. The children were especially fascinated, above everything else, by Bill's footwear and his walking stick. Somehow he had procured two lengths of rubber tyre, possibly from a motorcar or lorry, and cut them to fit his huge feet. These were tied with frayed lengths of rope threaded through holes punched in their rims.

Bill's walking stick was nothing less than the branch of a tree. He renewed his stick from time to time by simply tearing a fresh one out of the hedgerows whenever he broke or lost one. He always chose branches with a right angle at or near the top of them to serve as the handle. In spring and summer the various walking sticks sometimes continued to generate new greenery, the only colour to relieve the encrusted drabness of Bill's appearance, for the huge tramp was spectacularly filthy. It was quite possible that he never washed any part of himself from one year's end to the next.

If Bill shambled past the schoolyard while the children were playing, they would all gather at the iron railings to watch him pass, in total dumbstruck silence. Usually, Bill kept his eyes on the road ahead, but if he ever did glance sideways at the staring children, then the more timid ones would shrink back and perhaps burst into tears. Even the bigger boys refrained from catcalling or possibly lobbing the odd handful of grit at the giant, for to them that's what Bill Fletcher was, a huge, filthy, frightening giant.

Tat Taylor and the Machin boys, Allen and Dick, and their cousin Brian, always walked to and from school together. They would wait for one another every morning at eight-thirty where the two farm tracks met. The tracks were stony and deeply rutted with the constant passing of horses and carts. The Taylor's farm was only a few hundred yards from the meeting place. It stood on a wooded knoll fifty feet or so higher than the surrounding fields. Allen, Dick and Brian lived a mile further up the fell-side. Tat and Dick were ten and Allen and Brian eight.

Recently, the boys had devised a game. Whoever arrived first at the rendezvous had to hide from the others, never using the same hiding place more than once. As he was often the first to arrive, Tat quickly introduced his own variation into the game. He would hide some distance from the area that had been agreed upon as the hunting ground and watch the Machin boys arrive and take up their hiding places. Tat would then saunter up and flush the others out with nonchalant ease or creep up on them from unexpected directions and frighten them out of their wits.

After a couple of weeks the game was losing its edge and the original good humour with which the boys engaged in it was turning to argumentative boredom. As they proceeded down the track one particularly sunny spring morning, bickering about Tat's dominance of the game through what the Machins decided was cheating, they reached the point where the whole Eden Valley opened up before them. This spectacular view meant little or nothing to the boys so inured were they to their surroundings. They were approaching the lane which led to Winton. Once they joined it they would be no more than ten minutes' walk away from school. Allen suddenly hissed at the squabbling group to shut up and keep still. He pointed ahead, his eyes wide with excitement.

"Bloody hell!" he gasped, "Bill Fletcher's in the lane."

Ducking low, the boys scuttled forward to get a good look at the huge tramp. They hid behind a chestnut tree about twenty-five yards from the lane. Dry stone walls flanked the narrow roadway. Any normal adult walking along it might show the top of their head from time to time. As he moved from right to left, opposite their hiding place, the tramp towered above the stone walls. They all agreed that a normal adult could only have appeared so tall if they had been on horseback.

"A bloody big horse an' all," Brian had added gravely.

As they watched, Bill reached a point where a branch from a Scots Pine grew straight as a die over the road. The boys held their breath as Bill Fletcher ducked his head to pass under it. A few moments later he had shambled out of view.

The boys trotted over to the lane. They jostled each other for position, bickering over which of them should be first to climb the stile cut into the wall. The group stood on the road gazing up in awe at the branch which had caused Bill Fletcher to duck. To them the branch might as well have been twenty feet off the ground. Nonetheless, they agreed that this would provide them with the opportunity to gauge the tramp's height with some accuracy.

By the time they reached the school, which stood by itself upon the village green, the boys had decided how they would measure the distance from the road's surface to the overhanging branch. They would need a length of string with a stone secured to one end of it. This they would toss over the branch while keeping hold of the other end of the string. With care, they ought to be able to lower the pebble to the surface of the road. The weight of the stone would ensure that the string hung straight down like a bricklayer's plumb line. The boys decided to add the final details to their plan at the lunch hour when, after consuming whatever their mothers had packed for them to eat, they would meet together for half an hour in the playground.

Tat was the undisputed champion tree climber at Winton Primary School. He was a complete natural who not only had no fear of heights, but at least as far as tree climbing was concerned, no fear at all. During their playtime the boys quickly agreed that Tat's skills would be needed on the way home after school. Somebody would have to climb the Scots Pine back up the lane and shin out along the protruding branch and mark the string at the appropriate point. Allen, who regarded himself as an accomplished petty thief, offered to steal a piece of blue chalk from the chalk box underneath the black board. This would be the all-important marker. He would relieve the school of a one-foot ruler, to be secretly returned next day, so they could accurately measure the height of the branch. Tat agreed to pinch a suitable length of string from the big ball in the cupboard next to the cloakroom. Luckily, he had his penknife with him, newly sharpened by his brother Michael.

As soon as Miss Hollis, the headmistress at Winton School, released the children at four o'clock the friends quickly gathered up their belongings so as to make a quick exit. Miss Hollis delayed this for an annoying five minutes or so when she called Tat over to give him a sealed envelope addressed to his mother and father. Finally, she concluded by saying, "Give this to your parents as soon as you get home today please, Thomas." Miss Hollis was the only person who called him Thomas. Christened Thomas Arthur Taylor, he was known to everyone as Tat and had been all his short life.

Allen, Dick and Brian heard this brief exchange as they waited for Tat in the cloakroom. Tat knew what he was in for.

"Oh dear me, it's Master Thomas. Do you think we might be allowed to proceed on our way now, Master Thomas?" Dick sneered sarcastically. The other two giggled inanely and swept off their caps and bowed mockingly.

"Oh yes please, Master Thomas, do let us proceed," they piped in stupid voices.

Tat, though inwardly seething at this open onslaught upon his dignity, knew one of his friends would expose a weakness sooner or later which he could exploit in revenge. For now he satisfied himself by tripping Dick up once they were clear of the school and telling Allen and Brian, two years his junior after all, that he would kick their arses and deposit their caps up the Scots Pine if they didn't watch out.

Once they reached the tree, Tat made short work of climbing it. As he worked his way along the protruding branch, he realized that all he needed to do was hang the weighted string down until it reached the road's surface, then mark it appropriately with the chalk which he had put in his pocket. This would have deprived his friends of full participation in the scheme, so he decided not to mention it, although it would have paid them back handsomely for mocking him earlier.

Dick, Allen and Brian looked very small from Tat's vantage point on the branch, especially as they were so foreshortened. Allen called up to him in an exaggerated stage whisper, "Tat, you'd better make sure Bill isn't knocking around; we don't want him catching us."

Tat saw the sense in this and looked in both directions along the lane. It was all clear.

"Come on then Dick," Tat hissed, "let's be having the bloody thing."

Dick drew back his arm and let fly with the stone attached to the string. It whizzed past Tat's head, causing him to duck, and swung to and fro below the branch. The near miss caused Allen and Brian to break into hysterical giggles until Dick cuffed them into silence.

Tat lowered the string until the pebble touched the road and quickly marked it with the piece of blue chalk. He let the string go and the three Machin boys pounced on it.

"Don't bugger the chalk mark up," Tat called with strangled urgency. He scrambled down the tree in double quick time. They stretched the string out tautly on the road whilst Allen produced the 'borrowed' one-foot rule. Each foot was marked along the length of the string. The friends stared at each other in open-mouthed disbelief. The crucial blue mark measured seven feet eight inches from the pebble. Bill Fletcher was a giant all right and they had proved it. They added three more inches to allow for the fact that Bill had ducked to pass under the branch.

A TURNING POINT

Mary Hollis cycled most of the way to Fell End, the Taylors' farm. She was obliged to dismount, however, when she left the tarmac lane and began to climb the rutted track which led directly to the farm itself. It was a beautiful bright spring afternoon. The clouds scudded swiftly across the clear, blue sky sending huge shadows chasing across the fells, followed by patches of luminous sunlight. Curlews wheeled high above Mary's head, calling continuously, and peewits tumbled madly about, attempting to attract her attention so that she wouldn't stray into the vicinity of their nests.

Jack Taylor saw Mary approach from the vantage point of the hill upon which the farm stood. His wife, Ivy, had made him promise to be close to the farmhouse at the time of Mary's arrival. Her letter, which Tat had delivered a couple of days earlier had stated that she would arrive at around four-thirty. It had also stated that she wished to talk to Jack and Ivy about young Tat's future.

Long before Jack had married Ivy and brought her to the farm, he had been sweet on Mary. However, Mary had seen going to Teacher Training College in Lancaster and following a profession as much more important than returning Jack Taylor's affections. These days their paths rarely met, but Jack felt shy in Mary's company. He wasn't looking forward to the next hour or so. Anyway, just how could 'young Tat's future' possibly have anything to do with Mary Hollis? She must know that Tat would be needed on the farm once he'd finished at the council school in Kirkby Stephen. Tat would be fourteen by then, big and strong enough to join his two older brothers on the farm. Jack wanted his three sons by his side, just as he had been by his father's side. This was the way of things as far as Jack Taylor was concerned; it always had been and always would be. Family farms like Fell End depended upon the simple principle of sons following their fathers onto the land. Jack considered himself lucky in having three sons. He'd had two sisters so his father had struggled on until Jack had left school, hiring a succession of farm labourers to help with the heavy work.

Mary entered the farmyard pushing her bicycle which she leant against the big stone water trough. She was flushed with the effort of climbing the knoll. Her hair, which was tied up in a respectable bun at the back, had become loosened by the gusty breeze. Rather than attempt to rearrange this, she removed her hairclip and let her thick brown hair fall free over her shoulders.

"Now then Mary," Jack called, stepping forward a few paces, too shy to approach Mary and shake her hand. He cast about in his mind for something else to say and failed. He began to blush.

"Good afternoon Jack," Mary said breathlessly. She always sensed Jack Taylor's hesitance whenever they ran into each other. Now in Jack's farmyard, on his territory so to speak, Mary had hoped that Jack would be surer of himself. But there he stood, shifting from one foot to the other, unable to meet her gaze for more than a few seconds at a time. Suddenly, Jack yanked his cap off his head. His mother had always insisted that this should be done in the presence of women.

Mary was approaching forty now and by any standards she was a fine-looking woman. Jack couldn't help noticing that she had kept her athletic figure and all that wavy brown hair falling over her shoulders made her look positively girlish. Mary had never married, although plenty of men had tried their luck. None of them had got anywhere, including Jack.

Ivy Taylor appeared at the side door of the farmhouse. She was plumpish and her flowered apron stretched tightly across her ample bosom. Jack glanced across at his wife and couldn't help comparing her with Mary Hollis. He was vaguely ashamed of these thoughts and felt even more awkward in the company of both women at once.

"Come away in, Mary," called Ivy, "I've got a pot of tea mashing and some fruit cake if you fancy some."

Ivy was pleased to see Mary whom she had always liked. Visitors to the farm were few and far between and it gave Ivy great pleasure to get out the best china and bake a cake to give the visit a sense of occasion. She had set the table for tea in the front parlour, not the kitchen where her family took their meals. Ivy rarely got the chance to put on a bit of a fuss, so when an opportunity presented itself she made the most of it.

Mary smiled warmly as she approached Ivy.

"You look well, Ivy," she said as they shook hands. "Did you mention fruit cake? Well lead me to it; I've worked up quite an appetite. I'd forgotten what a climb it is. Isn't it a beautiful day?"

"Aye, it's grand. Come away in and make yourself comfortable. Jack scrape them muddy boots before you come in," she called over her shoulder. "We'll be taking tea in the parlour."

Jack scowled at the prospect of being stuck with the two women in the parlour. He never felt comfortable in there with the piano and little-used furniture. It made him feel awkward and clumsy; he always feared that if he was obliged to eat or drink in there he would be sure to break a piece of Ivy's treasured china or drop food down his waistcoat. He not only scraped the mud off his boots but gave them a going over with the yard brush as well. He followed his wife and Mary Hollis along the stone flagged passage which led past the kitchen, hung his cap on one of the hooks there and cautiously entered the parlour, where the two women were already seated. Ivy was pouring the tea.

Jack was frequently surprised at the way women could talk to each other without any inhibitions. There they were going at it as though they were best friends and saw each other every day. They laughed frequently and used their hands easily to emphasize whatever point they were making. They were totally at ease in each other's company. Jack felt as though he spoiled the atmosphere by joining them, but knew he had to. He lowered himself into a chair at the table and his wife handed him his tea in one of the dreaded china cups. Jack postponed drinking his tea in case he made noisy gulping sounds. The idea of eating Ivy's fruitcake, which he loved, was out of the question; the two women would hear him chewing it for sure. So Jack sat still and silent, wishing he was out with the ewes up the fell-side whilst the light lasted.

After five minutes or so Mary said, "Anyway, can I get down to business? I don't want to be cycling down your track in the dark now do I?" Ivy folded her hands over her bosom and made what

Jack thought was an over eager face at Mary.

"Well," said Mary, "I've taken the trouble to struggle up here today because I think Thomas should continue with his education. I know you will assume that I'm poking my nose in where it's not wanted, but Thomas is a very clever boy and has the most beautiful singing voice. Honestly, I think he could be something in the world if he's given the chance. I'm here today to persuade you to let Thomas carry on at school. I can help to sort it all out if you agree."

Ivy positively swelled at the suggestion. She knew Tat was clever but she'd never heard him sing, not properly anyway. He sang carols at Christmas time quite sweetly, but what was all this about him having 'the most beautiful voice?' What a lovely thing to hear said about her treasure, her Tat.

"What do you have in mind, Mary?" asked Ivy.

"Well, I'm sure Thomas would have no difficulty in taking the open exam for Appleby Grammar School later this year. He could start in September. Believe me, I can quite see him going on to university. Who knows, ten years from now Thomas might be a doctor or a lawyer or even a professional singer."

Mary gave a start as suddenly the outside door banged open and Michael, the second oldest of the Taylor boys clattered noisily down the passage shouting, "Our Dad, our Dad, you've got to come quick!"

A second later he skidded to a halt in the parlour doorway. The unaccustomed sight of his parents taking afternoon tea with a visitor rendered him speechless. His confusion was made worse when he recognized the visitor as his former primary school teacher.

"Good afternoon Michael," Mary said pleasantly. Before Michael could summon up a reply his mother rose from the table and strode purposefully to the doorway to prevent Michael from entering her freshly cleaned and polished parlour.

"Our Michael," she said sternly, "where's your manners? Get that cap off your head; there's a lady present and look at the state of them boots!"

"Sorry Mam," Michael stammered. "How do Miss Hollis, but our Dad's got to come up to the ewes. There's twins, one's out, but the last one is stuck fast. There's nowt else I can do, please Dad, let's be going."

Jack was already on his feet, his tea and cake untouched. He was relieved to be called away to do something practical, something he knew about. Although he had contributed nothing to the conversation, his heart had begun to feel heavy in his chest. After only ten minutes in the company of the two women he knew instinctively that he would have to make do with his two oldest sons on the farm. Deep down he knew that between them Ivy and Mary would get their way.

"Come on then lad," he growled at Michael, "let's see what's going on." Just as he pulled his cap from the peg in the passage he remembered himself in the nick of time. Poking his head around the parlour door he said, "Excuse us Mary, duty calls."

Jack and Michael clattered across the cobbles in the farmyard. At least four sheep dogs ran after them barking excitedly.

Ivy returned to her seat and shaking her head said, "Eh dear, I'm sorry about that Mary, you never know what's going to happen next come lambing time."

"Don't worry Ivy, I know what comes first on the farm."

Pouring more tea for them both, Ivy sighed and said, "I think it's grand what you say about our Tat. But Appleby is twelve miles away. How would he get there in all weathers, poor little mite?"

"Well, they have a significant number of boarders at Appleby. I know the headmaster's wife quite well; she was at Lancaster with me. She looks after the boarding side of the school with a couple of matrons as well as the domestic staff. Why don't you let me make some enquiries, then we can talk again?"

"But surely that must cost, boarding I mean?" Ivy said looking worried.

"Well yes, but I'm sure it won't be much. Come to see me next

Sunday after chapel and I'll make sure I have all the details for you. I'll be able to give you some of my cake; say about two o'clock." Mary stood up, smiling, "Now it really is time I made my way back."

Ivy accompanied Mary across the farmyard to where her bicycle leaned against the stone trough. The light was just fading towards evening.

"Thank you for the tea and cake. I'm sorry to have caught Jack at a bad time"

"Leave Jack to me," Ivy said conspiratorially. "His bark is worse than this bite. I'll make him see sense; in the long run he won't stand in Tat's way. After all, he's got two lads out of three on the farm already. He'll see that those are good odds. Our Jack may be stubborn, but he's not a fool!"

Ivy watched Mary struggling along the rutted track and smiled when she saw her dismount and walk along the verge pushing her bike. Soon Jack and the lads would have to get round to filling in the ruts and potholes, certainly before the back end when the threshing machine came. Ivy felt a current of excitement surging through her; today had been a turning point. Now the battle would begin with Jack, but she knew that he'd give in sooner rather than later. Tat was going to break the mould.

Tat, who had been playing with the dogs outside the big hay barn, saw his father and Michael leave the house and head off towards the field where the ewes had begun lambing a week before. The dogs chased after them both, leaving Tat suddenly alone. He longed to catch up with his father and Michael, but a growing anxiety held him back.

Tat had seen Miss Hollis arrive earlier wheeling her bike up the track into the yard. She must have been in the house at least a quarter of an hour before his brother and father emerged; the latter's face as black as thunder. He was sure he was in for a dressing down. Obviously, Miss Hollis had discovered the missing chalk and string. Allen had been extremely efficient at returning the ruler without drawing attention to himself. The boys had decided to keep the blue chalk stick, and the all-important length of string. So, they had been found out. Miss Hollis was a clever one all right. Not only had she discovered the crime but she also knew he was one of the culprits. No doubt his mother and Miss Hollis were deciding upon how best to punish him at this very moment. Tat decided to lie low and await developments. He took up a spying position in the cart shed which gave him a clear view of the side door of the farmhouse. Tat settled down in the heavy wagon and waited for Miss Hollis to leave.

After what seemed like a lifetime, Tat saw Miss Hollis and his mother leave the house together and stroll over to where Miss Hollis's bike stood. They were laughing and seemed very friendly, as if they didn't have a care in the world. This, plus the fact that they had been closeted in the house for at least an hour, puzzled Tat. Surely any discussion about his collusion with the Machin boys in the theft of school property would only have taken a minute or two at best. Tat wondered whether further misdemeanours concerning himself and the Machins might have been up for discussion. It was all rather worrying. Tat would have to face the music. He knew that; but when and how; that was the problem.

He watched his mother re-enter the farmhouse and waited until Miss Hollis had faded from view as the first hint of dusk gathered across the fields. His mother would be getting the tea on for all of them. They sat down around the big scrubbed table in the kitchen at six o'clock sharp at this time of year, earlier in the winter. Tat hated the idea of receiving his comeuppance in front of his two older brothers so he resolved to seek out his mother immediately and take what was coming. He thought that if his mother had already dealt with him, his father might leave it at that. This had happened before.

Tat climbed down from the cart and reluctantly sauntered across the yard towards the house. He scraped the mud off his boots and once he was in the passage decided to take them off to be on the safe side.

"Is that you, our Tat?" his mother called from the kitchen. "Come away in and help me get the tea on."

"Now then my little treasure," Tat's mother said with what seemed to him to be a particularly radiant smile. "Set out the knives and forks and put this loaf in the middle on the board with the sharp knife. They'll be in in a minute, starving as usual," she added.

Tat, bewildered and relieved in equal measure, did what he was told with unnatural eagerness. His mother watched him, still smiling, and shook her head. Suddenly, the outside door burst open and his two brothers entered the passage. They emerged out of the gloom into the kitchen, bringing the freshness of the cool outdoors with them. Although John and Michael were of average height, to Tat they seemed large and impressive.

"Now then our Tat," said John, the oldest, in his man's voice. Michael passed close to Tat and pretended to throw a punch at him. Tat knew the routine and ducked dramatically. He felt giggles building in his throat but suppressed them. Tat's brothers jostled each other at the stone sink, bickering about which of them should work the water pump. They were noisy and boisterous; their very presence seemed to change the temperature in the kitchen.

"Now you two," Tat's mother said abruptly, "I don't want the floor swabbing right now, thank you very much."

John and Michael tugged a cloth between them as they dried their hands. John asked, "Should I light the lamps, our Mam; we'll all need white sticks afore long?"

"Aye, there's a good lad," said his mother who was selecting eggs from a bowl. The oil lamps created pools of soft light in the kitchen, throwing dark shadows all around the space.

Tat's heart lurched as his father bustled into the passage where he paused for a few seconds, hanging up his jacket and cap. Feeling apprehensive, Tat shrank back a little into the shadows. Was this to be the moment of truth?

"Now then," Tat's father said rubbing his hands together. "I'll have three of them, our Ivy, if you please."

"Bit of ham to go with 'em?" Ivy asked.

Tat's father crossed the kitchen to wash his hands and chatted to the older boys about the lambing. As he dried his hands he spotted

Tat and said, "Now then our Tat, I thought I was going to have the pleasure of your company over at the ewes. Two grand new lambs up there, born about an hour ago. Never mind, you'll see them tomorrow."

Tat came forward to the table to take his place as the kitchen filled with the sound and smell of frying eggs. His father tweaked his ear. Although confused, Tat allowed himself to relax and was happy to let the conversation about the day's work wash over him. His mother served up the ham and eggs noisily. She winked at Tat.

John left to watch the ewes immediately after supper. Michael went to bed the earliest, as he was to relieve John in three hours or so. Tat was next, after he had washed his hands, face and neck. His mother always gave him a quick inspection before he took his candle and went up the dark, creaking staircase to the bedroom he shared with Michael. His brother was sound asleep, snoring softly. Tat undressed and put on his faded, striped nightshirt, an old one of John's, first cut down for Michael and now for him. He snuffed out the candle and snuggled down into the yielding mustiness of his bed.

Tat enjoyed the initial chill of the bed, knowing that he would soon be warm and comfortable. The winter had seemed as though it would never end; bedtime then had been an ordeal to be dreaded and endured. There was still a deal of snow on the tops. Now he had spring and summer to look forward to. He and the Machin boys intended to spy on Bill Fletcher and in particular find out where he spent the nights. This had always been a mystery.

Another mystery was just why had Miss Hollis visited his home? If not to report her suspicions about his involvement in the theft of chalk and string, then why had she made the visit at all? He decided that to be on the safe side he would persuade Dick to get rid of the blue chalk stick, for it was he who had kept it. For his part, he would hide the length of string marked with blue chalk in one of his most secret hiding places in the big hay barn. After all, this was the all-important proof of Bill Fletcher's gigantism. He decided that the best place would be behind a loose stone in the wall where he had already hidden some other treasures. He'd do it tomorrow, choosing a moment when no one was around.

Tat began to drift into the delicious, drowsy stage just before the onset of sleep. He was aware of the distant baaing of the ewes over in the lambing pasture. His big brother John would be up there now with his twelve-bore watching for foxes and any new births. Tat could imagine him rolling one of his thin, untidy cigarettes prior to lighting it. He felt he could see the flare of the match and smell the sulphur. Just as Tat slipped away Michael farted loudly in his sleep. Tat was convulsed with giggles and had to bite his sheet to stop laughing out loud. He had begun to recognize notes in an instinctive sort of way. He reckoned Michael had farted in B flat.

THE PLAN

The subject of Tat's possible entry into Appleby Grammar School was simply not mentioned in the few days following Mary Hollis's visit to Fell End. The idea hovered in the air surrounding Jack and Ivy Taylor but didn't take concrete form. Ivy made her plans secretly; she knew that when she confronted Jack over Tat's future, she would stand the best chance of winning Jack over if she had a practical strategy, something which Jack would find it difficult to oppose.

Ivy's mother, Jane Watson, was a widow. She ran the Black Bull, a thriving public house on the main street in Kirkby Stephen, which also took in lodgers. Some of these were unattached young men who had full time employment in the town. There were two bank clerks and a schoolteacher, as well as a young mechanic who worked on the railway. Others came and went, mostly commercial travellers passing through doing their rounds. Mrs Watson's husband had built up the business with herself mostly behind the scenes. After her husband's death from a heart attack seven years previously, nobody had expected her to step forward and take over the Black Bull. This is precisely what she had done, however, making a huge success of the enterprise. She employed six staff and was a woman to be reckoned with.

Ivy was her only child and when she left school at fourteen began working for her mother. She did a bit of everything in the kitchen, cleaning and laundry work, waiting at table and eventually serving in the bar. Ivy loved it all. It meant she was continuously in the swim of things, meeting people of all different types and age groups. Although she was not conventionally pretty, Ivy was striking. She had a mass of dark red hair, which was usually piled up and pinned skilfully in place. Her figure was decidedly voluptuous, which eventually caused her to be the main attraction at the Black Bull. Many of the young men who frequented the place lusted after her. She handled this with a light touch until Jack Taylor came along. They had fallen for each other hook, line and sinker.

Mrs Watson, although sorry to lose her main support in running the Black Bull, saw that there was no point in standing in the way of the young couple. They obviously adored each other and, as Jack Taylor would eventually take over the family farm, a secure future for her daughter was more or less guaranteed. All in all, it had turned out very satisfactorily.

Of her three grandchildren, John, Michael and young Tat, it was the last upon whom she doted. There was something about him which had appealed to her from the outset. As a baby, Tat was so beautifully rounded and placid that Mrs Watson would find any excuse to take him off Ivy's hands. He was simply irresistible. Her initial affection for Tat never faltered and she made no secret of the fact that out of the three boys Tat was her favourite.

During the week before Ivy was due to take tea with Mary Hollis she visited her mother. She chose the mid-afternoon when there was something of a lull at the Black Bull. She walked the two miles into Kirkby Stephen which gave her ample time to prepare her case.

"Come away in, Ivy," her mother said embracing her daughter warmly. As they made their way to Mrs Watson's private sitting room at the back of the building, Ivy became conscious of all the familiar smells of the place. The two women chatted easily about the pub. Ivy's mother had recently taken on a new lad to help look after the horses, although just as many motorcars were currently taking up spaces in the stables. Ivy was surprised when her mother suggested that she was thinking of buying one herself, as the new lad was a very keen driver.

She said, "We'll be able to go off all over the county. I bet young Tat would love that."

Ivy saw her opening. "Mother," she said, "Mary Hollis came to see us a few days ago. She says that our Tat is very clever and should go on with his studies at school. She thinks he could easily pass for the Grammar School at Appleby and could make something of himself. I've come over today to see what you think about it all."

"Well I never," said Mrs Watson, "whatever next? Never mind what I think our Ivy, what does Jack think? He'll not be keen if I know owt about it. He'll want Tat on the farm."

"Well," Ivy said hesitantly, "to be honest we haven't really talked about it yet. I don't think Jack will stand in Tat's way if he can see the benefit. I wanted to talk to you first."

"Well you know Jack better than me, our Ivy. But surely a farmer who's lucky enough to have three lads as bairns, well, I mean…"

"Aye I know, but just think about it Mother, I mean Tat might become a doctor or a lawyer. Aye and Mary says he's got a beautiful singing voice, not that I've heard him sing that much, the little pet. Honestly, Mother, Mary Hollis thinks our Tat is special, out of the ordinary." Ivy stopped, realizing that she was running out of breath in her excitement.

"Aye well, he'll get his singing voice from my father no doubt. Lord above, he could make the windows rattle, our Dad. Proper man he was," Mrs Watson said wistfully.

"The thing is," Ivy went on, "Tat could take the exam this summer and start at the Grammar School this back end."

"That's a bit quick off the mark isn't it?" said Mrs Watson, raising her eyebrows. "Anyway, never minds all that, how on earth would little Tat get to and from Appleby every day? Have you thought of that? I don't think he's even been to Appleby, has he?"

Ivy knew that she had reached the highest hurdle. She drew in her breath and said, "Mary Hollis says that Tat could be a boarder at Appleby, stop over like and come home in the holidays. Lots of lads do it, she says."

"You mean leave Fell End at, what is he, ten?" Mrs Watson said aghast, "He's nowt but a bairn. It would break his little heart, our Ivy. What are you thinking of?"

Ivy said, "Well Mother, Tat is eleven in May. That's why it's quick, as you call it. Lads start at the Grammar School at eleven, just like the lasses do here in Kirkby Stephen. Lots of them are boarders, just over the street."

Mrs Watson got up and yelled down the passage to the kitchen, "Clarrie bring us a pot of tea and some shortcake will you?"

Ivy knew she was playing a trump card. Her mother had always expressed an admiration for the lasses at Kirkby Stephen Girls' Grammar School. She had watched them come and go from the big grey stone building just up the main street which was where about fifty of them boarded. She knew Dora Walsh, a woman she had grown up with, and who was the head cook at the school boarding house, and liked her. She liked the black gymslips and soft grey blazers the girls wore.

She frequently said that those lasses had style; they'd go places some of them. She'd noticed that, when the parents came to fetch their girls at the end of term, they frequented the King's Arms, a proper hotel where the maids wore black uniforms with starched white aprons. Not many of them used the Black Bull; that she did notice.

By the time the teapot was empty and only a few crumbs were left on their plates, Mrs Watson had taken charge, as Ivy reckoned she would. Ivy was to find out all the particulars from Mary Hollis, who herself had been a pupil at the Girls' Grammar School, Mrs Watson remembered with a bit of prompting from Ivy. She should find out what the cost would be for Tat to board at Appleby, how much the uniform would be and anything else for that matter. She would pay. After all she could afford it and wasn't Tat her little treasure? Nothing was too good for our Tat.

As Ivy walked back to Fell End to get the tea on she was satisfied that the main part of her plan had fallen into place. Jack might go on a bit about her mother interfering, but he was enough of a businessman not to look a gift horse in the mouth. Ivy decided she would postpone talking to Tat, as yet blissfully ignorant of his immediate future, until she had visited Mary Hollis on the coming Sunday. She would go to chapel in Winton first.

Ivy had never been to Mary's house before. She knew the schoolteacher lived with her mother who had suffered a stroke some years ago. The house was a detached stone-built affair with a neat front garden on one side of Winton green, a mere stone's throw from the school. Ivy realized she felt vaguely nervous as she knocked at the Oxford blue front door.

"Ivy, how nice to see you, come in," Mary said pleasantly on opening the door. She led the way into an elegant sitting room where a fire crackled in the grate. Mary's mother sat in a wingback armchair with a rug across her knees. She was rather hunched but pleasant in appearance; her grey hair neatly pulled back into a bun. She smiled and nodded as Mary introduced her to Ivy, but didn't speak. Ivy took in the discreet antique furniture and attractive paintings; very tasteful, she thought rather enviously.

Mary asked Ivy if she wouldn't mind helping her bring in the tea things and when they were bustling about in the kitchen, which Ivy thought very up to date, Mary said, "My mother can't really speak since her stroke, poor dear, but she loves having company. Now then, I think that's everything, I'll take the tea tray if you can manage the cake, victoria sponge. I'm rather pleased with the result. Let's put it to the test shall we?"

As they sampled the sponge cake, which was delicious, Mary consulted a notebook in which she had jotted down various details regarding Appleby Grammar School.

"First of all, Ivy," she said, "I've got some excellent news. Mr and Mrs Machin up at Rookby Scarth have expressed a desire that Richard should sit the exam for Appleby. He's an excellent candidate and should have little or no trouble gaining entry. As you know Thomas and Richard are virtually inseparable and just knowing that they would start together should be a huge encouragement to them both."

"Why that's grand," said Ivy genuinely pleased. She felt almost light-headed. This would make it so much easier when it came to persuading Tat to cooperate. "Will Dick be boarding as well then?"

"Well, apparently Richard has an uncle and aunt who live at Dufton, a few miles beyond Appleby. Their oldest boy went to the school and is in his first year at Newton Rigg Agricultural College near Penrith. I think Mr and Mrs Machin have something similar in mind for Richard in the long run. Richard will be a weekly boarder I believe, staying the weekends with his relatives."

Ivy realized that even though the Machins only lived a mile away further up the fell side, she knew precious little about them. They seemed nice enough and with their farm being considerably bigger than Fell End, Ivy assumed that they could probably afford to have Dick board at school without feeling it too harshly.

"So Mary, can you give me an idea what it will cost for our Tat, say on an annual basis and then there's the uniform and such like?" Ivy asked. "Maybe I should tell you, just between ourselves, that my mother is ready and willing to pay for it all. Not that Jack knows that yet, mind you."

Mary giggled slightly at this, "You've got quite a devious side haven't you Ivy?" Both women laughed and even Mary's mother managed a smile. Mary was still chuckling as she helped her mother finish her cake, brushing the crumbs off her blanket into the grate.

"Right, I've got it all here. I've spoken to Jane Randle, the headmaster's wife. Remember I told you she was at Lancaster with me? She has room for fourteen new boarders and has promised to treat our two Winton candidates as priorities. See, it pays to have a bit of influence in these matters," Mary said narrowing her eyes conspiratorially.

"For a full boarder the fee is fifty pounds a year. The uniform and various extras such as sports wear, rugby, cricket and gym in particular, will cost about fifteen pounds, say five pounds for pocket money and end-of-term travel. I think it could all be managed for say seventy five pounds per annum. What do you think your mother will make of that, Ivy?" Mary looked up from her calculations expectantly.

"Well, she told me that she would be willing to put one hundred pounds a year into it. She'll do owt for our Tat, so I think, knowing my mother, that she'll be very glad to have twenty five pounds change," Ivy said grinning broadly.

"Wonderful, wonderful," Mary almost shouted with pleasure.

"Isn't that wonderful mother?" Old Mrs Hollis smiled and tried to clap her hands.

"Well, what progress we are making. Let's have a sherry to

celebrate. I know it's Sunday but this is all so exciting," Mary said, standing up hugging herself with pleasure. She positively skipped across to the corner cupboard to fetch the Bristol Cream and glasses.

Ivy felt as light as air after what turned out to be two helpings of the delicious sherry. She took the same route home as the boys, passing under the horizontal branch of the Scotts Pine which held such significance for them. Ivy felt a surge of new confidence within herself. She almost looked forward to the inevitable confrontation with Jack; she was well and truly prepared. Tat would have to be handled with care, but she felt positive that he would rise to the occasion once he knew about Dick Machin. What a stroke of luck!

As Ivy reached the point where the rutted tracks diverged, she could see Fell End standing proud upon its wooded hill. She was consumed with a profound love for the place and her family. She would make a special effort over the Sunday tea and began to plan it, taking delight in selecting each item. After cold beef with fried potatoes and pickled onions, they would have apple pie with fresh cream, then fruit cake with Wensleydale cheese, all washed down with gallons of tea.

Afterwards, when John had left to take the first watch with the ewes and Michael and Tat had gone to bed she would produce the bottle of whisky, which her mother had given her, and talk to Jack about Tat's future. She knew it was essential for her to stay calm and present her case as a desirable and, above all, workable proposition. She was already wearing her best dress owing to her wish to appear presentable whilst visiting Mary Hollis. Perhaps she would take a minute or two to rearrange her hair which was escaping from underneath her bonnet in the strong breeze. She'd also splash on some rosewater.

After clearing the table and washing up the tea things, Ivy gave Tat a going over with soap and warm water. He squirmed and complained as usual, especially as he suffered the indignity of having his hair washed, a Sunday night ritual. She kissed him as he reluctantly took his candle and went to bed.

Jack was cleaning his boots and leggings with dubbin, another

Sunday ritual. Ivy smiled across at him asking, "How about a whisky Jack? Our mother gave us a bottle in the week."

"Aye, grand," agreed Jack. "She's certainly got her uses, your mother."

Ivy brought the bottle and two glasses from the pantry, whilst Jack washed his hands. They both sat at the table and Ivy poured generous measures of liquor for them both. "Still no pet lambs yet then? I've usually got two or three by the range by now," said Ivy.

"No, touch wood, they're all in good fettle so far; a couple of stillborns like; not too bad at all considering," Jack replied. He took a sip of whisky and grimaced.

"By, it's grand is that," he said, coughing a couple of times.

Ivy held her breath for a moment and said, "Jack, I know we haven't discussed what Mary Hollis had to say about our Tat. You've been that busy with the ewes and the ploughing that I haven't wanted to bother you with it."

"Now Ivy…" Jack said in a soft voice.

"No, Jack love, let me finish, then I'll hold my peace," Ivy said putting her hand over Jack's where it lay on the tabletop. "I went to see my mother during the week. You know I value her opinion; she's been that good to me, all of us, in fact. Well I asked her what she thought about our Tat going on with his studies," Ivy took a gulp of whisky which momentarily stung her throat and made her nose tingle.

"The long and the short of it is, Jack, that my mother agrees with me that it would be grand if Tat spread his wings and had a chance to get on in the world. She'd do owt for our Tat, you know that, and, well, not to beat about the bush Jack, she'll pay for it all."

"Bugger me," said Jack, rubbing his short hair backwards and forwards until it stuck up like a scrubbing brush. "Pour us another whisky, lass." Ivy noticed a flush in Jack's weathered cheeks whilst she refilled his glass.

"Mind you Jack, she told me that you had to give your permission first!" Ivy cringed inwardly as her mother had not said any such thing. She gulped and went on knowing that she only had a few minutes left to state her case. The whisky was flooding through her veins, filling her with conflicting measures of courage and trepidation. She went on, "As you know Jack, I went to see Mary today, after Chapel, and she gave me these details." She fumbled in her pocket and produced the jottings Mary had made for her.

Two tears had formed on Ivy's cheeks; she dashed them away and they were immediately replaced by two more. In a final effort to control her surging emotions she said, "Dick's going to take the..." She faltered and stopped, her heart hammered in her throat and she saw through her tears that Jack's shoulders were shaking. He was suppressing laughter.

"Ivy, lass," Jack wheezed, "You must think I'm bloody slow on the uptake. Settle yourself, I've got a couple of things to tell you." He took both Ivy's hands in his. She felt the callouses rasping against her skin.

"Now then," Jack said, "on Thursday I went to get some cartridges in Kirkby and thought I'd have a pint at the Black Bull. Your mother spotted me and took me off to her den in the back. She gave me the whole thing with both barrels. Told me I'd be daft to stand in the way of 'progress.' Not a word of a lie, that's what she called it, 'progress.'

'Our Tat's going to be a doctor,' she said." Jack released her hand and drained his glass. Ivy felt a deep crimson blush creep up her neck.

"Then, lass," Jack continued, "I ran into George Machin, up by the railway. He'd just shot a lovely hare. Anyway, he wasted no time in telling me all about Dick taking the exam and how he was going to go to Newton Rigg and be a proper up-to-date farmer. Not like us lot, cheeky bugger." Jack looked at Ivy with a sly sideways cock of his head whilst he poured himself another whisky.

"Oh Jack," Ivy whispered, tears freely coursing down her cheeks. Jack put a finger up to her lips.

"Shush now," he said tenderly. "If our Tat wants to go, then so be it. I don't know how we'll manage without him, mind you. John and Michael will just have to knuckle down all the harder. So will I, I suppose."

Ivy stood up and hugged Jack to her ample bosom. Tears of relief and joy fell from her cheeks and lodged twinkling in Jack's hair.

"Thank you Jack," she sobbed, "you're a good man."

"What I can't wait to see," said Jack, his voice muffled, "is your mother queening it over everybody in her new motor, whatever will she do next? My God, she's a character."

They clung together convulsed with laughter. Jack ran his hands down Ivy's back, pulling her close to him. Ivy woke early next morning. Jack had been gone for two hours, relieving Michael around dawn. She lay for a luxurious minute or two recalling the moment when Jack, stimulated by whisky and humour, had ushered her upstairs. She felt momentarily anxious when she remembered the frantic creaking of the bedsprings. Could Michael and Tat possibly have heard, she wondered?

Collecting her thoughts while she took a pitcher of hot water upstairs to wash, she resolved to speak to Tat before he left for school.

Things were moving beyond her control. Dick Machin could blurt everything out to Tat this very day. After dressing, she roused Tat even though it was barely six o'clock.

While Tat was wolfing down his porridge, his eyelids still puffy with sleep, Ivy said she wanted him to help her collect the eggs. She made the excuse that they had been left all through Sunday, which as it happened, was true. Tat's expertise in egg collection was needed, she said.

Whilst washing, Ivy had remembered an incident in March when James McLeod, the Scots vet, had been to the farm to treat Rosie, the big mare. She'd had a cruel time producing a foal a week before. Reluctantly, Jack had no alternative but to call the vet. Tat had watched it all with unflinching fascination. Mr McLeod had noticed this and got Tat to fetch and carry for him. After a gory hour and a half he had given Tat a shilling, whilst he'd drunk a restorative whisky in the kitchen.

"He's got a way with him, the youngster," Mr McLeod had remarked. "Not many lads would have stayed the course in the stable today like he did; it was a messy one."

Later, Tat had asked his mother, "Mam, how do you get to be a vet like Mr McLeod? Could I be a vet one day?"

"Don't be daft our Tat," she had answered, carelessly, she now realized. As she and Tat gradually tracked down the eggs whilst the chickens cackled and strutted around them, Ivy thought, now or never.

"Tat," she said, "can you remember asking me a bit back, when the vet was stitching up poor old Rosie…?"

Before she could finish, Tat said, "You mean when I asked you if I could be a vet, like Mr McLeod? Anyway he told me when I helped him carry his stuff to the car, can you remember he had to leave his motor at the lane end, 'cos our track was too rough? He said to be a vet you had to study hard and go to a university."

Ivy stood up arching backwards to relieve her aching spine. She looked at Tat with her head on one side and asked, "Did he say how you got to this university then?"

"He just said you had to work hard and pass lots of exams," said Tat depositing four eggs in the almost full basket.

"Tat, do you still fancy being a vet, really and truly I mean?"

"Aye Mam, Mr McLeod said he thought I'd make a good one, and he gave me a shilling." Tat replied, and then added, "Can I be a vet, Mam?"

"Course you can pet," Ivy said gathering Tat to her, "you can be owt you like. Come away in and I'll tell you all about it. We'll have some hot milk and a bit of fruit cake afore you set off for school." After all her anxiety, it was typical of Tat to make it easy for her.

THE PLAYGROUNDS

The boys had a number of favourite places where they spent time playing together when their various chores were completed. Feeding the hens and farm dogs and egg collecting were regular responsibilities, whilst general fetching and carrying occurred to a greater or lesser extent depending upon the time of year. As the evenings grew lighter and the temperature gradually climbed, the boys would meet up after school, rarely straying much further afield than the boundaries of their parents' farms. At the weekends, however, the friends would venture out into the surrounding territory, concentrating particularly upon three or four locations.

The fells, which rose above the stone walled fields, were of little interest to them. They were on the whole treeless, boggy and alienating, containing little to hold their attention for long. Consequently, the boys sought out areas which lay within the landscape at lower levels. The River Eden, a considerable watercourse of great contrasts, ran through the fertile valley which dominated the area. The mountainous sides of the valley were at intervals many miles apart and elsewhere surprisingly close together. Market towns and villages were scattered across the floor of the valley. On the whole the more prosperous farms were located here. Several boasted large dairy herds supported by lush grass growing on the alluvial soil laid down over centuries by the river. Tributaries made their tortuous way from the heights on either side of the valley to join the Eden. Many of these had cut out their own subsidiary valleys. They were often steep sided and wooded. Outcrops of limestone created the most unlikely twists and turns in these streams as well as rapids and waterfalls. During the wetter parts of the year these otherwise innocent tributaries would transform into raging torrents of brown water, capable of uprooting trees and tearing great swathes of riverbank away. During spring and summer however, such places were the perfect playground for the boys. Their favourite was Podgill. There they could be cowboys and indians, Stone Age tribesmen, soldiers fighting a multitude of enemies or explorers discovering Africa.

About a mile from Fell End a stream emerged sluggishly from a treacherous bog on the lower slopes of the fell. Within half a mile of this, a cleft in the limestone suddenly opened into a vertical sided gorge. The stream plunged down this narrow funnel and emerged from it a hundred feet below, transformed into a fast flowing beck which chattered between mossy boulders at considerable speed. This chasm, known as Ewbank Scar, was where the friends invariably entered the upper reaches of Podgill. The stream slowed and meandered through a rock-strewn wooded valley with steep sides. Eventually, the tributary reached the Eden, joining it at right angles where a deep black pool of very slow water was a favourite with fishermen after brown trout.

Sometimes the boys would spend the whole day in Podgill; more than once they had dammed the stream with stones and sods of earth. This would necessitate the removal of boots and socks and the rolling up of trousers. They were oblivious to the freezing cold mountain water which numbed their feet. If they were successful, a considerable pool would be created. In hot weather they might be tempted to strip off all their clothing and engage in a water fight. As a consequence the pool would turn to a muddy brown especially as, more often than not, they would hurl clods of earth at each other torn from the banks of the stream. Afterwards, if they had remembered to bring matches, they would build a fire to warm their white goose-pimpled bodies; otherwise they lay in the sun until they were warm and dry enough to put their clothes back on.

The woods were cacophonous with birdsong throughout April and May, particularly. The boys robbed nests by the dozen and sometimes had running battles throwing eggs at each other, dodging between the trees and seeking refuge in thick undergrowth. They flushed out pheasants and chased them until they took flight. The boys were fascinated by their staccato calls and metallic, whirring wing beats. The place was teeming with rabbits, which they were never able to hit with the bows and arrows they painstakingly made from dead-straight cuttings extracted from the thickets of hazelnut trees. They gorged themselves on the sweet nuts which hung in clusters during the autumn. All except Tat, whose throat itched violently at even the smallest contact with the tempting white kernels. Often they would return home with their hands and mouths stained purple after consuming fat juicy blackberries which grew in abundance in the sun-drenched clearings.

The most impressive feature in Podgill was the viaduct. This many-arched stone built structure spanned the wooded valley carrying the railway. None of the boys had yet travelled in a train, but they watched them often. The closer they could get to them the better. Whilst playing in the wood they kept alert so that they could hear the distant whistle of approaching trains. As soon as this occurred, the boys would sprint towards the viaduct so as to gather under its vast arches. When the train passed directly overhead the deafening sound was conducted down the massive supports. The stonework vibrated and the earth shook, filling them with an hysterical mixture of terror and excitement.

If the breeze was in the right direction, the billowing smoke from the engine tumbled down the sides of the viaduct, momentarily engulfing the shouting boys.

When they felt sufficiently brave, they would climb the slippery sides of Podgill and squeeze through the heavily built fence which flanked the railway lines so as to gain access to the viaduct itself. Ignoring the cast-iron signs, which warned them to keep off the tracks, the boys would pause, listening intently to ascertain whether a train was in the vicinity. If the coast was clear they would sprint across the viaduct stepping skilfully on the blackened wooden sleepers. Of course, they were aware that if a train had made a sudden appearance on either of the two tracks when they were executing this feat of daring, they would have been trapped by the stone parapets of the viaduct. This quite terrifying prospect made the experience all the more attractive in their eyes.

The railway passed through the higher fields farmed by the Taylors and Machins. Several steep-sided cuttings had been hewn through the rocky, uneven terrain to make way for the tracks. About half a mile from the viaduct a branch line joined the railway and curved into such a cutting. Beyond this was Hartley Quarry, a huge, seemingly chaotic void scooped out of the fell side. Limestone was blasted out of the quarry, and after being crushed, taken by iron wagons down the branch line and then on to the steel works in Yorkshire and the Midlands.

Hartley Quarry could be approached from dozens of different directions. Red flags flew on tall poles to warn the public when blasting was imminent. Numerous signs stood around the perimeter of the quarry warning any stray walkers to keep out. They were painted red, and each bore a white skull and crossbones to emphasise the danger of the place. Depending upon the season, the quarry was either a dust bowl or a sea of slimy mud. The boys usually chose Sunday to explore the place. It was eerily quiet and so far as they could tell completely deserted. Rough limestone cliffs soared upwards from the floor of the quarry, the base of the cliffs piled with boulders which had been blasted out with explosives. The quarry was criss-crossed with miniature railway tracks which carried wooden wagons that were pushed along by hand. The boulders were loaded into the wagons and pushed along to the crusher, a vast noisy machine which ground the boulders down. Given the opportunity, the boys delighted in pushing the empty wagons along their tracks and crashing them together with satisfyingly loud reports.

Above all, however, what really attracted the friends to the quarry was the blasting itself. During the school holidays they would take cover behind rocks up on the perimeter of the quarry with a clear view of the cliff side where the quarrymen were drilling holes into which explosive charges would be placed. A strident siren began to wail, echoing off the cliffs, whilst the men withdrew into a portable shelter. The boys could clearly see the long fuses spewing out sparks and smoke. They crouched low as the fuses reached the charges. The cliff sides erupted in a maelstrom of smoke, dust and flying rocks with a brief crimson flash at the center of each explosion. The detonations were set off two seconds apart and covered about fifty yards of a given area of the cliff.

The explosions echoed thunderously around the surrounding hills as the boulders showered down the cliff to settle at the bottom. On quiet days the resulting dust cloud drifted slowly across the quarry covering everything in its path. When strong winds blew the dust was whisked into madly eddying rhythms which were gone in a few seconds. The whole spectacle left the boys dazed and exhilarated. They conversed in unnaturally loud voices for at least half an hour afterwards unaware that they had become temporarily deaf. On more than one occasion they had misjudged the distance of their hiding place from the point of detonation and seen and heard shards of stone whine over their heads, clattering through the trees behind them. They loved every dangerous minute of it.

Fell End and Rookby Scarth both had the remains of old lead mines within their boundaries. The old spoil heaps created strange hummocks of roughly equal size long since overgrown with grass and nettles. The boys had uncovered the entrances to several tunnels; they were mostly blocked with tangled undergrowth which could, with an effort, be dragged out of the way. After entering these for only a few feet, the friends became scared however, as the candles they had brought with them showed just how fragmentary and unsafe the dripping tunnels were.

Their desire to get underground was eventually satisfied when they discovered the most spectacular gorge in their locality. Stenkrith was a huge rift in the limestone through which the River Eden raced at breakneck speed just to the south of Kirkby Stephen. The river had eroded the limestone into fantastic sculptural shapes. Over millennia pebbles had found their way into crevices and been swirled around eventually scouring out perfectly cylindrical holes. Many of these were deep enough for the local children to stand in them up to their necks during the hot weather. They learnt to avoid the deeper ones after a few frightening incidents.

The place was honeycombed with caves some of which were wide and tall enough to allow adults to enter them with ease. For a while the boys became addicted to exploring the cave network. Many of them converged, sometimes more than once, and several had icy water coursing through them. Although the caves were cold, wet and dark, nothing thrilled the boys so much as their excursions into this subterranean world. The guttering candles they carried threw fantastic shadows across the smooth surfaces and occasionally illuminated clusters of glinting stalactites. They had managed to break off several finger-sized examples which they kept as treasured possessions. With these they could prove that they were amongst the elite few who had penetrated the caves in Stenkrith.

Eventually, their enthusiasm waned, however, when three teenage boys from Kirkby Stephen were drowned. A cloudburst had occurred several miles up the valley filling the many tributaries with huge volumes of water. This eventually joined the mainstream and swelled massively by the time it reached Stenkrith. The wall of water crashed through the gorge with terrifying velocity carrying with it whole trees, drowned sheep and even a couple of fell ponies. The boys had been caught in a cave and perished. Their bodies were catapulted out of the cave to join the now deadly torrent of the Eden in full spate. They were found terribly mutilated, caught up in the branches of overhanging trees where the river ran past the outskirts of Kirkby Stephen. For several weeks the local children, including the four friends, avoided Stenkrith. Gradually, they returned and began to take up where they had left off. The bigger, more confident boys even began caving again as the memory of the grisly events faded. The friends were too shaken, however, and avoided the once magnetic dark entrances to the caves like the plague.

They found a number of side pools with slow moving silky brown water which were extremely deep. A quarryman from Hartley had shown them how to feel under the smooth stone edges of the pools where numerous brown trout sheltered during the day. With patience and skill it was possible to locate these by touch and tickle their bellies. This seemed to put the trout into a kind of trance so that they could be whipped out of the shadowy water in one swift movement. Tickling trout soon had their undivided attention, and both families enjoyed fried trout for supper when the boys were lucky.

TRACKING THE GIANT

As spring gradually transformed into early summer the boys forsook their favourite haunts in favour of tracking Bill Fletcher. In the most obvious way this was not difficult as Bill was so big. He never attempted to hide himself. He simply went about his business, which mostly consisted of tramping the lanes around Winton. After a while the boys realized that Bill had never been to Kirkby Stephen which, in comparison to the smaller villages and hamlets, was a busy place. Cattle and sheep markets were held there every Wednesday which brought most of the local farmers into Kirkby with their beasts. The town boasted six pubs, three butchers, five grocers, a saddler and blacksmith, as well as numerous businesses and shops. The railway had brought prosperity to the place, facilitating the swift movement of goods and people in and out of it.

On one occasion when the four friends were following Bill Fletcher at a safe distance, it became clear that the giant was heading purposefully for Kirkby Stephen. The town had within it several very rundown areas. These were mostly at the lower end of Silver Street, where dingy, narrow passageways gave access to a network of stone-flagged yards. There, dilapidated cottages crowded together facing onto the yard where there invariably stood a communal water pump and stone trough. The families who lived in these yards were the poorest in the town. The children ran wild and were filthy and barefoot. The older boys hung around in gangs often setting upon unsuspecting strangers who wandered through what they considered to be their territory. The friends had learned to avoid these areas of the town unless they were accompanied by adult members of their families.

Bill Fletcher strode into Kirkby Stephen via Silver Street. The friends took cover behind a stone wall on a hillock that overlooked the full length of the street. A group of teenage boys were idling about in the sunshine as Bill came into view. They immediately gathered in the middle of the road and began to pick up loose stones from the gutters. Two of the bigger boys carried cudgels and seemed to have some control over the group.

The boys began to shout and jeer at the huge tramp who by this time was only a few yards from them. Without warning a punishing volley of missiles stopped Bill in his tracks. More children emerged from the yards and passageways attracted by the commotion. Within a minute there must have been twenty or more children in the street all gathering up stones and hurling them with varying degrees of accuracy at Bill Fletcher. Several stones found their mark, striking the tramp about the head. One boy had produced a catapult that he used with great rapidity and accuracy. Within no time blood was flowing from Bill's face and he had begun to roar with fear and rage, laying about him with his huge walking stick. The nimble children evaded his clumsy lunges with ease and intensified their attack.

Eventually, several men appeared on the scene bringing their dogs with them. Bill, despite his size and ferocious bellowing, was soon overwhelmed by the onslaught and retreated back down the street with half a dozen dogs snapping at his heels and stones raining down on him from all sides. One dog fastened its teeth into his right ankle; he reached down and tore the creature free and flung it in a scrabbling yelping arc back towards his tormentors. The dog struck the road with a sickening thud and howled in agony. When it attempted to scamper back to its furious owner it dragged its back legs behind it. The crowd gathered around the injured dog as Bill made his escape through the nearby sawmill yard and across the fields towards the river. The four friends had witnessed the whole incident and were shaken by the suddenness and violence of it.

"Let's be going before they spot us," Dick said urgently.

The friends kept low behind the cover of the stone walls and made their way as quickly as possible to the river bank. They spotted Bill about two hundred yards downstream. Thick stands of trees grew over the river beyond which a humped road bridge spanned it at right angles. The tramp was splashing through the shallows making for the bridge; once there he crouched down beneath its curving arch and began bathing his wounds. Cautiously, the four boys approached the spot and crouched amongst the trees about twenty feet from the stricken tramp. Above the rushing of the water they could hear Bill muttering and groaning as he tended to the cuts and bruises he had sustained.

"Bugger me," Allen whispered, "he's crying."

And so he was. Bill Fletcher, the invincible giant, was sobbing, his massive hunched frame shuddering uncontrollably. The boys quietly crept away feeling that they had no business intruding into Bill Fletcher's grief and shame. To their knowledge, Bill never ventured into Kirkby Stephen again.

After a few days the friends decided that their main objective should be to discover where Bill went at night. As far as they were aware he never knew that he was being observed or at least never gave any outward sign of it. One sunny afternoon the boys had decided to cut fresh hazel rods from the thickets in Podgill. They needed to renew their tattered and split bows and arrows with which to pursue their rabbit hunting.

By the position of the sun the boys assessed that they should gather up their hazel cuttings and head for home. Tat suddenly noticed a thin column of blue smoke coming from a section of the wood they never visited. It was in a boggy corner of Podgill that, no matter how dry the summer weather, always remained wet and treacherous. The four friends approached the edge of the bog peering through the dense trees that flourished in the wet earth. The ground rose steeply beyond the swamp and at the summit lay the railway. They could see that the smoke came from a small fire at the top of the high ground.

"That's rabbit cooking isn't it?" Tat said sniffing the air.

"Aye I reckon it is," said Dick.

The necessity to reach their farms before teatime prevented the boys from either finding a way through or around the swamp in order to discover who was cooking rabbit up on the edge of Podgill. Before Tat left the others where the farm tracks diverged, they had agreed to find a way through to the high ground and solve the mystery.

It was two days before the boys met again. Tat had taken time to work out that the best way to find the place where the smoke came from was to approach it along the railway tracks. That way they would avoid the bog with all its pitfalls. One thing that had occurred to Tat was the possibility that they might be discovered halfway across the swamp. If they were surprised in such a place by unfriendly forces, such as rough boys from Kirkby Stephen, or gypsies who frequented the area in the summer, they would be unable to make a quick escape. Also, they would have to remove their boots and socks in order to enter the bog, as the possibility of losing their footwear in the sucking mud was a real one. Bare foot and stuck up to their knees in the swamp they wouldn't stand a chance.

One train pulling quarry wagons full of crushed limestone passed them as they made their way along the railway line towards Podgill. The boys skipped crazily amongst the pungent, white steam that gushed from the valves along the side of the green engine. The black smoke, which shed even blacker showers of soot, was whisked away across the fell side by the strong breeze. The driver and fireman waved at the boys, glad to relieve the monotony of their routine.

As the trees of Podgill showed in the distance, the friends stopped their noisy banter and began to gauge just where the smoke had been located from this unfamiliar angle of approach. When they had first seen the smoke they had been on the floor of the valley, now they were high above Podgill, level with the treetops. Just as they left the railway track, Bill Fletcher emerged as if from the ground itself about ten yards ahead of them. The boys sank down into the bracken as Bill strode away. He disappeared into the trees without looking back.

"Bloody hell, that was close," said Tat as they cautiously emerged from their hiding place.

"What's old Bill doing up this way?" Dick said, genuinely puzzled. The boys edged forward until they reached the place where Bill Fletcher had appeared, after waiting about ten minutes to give him time to get clear. After they were sure that Bill was no longer in the vicinity they began to explore. They discovered a well-worn path beaten through the bracken that was clearly used regularly. The path disappeared into a thicket of hazel trees and blackthorn. The boys pushed their way through this and discovered a clearing beyond which stood a derelict lime kiln. In the centre of the clearing lay the embers of a fire set amidst a circle of stones. The area was littered with animal bones, mostly rabbit. Decaying guts and skins hung from the bushes around the edge of the clearing, covered with swarming flies. The smell was overpowering.

Holding their noses, they approached the arched entrance to the kiln. In the dim light they made out a bed of crushed bracken covered with filthy sacks. More rabbit bones littered the floor. Two battered saucepans with broken handles chinked suddenly as Brian accidentally dislodged them with his boot. The sound made them jump, arousing them from the daze into which they had fallen since discovering the place. Panicking suddenly, they raced across the clearing and burst through the thicket. They left the path trodden down by Bill Fletcher's huge feet and regained the railway within a few seconds. They sprinted along the tracks for two hundred yards or so, before throwing themselves down upon the springy turf of the embankment.

"Christ, what a bloody stink!" Allen gasped, "I don't know how even old Bill can put up with that. What a shit heap!"

In truth, the boys had been shocked by what they had found. None of them enjoyed the daily chore of keeping themselves clean. Above all, hair washing and teeth cleaning repulsed them more than anything else. They took the cleanliness of their homes for granted, and the regular supply of appetizing food. Now they had seen at close quarters what real filth and squalor were like. They had seen it and smelt it. Even though they were shaken by the experience they resolved to keep the whereabouts of Bill's hideout a secret. The truth was that ever since the shocking incident in Kirkby Stephen, followed by their witnessing Bill's emotional collapse under the bridge, they had begun to feel sorry for the giant. He was feared and mocked and reviled by everyone. He didn't have a friend in the world and lived amongst filth of his own making.

David Thompson

THE EXAM / & GYPSIES GATHER

Tat and Dick took the entrance exam for Appleby Grammar School for Boys early in the summer. John Braithwaite, whom neither Tat nor Dick liked very much, also sat the exam. Four girls were put forward for entrance into the girls' grammar school in Kirkby Stephen. It was an exciting day as about forty children from the various primary schools in the locality assembled in the Masonic Hall in Kirkby Stephen. The boys and girls sat in different areas of the cavernous space, separated by a wooden screen.

Seeing so many children of their own age who were strangers to them was a novelty to Tat and Dick. The day started with prayers taken by a booming-voiced vicar. Then they were given a lecture on how serious the day was and how everybody expected them to do well. Dick caught Tat's eye at this declaration and pulled his fish-face which almost got Tat giggling. Two severe-looking teachers sat at the front at high desks, and after consulting the big clock on the wall, told the children when to begin answering the questions set before them. None of the children had ever seen the teachers before. Later they learnt that they had come all the way from Kendal to oversee the exam.

They were to be tested in mathematics and English grammar throughout the morning. There would be a half hour milk break and an opportunity to play in the yard at the rear of the hall at ten-thirty. It was exciting to do something different which broke the familiar routine of life at Winton Primary School. During the morning break the boys ganged up to play tag and leapfrog, whilst the girls skipped and chanted strange rhymes whilst clapping. Basically, the two groups ignored each other. Tat and Dick agreed that the mathematics was 'rubbish,' which meant easy.

The English grammar gave them no trouble either and the friends were delighted to find that the lunch laid on for them was roast chicken with all the trimmings. The children concentrated so hard upon eating every scrap that almost total silence settled over the scene, apart from the clatter of knives and forks. The older of the two supervisors said an unfamiliar grace before and after the lunch which was rounded off with delicious sponge pudding and custard.

After lunch there was a brief playtime in the yard, when Tat secretly wished he could skip like the girls who were so skilful and daring, inventing seamless variations into the graceful game. History and geography occupied the afternoon, both of which Tat excelled in. He was almost sorry when the older teacher told them that they had ten minutes left to complete their papers. When he told the children to stop writing in a ridiculously loud voice full of self-importance, Dick looked across at Tat and the two of them had great difficulty suppressing inner waves of hysteria.

The papers were collected and the children began to file out of the hall onto the street. Outside some parents were waiting for their sons and daughters. Tat and Dick were instructed to go to the Black Bull where Tat's mother was waiting for them. Tat's mother and grandmother made a real fuss of the boys and peppered them with questions about the exam. Was it hard? How many children were present? Had they finished on time and what had they had for lunch? For their part, Tat and Dick were dismissive of the exam saying in unison that it was 'rubbish,' whilst they were ecstatic about the roast chicken and sponge pudding. They imitated the vicar and the teachers from Kendal which reduced the two women to tears of laughter. Despite the filling lunch they had already consumed, Tat and Dick demolished the generous tea Clarrie set before them in Mrs Watson's sitting room.

Ivy was itching with curiosity to know more about how the boys thought they had done in the exam. However, as they walked home, all the boys were interested in was running off ahead to chase curlew chicks which sprinted ahead of them through the long grass in the hay meadows, as yet unable to fly. Tat had become very attached to a curlew chick which he had visited regularly throughout the spring. It's tiny fluffy body and cheeping calls captivated him. He had held the chick in his cupped hands almost every day feeling its warmth and fluttering heartbeats. Gradually, as the chick grew and began to sprout recognizable feathers through its yellow down, it became so tame that it scuttled up to Tat whenever he visited it. Now it was just one of the many gawky chicks with primeval curved beaks which scattered in all directions ahead of Tat and Dick.

Gypsies had begun to camp along the verges and across the common land throughout the Eden Valley. They came every year in their hundreds to attend Brough and Appleby horse fairs. Two or three families camped in the lower fields of Fell End. They were regular visitors to whom Jack Taylor gave casual jobs during the summer and autumn. Jack and the older boys had deposited several piles of crushed limestone along the verge of the rutted farm track. The gypsies would be hired to haul the stones along the track and fill up the ruts and potholes. Later they would help with the haymaking and harvest.

As Ivy and the boys passed the gypsy camp, they were greeted by the swarthy men and women who invariably had a fire going and washing hanging up amongst the bushes. Barefoot children scampered around the brightly painted caravans, whilst piebald ponies, tethered to pegs in the ground, grazed the grass. The local people viewed the gypsies with mixed feelings. The middle class professional folk regarded them as a nuisance to be kept at arm's length. A certain amount of thieving did take place and drunken brawls would break out in the local pubs, as the gypsy numbers grew in the week of the main gypsy fair in June. Old scores and rivalries between different gypsy factions could go on for years. Now and again knife fights occurred and the police became involved.

The local youths tended to regard the dark skinned gypsy men, with their black curly hair and gold earrings, as rivals. Certainly, the gypsy men and youths were more than confident when it came to flirting with the local women and girls. If a flirtation went further, however, and some certainly did, violence would invariably be the outcome. As far as the local publicans and shopkeepers were concerned the arrival of the gypsies meant an upsurge in business, worth the inconvenience created by the odd fight or increased pilfering. The farmers, on the whole, welcomed the gypsy families, as they proved to be willing labourers doing rough work such as road mending and tree felling, as well as field work. They were good with horses and helped when it came to shifting heavy materials around the farms.

Dick, Tat and other Grammar School candidates at Winton School were questioned about the examination by Miss Hollis. She had received copies of the four exam papers and patiently went through them with the seven pupils. After considering the answers each child had given on the day, she confidently expected Tat and Dick to have done particularly well. However, she kept her opinions to herself, as four weeks would elapse before the official results were published. The children quickly put the experience behind them, and got on with their lives with little or no thought of how dramatically different the future would be for them.

The gypsies began work on renovating the farm tracks over the following days. They preferred to take part of their earning in eggs, milk and pig meat. Such things were in short supply when they were on the move. Jack opened up a rough pasture for the gypsy ponies. Several had foals which Tat loved to watch. A couple of gypsy boys about Tat's age became regular playmates of the four friends. They taught them how to cook hedgehogs wrapped in mud and roast eels from the beck in Podgill threaded upon sticks. These strange feasts cooked and eaten in the woods proved to be delicious. Despite the persuasive efforts of the boys, neither the Taylor or Machin families could be tempted into including these culinary experiments into their diets.

One of the gypsy mothers carried a beautiful baby girl on her back tied in a shawl. The little girl was almost a year old and to Tat's amazement already had a small gold ring in her left ear. The baby took a liking to Tat and always became animated in his company. Ivy adored the child and sometimes looked after her when the mother went off with her friends selling clothes pegs around the villages. The gypsy women made the pegs out of hazel cut from the hedgerows, bound with strips of copper wire. They did a roaring trade, as their pegs were cheap and efficient. To Ivy's surprise Tat, and sometimes even the Machin boys, would spend considerable amounts of time playing with the baby. Often they would spread a rug in the orchard beside the farmhouse and vie with each other for the little girl's attention.

Hannah, the baby's mother, was a striking looking woman. She was tall and had beautiful posture. Her skin was nut brown and when she let her black hair down it reached almost to her knees. As a contrast to her fine looks, however, her strange guttural speech was hard for the locals to understand, and she smoked a pipe. Even when this wasn't lit she held it clamped between her teeth. She wore several gold rings in each ear as well as numerous gold bangles and a necklace made of sovereigns.

Bill Fletcher took no more notice of the gypsies than he did of anybody else. He passed their encampments on a daily basis as he tramped through the lanes. Most of the gypsy families had got used to him over the years. Their children were forbidden to tease him, and those who were stupid enough to try would receive a thorough beating from their parents. Until the piebald ponies tethered along the verges became accustomed to Bill's fearsome appearance they might shy at his approach. Some snapped their tethering ropes and galloped off for a short distance. The gypsies were used to this, however, as stray dogs or even motorcars, which were becoming more numerous, had the same effect.

The group to which the baby girl's mother belonged had camped on a stretch of common land near to the Winton road. The campsite was close to the Scots pine which had provided the boys with their means of measuring Bill Fletcher's height. Tat had shown the two gypsy boys the string marked with blue chalk and pointed out the horizontal branch under which Bill had ducked.

Tat and Dick had by now learnt that they had been successful in gaining entry to Appleby Grammar School. They treated the news with studied indifference, although they were inwardly thrilled. They told the gypsy boys about it, as they knew that their families would soon set out for Appleby to spend two weeks at the horse fair. They vowed to meet up in Appleby in the future; little knowing what difficulties this would create. Tat's mother had almost suffocated him with hugs and kisses when the official letter arrived from the Education Authority in Kendal. Much to Tat's embarrassment, she had wept with pure pride and joy. She insisted on carting Tat down to the Black Bull so that she could tell Mrs Watson the good news in his presence. He was given a gold sovereign by his grandmother, as well as a large slab of chocolate and a glass of lemonade.

Mrs Watson gave Ivy a bottle of whisky so that she and Jack could drink Tat's health at supper time. In fact, they had all drunk his health that night, even Michael was allowed a generous tot of whisky that made his eyes water and his ears hot and red. Tat had to withstand a good deal of teasing from his brothers who called him Professor Taylor, and suggested that he'd be too grand to do menial tasks any more, like egg collecting and feeding the dogs. It was good-natured and Tat couldn't help feeling proud, at least for that one special supper time. Tat's father suggested that as it was Saturday the following day Tat should be allowed to sleep in; this had never happened before.

Early the following afternoon Tat met the Machin boys at the viaduct in Podgill. The plan was to place some old pennies on the railway lines to see if a passing train would, as they had been told, cut them in half. As they were discussing which line to put the coins upon, Brian, who was acting as lookout, gave a low whistle. When the others looked up they saw Brian gesturing wildly at them to join him. When they reached him he pointed down into the wood.

"See yonder," he hissed, "it's Bill, and he's got summat in his hand."

The friends craned over the parapet of the viaduct just as Bill Fletcher splashed across the beck. In his left hand he clutched a small bundle which the boys couldn't see clearly. Suddenly, they stiffened as the unmistakable cry of a baby drifted up to them.

THE PURSUIT

"Christ Almighty," Tat gasped, "he's got a baby!" Horrified, the boys watched Bill Fletcher vanish under the tree canopy. He was moving at some speed towards his hideout above the swampy corner of the wood. The friends were immobilized with shock, which was compounded by the sudden appearance of a passenger train at the opposite end of the viaduct. So extreme was their confusion that they hadn't even heard the engine whistle in the distance, or the thrumming of the tracks upon which they stood. They scrambled up the embankment and were completely incapable of returning the waves from the engine crew and passengers. They ignored the smoke and steam that billowed around them. Brian was crying as the train clattered into the distance.

"What are we going to do?" he sobbed.

Tat struggled to control the panic that threatened to overwhelm him. He realized that they were nearer to Kirkby Stephen than either of their homes. If he ran all the way, which was downhill for at least half the distance, he could be in the town in not much more than ten minutes.

"We'll get wrong, I know we will," Brian sobbed.

"Shut up, you silly sod!" Dick said harshly, "Come on, let's get going."

"Be as quick as you can," Tat yelled after the Machin boys who were struggling up the embankment. Tat skipped across the railway tracks and caught a brief glimpse of the two severed halves of a penny lying on either side of one of them. Even though he knew Bill Fletcher was well clear, Tat was terrified as he dodged between the trees and vaulted over the mossy boulders. He felt enormous relief as he ran out of the woods onto open ground and started down the steep grassy slope. His feet were pounding so quickly that he stumbled and fell, rolling uncontrollably down most of the incline. Tat was winded and dizzy when he picked himself up; he was covered in grass stains and one of his shirt sleeves was torn.

Beyond This Horizon

He trotted past the cricket field on the outskirts of the town and considered whether he should stop the white clad players engaged in the regular Saturday match and tell them about what he had seen. He was too shy to attempt this, however, and decided to carry on to the Black Bull. Several people turned to stare at the dishevelled boy as he stumbled across the Market Square.

The crowded public bar fell silent as Tat crashed through the swing doors and stood blinking through his tears.

"Now then lad, will you have a pint or what?" said a big red-faced man with a cigarette stuck to his bottom lip. The bar erupted with coarse laughter and Tat shrank back against the doors unable to cope. Mrs Watson looked up from behind the bar where she was pulling beer and was shocked to see her grandson amongst the jostling crowd of Saturday drinkers. She elbowed her way across to Tat and bent down towards him and asked kindly, "Our Tat, what is it love? Eh, what a state you're in."

Tat collapsed into his grandmother's arms and allowed himself to be carried through the now subdued men to Mrs Watson's sitting room. Tat's grandmother stroked his face and waited for him to recover a little. After a minute or two, she shouted through the open door, "Clarrie, bring a glass of lemonade in here double quick please."

Turning back to Tat she asked, "Now then our Tat what's going on? Have you been caught by them rough-necks down Silver Street? I'll murder the buggers if they've done this to you."

Tat took a deep breath, "No Gran, it's Bill Fletcher. We were up in Podgill playing and we saw Bill in the woods. Gran, he's got a little baby with him."

"God Almighty," Mrs Watson gasped. Just then Clarrie bustled in with a glass of lemonade and a plate of chocolate biscuits.

"Hello my treasure," she said to Tat, "Have you been in the wars then?"

"Clarrie," Mrs Watson said, "get away up to the police station and bring Sergeant Crowther down here. Quick now."

"Now then, Tat, love," she continued, "why did you come here instead of getting your Mam and Dad?"

"I knew I could get here quicker, Gran." Tat said after gulping half his lemonade. "Dick, Allen and Brian have gone to Fell End to tell our Mam. What do you think will happen, Gran, to the baby and Bill I mean?"

"God only knows," Mrs Watson replied. "How on earth would Bill Fletcher get hold of a baby? Are you sure it was a real baby, our Tat? It might have been an old doll somebody chucked out that Bill just found."

"No, honest, Gran," Tat insisted, "we heard the baby crying, plain as day."

"Well I never," Mrs Watson said wringing her hands. "Bill Fletcher with a baby, well I never did!" Suddenly, the doorway darkened. Tat and Mrs Watson looked up to see the imposing figure of Sergeant George Crowther standing half in and half out of the sitting room. He was removing his helmet.

"Now then, Missus, what's this all about? Gypsy trouble no doubt."

"Come away in, George," Mrs Watson said. "No for once it's not. Our Tat here tells me he's seen Bill Fletcher up in Podgill; he's got a baby with him."

The sergeant lowered his bulk onto the sofa next to Tat and looked at him. "Now then, lad," he said quietly, "you'd better tell me just what you did see. Just the truth now, no fibbing."

"Honestly, it's true," said Tat. "I was playing with my mates in Podgill and we saw Bill carrying a baby. We heard the baby crying." Tat was crying himself by now.

"How long ago was this then?" Sergeant Crowther asked.

"About half an hour ago," said Tat miserably. "I came to me Gran 'cos I thought it was nearer than Fell End. Dick, Allen and Brian have gone to tell our Mam and Dad."

"That'll be the Machin lads then will it?" Sergeant Crowther said gravely. Tat nodded, his bottom lip quivering. The sergeant stood up and looked at Mrs Watson.

"I don't like the sound of this," he said. "Your stable lad is a good rider isn't he, Missus? Get him in here if you please and I'll give him a message to deliver to Jack and Ivy Taylor."

He took out his notebook and scribbled a message informing Tat's parents as to his whereabouts. He wrote a brief explanation of what Tat had told him about Bill Fletcher and the baby. Lastly, he suggested that Jack and his two older boys meet him with Tat under the viaduct in Podgill in one hour's time.

The stable lad, as ever eager to please, took the note and after tacking up the quickest pony in the stables, clattered out of the Black Bull yard. He was excited to be doing something different, especially as the sergeant had told him to ride as fast as possible and speak to nobody on the way.

Sergeant Crowther sat down again next to Tat. "So Tat, can you remember what direction Bill Fletcher was going in when you saw him?"

"Bill has a hideout up near the railway; it's an old limekiln. We found it a few days ago. I reckon Bill would be going there," Tat mumbled hanging his head. He felt guilty already about divulging this knowledge to Sergeant Crowther. He and the Machin boys had vowed to keep Bill's hideout to themselves. It was to be their secret.

"Can you show me where it is, lad?" the sergeant asked, keeping his tone light and conversational.

"Bill won't hurt the baby will he?" Tat asked fresh tears staining his cheeks.

"Nay lad, Bill's got no harm in him," Sergeant Crowther replied. "Now what do you say, will you show me where this hideout is?"

Tat looked at his grandmother, "Do I have to Gran?"

"I reckon you should, our Tat. Just point to where it is and George here will take care of everything." Mrs Watson replied as cheerfully as she could, although she could not conceal the anxiety that showed in her face.

"Right then," said Sergeant Crowther. "I'll need about quarter of an hour to get things organized. I'll get back here to collect the lad as soon as I can." Passers by witnessed the unusual sight of the stately figure of the sergeant running at top speed up the High Street towards the police station.

Hannah had discovered that her baby girl was missing about ten minutes after she left the child on a blanket in the shade, while she hung out washing on the gorse bushes close by. Her father, a wizened seventy years old, had been sitting smoking his pipe on the steps of their caravan watching over the baby. He had dozed off in the sunshine and seen nothing. Hannah and her father had been the only adults close to the roadside. Her husband and his brothers were breaking a pony more than a hundred yards away across the stretch of common land where they had been settled for almost a month. Most of the children were watching the men folk as they attempted to mount the wild pony.

Hannah soon established that her baby was nowhere in the vicinity of the camp. She cursed her father for falling asleep. The old man, befuddled by sleep and unable to offer an explanation, was cowed and crestfallen. Hannah ran over to the group of men who had got a youth onto the pony's quivering back. By this time she was sobbing hysterically and had some difficulty making her husband understand that their baby had disappeared.

Hannah's husband mounted one of his ponies and quickly made a tour of the neighbouring campsites. He was hoping to discover the baby, perhaps in the company of some of the children who tended to wander between the various camps. Soon he was back, however, having discovered nothing worthwhile.

Hannah by this time was inconsolable. He found her sitting on the ground with her shawl over her head rocking to and fro. After a while he raised her to her feet with the help of two other women. He persuaded her to think hard to discover if anybody they knew might have taken the baby, perhaps in all innocence. Hannah suddenly remembered that the boys up at Fell End often played with the baby and that possibly they had taken the little girl. Fell End was barely a mile away across the fields and within fifteen minutes Hannah and her husband, both mounted on an older pony, clattered into the Taylor's farm yard.

Dick, Allen and Brian had arrived at Fell End about ten minutes earlier. They were out of breath and dishevelled, and found Ivy Taylor hanging out the washing in the orchard. Dick was the only one who could coherently explain what they had seen in Podgill, as both Allen and Brian were in tears. Ivy was at first angry and inclined to dismiss Dick's explanation as pure mischief. When she learnt that Tat had taken it upon himself to run off into Kirkby Stephen to raise the alarm at the Black Bull, however, the full enormity of the situation began to sink in.

Jack, along with John and Michael, was with the ewes when they had seen the stable lad from the Black Bull gallop into view. They had intercepted him on the farm track. The lad slid down from his lathered pony and handed Jack the message from Sergeant Crowther.

"Christ Almighty!" Jack Taylor gasped, handing the by now crumpled message to John and Michael.

"Get back to Kirkby as quick as you can, lad," Jack barked. "If you can catch Sergeant Crowther, tell him we'll be in Podgill in half an hour."

The stable lad mounted again and sped off towards the town, clods of earth flying from under the pony's hooves. Jack, John and Michael ran as fast as they could towards the farm. As they approached, they could see a gypsy piebald tethered to the farmyard gate. High-pitched sobs cut through the balmy air.

On entering the farmyard Jack and his sons saw an oddly assorted group gathered around the side door of the house. The Machin boys, who were white faced and tearful, were watching Ivy attempt to console Hannah, assisted by her husband.

"Get her inside," Jack rasped. "Give her some whisky Ivy before she passes out. John get the shotguns and some cartridges." Turning to Hannah's husband, Jack said, "Now then lad, what's your name?"

"Patrick Kenny," the gypsy replied. "Do you know what the hell's going on?"

"Aye Patrick lad I do," Jack said, "and its not good news! These boys here, and our son Tat, have seen Bill Fletcher away off in Podgill with a baby."

"You mean the giant?" Patrick said horrified. "You mean he's got our baby?"

"It looks that way, I'm afraid," Jack said, putting his hand on the gypsy's arm. "Let me read you this message, it's from the police sergeant in Kirkby Stephen."

As Jack read out Sergeant Crowther's message, Patrick Kenny buried his face in his hands. Jack gave him a minute before saying, "Come with us lad, you'll be needed." Then turning to Michael he said, "Michael, you take the Machin boys up to Rookby Scarth, take this message with you and explain as best you can. Come back down the railway track and wait above Podgill till you see us. Try to get Dick to show you where, and bring his dad."

Jack went into the kitchen where Ivy sat with her arm around Hannah's shoulders. The whisky had calmed her slightly but her face was drained of colour and her eyes swollen with crying. Ivy looked up at Jack and shook her head.

"We'll be off now, Ivy, do your best with the lass. Don't worry about our Tat; he's done the right thing and the Machin boys an' all. Patrick's coming with us, Hannah. Don't worry; we'll get your baby back."

Jack and John took the two shot guns and left the farmyard with Patrick Kenny. Jack whistled up the sheep dogs which raced after the men excited by the unexpected activity. The way to Podgill viaduct was mostly down hill and they soon saw the massive structure jutting clear of the tree tops.

Tat had recovered his composure by the time Sergeant Crowther returned to the Black Bull. He was accompanied by a young constable and a local gamekeeper. The latter was an auxiliary policeman and wore a black and white striped armband on his shirt sleeve. He carried a twelve bore shot gun and had a lurcher on a chain.

"All right then, Tat, let's be having you," Sergeant Crowther said cheerily. Looking at Mrs Watson, he added, "Don't worry now, Missus, we'll look after him."

"Mind you do," Mrs Watson said with tears glittering in her eyes. She stood in the yard watching the strange group cross the road. Several drinkers had assembled in front of the Black Bull and began to speculate as to what the policemen, accompanied by young Tat, were up to.

As they passed the cricket ground, not only the spectators but also the players themselves looked over at the three men, the little boy and the lurcher, as they strode purposefully along the river side towards Podgill. Sergeant Crowther was seen to reach down and hoist the boy onto his shoulders.

Tat began to enjoy riding on the sergeant's shoulders. George Crowther was six feet four and Tat was amazed at the different view of the world he experienced from this new vantage point. The three men joked with Tat in order to keep his spirits up and divert attention from what they might find in Podgill.

"By God, you weigh a ton, lad," the sergeant said after about ten minutes. "Come on, Norman, you take a turn." Tat was transferred to the young constable's shoulders for the remainder of the journey. The sergeant pulled ahead slightly with Joe Harker, the auxiliary policeman, and began to discuss how best to deal with the problems ahead of them.

On entering Podgill, they could see the arches of the viaduct through the trees. Tat thought he recognized the familiar barking of the Fell End dogs above the splashing of the beck. Then he saw his father and his brother John waiting under the viaduct with the four dogs. They held shotguns under their arms. A stranger stood slightly apart from them, he had hunched shoulders and was smoking a cigarette.

"Dad," Tat yelled excitedly. The constable lifted Tat from his shoulders and lowered him to the ground. Tat raced across the beck, which had very little water in it. Jack stooped down and gathered Tat up in his arms. He held his son tight whilst telling him how brave he'd been and how proud he was of him.

"Now then, Jack, you've got a grand lad there," said the sergeant as he approached.

"How do, George," Jack said as he placed Tat on the ground and shook hands with the sergeant. Tat ran over to his brother and began fussing the dogs who were delighted to see him in such unfamiliar surroundings.

"Who's yon gypsy lad then?" Sergeant Crowther asked Jack.

"That's Patrick Kenny. He's the baby's father." Jack went on to explain how Hannah and Patrick had ridden up to Fell End searching for their missing child.

"Bloody hell, Jack, it's a bad do," the sergeant said. "The thing is Bill Fletcher hasn't ever done owt wrong, not really, in all the years I've been on the force. Anyway, I'll have a word with the lad, then young Tat's going to show us Bill's hideout."

"Aye the Machin boys told us about it, it's up there somewhere." Jack gestured towards the high ground beyond the viaduct where the railway tracks curved away from Podgill. Patrick Kenny had no love of the police. However, on the way to Podgill Jack had explained to him that George Crowther was a good man and could be trusted. He had emphasized that they all wanted to retrieve the baby and would have to act under the sergeant's supervision, and above all stay calm.

Sergeant Crowther approached Patrick Kenny and held out his hand to him. The gypsy reluctantly shook it.

"I'm glad you're with us lad, your little lass will be glad to see you. Let's face it, she won't be too thrilled with all our ugly mugs. Now then, young Tat over there is going to show us where Bill Fletcher hangs out. I reckon that's where your little lass is. I must insist that you stay in the background and don't do owt without my say so. Have you got that?"

Patrick Kenny looked the sergeant square in the eye and said between clenched teeth, "If that bastard has harmed a hair of her head I'll kill him."

"Aye well lad, I can sympathise with you on that score. I'm sure I'd feel exactly the same if I was standing in your shoes," Sergeant

Crowther said, patiently. "The thing is though, that way you'd swing for murder. Your little lass would grow up without her dad and you'd never see her again. So think on. You've got to leave this to us."

Patrick Kenny hung his head and bunched his fists at his side.

"Now listen, lad, every minute we waste talking means your lass is all alone with Bill Fletcher somewhere in these woods. If you can't promise me that you'll stay in the background till you're wanted I'll cuff you to the bloody viaduct. Is that understood?"

"Aye," Patrick replied, his dark features contorted and tears shimmering in his bright blue eyes. "I'll do as you say!"

"Good lad," said the sergeant, "let's get organized. Now then young Tat, show us where Bill's hideout is, if you please."

Tat pointed in the direction of the high ground beyond the boggy corner of Podgill. "It's up there, but the quickest way is across the viaduct along the tracks."

"All right let's get up there. Jack keep them dogs close; we don't want them running ahead," the sergeant said.

Tat led the way up the wooded slopes until they reached the fence.

After climbing this, they paused, listening for any approaching trains. Once the sergeant was sure the coast was clear they sprinted across the viaduct and paused to regain their breath when they reached the other side.

"Now then Tat, how much further?" Sergeant Crowther asked quietly.

"It's round the bend. There's a path that Bill uses; it sort of vanishes into the bushes. On the other side there's this old limekiln. That's where Bill sleeps at night."

As they edged forward keeping to the thick bracken at the side of the tracks, Tat tugged at the sergeant's sleeve and whispered, "Look there's the path, and further on that's the spot where the bushes cover it over."

"Right," said the sergeant, "that high ground beyond, I dare say you can look down on this old kiln from there. What do you think, Tat?"

"Aye you can, but there's brambles and nettles in the way," Tat answered. Then he suddenly pointed up the curving tracks.

"Look yonder," he said, "it's our Michael with Dick and his dad." They peered up the railway line and about two hundred yards away saw the approaching group walking towards them through a steep sided cutting.

"I never thought they would get here this fast," said Jack Taylor.

"We'll have to stop them before they get too close," the sergeant said urgently.

"I'll go," John said.

"Good lad," said Sergeant Crowther, "keep to the grass on the embankment, otherwise you'll make a hell of a racket. Tell them to come forward quietly and get on that high ground above Bill's hideout. Tell them to do nowt until I join them up there. Get going."

Turning to the others, the sergeant said, "Now then lads, if we can surprise old Bill we'll get away with this. Remember he's none too bright and doesn't move very quickly. If we can get in there and snatch the little lass, we'll be out again before he's gathered his wits. After that he'll probably get nasty and break cover. Tat, is there any way out of there other than the path?"

"No, I don't think so," said Tat.

"Right, so he'll break out this way along the path. If he gets as far as the railway he can only go one of two ways. We've got him boxed in. Now listen, if you need to use your guns shoot over his head or at the ground. If he gets through us let the dogs go to slow him down. Right, I'll get up there. Watch for my signal."

As Sergeant Crowther scuttled forward to join the others on the high ground, the faint sound of a baby crying floated on the air. Patrick Kenny winced and ground his teeth. Jack hissed, "Steady now, lad," and put a restraining hand on his arm. "We're almost there, keep calm. You'll be needed soon enough."

George Machin saw the sergeant approaching them first. He

nudged Michael and John Taylor to alert them and put his finger to his lips. Dick, who seemed terribly small amongst the men, crouched at his father's side. He had led them to the position directly above Bill's hideout. Sergeant Crowther was dripping with sweat by the time he lowered himself into the grass beside them.

"Now then," he whispered, "can you see owt from up here?"

"Not a lot," replied George Machin, "But the baby's alive at any rate."

"Aye, I heard her crying just now," replied the sergeant, "that's a Godsend if nowt else." He began to remove his tunic and helmet. "Right," he said, "we'll have to make a move while there's still time, I'm going to crawl up a bit further to see if I can spot Bill and the baby."

As the sergeant peered through the brambles he caught sight of the top of Bill's head and could hear him muttering to himself. Suddenly, he heard the baby cry again and felt a knot of anxiety in his stomach. He craned forward a few more inches and, to his great relief, saw the baby lying on a bed of bracken right in the middle of the clearing. The sergeant wrinkled his nose as the foul smell from the place reached him.

He slithered back down the incline to join the others. "Right, the baby's in the middle of the clearing and Bill is on the side nearest us, just outside the entrance to the kiln as far as I can tell. I'm going to show myself to Bill and try to get his attention. Michael, get over to the others and tell them to be ready. Tell Joe Harker to get up close to them bushes and wait for me to shout, 'right Joe.' Then get in there fast, grab the bairn and get out again as quick as he can and give the baby to Patrick Kenny. After that we'll have Bill to sort out. Now get going."

Michael delivered the message and held Joe Harker's lurcher whilst he took up his position just where the path disappeared into the thicket. Sergeant Crowther glanced all around him to check that everybody was ready and carefully got to his feet.

Bill Fletcher tried to ignore the grating cries the baby produced.

He knew the squirming infant must be hungry. He didn't fully understand why he had scooped the baby up with one hand as he'd passed the gypsy camp. He had seen that the only person in the vicinity had been an old man asleep on the steps of a caravan. He liked the look of the baby so he'd just picked it up and kept walking. He'd thought that the baby would like his camp, and would be company for him. The shouting baby had amused him initially, but now it was getting on his nerves. So he would light a fire and cook some rabbit to feed the baby. That would stop it screaming.

Bill tore up some bracken and made a bed for the baby. He hoped she would go to sleep whilst he prepared their supper. He had a box of matches in his pocket and was fumbling with these trying to light the dry grass under some twigs when he heard a voice above him.

"Now then, Bill," the voice said, "are them matches damp? Try these." Bill straightened up and turned in the direction of the voice. Silhouetted against the sky up on the embankment stood a man. He was holding something out to him. The voice came again.

"Here you are Bill, try these matches; they're dry as a bone, I'll chuck them to you." As Sergeant Crowther prepared to toss the matchbox down to Bill Fletcher, something squirmed past his right leg. The brambles shook and in an instant Dick Machin appeared on the crumbling roof of the old limekiln. Without warning, Dick vaulted right over Bill Fletcher's head and landed sprawling behind him in the clearing. In a split second Dick was on his feet and had snatched the baby. He didn't look back and dived through the bushes with the baby tucked firmly under one arm. He cannoned into Joe Harker who was still awaiting the signal from Sergeant Crowther.

"I've got the little bugger," he said to the shocked auxiliary constable, grinning from ear to ear. Joe Harker took Dick by the scruff of the neck and frog marched him along the track to where Jack Taylor lay in wait with Patrick Kenny and the constable. Patrick ran forward and took the baby from under Dick's arm. He hugged the child to his chest and rocked it to and fro.

Meanwhile, Dick's father had scrambled up the bank and, standing next to Sergeant Crowther, yelled, "Dick get back here now, you little sod."

"He's been and gone has your Dick," Sergeant Crowther said, unable to suppress his surprise at the speed with which Dick had intervened. John joined the two men and they all looked down at Bill Fletcher who was only just beginning to take in what had happened.

The giant whirled round in lumbering circles, then stood still, staring at the shaking bushes through which Dick and the baby had escaped. With a roar he charged at the thicket tearing it aside with his enormous hands.

"Stop there Bill," the sergeant shouted. "Look out lads, he's coming your way," he added urgently.

Bellowing like a mad man, Bill emerged from the thicket and lurched along the path onto the railway lines. Jack Taylor grabbed Dick and Tat, dragged them across the tracks and pushed them up the embankment on the other side.

"Get up to the top and stop there," he rasped.

He turned and saw the young constable and Joe Harker moving to block Bill Fletcher's path. Michael was struggling to restrain Harker's lurcher. He heard the far-off whistle of a train.

Sergeant Crowther heard it too; he looked back up the line and saw the smoke in the distance.

"Get off the bloody tracks," he yelled, "there's a train coming. Get off the tracks now." The constable and Joe Harker climbed up the embankment and Michael pulled the lurcher into the bracken on the opposite side.

Bill watched his tormentors withdraw and took his chance. He began to run along the tracks towards the viaduct; he almost fell more than once as his ill-shod feet faltered on the sleepers.

The train passed, puffing out dense smoke and shedding soot. The crew and passengers waved, especially at the two little boys high up on the embankment. They wondered why the two policemen were present and what the shotguns and dogs were all about. Tat and Dick looked down on the whole scene. As the train rounded the curve, the driver spotted the shambling figure of Bill Fletcher who was by now starting to cross the viaduct. He blew a long blast on the whistle and applied the brakes. Tat tugged at Dick's sleeve and pointed to the further end of the viaduct.

A train was speeding into view from the opposite direction. Bill was almost half way across the viaduct before he realised that he was hopelessly trapped. Both trains blew their whistles continuously, whilst their brakes screeched and threw out red-hot sparks. Bill whirled around like a gigantic scarecrow before he scrabbled his way on to the left hand parapet of the viaduct. As the trains passed each other Bill stood up straight, spread his arms and pitched forward. His last sound on earth was drowned out by the metallic cacophony. As he plummeted towards the beck over one hundred feet below, he shouted one word, '*B A B Y!*'

THE INITIATION

The ball skittered off the muddy ground and spun into Tat's hands. Instead of running with it he side-stepped two Wigton forwards and chipped it into a gap some fifteen feet ahead. Running into the space Tat gathered the ball and pelted the remaining ten yards handing off the Wigton fullback. With elegant ease, he grounded the ball between the posts. The try was easily converted by Norman Dixon, Appleby's captain, putting them five points ahead. Appleby kept control of the game for the remaining eight minutes, securing their fourth victory of the season.

John Heatherly, who doubled as history master and the school rugby coach, walked off the pitch with William Randle, the headmaster. "Well, William," he said, "I think it's becoming clear as to who we can replace Dixon with as captain after he leaves. Young Taylor just gets better and better. We only practiced that manoeuvre fully a fortnight ago. I've rarely seen it done better."

"I agree absolutely," Mr Randle replied, "The boy is a natural. However, isn't there an understanding that the captaincy always goes to a three-quarter?"

"Yes, that is invariably the case. There is no written ruling on the matter, however. I think it has always been assumed that the backs are free to exercise their intelligence, whilst the pack are the pick and shovel types. Quite frankly, all that is nonsense. With your approval I want to bring Taylor on with the intention that he take over the captaincy when he enters the lower sixth. What do you think?"

"Of course, of course, John," the headmaster replied. "I will, as ever, leave it in your capable hands."

The Wigton party left within the hour, subdued and surly, to start their two and a half hour train journey home. They were one of the best school teams in Cumberland and didn't take kindly to being beaten by a smaller school from the smaller county of Westmorland.

It usually took about two hours before the aches and pains set in.

Tat felt them keenly as he collected the lantern from the boiler room. Next day he would be worse unless he ran a mile or two to loosen up. Tat was on locking up duty for the week and attempted to sort the keys into a semblance of order under the yellow glow of the gaslight, which burned all night in the entrance hall.

There were eight gates to lock at various points around the perimeter of the school grounds. Tat hunched his shoulders against the cold and held the lantern out in front of him. He left the main gate until last. This was a double wrought iron affair with the school crest set upon both parts. Tat looped the chain securely and snapped the large padlock together. By now his hands were chilled from handling the cold metal of the gates. He walked down the drive looking forward to spending a few minutes in the boiler room whilst he returned the carbide lamp to its shelf. Halfway down the drive he looked up at the looming bulk of the school which had become his second home for much of the last five years. He was fifteen and preparing to take his matriculation exams in the summer.

The windows of the gaunt red and grey sandstone building were lit up. He picked out his own dormitory high up to the left, just under the eaves of the roof. He shared this with eight other fifth year boys all of whom had started along with himself and Dick. They got along tolerably well and had, by now, learned how to avoid rubbing each other up the wrong way. He had heard the headmaster remark that by the time they reached the fourth and fifth years most boys had 'had the corners knocked off them.' Tat's gaze wandered across to the far right of the upper storey to where the junior dormitories were situated. The lights in these quarters would be turned off at eight o'clock. Tat found himself wondering what would befall the younger and weaker boys in the following hour or so.

Five years previously, Tat and Dick, accompanied by their mothers and Mrs Watson, had visited Appleby initially in order to be fitted with their school uniforms and sports gear. The stable lad, resplendent in goggles and cap, had driven them all from Kirkby Stephen in Mrs. Watson's shiny new eight-horse power Rover, with the canvas hood down. They had already undertaken several journeys along the lanes through the Eden Valley. The novelty of travelling at what to the boys seemed to be unlimited speed, in the noisy motor with its petrol smells and continuous vibrations, was still in its infancy. They couldn't get enough of it.

The trip to Appleby was just over twelve miles. It took them way beyond their familiar surroundings, through villages and hamlets they had barely heard of. The town wasn't much bigger than Kirkby Stephen but with the Eden running through it, dividing it into two halves connected by an impressive sandstone bridge, it felt very different. The buildings in Kirkby were built from grey brockram. Appleby was in an area of red sandstone that they later discovered stretched all the way along the Eden Valley beyond Penrith to Carlisle.

Many of the buildings in Appleby were bigger and grander than those of Kirkby Stephen. Appleby was, after all, the county town of Westmorland. A large castle stood on a hill dominating the place. It boasted the County Law Courts and an ancient town hall known as the Moot Hall that stood on its own at the bottom of the castle hill. Indeed, Appleby was a town of hills.

Whitehead's, the school outfitters and bookshop, was situated close to the bridge on a street at right angles to the river. The lad parked the motorcar outside the Tufton Arms where they would take tea later. Whitehead's occupied three floors of the building and had the monopoly of supplying pupils at the grammar school with all that they required. After an hour of much fussing and endless parading in front of the women folk, Dick and Tat were fitted out with black school blazers, grey short trousers and socks and black boots. They were dismayed with the stiffness and severity of these combinations.

The games outfits crackled with newness. The boys, used only to kicking homemade footballs about, couldn't see the point of the red and black hooped rugby shirts and voluminous navy blue shorts. When they viewed themselves in the full-length mirror they erupted into giggles as the shorts stuck out, maintaining the stiff creases in which they had been folded. The studded leather rugby boots were as rigid as cast iron and neither Tat nor Dick could walk naturally in them. Mercifully, they were spared trying on cricket whites as it was decided that this could be postponed until summer. The numerous boxes and parcels were stowed in the car whilst they consumed a generous tea in the Tufton Arms.

Before the return journey they took the road to Penrith. After climbing a steep hill they reached Appleby Grammar School, set back in its own spacious grounds about a quarter of a mile outside the town. They had pulled up outside the school gates which were shut. The women made favourable remarks about the large sandstone building with its many gabled slate roofs and numerous tall chimneys. A circular lawn was situated immediately outside the double doors which were clearly the main entrance to the school. Conifers flanked the right hand side of the driveway, whilst on the left were well kept lawns and flower beds. Through a garth of full-grown chestnut trees way over to the left of the main building, the white painted rugby posts indicated the position of the playing fields. Tat and Dick glanced at each other in silence, each of them experiencing a sudden sinking feeling. It dawned on them for the first time that this gaunt building, which the women so admired, would be where they were to survive without their families in just over ten days time. On the way back to Kirkby Stephen the boys were decidedly subdued.

Tat had said his farewells to his brothers and his father bravely enough. He had spent ten minutes or so fussing the farm dogs and endured his mother's scolding when she discovered the multitude of hairs they had transferred to his school blazer. His father had delivered Tat and his mother, along with his trunk and tuck-box, in the pony and trap to the Black Bull. Dick and his mother were already there. Mrs Watson insisted upon a thorough inspection of both boys whilst the lad loaded their luggage in the boot at the back of the motor. She told them they looked grand, though both Tat and Dick felt stupid in their unfamiliar, stiff uniforms. They dreaded being spotted by any Kirkby lads and kept close to the car in the relative safety of the stable-yard.

The boys grew less and less boisterous as they approached Appleby. By the time they drove through the town and saw the chimneys of the school standing clear of the surrounding trees, they were silent and settled in their leather seats closer to their mothers.

The scene which met them when they swung through the double gates, now fully open, couldn't have been more different from their last sight of the school. The place was alive with activity, numerous traps and light carts stood around the circular lawn. They edged forward in turn until each of them stopped opposite the main entrance to the building. Piles of luggage stood at intervals, gradually being added to by each new arrival. Boys and their parents milled about greeting each other. Only two other motorcars were present, carefully manoeuvring through the crush so as to avoid frightening the horses. Plentiful piles of horse dung were quickly spirited away by two stable lads wielding shovels and a barrow.

A bald man with spectacles, wearing a flowing black gown over his well-cut tweed suit, seemed to be in charge. As Mrs Watson's motorcar drew up opposite the front entrance, he smiled and approached the vehicle. He was followed closely by a tall fair-haired woman dressed in black.

"Good afternoon, ladies," he said pleasantly, leaning into the car. "What an impressive vehicle. I can see I'm falling behind the times. Let me introduce myself. I am William Randle, the headmaster. Now by the look of these two fine chaps I'd guess they must be new boys. Let me help you all out."

Mrs Watson, confident as always, took charge of identifying themselves as the Taylor and Machin party. The tall lady was introduced as the headmaster's wife. Whilst the group exchanged pleasantries, Tat noticed how shy his mother was, only speaking when spoken to. This baffled him as his mother was normally so outgoing. He glanced up at the large many windowed façade of the school and was momentarily overawed by the sheer size and complication of the building. He glanced at Dick who was unnaturally pale and wide-eyed.

"Now, my boys," the headmaster said, leaning over Tat and Dick, "which one of you is which?"

Mrs Watson stepped in and said, 'This is my grandson, Thomas, and this is Richard.' The boys took the outstretched hand of the headmaster shyly and repeated the performance with Mrs Randle. In truth, this was the first time either of them had actually shaken hands properly with a stranger. The two boys stood close to their mothers as the headmaster continued to chat. Eventually, he said, "Now lads, say your goodbyes and wait with the other new boys just inside the entrance. A prefect will show you where to go and what to do."

Tat and Dick were hugged and kissed by their mothers and Mrs Watson. The women wore brave expressions but Tat noticed that tears glinted in his mother's eyes as she whispered in his ear, "Off you go Tat, be a good lad and do your best. It won't be long afore we see you. Tat I love you, remember now."

Tat felt an upsurge of emotion far beyond anything he had previously experienced. He was on the verge of panic but forced himself not to cry. Mr and Mrs Randle ushered the women away towards their own quarters where tea was being served to the ever-growing throng of parents.

Dick's white face was streaked with tears as they shuffled through the double doors. He brushed them away roughly, furious with himself for showing his feelings. Inside, a long corridor stretched seemingly forever in both directions. A group of boys stood awkwardly along the outer wall, all dressed identically in their stiff new uniforms. Two or three of the newcomers were noticeably smaller than the rest and their uniforms were painfully large for them. Nobody spoke.

Older boys hurried to and fro calling out to each other. Trunks and cases were being moved towards the bottom of a wide stone staircase on handcarts. Three or four tough looking men proceeded to haul the luggage up the stairs. Nobody took any notice of the new boys until suddenly a youth of about seventeen approached them. He spoke loudly and distinctly to make himself heard above the general hubbub.

"Now you lot." he said, "my name is Johnson. I'm a prefect and it's my job to show you the ropes. Follow me and look sharp about it."

He turned away and started up the staircase which was thronged with jostling boys of various sizes and ages, dodging the sweating men carrying trunks and boxes. The new boys were frequently barged out of the way with apparent indifference. After what seemed to be an eternity of passing down corridors and up further staircases, Johnson halted the group outside a large panelled door. A painted sign declared this to be the 'Junior Dorm.' Trunks, boxes and cases were piled up on either side of the entrance.

Johnson opened the door and ushered the new boys inside. The room was long and wide with windows at the far end. Tat glimpsed the outline of the fells in the distance. About thirty iron-framed beds flanked the walls, each covered with identical grey blankets. Small, much used wooden lockers stood by each bed at the head end. Two washbasins, with discoloured taps above them, stood in an alcove in the far right corner. The floorboards were bare and much scrubbed. There was a smell of carbolic in the air.

"Right," Johnson said, 'Home sweet home, eh lads! Each one of you will find a card with your name on it placed on the pillow of the bed which you will occupy. It looks as though your luggage has found its way here ahead of you. Sort it out between you, put your trunk at the end of your bed, anything else under it. I'll be back in ten minutes to give you the grand tour. Look sharp now." He turned and left.

The group moved hesitantly to begin the task of sorting out their luggage. They hardly spoke to each other. They were numbed by the abruptness with which their loved ones had been taken from them, and the realization that they were on their own for the first time in their lives. To Tat's relief, Dick had pulled himself together. Although pale, he was dry-eyed and took charge of dragging the trunks and boxes into the dormitory. He even got a few of the new boys to laugh at his silly antics.

Johnson showed them around the school. He pointed out what they could and couldn't do in various parts of the cavernous building. They were shown the classroom where they were to be taught for the coming year. It was a high ceilinged room with rows of battered desks and chairs. There were windows down one side, placed too high in the wall to afford a view of the outside world.

A scuffed blackboard stood next to the tall desk and chair which their teachers would occupy in front of the classroom. The room smelt of chalk, ink and dust.

The communal washroom and toilets filled the boys with dread. Four huge baths stood in the centre of the room. They were stained and chipped, as were the washbasins fixed in a row along one wall. Toilets with cast iron cisterns and dangling chains were visible through the open doors of dingy cubicles, dimly illuminated by a single gaslight. The place dripped with condensation, which streaked the peeling, lime-washed walls and gathered in pools on the flag-stoned floor. Sinister- looking lead pipes snaked across the walls and emerged from the floor. To the new boys, it looked for all the world like a medieval torture chamber.

As they re-traced their steps along the corridor which led to the Junior Dorm, one of the smallest boys began to sob quietly. Johnson took his hand and leaned down to whisper a few words in his ear. He spent a minute or two making sure that everybody knew which bed was theirs, and that the luggage was arranged correctly. He ordered each boy to sit on his bed whilst he shut the door and stood with his back towards it.

"Now, lads," he said, "don't look so anxious, you can't be expected to memorize every nook and cranny of the school just yet. In a few minutes the bell for supper will ring and we will assemble in the main corridor downstairs before entering the dining hall. You won't all sit together. I will show you to your individual places. During the meal do not speak unless you are spoken to.

"After supper return here, when the headmaster's wife, Mrs Randle, will introduce you to the matron, Mrs Chatterly. They will explain how we do things here, and you will meet the other occupants of Junior Dorm."

Johnson paused and looked at the little boy who had held his hand. The child had stopped crying but his eyes were puffy and red-rimmed. "Now I know some of you are upset and frightened. You might be surprised to know that I was just like you when I started here seven years ago. I can assure you that within a couple of weeks or so you will all settle in and feel at home. Here in Threlkeld

House we never tell tales; it is called sneaking. Meanwhile, be brave and do what you are told. Things may happen after lights out which…'

Just then the supper bell rang.

Tat held his numbed hands towards the gently rumbling boiler. How long ago it all seemed. He judged that he had ten minutes of privacy left before prep. He fumbled along the dusty shelf behind where the lamp stood until he found the loose brick in the wall. He removed the grubby packet of Woodbines and the box of matches and placed a slightly bent cigarette between his lips. He lit it and inhaled cautiously. Tat and Dick had taken to smoking the occasional cigarette. Neither of them felt too confident about this, but persevered nonetheless. He flexed his limbs and winced at the stiffness which was now well established since the game. Yes, he'd get up early tomorrow and run a couple of miles, it always seemed to work.

Tat and his fellow fifth year pupils occupied their own study for the purposes of prep. Although they were expected to carry out their increasing amount of homework unsupervised, it was understood that a prefect or, on occasions, the headmaster himself, would look in on them from time to time. This sufficed to keep them focused, on the whole. Dick and Tat had remained close friends. They were popular with their fellow pupils for different reasons. Dick remained small for his age. His enthusiasm for jokes and clowning kept him in the limelight. Dick could rarely resist the opportunity to take risks and this, plus his naturally cheeky disposition, made him a source of irritation to the prefects and masters. He was capable of keeping them amused simultaneously, however. His quick mind ensured that he kept abreast of his school work most of the time. He could have done better and knew it. He developed a knack for pulling all his studies together just in time to put him amongst the top dozen in his year.

Dick was, as ever, determined to enjoy himself and refused to take life too seriously. He gained a reputation as a ferocious fighter, despite his size. The headmaster disliked using the cane, but was obliged to beat Dick several times. Finally, he wrote to Dick's parents. One more serious misdemeanour and Dick could face expulsion. His father had put the fear of God into him during the next holiday. George Machin had told him he would leave school at fourteen and get a job at Hartley Quarry hacking stone, until he had paid back every penny of his school fees. Dick hadn't liked the sound of that and promised to mend his ways and concentrate upon gaining a place in the sixth form.

Dick's attitude to games was flippant. He was nimble and tough and could have been good but he rarely stretched himself. He just couldn't be bothered. Tat, however, excelled on the sports field. Although he had never before even seen a rugby ball, the very first time he touched the strange oval object it seemed right to him. From the outset, he found he could catch, throw and kick it with natural ease. He established himself as a leading light in the junior team and at thirteen had been picked for the first fifteen. By this time he was five feet six and stockily built. He had replaced the regular hooker, temporarily laid up with a broken collarbone, and quickly secured this position as his own. Most hookers do their work in the scrum and throwing in at line-outs and rarely do much to affect general play. Tat however was keen to be in the thick of things and followed the ball everywhere. Much to the annoyance of the enormous second row forward, Charlie Moffat, Tat usurped him as pack leader whilst still only fourteen.

Just as at Winton, Tat found the schoolwork caused him little or no trouble. From the first year onwards he was consistently amongst the top three pupils in his form. His prowess at sport, especially rugby, ensured his popularity and perhaps because of this he was never branded a swot, unlike several of the more academic boys. Another thing that helped in this regard was Tat's talent for mimicry. At home he had frequently reduced his family to tears at meal times with his imitations of various local characters.

At school the opportunity to increase his range was vastly extended. There were at least fifteen teachers, including the headmaster and his wife, the matron, Mrs Chatterly, and the domestic staff, as well as the stable lads and Ben Jessop, the gardener, whom were all too good to resist. Until he learned how to avoid detection, Tat had been caught several times mimicking his elders and betters. His first caning had been brought about when he had been discovered regaling the class using the voice and mannerisms of Peter Broughton, the geography master. Tat had been severely shaken by the extreme pain of the beating. The three red stripes, equally spaced across his backside, took over three weeks to fade. Tat only received the cane two more times, once when he and Dick, accompanied by three other boys, were caught one moonlight night exploring the roofs and gables of the school in their pyjamas. The last time had been when their friend, Tim Hope, had been drowned during an illicit bathing excursion two summers previously. Tim's foot had become stuck fast between two boulders whilst the boys were swimming under water in a deep pool. Despite their efforts they couldn't free him. That time they had received six strokes in front of all one hundred and eighty pupils, who looked on in stunned silence.

That first supper at Appleby did little to reassure the new boys. Johnson placed them at the end of a long line of borders in the corridor at the bottom of the main staircase. After a minute or two, the headmaster and his wife emerged through a green baize door at the furthest end of the corridor. The headmaster paused and said, "Good evening boys" in a clear, loud voice.

"Good evening, sir" the boys replied as one. They all shuffled forward following Mr and Mrs Randle into the dining hall. As the new boys were about to enter, Johnson hissed, "Now remember what I told you lads, don't speak unless spoken to."

As the scraping of chairs and shuffling of feet gradually subsided, Johnson showed the last new boy to his place. Silence descended and the headmaster said grace. The chairs scraped once more and three maids stepped up to a long table at the kitchen end of the dining room to serve the food. The boys went up with empty plates to receive their portions on a table-by-table basis. Tat's table was the last to be served so the food, a grey looking mince dish with overdone potatoes and cabbage, was almost cold. The pudding, though simple, proved to be rather nice: stewed apples with a square of pastry and sweet custard. To most of the new boys, the meal passed in a blur of anxiety. Tat looked downwards throughout the proceedings and avoided catching anybody's eye.

He forced himself to eat every scrap set before him.

After the tables were cleared, the headmaster rose and silence fell once more. He made a short speech welcoming everybody back after the long summer vacation. He emphasized the need for the utmost effort on everybody's behalf to do their best to maintain the highest standards in the classroom and on the sports field. Above all he reminded his audience of the need to observe Christian Principles at all times.

He concluded by addressing the new boys, "You new members of our boarding establishment will find life away from your homes and loved ones somewhat strange initially. I want you to think of the school as your home, where you will be nurtured and educated in the best English traditions. My wife and I, and Mrs Chatterly and her staff might be looked upon as your second family. You must strive to fit in here and above all do your best. You can do no more. You are now members of Threlkeld House. Welcome to you all."

He then lowered his head and said a short prayer. Johnson was waiting in the corridor outside. When all the new boys were present he reminded them that they were to go to the Junior Dorm to meet the headmaster's wife and Mrs Chatterly. He made sure they knew exactly how to get there.

Mrs Randle and the matron were waiting for them when they nervously entered the dormitory. The two women were kind and efficient. They gave instructions about how to unpack their belongings and keep them neat and tidy. A large wicker basket stood under the windows; this, they were told, was for dirty laundry. A change of shirts, socks and underwear took place every Wednesday after they had all taken a weekly bath. Towels were hung upon pegs next to the two sinks where they were to wash every night and morning. The two gaslights were to be extinguished at eight o'clock sharp. Just before this they were to kneel by their beds and say their prayers.

At six in the morning they would be woken by a bell rung by a senior boy patrolling the corridors. After washing and dressing, they were to assemble at six thirty in the long corridor to await breakfast. They were to gather in the first form classroom at eight o'clock, when they would meet the new dayboys and receive instructions from their form master. A group of fifteen boys, who were now second years, had grouped together in the corridor during the closing stages of this address. Mrs Randle called them in eventually and introduced them. A bewildering confusion of surnames was bandied about; not many stuck in the minds of the new boys.

When Mrs Randle and the matron withdrew, the second year boys chatted easily amongst themselves. None of them spoke to the new boys; it was as though they didn't exist. Finally, once they had washed and changed into their nightshirts, the older boys knelt by their beds and began to pray. The new boys hesitantly followed suit, after which they squeezed between their tightly stretched bedclothes. Mrs Chatterly bustled through the door to extinguish the gas mantels.

A long silence followed. A few whispered conversations struck up for a while amongst the second years. The new boys lay stiff with apprehension not knowing what to expect. The beds were hard and creaked at the slightest movement. In the aching silence, one or two of the new boys sobbed, overwhelmed by the sheer loneliness of their predicament. Tat gritted his teeth as tears prickled beneath his eyelids. He felt a leaden pain in his throat and wondered if this was the strange condition referred to as home-sickness. He had overheard his mother use the expression in conversation with Mrs Machin and his Gran on the journey to Appleby. It didn't seem possible that he had been kissed and hugged by his mother only four hours previously. It seemed like a lifetime ago. Despite all this, Tat eventually began to doze.

Suddenly, Dick called out to Tat from the opposite side of the dormitory, "See you tomorrow, old lad."

"Shut your gob, farm-boy," snarled one of the second years.

Breakfast consisted of porridge with milk, bread and butter, and strong tea served from a huge gurgling urn. Tat noticed that the senior boys produced their own pots of jam or marmalade, presumably brought with them from home. Nobody spoke to the new boys.

By the time they reached their classroom, an influx of strange boys of all different ages were milling around the ground floor corridors. They were noisy and cheerful; there was much pushing and shoving. Through the windows of the main corridor Tat saw a steady stream of boys making their way through the main gates. Some were on bicycles but mostly they were on foot. A horse and trap scattered them as it clattered down the drive with at least ten boys on board. The dayboys were arriving.

When they reached the classroom, after threading their way between groups of jostling pupils, they found Johnson gathering a group of boys all dressed in stiff new uniforms like their own. They glanced about nervously trying to make sense of their new surroundings. Johnson herded the new boys into a line to await the arrival of their form master. After a few minutes a fresh-faced man in his early thirties appeared dressed in a tweed jacket and corduroy trousers. Over this he wore a rather tattered black gown.

"Morning, Johnson," he said breezily, "so this is my lot is it? That'll be all thank you," he added and Johnson took his leave without a backward glance.

He surveyed the new boys for a moment doing a quick head count. "Right then boys, let's get cracking. In you go. First things first, we'll get you all sorted out with a desk and do the register."

After ten minutes or so, each boy occupied one of the scarred desks on the principle that the bigger boys sat at the back and the smallest at the front.

"I am your form master; my name is Blandish; however, you will call me Sir. In fact, you will address all your teachers as Sir. You will have all your lessons in this classroom initially. I will write your timetable up on the blackboard and you will copy it into your jotter which you will find in your desk. Over the next few days you will be issued with exercise books and textbooks for each subject by the masters responsible for them. You will write your name in each book and be held responsible for them all. On no account damage or lose them."

He glanced at the clock on the wall behind him, "In a few minutes the bell will sound for assembly. You will form an orderly line and follow me to the school hall. You will occupy the front two rows."

The school hall seemed enormous to the new boys. The walls were oak panelled, with lists of names carved into the wood, picked out in gold leaf. Eventually, they came to understand that these were the names of former pupils who had gone to various universities. The earliest example referred to one Robert Langton, who had gained a place at Queen's College, Oxford, in 1470.

When all the boys were assembled, with the sixth formers at the back and the new boys at the front, the masters swept in, black gowns billowing around them, the headmaster entering last. The whole school rose as the masters took their place on the stage facing the boys. The headmaster stood to the left beside an elaborately carved chair with a large desk in front of it. He looked at the assembled school for a moment and said, "Good morning boys, please sit."

The headmaster remained standing. Tat tried his hardest to follow the proceedings. To his surprise, a piano struck up. Even though this was situated almost directly in front of him on the stage, until that moment he hadn't noticed it. Mrs Randle played the accompaniment for several hymns which were rousingly sung by the whole school. She was the only woman present. They stood up to sing and remained standing for prayers bowing their heads and closing their eyes. The headmaster made a lengthy speech, most of which went in one of Tat's ears and out of the other. Suddenly, it was all over and his fellow new boys were the first to file out of the hall. They kept their eyes on the floor.

The rest of the day seemed to fly by at breakneck speed. They met five masters who initiated them into their respective subjects. Tat was fascinated by their different hairstyles and choice of clothes. Some wore spectacles, others had moustaches. At least two had shiny, bald heads. They all wore long black gowns. Mostly due to nerves and anxiety, the new boys did exactly what was asked of them. There was a break at ten thirty, when all the pupils spilled out into the big yard behind the main school building. Tat was relieved to find the dayboys friendlier than the boarders, who had so far ignored them. They quickly got to know their class mates, exchanging information about where they came from and what their fathers did.

At lunch time the boarders lined up once more in the main corridor before taking their meal in the dining hall. It consisted of meat, which Tat failed to recognize, with the usual soggy potatoes and cabbage. The meat was tough and stringy and Tat's jaws ached from the prolonged chewing he found necessary to swallow it.

The dayboys were marched off in a long line, which seemed to be called a 'crocodile', to have their lunch in a canteen somewhere in the town. There was half an hour in the yard when the dayboys returned to work off the stodgy food. The new boys were left to themselves, which allowed them to discover each others' names. They even got as far as allocating the odd nickname. To his relief, Tat was to remain Tat for the rest of his time at Appleby.

Before supper on that first day, the new boys were introduced to homework for the first time. Each master had set them a task within their subject. The boarders gathered in their common room for one and a half hours before supper every evening except Sunday, to complete their homework under the supervision of a senior prefect. It was all carried out in silence although some prefects allowed the younger boys to ask their advice and guidance if they were completely stuck.

The prefects were all sixth formers. It became clear to the boys after a day or two that they formed a stratum of discipline and control that was almost equal to the staff. They had an air of authority about them which it was unwise to challenge. Their blazers were edged with red braid and many of them wore tight black waistcoats. Separate studies and an individual common room were set aside for fifth and sixth year boys. Once a term there was a Prefects' Court when boys found breaking one or other of the many complicated regulations of the school were tried and punished. All the boarders attended these courts, which were sometimes very funny and lighthearted, and on other occasions just the opposite. Punishments varied from a forfeit such as reciting a poem or singing a song, to caning on the hand or backside. No masters ever attended a Prefects' Court.

The new boys made their way up to the Junior Dorm after supper. They felt a little more confident, having got to know each other and rubbed along with the dayboys in their class well enough. They had survived the first day.

After lights out it started.

"Right you kids, out of bed and quick about it." It was David Reynolds, the biggest of the second years. One or two new boys obeyed instantly, others sat up and peered through the gloom unsure as to what was expected of them. Some pulled their bedclothes over their heads.

Reynolds and half a dozen second years were on their feet and began pulling the more hesitant new boys out of their beds. After a deal of pushing and shoving the new boys were formed into a line along the central space between the trunks.

"Right, you little weeds," Reynolds rasped, "we are all going to have some fun and games. I should think you're all thirsty. You're thirsty aren't you, weed?" he asked, stopping in front of the smallest new boy.

"I don't know," the boy replied almost inaudibly.

"Oh dear me, do you hear that lads?" Reynolds drawled sarcastically. "He doesn't know."

Reynolds grabbed a handful of the little boy's hair and twisted his head backwards.

"I said you're thirsty aren't you, weed?" Reynolds repeated with his face only an inch or two from the boy's ear.

Between sobs the little new boy gasped, "Yes I am."

"Yes I am, sir," Reynolds growled menacingly.

Some of the second years who were milling around began to giggle.

"Yes I am, sir," the child whispered and Reynolds gave his head a final shaking. Two of the older boys had drawn the curtains which allowed the moonlight to illuminate the dormitory. The sound of dribbling liquid came from the alcove where the sinks stood. Tat glanced around and saw a second year urinating into a milk bottle. When he had finished the bottle was only half full, another boy completed the job. They brought the bottle to Reynolds.

"Oh lovely," said Reynolds holding the bottle up, "just the job, nice and warm, just what you weeds need to make you grow big and strong."

He turned back to the snivelling new boy and said, "now weed, tell me again, are you thirsty?"

"Yes, sir," the boy replied.

"That's the ticket," Reynolds said cheerily looking round for the approval of his supporters. He was rewarded by a ripple of stifled laughter.

"Give me that straw, Joe," he snapped over his shoulder. One of his cohorts handed him a somewhat battered drinking straw from a bundle he was holding. Reynolds inserted the straw into the neck of the milk bottle and after ordering two older boys to pinion his victim's arms he said, "Now then open wide" as he inserted the straw into the little boy's mouth.

"Drink up, weed," Reynolds ordered menacingly.

The terrified child, unable to see an alternative, sucked at the straw and swallowed. He grimaced and coughed violently, then hung his head gasping. Tears and snot ran off his nose and chin and pattered around his bare feet.

Strangely, Tat was relatively calm. He watched the ritual repeated as each new boy was forced to drink from the bottle. He and the Machin boys had drunk their urine on more than one occasion just to see what it tasted like. It wasn't pleasant, but Tat knew he could do it and knew it wouldn't kill him. He looked across at Dick and noticed that he had a strange smirk on his face. Dick winked at Tat.

When his turn came, Tat showed no emotion of any sort. He ignored the coughing and retching of those who had already drunk from the bottle. He let his arms go limp so that when Reynolds' assistants grabbed them they were confused at his lack of resistance. Reynolds, a good head taller than Tat, pushed the bottle towards his face. Tat locked eyes with Reynolds and pulled on the straw. He filled his mouth with urine and calmly swallowed it. Despite the burning in his mouth and throat, he didn't flinch or make a sound. He continued to look straight into Reynolds's eyes throughout.

Reynolds quickly moved on to his next victim. Eventually, it was Dick's turn. Tat stiffened not sure what Dick would do. Reynolds had remembered that it was Dick who had broken the rule of silence by daring to say goodnight to Tat the night before.

"Oh it's the farm boy's turn, take his arms lads," he said with great relish. But before they could, Dick said, "Oh ta very much" with his brightest smile. He snatched the bottle from Reynolds and drained its reeking contents. He wiped his lips with the back of his hand and said, "That was grand, thank you very much, sir."

Reynolds glared at Dick unsure of how to react. The second years doubled up with laughter and despite their distress a few new boys sniggered.

"You cheeky bastard," Reynolds hissed. 'You can all have the slipper for that."

The new boys were forced to lean over their trunks. Their nightshirts were pulled up to expose their backsides. Reynolds gave each of them three of the best with one of his slippers. Most were reduced to tears. Tat clenched his teeth when it came to his turn and was shocked as to how painful the beating was. Dick received six blows and despite his cheeky disposition was obviously shaken by the experience.

"Now into bed you grubby, little weeds," Reynolds gasped, out of breath from his exertions. "You can blame the farm boy for that."

Although several new boys sobbed and sniffled for a considerable time, gradually they fell asleep.

Reynolds and his mates persecuted the new boys for the next two nights after lights out. He was obviously enjoying himself, although Tat and Dick agreed that the other second years in the dorm were less enthusiastic than their bullying leader.

Reynolds seemed to have an inexhaustible repertoire of cruelty. The new boys were forced to drink more urine. The sinks were filled, and the bigger second years, under Reynolds' orders, held the new boys' heads under the icy water until their breath gave out.

They were pushed and shoved into a line along the centre of the dormitory and forced to stand on one leg for what seemed to be hours on end. Alternatively, they were instructed to hold their arms straight up above their heads. When exhaustion or a failure to balance overcame them they were beaten on their bared backsides with Reynolds' slipper.

In the mornings they would frequently find their boots knotted tightly by the laces in a tangled heap. Items of their clothing were hidden until the breakfast bell rang when Reynolds would throw them contemptuously on the floor as he left the dorm. They were obliged to brush their teeth with carbolic soap at night and again in the morning. Dick refused to do this on the third night. He was overpowered and Reynolds forced him to bite off a lump of soap and swallow it. As a lesson to the rest Dick was given a terrible slippering, which reduced him to tears. Tat was aware of his friend's stifled sobbing for at least an hour after this before he managed to sleep.

Next day Dick, white faced and walking stiffly, approached Tat in the yard during the morning break.

"Tat," he said, "we've got to stop the sod before he kills one of us. The little lads can't take much more and I'm not bloody going to."

Tat looked hard into Dick's red-rimmed eyes and saw that dark patches had developed beneath his lower lids.

"But, Dick, what can we do? Reynolds is bigger than us. If we try to do owt it'll just make him worse."

"Look Tat, obviously it's Reynolds that rules the roost. I reckon his so called mates are frightened to death of him."

"You're probably right, but where does that get us?"

"Tat, we've got to face up to him. Me and you and the rest; we've got to, don't you see?" Dick said almost in tears.

"Christ I don't know, Dick, what if Reynolds gets worse?" Tat replied miserably.

"That's the point, Tat, he's got to be stopped before he does. Come on let's round the other lads up and see what they think," Dick concluded. Dick and Tat got the other new boarders together in a corner of the yard where the coke for the boiler was stacked. They had ten minutes or so before the bell would sound to signal the end of the morning break.

Dick did most of the talking. Tat did his best to support him.

"Look, you lot," Dick said urgently. "They are only one year older than we are. They're not as tough as they make out. I reckon they're all scared stiff of Reynolds. With him out of the way the others would probably pack it in. We could all be mates. What do you think?"

Three of the first years were small for their age, the rest were as big as most of the second years, give or take an inch or two. They agreed that Reynolds was the top dog and the rest followed his orders because they were scared of him. They also admitted that they were even more frightened of Reynolds than either Tat or Dick.

Dick kicked a piece of coke savagely and ground his teeth together in frustration.

"Look," he said staring hard, "let's get the second years together at break this afternoon, without Reynolds, and find out what they really think. I reckon they'll side with us if it means Reynolds is stopped."

As the bell sounded they reluctantly agreed to this. When they filed into the classroom Dick whispered to Tat, "I know we can do it Tat, we've bloody well got to."

With some difficulty they separated the second years from Reynolds and met behind the outdoor lavatory block during the afternoon break. At first, the second years treated them with contempt and made as if to leave. One of them began to pick on the smallest new boy and Dick rushed at him in a rage and flung him to the ground. Tat grabbed Dick before he did too much damage. The second year lay cringing in a heap and burst into tears.

Tat kept tight hold of Dick and hissed into his ear, "Dick calm down, can't you see he's frightened to bloody death. We've got to talk to them, not half kill them." Dick stood aside panting loudly. Tat stepped over to the little new boy, who was by now tearful, and put his arm around his shoulder.

"Look," he said, "this is what it's all about. That silly sod picks on the little one and Dick knocks him flat. We shouldn't be fighting each other, we should be fighting Reynolds. You lot only side with the swine because you're scared of him. Well, aren't you?"

The older boys shuffled their feet and looked uneasy. Tat helped the second year up to his feet and brushed him down. He dried his eyes and said, "You don't know what he's like."

Another said, "Reynolds says he'll kill us if we don't help him."

Dick spoke up having recovered his composure. "That's the bloody point, don't help him. If we gang up on the bugger, all of us together, he'll be knackered."

Tat persuaded Dick to shake hands with the boy he'd knocked down. Finally, they all agreed that after lights out Reynolds would find himself isolated. He didn't know it but he was living on borrowed time.

Tat's mind wandered throughout the closing stages of the afternoon's lessons. Had they done enough to convince Reynolds' minions to join forces with them after lights out? If they hadn't surely things could spiral out of control. He thought about Dick who had begun to show a side of himself which Tat, until now, had never really recognized. Dick was utterly fearless and single-minded. Tat realized that the key to the dilemma was probably Dick himself. If they managed to stand firm, Dick would somehow deliver them from Reynolds' clutches.

During prep that evening and later during supper, knowing looks passed secretly between the occupants of Junior Dorm, without Reynolds' knowledge. As the headmaster said grace Tat risked a glance at Dick who sat opposite him at the next table. Dick gave Tat a quick grin and winked. His face was pale and pinched with ever deepening violet patches under his eyes.

The duty prefect glanced around the dorm to check that everything was as it should be before he extinguished the lights.

"No talking now, get to sleep," he said. His footsteps echoed down the corridor and silence fell upon the Junior Dorm.

After a few minutes, Reynolds' bed creaked and he swaggered into the middle of the dormitory.

"Alright, boys," he said menacingly, "let's get the little squirts up for a bit of sport."

Reynolds hesitated and moved towards the smallest boy's bed.

"We'll start with the runt of the litter; come on you lazy sods, let's get started."

"I'll tell you what Reynolds you can start with me." Dick had slipped out of his bed and stood swaying from side to side. Reynolds turned and looked at Dick.

"Oh bloody hell, not the little farm boy."

Without hesitation Dick rushed at Reynolds ducking low. Reynolds went down like a sack of potatoes, legs and arms flailing. He squealed in agony as Dick grabbed his genitals and hissed, "Come on lads, get his arms and legs." Within seconds Reynolds was immobilized as all the boys jostled to get a grip on him. Once he was secured, Dick stood up and said, "Now Reynolds you're going to get some of your own medicine."

"Come on, Titch," he added to the smallest new boy, "Get the soap and see how much he can eat."

As it happened, Titch, who was to be called that for the remainder of his time at Appleby, proved to be too nervous to participate. Others took their turn, however. With his mouth choked with soap, he was tied to his bed with his socks and nightshirt sleeves. At this moment of his humiliation and defeat, Reynolds peed himself. The dethroned bully spent a sleepless night he would never forget; his mattress and his bed clothes soaked with urine and his soap caked teeth chattering against the cold. When eventually they drifted off, Tat lingered, and wondered whether Reynolds might rise again the next day and crush them.

The morning bell awoke the boys and they began to wash and get dressed. Dick and Tat approached Reynolds and began to untie him. He was shivering and sweat beaded his forehead and upper lip.

"Right, you bastard," Dick growled, "we're going to set you loose, but listen to me, if you lay so much as a finger on any of us again you'll get more of the same."

With difficulty, Reynolds raised himself into a sitting position. All the boys gathered round and stared at him.

Tat broke the silence, "Do you understand, Reynolds? It's over. You've got five minutes to clean yourself up and get down to breakfast. But first you've got to say you're sorry."

Reynolds was shivering more violently now. He hung his head and tears splashed down onto his legs and his urine stained mattress.

Dick grabbed a handful of Reynolds' hair and twisted his head back. "Say you're sorry, you bastard" he rasped into Reynolds' twitching face.

"I am, yes I am, I'm sorry," Reynolds croaked through his dry cracked lips. Dick let his head drop forward and as he did so Reynolds vomited.

The breakfast bell rang and the boys rushed for the door leaving their tormentor to fend for himself. As they clattered down the staircase, Tat hissed into Dick's ear, "Dick we've gone too bloody far. There's going to be hell to pay."

"I just don't care Tat."

The boarders jostled around with a few minutes to spare before they lined up for breakfast. Dick nudged Tat and pointed to the end of the corridor. Titch was pulling at Johnson's sleeve. The tall prefect bent down to catch what the little new boy said. Johnson patted Titch on the shoulder before turning to the House Captain, Peter Burton. After a brief conversation, Johnson pushed his way through the gaggle of noisy boys, and headed up the staircase two steps at a time.

Titch joined Tat and Dick; he was smiling like a Cheshire cat.

"What did you say to Johnson, Titch?" Tat asked.

"Not much really. I told Johnson that Reynolds was poorly. I said he'd wet the bed and been sick. Johnson's gone to sort it out. He said I'd done the right thing."

Tat and Dick looked at each other, then back at Titch. The little boy had outsmarted them all. He had thought it through and indeed had done the right thing, for all their sakes.

"Titch," Tat said, "you're a bloody genius."

Burton called for silence and they all lined up for breakfast.

When they returned to Junior Dorm to collect their satchels and caps Reynolds' bed had been stripped to the springs. A strong smell of disinfectant pervaded the dormitory. Mrs Chatterly poked her head around the door and said, "Now boys, Reynolds is ill as you know, he's been taken to the sick bay. Do any of you feel poorly?"

The boys shook their heads and mumbled.

Mrs Chatterly paused and said, "Right, well if any of you feel unwell you are to come to me or Mrs Randle at once, is that clear?"

Throughout the day the boys from Junior Dorm began to relax. At the morning break they sought each other out to discuss their triumph. It was decided that Dick and Titch were the heroes of the hour. They all agreed with what Dick had said so desperately the previous day. They could all be mates.

As they prepared for bed that night, the atmosphere in the dormitory was positively lighthearted. The cloud had lifted, and as if to underline this, Reynolds' bed stood starkly empty. Even his trunk had been removed. It was as though he had never existed.

Philip Johnson came to check the dormitory and see to the gaslights. The good humour of the boys communicated itself to him. Just before he left he called for silence.

"All right, pipe down you lot. I thought you ought to know that Reynolds has been taken to the Cottage Hospital in Penrith for observation. It would seem he has a dangerously high fever. It's a mystery how he became ill so suddenly."

He looked around at the boys who were by now all tucked up in their beds, then added, "Anyway by the look of you it isn't contagious. But then I suspect you are tougher than you look."

With a raised eyebrow and a faint smile playing across his lips he nodded and said, "Good night to you," before closing the door.

Eventually the occupants of Junior Dorm learnt that Reynolds had transferred to Penrith Grammar School. They never saw him again.

APPLEBY HORSE FAIR

Appleby Horse Fair was reputed to be one of the oldest and biggest of its kind. It took place for two weeks every summer in early June. For some time before, the roads and lanes leading to Appleby were choked with horse-drawn gypsy caravans. Their final destination was Gallows Hill, which was about half a mile from the grammar school, just to the north of Appleby. The gypsies brought hundreds of horses and ponies with them. They were driven on their way by youths and men mounted bare back. Frequently, individual herds of unbroken horses filled the thoroughfares from side to side, raising thick dust clouds as they trotted on unshod hooves. Most of the horses were eventually pastured on the common land surrounding the ever-growing gypsy encampment.

It was a testing time for the sedate county town, which boasted a population of barely two thousand. At its peak the horse fair attracted upwards of five thousand gypsies. Extra police were drafted in from as far away as Kendal and Carlisle. The gypsies were a rowdy, lawless bunch. When no further room was available on Gallows Hill, they camped along the verges of the neighbouring lanes. Tradesmen and publicans did a roaring trade, but it was at the expense of normal standards of law and order. Some years previously, a company from the Border Regiment had camped in the castle grounds. It was hoped that the mere presence of soldiers patrolling the area would stabilize the situation. If anything, it only served to inflame the already volatile atmosphere.

The road, which ran past the school, led directly to Gallows Hill. Caravans and thundering herds of horses passed the school gates in an almost unbroken stream. The headmaster addressed the boys every summer as to how they were to behave throughout the fair. They were forbidden to fraternize with the gypsies. They were to be vigilant at all times and report any gypsies found loitering in the vicinity of the school to a master or prefect. They were to avoid confrontation at all costs. Any pupils involved in fighting with gypsy boys would be punished. The dayboys were to take an alternative route, to and from the town, across the playing field. It was a time of great anxiety and tension for the headmaster and his staff. Although many of the pupils were wary of the gypsy boys and youths, the horse fair introduced a welcome diversion from their everyday school routine.

Horse-trading took place continuously throughout the two weeks. Groups of swarthy men gathered along the lanes to inspect the horses and ponies. They were trotted to and fro, held by the forelock by running youths who were often bare-chested, glistening with sweat. When a sale was made the men spat on their palms and slapped their hands together to seal the bargain. Huge sums of money changed hands; the men peeled off greasy bundles of notes with calloused thumbs. The drinking was formidable. A day's horse-trading always ended with hours of rowdy drunkenness.

The police patrolled the town as the noisy crowds were banished to the streets at closing time. They had sense enough to stay in the background unless things got seriously out of hand. Arresting brawling, swearing gypsies after several hours of drinking, was no easy matter. Many gypsy men carried knives and were willing to use them. The boarders would watch the shouting, singing men as they reeled past the school on the way back to their encampment, from their dormitory windows. Beyond, Gallows Hill was lit up with hundreds of campfires. As the days wore on the smell of woodsmoke and fresh horse dung filled the summer air.

At all times of the day scores of horses were driven down into the town to drink and be washed in the River Eden. The bareback boys and youths would ride their mounts into the river just by the bridge at breakneck speed. The unbroken horses would follow rushing headlong into the water sending up huge fans of spray. Often dozens of people would watch this extraordinary spectacle from the bridge. The gypsies often goaded the horses into the deep central channel of the river. Almost out of their depth, they would plunge about wild-eyed and snorting. The hope was that the water would dislodge ticks and maggots as well as cool them down. Once clear of the river they would shake themselves like huge dogs on the roadside, much to the annoyance of passers by who were often soaked by the spray. The continuous running of horses to the river and back to Gallows Hill, left the road caked in ever thickening layers of dung. Big, black flies bred in this by the million.

Tat and Dick looked forward to the horse fair. They were used to gypsies working on their parents' farms and camping on the common land around Winton. However, they had never seen such a huge concentration of them in one place before.

One Saturday afternoon in June 1913 Tat, Dick and Titch had joined the crowd on the bridge to watch the horses in the river. They were coming to the end of their third year at Appleby. Tat was considerably taller than the other two. Two gypsy boys were entertaining the crowd by stepping across the backs of the horses. Now and again they missed their footing and fell in. They held onto the nearest horse's tail and pulled themselves aboard again. They were naked except for ragged discoloured shorts.

The three friends were highly amused by these antics. The crowd on the bridge began to thin out as the horses were herded onto the bank by three men riding bareback. The two gypsy boys followed and stood close to the horses as they shook the water from their coats, so that they would get a good soaking. As the horses clattered off towards Gallows Hill, the gypsy lads sat on the riverbank to dry off in the hot afternoon sun.

As it was almost four o'clock Tat, Dick and Titch agreed it was time to set off back to school. They walked past the spot where the gypsy boys were sunning themselves. They were preparing to ignore any cheek that might be directed at them, when one of the gypsies sat bolt upright staring at them.

"Tat, Dick, it is you isn't it? Well, I'll be buggered!" he exclaimed in a strong Irish burr.

The other lad sprang to his feet and added, "Jesus and Mary where the hell did you two spring from? My God, what a pair of toffs you are to be sure." Tat and Dick were wide-eyed with surprise.

"Liam and Pat," said Tat, "I should have known it was you two showing off in the river." It was the gypsy boys they had played with back at home before they had started at Appleby.

"I said we'd see you sooner or later," Dick said grinning broadly.

"We've always known you would turn up. Me and Tat have kept our eyes peeled for you."

"Ah we've been travelling all over the damned place; this is the first time we've been here for donkeys years. It's grand isn't it?" Liam said. They were all genuinely thrilled to meet again. Titch was introduced, although he was fairly hesitant about it, constantly looking over his shoulder. Tat suddenly realized why. They might be seen at any moment by a prefect or master, many of whom would pass this very spot on their way back to school. Tat began to panic then he suddenly thought of a way out of their predicament. He pointed in the opposite direction from the school and Gallows Hill.

"Look," he said, "back there near the bowling green there's a path that runs through the big trees down to the river. We'll get some ice-creams and meet you there in five minutes, all right?"

Dick trotted off with Liam and Pat whilst Tat and Titch bought vanilla cones from the little café on the corner of the bridge. They managed to make the rendezvous without losing too much ice cream. Liam and Pat had probably only tasted the stuff once or twice before. They demolished the cones in double quick time, ice cream dribbling from their chins.

"Jesus that was good! Have you come into money Tat, or what?"

"No, we get pocket money, sixpence a week to spend on Saturdays." He paused, looking at Liam and Pat and then at Dick and Titch. He knew he had an unexpected mountain to climb.

"Look, you two," he said slowly. "We've got to get back to school. It's the rules, five o'clock prep, no way out of it. That's right isn't it, Dick?" Dick blushed and mumbled something, Titch nodded.

"What the hell are you talking about?" Liam said. "Look at that pool down there. We could catch some trout; I can see the buggers from here. Get them fancy jackets off, it'll be grand."

Tat stood up and blew a long, low breath. He tried again.

"We've got to get back; we'll get hell to pay if we're late," he said. "Honestly, I mean it, we've got to go."

Titch suddenly stood up straight and said, 'We'll meet you here at four o'clock tomorrow morning; the fish are lazy then.''

"You're on, little man. I'll bet we're here first," Pat said.

As they ran back to school, sweating in the late afternoon heat, Dick panting heavily said, "What the hell were you talking about Titch, four o'clock in the bloody morning!"

"I don't know," Titch said wiping his forehead, "it's all I could think of."

"You silly sod," Dick said, "honestly, you bloody are a silly sod."

They were approaching the back entrance next to the coke heap when Tat said, "No Dick, Titch is right, it's the only way. They'll think we don't like them anymore. We can use the fire-escape and be back in time for the morning bell."

Next morning, with their uniforms stowed away in their satchels and dressed in their gym gear, Tat, Dick and Titch skirted the playing field as the sun came up. The grass was drenched in dew and before long their feet were soaked. The town was deserted. In the clear, morning light they became aware for the first time as to how much horse dung smothered the road along the riverside.

They discussed the headmaster's dire warnings regarding fraternization with the gypsies. How on earth could they tell Liam and Pat that they were forbidden to even be seen in their company? It was impossible.

"Look," Titch had said, "the first week of the fair is over. It's Sunday morning now, so there's one more week to go. We can meet them early like now, if we're careful, say twice more. Then next Saturday instead of going into town, we could go up the river with them. We'd have two or three hours to do owt we liked."

"Aye," Tat agreed, "I see what you mean. We'll say we have to abide by the rules and regulations. I just hope they believe us that's all."

"Listen, we'll just have to box clever," said Dick. "If they get the idea that we are avoiding them… well, they're tough lads, that's all I'm saying."

Liam and Pat were not there first. They sauntered through the trees about ten minutes later. Tat and Dick teased them for sleeping in, although Titch kept in the background, not yet sure of the tanned, blue-eyed gypsies.

Safe from prying eyes, they waded about in the river. Eventually, further upstream they found a deep pool with big flat rocks tumbled about its edges. It was just the sort of place where the trout would hide as the sun, now fully up, got hotter. Liam and Pat concentrated on tutoring a hesitant Titch in the art of tickling fish, without much success. After an hour of patient work, four good-sized trout lay on the stones clear of the water, in the shade.

Tat casually suggested that they should meet at the same time in the same place on the coming Tuesday.

"Why not?" Pat had said cheerfully. "Sure, we've got all the time in the world. Not like you poor sods. What in the hell do you find to do all day in that funny, old place?"

Liam asked, "Why don't we meet in the town? You could buy us some more ice creams, eh Tat?"

"Oh, we're not allowed in the town during the week; it's the rules," Tat replied hesitantly.

"Christ Almighty!" Liam said. "You're sure it's a school you're at, not a prison?"

The clock on the tower of St Lawrence's Church in the town struck five. "Come on you two," Dick said, "we'll have to run all the way back if we're not going to be caught."

"Don't forget your two fish, boys," Pat said.

"No, you have them," Tat said, slinging his satchel over his shoulder. You can tell us what they tasted like on Tuesday. Come on, you buggers, we've got to shift."

They met up in the same place on the following Tuesday and Thursday, just after dawn. They were lucky not to be caught. A policeman standing on Bongate Bridge, having a sly early morning cigarette, stared at the three schoolboys rather intently. As they were wearing shorts and singlets however and trotting along purposefully, he must have assumed that they were out for an early morning run and not up to mischief.

They arranged to meet at one-thirty after lunch in the usual place on Saturday. Tat promised to bring ice creams. Dick and Titch bought a bottle of lemonade and some currant buns. They had agreed to go upstream. Previously, on the long Sunday afternoon walks the boarders took with a couple of prefects in charge, they had been up that way. They knew that in the thick woods, which crowded in on the river, they could lose themselves there for a couple of hours. Liam had a filthy, old sack with him. He proudly displayed two dead hedgehogs he had caught during the night.

"We can cook these little beauties later," he said, grinning broadly.

Tat and Dick were thrilled at the prospect, although Titch didn't share their enthusiasm. They took off their blazers and caps and hid them in a gorse bush. As they made their way up the river, they passed under the looming walls of the castle on their right. Soon they left the town behind them and saw the beech woods in the distance. Rabbits scattered ahead of them. Pat produced a catapult and took a shot or two at them, without success. Once in the woods they found an enormous complex of badger setts, which must have remained undisturbed for hundreds of years. The river ran silent and deep beneath the tree canopy. The boys stripped off and swam for a while. Titch panicked when he spotted a large eel gliding by only a couple of feet away. He scrabbled onto the bank and refused to enter the water again, much to the amusement of the others.

When they had dried off and got dressed, Liam prepared the hedgehogs and lit a fire. They sat around chatting as the mud hardened in the red-hot embers. Titch reluctantly took his first mouthful of hedgehog and was amazed at how delicious it was.

"Good on you, little un," Pat said. "It'll put hairs on your chest to be sure."

Liam had just cracked the baked mud off the second hedgehog and begun to share it out, when a shiny black Labrador scampered amongst them without warning. It was wagging its tail furiously and showed great interest in the bones and scraps strewn about on the ground. The boys began to make a fuss of the dog when they heard a whistle some way off, amongst the trees, followed by a man's voice calling, "Jet, Jet, come away back here!"

Liam and Pat were on their feet in an instant staring through the trees. Pat was the first to see him; he pointed and said, "Oh hell, it's a bloody keeper."

Then they all saw the man about fifty yards off. He was dressed in matching tweeds with brown boots and leggings, despite the heat. A game bag was slung over one shoulder and a twelve bore on the other. He stopped and stared straight at them.

"What the hell do you think you're doing?" he yelled, unslinging his shotgun. Without a word the boys ran for it, dodging through the trees as fast as their legs could take them. "Go on Jet," the keeper shouted, "after the buggers."

Mercifully, Jet was more interested in consuming the second hedgehog, otherwise the dog would easily have out run them. A shot rang out and pellets rattled through the branches above the scampering boys.

"Stop, you bloody gypos," the keeper shouted pointlessly. Without his dog's cooperation, he knew he couldn't catch them. The boys heard the dog yelp as they ran out onto open ground. No doubt the keeper was giving Jet a good thrashing, poor thing.

They didn't stop laughing all the way back to Appleby. The church clock was striking five when Tat, Dick and Titch struggled into their crumpled blazers and crammed their caps onto their sweating heads.

"Come on, lads," Tat said, "we're bound to be late for prep." They said their hurried goodbyes to Liam and Pat, and then braced themselves for a further sprint back to school.

The two gypsy boys watched them till they were out of sight, wondering how their friends could live such a constricted life. What was it Tat had said, 'Rules and Regulations?'

WAR IS DECLARED

Towards the end of the long summer holiday of 1914 Tat, Michael and Jack Taylor were driving eight steers into Kirkby Stephen for the Wednesday auction. It was hot and close which made the beasts relatively lethargic. Tat led the way in order to block off the side lanes and tracks, whilst his father and Michael brought up the rear with two dogs. They reached the cattle pens which surrounded the circular auction building at ten o'clock. The place was already busy with sweating, cursing men herding their beasts into pens. Jack left Tat and Michael to settle the steers while he went in search of the foreman to ascertain the time at which they would enter the ring. The air was thick with the smell of fresh dung. The cattle, unsettled by the unfamiliar surroundings, and plagued by flies, became belligerent and noisy.

As their turn to put the steers into the auction ring was almost two hours away, Jack and the boys wandered into the town. When they reached the Market Square there was a tangible air of excitement about the place. Groups of people were engaged in animated conversations, many of them shared newspapers, looking over each other's shoulders absorbing the contents intensely.

Jack was greeted by Charlie Akrigg, a farmer from Winton. He carried a folded newspaper and looked gravely at Jack saying, "Well, the buggers have done it Jack, I always said it would come to this."

"Come to what?" asked Jack.

"The bloody Germans have invaded Belgium. There's a war on. Look here!" He shook out the newspaper and held it so that Jack could see the front page. The large headline was unambiguous, 'Britain at War with Germany.'

Jack took the newspaper and scanned the front page. He shook his head and blew out a long low whistle. Tat and Michael looked at each other and shrugged. The news meant little to them, although the shocked expression on their father's face as he talked to Charlie Akrigg, indicated the seriousness of the situation. Tat looked around at the knots of adults and saw that many looked equally grave. Some shook their heads in disbelief.

As the day wore on the news of the war in Europe became the sole topic of conversation. Jack went to the Black Bull with three or four other farmers who were in town for the cattle market. Tat and Michael ate a delicious pork pie apiece bought from Longdon's, the butchers closest to the Market Square. They fell in with a group of Kirkby Stephen youths all roughly Michael's age; even they were expressing their opinions about the unexpected outbreak of hostilities.

"Our lads'll sort it out sharpish when they get over there," one of them said pompously. "My uncle George is a sergeant in the Border Regiment. He says there's nowt to beat the British infantryman."

Another, who had struggled through the front page of the London Times, reckoned that the first British contingents would be deployed in Belgium within three weeks. He explained that the French had a sizeable army which had failed to modernize and might not stand up to a major incursion into their eastern territories. Ominously, he had added that the Germans, however, had the biggest standing army in Europe, which was well trained and well equipped.

Tat listened to all the conflicting gossip as he wandered amongst the market day crowds. He picked up a general air of nervous optimism. Most people, as far as he could tell, seemed to think that it was all likely to be over in a month or two, possibly even by Christmas. Eventually, Jack completed the business at the auction and was reasonably satisfied at the price the steers had fetched. They spent half an hour or so buying provisions at various shops in the town. Jack consulted a list Ivy had given him and once he was satisfied that he had procured everything they set off on the return journey to Fell End.

Supper that night was a subdued affair. Ivy was shocked at the news they brought back with them. Jack had bought one of the last newspapers available and after supper he and Ivy spent a considerable length of time with it spread out on the kitchen table trying to make sense of it all. In truth, very little of what was evolving internationally filtered down to the rural community, especially on the isolated farms.

Newspapers were not commonly read, and Jack and Ivy found the tangle of information difficult to decipher. On the third page of the newspaper was a diagrammatic map of Europe, illustrating the size and relationship of the protagonists. However, after more than an hour they eventually gave up when it came to making sense of the Balkans. There were so many individual countries and allegiances, all with unpronounceable names. How strange to read in the leading article that the incident which had eventually set the whole tinder box alight was the assassination of a Hapsburg Archduke at Sarajevo two months earlier. Ivy was left thinking that it was most improbable that a murder in a strange country, which the map showed to be on the far side of Europe, could possibly result in Britain being at war.

Michael spoke up and said that his mates had told him it would all be over in a few months. Ivy looked stern and said, "Aye that might be true our Michael, but there'll still be lads killed and maimed. Bairns'll grow up without their dads. That's one thing you can be sure of my lad. God knows where it will all end up."

Ten days later Tat and Dick were driven back to school in the motor. Since they had started four years earlier more motorcars had appeared, reducing the number of horse-drawn vehicles significantly. The headmaster had bought one, which created quite a stir in the district.

All anybody talked about was the declaration of war. When Mr Randle addressed the boarders after supper he referred to it as 'having grave implications for the whole country.' He asked all the boys to pray for our brave soldiers and sailors that night. The headmaster told them that he would speak to the whole school at assembly in the morning.

The fourth and fifth year boys, who shared Tat's dormitory, thought that the outbreak of war was extremely exciting. They cursed the fact that they were too young to join the army and take a crack at the Germans. Dick said, "You could always lie about your age."

"You couldn't though could you, short arse!" one of them snorted.

Dick flung a pillow at the boy; he was smiling, however, and didn't intend to take the jibe seriously. He knew he was the toughest boy in the dorm.

"Anyway," Tat said, "I heard some lads say that it'll all be over in a few months, so there's no hope of any of us getting involved." Then he added after a moment's thought, "Mind you some of the six formers could, though."

They speculated as to which senior boys might join up. Several big rugger players seemed to be the most likely. An aimless conversation developed about which sixth formers would look good in uniform.

"Good morning, boys, and welcome," the headmaster said, looking across the sea of up turned faces before him filling the Assembly Hall.

"I have no doubt that every one of you has heard the grave news regarding the outbreak of war with Germany. This will affect every citizen of our country including all of you. Many of us have feared this outcome for months. Now it has come about. The background to this conflict is long and complicated. I have asked your form masters to explain this to you as best they can in front of a map of Europe. I want you all to make an effort to understand how and why our country stands on the brink of war. You'll learn who are our allies and who our enemies. There is a rumour doing the rounds that hostilities might be over in a matter of months. Let us pray that this is true. Personally, I doubt it.

Four of your masters, including myself, have had the honour to serve our country in time of war. We all served in South Africa fourteen or fifteen years ago. We also heard rumours of being back home for Christmas. In fact it was three or four years before we saw our loved ones. You all know I am from Lancashire originally. I served as an officer in the Lancashire Fusiliers in South Africa. My former Commanding Officer, Brigadier Mason, has already been in touch with me. He has asked me to re-enlist with the rank of major. Naturally I am deeply honoured to be asked to do this and have accepted. Boys, I must tell you therefore, that I will be leaving my position as your headmaster in three weeks' time. Mr

Elliot, my deputy, has agreed to take over my responsibilities until my successor is in post."

A confused buzz of noise greeted this wholly unexpected and unwelcome news. The staff and Mrs Randle, having been told of the headmaster's intentions, were relatively undemonstrative. The boys, however, took some time before settling down and even then the atmosphere remained charged. Mr Randle was regarded as a fair and sympathetic headmaster. The school was shocked at the speed with which the declaration of war had affected their own community. What might happen next?

The headmaster concluded his speech with a warning to the senior boys, especially the sixth formers. "I know that some of you senior pupils will feel compelled to join up as soon as you are able. I appeal to you to complete your studies here and above all not do anything rashly. Take advice about what you should do and especially consult your parents and your God. Now let us pray."

In the light of all this drama Tat felt almost ashamed of his own private anxiety. During the summer vacation he had been happy to call on Mary Hollis several times to go through a selection of songs he had been practicing. Miss Hollis accompanied him on the piano in her sitting room.

Tat had become less sure of his voice latterly. He noticed a roughness in his tone and difficulty in controlling some high notes. During his third visit they were practicing a Scottish air called 'My Love is Like a Red, Red Rose,' which Tat felt he sang particularly well. Some weeks earlier his father had noticed him humming the ballad when he thought nobody had noticed. He had persuaded Tat to sing it for him one afternoon when they were scything thistles. Somehow singing the song, unaccompanied, in a rough pasture with the curlews calling overhead, had proved to be a singularly moving experience for both of them. It was the closest moment they had so far shared and ever would do. Neither told anybody else about it.

It was the last occasion when Tat sang flawlessly. Mary Hollis had been tactful when eventually it became obvious that Tat was experiencing difficulties. After their last practice she made tea for them both and at last said, "Thomas, you are fourteen now aren't you?"

"Yes I am," Tat replied gulping to finish a mouthful of cake.

"Can I ask if you are finding it more difficult to sing up to your normal standard?"

Tat blushed and hesitantly replied, "Aye, I am, I suppose miss, the fact is I think my voice is breaking. Most of the other singers in my year at school are going through the same thing. They sound funny when they talk. I think I do sometimes."

"Well, it is inevitable you know, Thomas," Miss Hollis replied with a smile. "I mean it's got to happen and around fourteen or fifteen is the usual time when it does."

"What should I do, miss?" Tat asked. "I don't want to crack up when I'm singing a solo. I'd be so embarrassed."

"Don't worry. I'll have a word with Jane Randle and suggest that you take a back seat in the choir. She'll understand, after all she's seen it all before over the years."

"Thank you, miss," Tat answered miserably.

"Come on, Thomas, cheer up. In six months or so you will emerge as a wonderful tenor or baritone. Now that will be something worth waiting for won't it?" She chuckled and squeezed Tat's arm.

As Tat walked home he experienced mixed feelings of relief and disappointment. He had enjoyed his singing opportunities at school. Performing in front of an audience had built up his confidence. If the truth were known he had grown to enjoy the popularity and acclaim it had brought him. However, he knew he would let himself down sooner rather than later.

Mrs Randle was in charge of musical matters at Appleby, as well as being responsible for the smooth running of Threlkeld House. She had received information in advance from Mary Hollis that one of her new boarders, one Thomas Arthur Taylor, had an outstanding alto voice.

Soon after the arrival of Tat and the other new boarders, Mrs Randle had gathered them around the piano in the Assembly Hall.

She played a series of scales for each boy to copy. Several of them had pleasant voices, some were just about acceptable and others had no musical ability whatever. Tat sang his scales like an angel. She tried him at a higher scale and realized that he possessed an impressive range. Wisely, she placed him in the alto category. After all, she decided, such a gift should not be placed under unnecessary stress.

Tat became a junior member of the school choir within a few weeks and soon began taking solo parts in church on Sundays. At special events such as the Christmas Carol Service and Easter celebrations, Tat was the main attraction. On one particularly triumphal occasion, several schools were invited to take part in a special Carol Service in Carlisle Cathedral. Tat had sung two solos and had been amazed when his strong, clear voice echoed back to him from the furthest reaches of the gigantic building. It was the first time he had heard himself, even if it was in brief abstract snatches of sound. The two hour train journey to, and eventually back from Carlisle after dark, was what excited Tat and his fellow choristers most, however.

The question of Tat's faltering voice on his return to school at the end of August 1914 was overshadowed by the all-consuming talk of war and the loss of the headmaster. Mrs Randle had been understanding but had more pressing matters to deal with. Tat's singing days it seemed were over, at least for the time being.

A NEW HEADMASTER

Within two weeks of the departure of Mr and Mrs Randle and their family the new headmaster arrived. All day the furniture van stood outside as the removal men laboured to unload the goods and chattels of Mr and Mrs Cedric Hargreaves. Eventually, the Hargreaves themselves arrived with their five children; the youngest was only a tiny baby. The four older children seemed to be aged barely a year apart from each other. Somehow they had all found room in the family car, a black Ford saloon. As this all took place on a Saturday only the boarders and the domestic staff witnessed the event.

Mr Hargreaves soon made his presence felt. Within an hour he was striding along the echoing corridors of the school flinging doors open inspecting every nook and cranny of the place. His highly polished, steel-tipped, black shoes rang out loudly on the stone flags and stairways.

Saturdays at Appleby were relatively relaxed. Boys were allowed to go about their business in shirtsleeves without ties or blazers. Some were preparing to kick a ball about on the playing field, whilst others had returned from a run across local farmland, spattered with mud. Later in the afternoon most of the boarders would spend two or three hours in the town before returning for Saturday prep, followed by supper. Some had been collected on Friday evening in order to spend Saturday and most of Sunday at their homes.

Mr Hargreaves burst into the communal bathroom as the runners were sluicing themselves down. Heaps of muddy shorts and singlets were strewn about untidily. The boys were noisy and looking forward to the rest of the day.

"Stop that infernal racket at once," Mr Hargreaves bellowed, his considerable bulk filling the doorway. "You sound like a cage full of apes."

The boys, mostly third years, fell silent immediately unsure as to the identity of the red faced man with his bristling moustache. The only sound was the intermittent dribbling of water from a faulty tap.

Mr Hargreaves walked slowly amongst the boys, regarding them with utter contempt. He disturbed a muddy running pump with the toe of his shoe and asked, "To whom does this disgusting article belong?"

His voice was deep and sonorous. The boys looked at each other hesitantly and after a second or two one of them spoke.

"I think it's mine sir," he whispered.

Mr Hargreaves fixed the terrified boy with a long, slow stare and said very quietly, "Your name boy?"

"Fothergill, sir," the boy replied.

"Come forward Fothergill," Mr. Hargreaves ordered; his voice was little more than a purr.

Fothergill, who was naked, and dripping with water, did as he was told. Without warning Mr Hargreaves slapped the boy across the face with the flat of his hand. Fothergill reeled sideways and sprawled across the soaking flagstones. Mr Hargreaves bellowed at the top of his voice, "You are filthy, noisy animals, every one of you. You will assemble outside the main entrance in the driveway in exactly ten minutes. You will be properly dressed, blazer, tie, polished boots and caps."

Without looking back he swept out of the bathroom slamming the door shut behind him. The panicking third years had experienced great difficulty in pulling their uniforms onto their still damp bodies. All the boarders, including sixth years and prefects, were drawn up in a circle in the drive. Mr Hargreaves stood in the centre of the circle, his face as dark as a thundercloud. He was tapping his leg with a thin bamboo cane. As the third years emerged cautiously from the front entrance he smiled broadly and called out to them.

"Come on, my lads, to me, stand in a row, smallest to the left, biggest to the right, that's the ticket." The boys did as they were told, their eyes downcast, heads low.

Mr Hargreaves looked all around the circle for a full minute in silence. He was a big, hefty man of about fifty. His salt and pepper hair was cut short and had the same prickly appearance as his moustache. His eyes were deep set and his jowls blue grey. He wore an immaculate three-piece, charcoal grey suit.

"I am your headmaster. My name is Cedric Hargreaves. I have found you out my boys. Without exception you are improperly dressed, your quarters are filthy and chaotic. You are noisy and undisciplined. I, my boys, intend to change all this." His voice rose as he spoke and a strange smile played across his lips.

"This bunch of filthy hooligans," he said indicating the line of third years, "have already made my acquaintance. They are about to meet my little helper, my right hand man." He swished the bamboo cane back and forth. "Right, my lads, bend over and touch your toes." He positioned himself behind the smallest and landed three cutting blows across the boy's backside. With surprising rapidity he administered three of the best along the row. When he had completed his task he was breathing heavily and ceased to smile. His victims straightened up with some difficulty, their pale faces contorted with shock and pain.

Two or three were tearful. "You will notice the effect this episode has had upon these hooligans," Mr. Hargreaves said, still slightly out of breath.

"When I beat a boy I make sure he won't forget it. You can avoid my little helper by doing exactly as you are told. I insist upon absolute obedience at all times." He continued, smiling, "I understand that you visit the fair town of Appleby on a Saturday afternoon. Not today I fear. You will spend the rest of today smartening up yourselves and your quarters. The prefects will supervise the rest of you. I will inspect the whole school half an hour before prep."

Life at Appleby was going to be very different from now on. Cedric Hargreaves could not have been more different from his predecessor. Mr and Mrs Randle had exercised a benign influence on the school. Although they had turned a blind eye to the more routine forms of initiation and milder episodes of bullying, they were fair-minded and just. Canings were regarded as punishments of last resort. Mrs Randle had run Threlkeld House in a scrupulously fair manner. She liked to think of the boarders as an extension of her own family.

Over the next few weeks Cedric Hargreaves established his harsh regime. The former happy and contented atmosphere of the school turned to fear and apprehension. Soon the cane was being used on a daily basis. Mr Hargreaves never delegated this task, preferring to carry out whippings himself, frequently with an audience. The weaker masters soon found they had an extra strategy at their disposal. They quickly discovered that all they needed to do, if a pupil misbehaved, was send the offender to stand outside the headmaster's study. As soon as they were discovered there, Mr Hargreaves caned them, rarely bothering to enquire what the unfortunate boy's misdemeanour had been.

As a result of this reign of terror the discipline in the school certainly did tighten up. The place was as neat as a new pin. Every pupil dressed correctly according to the school code at all times. No boy was allowed to have his hair growing over his shirt collar and hair oil was banned. The local barber from the town was hired to cut the boarders' hair once a month. Shoes and boots were brightly polished and garters were worn with socks. Even the food improved, despite growing shortages that were beginning to bite nationally. A stranger visiting the school would have concluded that the place was a model of high principles and educational perfection.

However, the school lost its spirit under Cedric Hargreaves. He was a clever bully, ruthless and cunning, frequently astounding pupils and masters alike with his ability to charm the parents. Whenever it was called for he would act the part of the smiling kindly patrician. He was particularly attentive to the mothers, the younger and prettier they were the more charming he would become. He was completely convincing, so much so that whenever boys attempted to explain to their parents just what Cedric Hargreaves was really like in everyday terms, they would be scolded for telling tales. Even Tat's mother and Mrs Machin would not have a word said against the headmaster. Mrs Watson did have her reservations but kept them to herself.

It turned out that Mrs Hargreaves was the headmaster's second wife. Nobody ever found out what had happened to his first. She was some fifteen years his junior and completely pre-occupied with her sizeable brood of young children. The departure of Mrs Randle meant that Mrs Chatterly, who was far from young, was in sole charge of the boarding house. Soon it became clear that she could not cope alone.

A housemaster was engaged to take over Threkeld House. Alan Mott was in his early thirties and had a pronounced limp. It emerged that he had suffered multiple fractures in a fall while rock climbing in Scotland. He was accompanied by his wife Joan, who was to assist Mrs Chatterly as second matron. Mrs Chatterly left shortly afterwards, unable to stand the bluntness and interfering of Mr Hargreaves.

It turned out that the presence of Alan and Joan Mott was to prove to be of huge importance in ameliorating the influence of the new headmaster. They were an attractive couple, full of good humour and an innate sense of fair play. Alan Mott, in particular, quickly developed strategies for keeping the headmaster at bay. He made sure that everything ran perfectly, leaving very little room for criticism. No matter how Mr Hargreaves tried to provoke him, Alan Mott never rose to the challenge. The headmaster seemed to be baffled by the man. The boarders were beaten less often, especially over the weekends. An uneasy truce was maintained as the headmaster concentrated his attention on the dayboys and staff.

Within a month or two of the outbreak of war several of the younger masters left the school in order to enlist. Despite the advice Mr Randle had given to the sixth formers to complete their studies first, several left prematurely to join up. A number of elderly masters arrived to fill in the gaps in the teaching staff. Many of them had been retired for several years. The headmaster found these easy to dominate; several only lasted a few months.

It wasn't long before lists of servicemen who had been killed serving overseas, especially in Flanders and France, began to be published in the newspapers. One of the first names familiar to the boys at Appleby was James Blandish, who had been the first formmaster to Tat and Dick's intake. Philip Johnson, the prefect who had been so kind to the new boys four years previously, had joined his father's accountancy firm in Appleby upon leaving the sixth form. News that he had enlisted gradually filtered down to the boys. It was Dick who spotted Johnson in Appleby one Saturday afternoon sitting in the church cloisters with his mother. His head had been swathed in bandages with a gap across his mouth. Dick had spied on them from a safe distance and noted that Johnson didn't move a muscle for over ten minutes. Weeks later Tat and Dick saw him being led across the market square. The bandages were off and poor Johnson's face was puckered and red raw. Most of his nose had gone and what was left of his eyelids lay moistly over empty sockets. Phil Johnson shot himself with his service revolver, shortly after Christmas.

Without Mrs Randle to oversee the musical agenda, including the school choir, the question of Tat's vocal dilemma simply faded away. Tat was on the whole relieved as he found he didn't have to face what he had foreseen as acute embarrassment. Much quicker than he had imagined his voice had broken fully and even if he'd wanted to, he was no longer able to sing at all, let alone as an alto. With the odd unexpected change in pitch he spoke like a young man and was proud of doing so.

Alan Mott, it turned out, was an excellent pianist. Although he didn't teach music as such, he re-formed the choir and played the piano during assembly. Alan and Joan Mott lived in rooms not far from the fourth and fifth year dormitories. Sometimes in the evening Tat would hear music as he passed their quarters. It was mostly orchestral and operatic. At first he didn't take much notice of this. On one occasion however, a male voice stopped him in his tracks. As he stood transfixed, Joan Mott appeared from a side door further up the corridor. She approached Tat slowly smiling, "Taylor, just what are you doing lurking outside our front door?" Tat jumped slightly, "Oh sorry, Matron, I was listening to that singer. He was singing in a foreign language, French or maybe Italian. It was beautiful."

"Oh yes," she said, "I only heard the last little bit but I know the piece you mean. That, Thomas Arthur Taylor, was Enrico Caruso. Ever heard of him?"

"I think so, but I've never head him sing before."

"Come with me, young man," Mrs Mott said opening the door of their flat. "Alan, we've got an opera fan on our hands," she said, pulling a somewhat embarrassed Tat into the sitting room.

The place was simply furnished but comfortable. The coal fire and oil lamps created a slightly secretive atmosphere. Alan Mott was bending over a large gramophone with a spectacularly shaped brass horn. He lifted a black shiny record off the turntable, handling it carefully by its outside rim. Looking round he said, "Hello darling. Ah a visitor, I see. To what do we owe the pleasure, young Taylor?"

Tat was too embarrassed to speak and began to blush.

"I found him outside listing to Caruso. I think he's rather impressed. It was Caruso wasn't it?" Joan Mott asked.

"It most certainly was," Mr. Mott replied. "That, Taylor, was Una Furtiva Lacrima from Donizetti's L'elisir d'Amore sung by the one and only Enrico Caruso. I tell you what, you've got at least fifteen minutes till prep. Park yourself by the fire and listen to it properly. Come on then boy, take a pew."

Chuckling slightly, he turned back to the gramophone, replacing the record, and wound the handle on the front of the machine enthusiastically. He lowered the needle arm onto the first groove of the spinning disc. Instantaneously a surprisingly loud hissing noise emanated from the bell of the horn. Within seconds this was replaced by the keening strains of an orchestra. When Caruso sang the hairs immediately rose on the back of Tat's neck and forearms. As he continued Tat began to feel weightless. The aria sounded unbearably poignant. The singing was effortless, a mixture of silky softness and almost bullish power. When it was over Tat felt a lump in his throat and was alarmed to feel tears forming in his eyes. All his musical experience as an alto seemed dwarfed into insignificance in comparison to what he had just heard.

"Now then, just what did you think of that Taylor, my lad?" Alan

Mott asked as he stopped the gramophone.

"It was, it, it was," Tat stammered hoarsely.

"My God," Mr Mott said leaning towards Tat, "that really hit the spot didn't it? Well, well, well!"

Joan Mott, who had gone through to the adjoining kitchen, came through with two glasses of sherry and some lemonade for Tat.

"Essential supplies to the ready," she said cheerfully.

"Do you know darling, I think we've got a genuine opera lover in our young friend. You loved it didn't you, Taylor?"

"Aye I did, sir," Tat replied bashfully. He never forgot this experience and had no idea how important it was to be to him.

The school became inured to Cedric Hargreaves' brutal ways. Those who started after 1914 accepted it as normal; they had, after all no other example to go by. The beating of schoolboys at every kind of school throughout the country was regarded as normal. What made Cedric Hargreaves different was the sheer amount of beatings he administered and his lack of interest, on the whole, as to what his victims had done to deserve it. It was difficult to avoid the conclusion that he simply enjoyed doing it.

Nobody at Appleby could recall the whipping of a prefect. In the autumn of 1917 when Tat and Dick entered the lower sixth the unthinkable happened. Trevor Brewitt, an all round sportsman, who was a member of the first eleven and the rugby fifteen, had been seen without his cap, tie and blazer, one Saturday in town by Mr Hargreaves. An altercation had occurred in the Market Place. The headmaster had attempted to slap Brewitt across the face there and then. The sixth former was a big muscular youth. He had caught Mr Hargreaves' wrist just before the blow landed. Boys from the school had witnessed the event, as well as several citizens of Appleby going about their normal business. The headmaster had become hysterical with rage.

Later he succeeded in giving Brewitt six of the best whilst he was held down by the gardener and boiler man. Brewitt had taken the punishment well enough but Cedric Hargreaves had crossed the line. Unbeknown to the headmaster, the incident in the Market

Place had been seen by the Reverend Harry Marston from his study window in the vicarage. Trevor Brewitt had been helping his verger shift some chairs in the church. The vicar had suggested that the prefect remove his blazer and tie. He had also asked Brewitt to post a couple of letters for him. It was on his return journey from carrying out this errand when Mr Hargreaves had, by coincidence, encountered him. The Reverend Marston had been concerned about the amount of whipping up at the school for some time. He was a governor and had already discussed the matter with several colleagues.

That evening Ben Jessop, the gardener at the school, had called to see him. Ben was a regular churchgoer and helped out keeping the graveyard neat and tidy. He had been disgusted at having to help restrain Trevor Brewitt whilst the headmaster thrashed the prefect. The beating had been a savage affair and he knew that in all the years he had worked at the school no prefect had ever been caned. Ben had discussed the situation with his wife, who worked in the kitchens, and between them they had decided to approach the vicar.

When the boarders arrived for Matins the following morning, the Reverend Marston kept an eye out for Trevor Brewitt. He noticed that the boy was walking with difficulty and lowered himself painfully into the pew reserved for prefects. He gave the verger a note he had written earlier and asked him to deliver it to Brewitt once the service had started. Now and again the vicar glanced at Cedric Hargreaves, who sang the hymns with great gusto and read the lesson in a particularly sonorous voice. He checked that Doctor Gibson was present in the congregation - he was a fellow governor. As soon as possible after saying his goodbyes to the congregation the Reverend Marston hurried across to the vicarage. Dr Gibson was waiting for him at the front door.

"Thank you for coming, Charles," the vicar said, ushering the doctor into his study. When they were seated he looked gravely at Dr Gibson and said, "Charles, I believe we have reached the point of no return regarding Cedric Hargreaves."

He described the event he had witnessed the day before and

the severity of the flogging relayed to him by Ben Jessop. He concluded by saying, "I have asked Trevor Brewitt to join us; he will be having a cup of tea with my wife in the kitchen. I'll fetch him."

Brewitt was in a bad way when the vicar brought him through. His face was drawn and deathly pale. He declined to sit and supported himself, stooping forward slightly, by gripping the back of a chair.

"Trevor, my boy," the vicar said, "you know Dr Gibson, of course. I want you to allow him to examine you. You will do that for us won't you?'

Brewitt hung his head and said nothing. After a few seconds he gathered his composure and, assisted by the doctor, lowered his trousers.

"My God!" Dr Gibson gasped. "This is outrageous. Just look at this, Harry." Six raised weals crisscrossed the prefect's buttocks and lower back. Multicoloured bruising spread from each and the skin was cut wide open in several places. Brewitt's shirt-tails were stained with fresh blood.

"Come on, Harry, help me to get him onto the couch," Dr Gibson said urgently. As they struggled to support him suddenly Brewitt fainted. The two men laid him face down as best they could.

"Right, Harry," the doctor said, "I'm going to get my bag from the surgery, I'll be back in five minutes. Kindly have some hot water brought in as soon as possible."

By nightfall Brewitt was admitted to the hospital in Penrith. Dr Gibson had driven him there himself. A special meeting of the school governors was called on Monday afternoon and Cedric Hargreaves was dismissed from his post on the grounds of cruelty. As well as this, irregularities were discovered in the accounts of Threlkeld House. He was given three days to pack up and leave Appleby. David Elliot, the deputy head, was offered the post of headmaster, which he accepted. He was well liked and trusted and although at sixty one he might, under normal circumstances, be regarded as rather too old for the job, the war had put paid to such considerations.

Trevor Brewitt returned to the school after a month. He had spent two weeks in hospital and a further period building up his strength at home. Despite his father's anger at his son's treatment, he was persuaded not to press charges against Cedric Hargreaves. It was agreed that a court case would only make matters worse than they already were. His rugby and cricketing days were over, at least for the remainder of his time at Appleby. Just before his return, the school captain had unexpectedly joined up and Mr Elliot awarded Brewitt the position.

On entering the lower sixth Tat had become captain of the first fifteen. As expected, he had a natural aptitude for this. His sheer enthusiasm for the game communicated itself to the rest of the team. He had even managed to involve Dick. His old friend's fearlessness and cunning eventually turned him into one of the most ferocious scrum-halfs the school had ever known. The team did very well under Tat's influence, but the loss of older boys from schools all over the country made standards difficult to maintain.

Meanwhile, Alan Mott had formed a music club in Threlkeld House.

On the first Saturday evening each month he transferred his gramophone into the boarders' common room. Boys of all ages were welcome to attend these occasions. He played records of concertos, symphonies and operas and gave talks about their composers and performers. After a hesitant start, the music club became a huge success.

Tat looked forward to the meetings with enthusiasm. The examples of opera that Alan Mott selected thrilled him in particular. He already knew what it felt like to sing. To have one's instrument in one's body struck him as special and different. When he listened to the great arias being performed by the likes of Caruso, Gigli and Pinza he felt as though he was in the grip of magic.

Tat had resisted the temptation to sing on his own account ever since his voice had broken. Now and again he recalled what Mary Hollis had said to him years before about the likelihood of his developing a fine tenor or baritone voice. He knew something was there when he sang along with everybody else at assembly and in church on Sundays. He felt the potential strength of it but he never dared sing out fully for fear of disappointment.

THE BARITONE'S FUTURE

One day, during the Easter holidays of 1917, Tat got up at dawn and climbed the slopes high above Hartley Quarry. He walked on until he was about five miles from Fell End. He stood on a rock and took a long look around him; the fells rolled away in all directions. Apart from a few sheep off to his far left, it seemed to Tat that he was the only living creature on earth. Although he knew the gist of what the arias meant, his gift for mimicry enabled him to memorize phonetically the Italian he had heard on the records Alan Mott had played at the music club. Tat cleared his throat and took a deep breath. He sang 'Una Furtiva Lacrima' in the same key he had learned from the recording by Caruso. When he had finished the aria he found that he was shaking slightly. A sensation of total freedom engulfed him. The power and clarity of his voice exceeded all his expectations. The high notes came to him with relative ease; indeed, he felt as though he could have sung even higher, although this would have put his voice under some stress.

Curious to discover how he would tackle a lower register he steadied himself and began 'Una Fatale', a baritone aria he had heard performed by Tito Ruffo. Without any real effort on his behalf Tat's voice found its natural centre. He revelled in the vibrato pulsing through his chest and throat. Almost afraid to break the spell Tat chose another of his favourite baritone pieces, 'Di Provenza il mar, il suol', from La Traviata. Tat gave it everything he had; without an audience he felt no inhibitions about expressing the emotions of the song. As the final notes drifted across the fells, tears of exhilaration swam in his eyes. Tat sprang from the rock and ran all the way back to Fell End scattering sheep as he went.

As Tat grew older his interest in becoming a vet had gradually faded. Although he helped out on the farm during school holidays, he felt less connected to the land. By the time he reached the sixth form, like most boys of his age, he assumed that he would be conscripted into the army when he left school. Tat and his friends discussed the idea of enlisting. It had become routine for lads to lie about their age. Once they looked eighteen, or thereabouts, the army rarely questioned the matter. Tat and Dick's parents had extracted solemn promises from them both not to contemplate this strategy until they had completed their final exams. Obviously, they were praying that hostilities might have ceased by that time.

David Elliot had observed Tat's progress through the school with interest. He decided that the boy was developing an analytical mind. In his opinion Tat's talent on the rugby field was mostly to do with tactics. No doubt about it he was tough and resilient but he seemed to have the ability to think ahead and create opportunities for his team. If the worst came to the worst, Mr Elliot could foresee that Tat would make an outstanding soldier, precisely because of these characteristics. If this could be avoided, however, he thought that Tat would be comfortable as an academic, possibly becoming a teacher, or at any rate entering one of the professions.

He shared his opinions with Alan Mott, who said, "I couldn't agree with you more, David. Young Taylor is certainly university material. I find the way he thinks things through very attractive. You will have noticed how good he is with people too. Persuasive, that's what Taylor is, persuasive."

"I intend to talk to the sixth formers shortly about their aspirations. Of course, this ghastly war has changed everything for them, God knows when it will end," Mr Elliot said frowning.

"Taylor reminds me of my older brother, Philip. He's the senior partner of a law firm in Carlisle. They have a similar attitude to the world, patient and persuasive. There you are, I keep coming back to that, don't I?"

"The law," said the headmaster, "now there's a thought." Rubbing his chin he added, "I might ask old Geoffrey Heelis to have a word with Taylor. He might show the lad around the office, show him how things tick."

Heelis, Harker and Burton were the school's solicitors. They occupied very old premises in Appleby; these were positively Dickensian, all nooks, crannies and cobwebs, with desks piled high with papers and books. Geoffrey Heelis was Chairman of the Governors.

"Actually, David," Alan Mott said, "I can't help thinking that an eighteen year old visiting our illustrious solicitors' somewhat picturesque offices might well be put off the law for life."

The headmaster smiled and said, "You have a point there, Alan."

"I'll tell you what, Philip is coming to Appleby for a spot of fishing in a fortnight. He and his wife will be staying at the Tufton Arms. Why don't I ask young Taylor to join us on the Saturday? He can help me out. I'm at a slight disadvantage these days." He tapped his left leg.

"That sounds like a good idea. Can I leave it with you?"

"Well, young man, have you done much fishing before?" Philip Mott asked.

"Yes sir," Tat replied, "I've often been out with my father and my brothers."

"Whereabouts was this then?"

"Along the Eden, further up river, mostly around Kirkby Stephen."

"Ah you lucky blighter," Philip Mott replied. "I have friends who've fished up there. First rate apparently."

They were passing under the walls of Appleby Castle heading upstream. Tat smiled to himself, remembering the excitement he and Dick had encountered in the beech woods up ahead with Liam and Pat. Before long they entered the woods. Philip Mott said, "Just the job, eh Alan? This will do I think."

The trees met over the river, shading the deep slow moving pools. At intervals, shallower water chattered over the pebbles, providing exactly the kind of contrasting conditions trout fishermen favoured. They spent ten minutes or so assembling the rods and selecting appropriate flies. Tat helped Alan Mott. They all wore thigh waders. Tat had been loaned a pair from the well-stocked tack room at the Tufton Arms. They fished for three hours, moving location every thirty minutes or so. Philip Mott caught three good-sized trout but Alan and Tat were unlucky. At twelve thirty they unpacked the picnic they had brought with them. There were three pork pies, some Wensleydale cheese and a jar of pickled onions.

They had placed three bottles of beer in the shallows to keep cool. These were quickly opened and they all took long swigs.

"Just the job," Philip Mott said, licking his lips. "We should have brought three more, eh?"

"Never mind," Alan replied. "Just think what your first pint will taste like when we get back to the Tufton."

As they ate the two men discussed the progress of the war. The newspapers were full of expressions such as 'The Tide Turning,' and 'The End in sight.' Indeed the Allies had sustained a series of victories latterly. Significant amounts of territory had been captured, or rather, re-captured. The losses on both sides couldn't be sustained at such a punishing rate indefinitely. Something had to give, one way or the other.

"I suppose if I'd been younger I'd still be over there myself," Philip Mott mused. "I should be grateful for that spell of pneumonia."

"Phil was with the Legal Division in France for two years," Alan Mott explained. "Then he got too ill to continue."

"What did you do there, sir?" asked Tat hesitantly.

"I had the misfortune to organize Courts Martial, young man! Mostly deserters and discipline cases. Not very pleasant but somebody had to do it. I was over the hill so far as active service was concerned. The war broke out just before my forty first birthday. I'm rather ancient you see." Philip Mott laughed.

"Anyway, with luck you and your friends might escape the rotten bloody mess. I hope for your sakes you do," he said, crunching a pickled onion.

"Phil, young Taylor and I have discussed the idea of him studying law at university. I think I'd be right in saying he's got the right kind of mind."

"Some of my enemies would say the last thing you need to be a lawyer is a mind," Philip Mott said grinning. "No, no, I'm only joking. The law is a fine profession. It combines the prospect of doing some practical good in the world and earning a very respectable salary into the bargain, eventually at least."

He gave Tat a long look and asked, "Is it what you really want?"

"I don't really know, sir. It's only come up recently," replied Tat.

"Well tell me this, what did you most want to be, when you were a youngster I mean?" Philip Mott asked.

"A farmer, like my Dad, or a vet maybe. But I've sort of drifted away from both of those really. I feel as though I want a complete change of direction," Tat said confidently. He was warming to this tough, jolly man.

Alan Mott said, "Well I'm going to explore these gorgeous woods for half an hour. They say one of the oldest badger sets for miles around is in here somewhere."

"Oh, it's there, up over the rise," Tat said pointing through the trees.

Philip Mott was a natural talker; in fact once he got going he was difficult to stop. Naturally, the law was his favourite subject. He gave Tat an explanation of the various routes open to young men hoping to enter the profession. Tat was surprised at the range of specialisms within the subject. He hadn't ever really thought about the fact that the bewigged and gowned judges and barristers who paraded from St Lawrence's Church to the Assize Court in Appleby, twice a year, all started out as students studying law. Philip Mott explained the differences between criminal law and property and commercial law. Divorce statistics, he said had rocketed up due to the separation of married couples during the war. At the same time, criminals of every description had taken advantage of the war to feather their grubby nests.

"I believe there has never been more work for lawyers," Philip Mott said. "The courts are groaning under the number of cases on their books. Industry has expanded out of all proportion and international trade will grow enormously when the war is over. A housing boom will follow, believe me." He paused to drain his beer bottle.

"Can I ask how long it takes to qualify?" Tat asked.

"Well, actually it takes about the same time as a vet. Many students are put off by the hard work and length of time it takes. But for the determined types, the clever ones, great rewards await them. It's all fascinating and," he said, putting his finger alongside his nose, "it pays bloody well, especially if you join the right firm."

"Mr Mott went to Oxford didn't he, sir?" Tat asked. "Did you go there too?"

"Indeed I did, for my sins. But the best law department these days is at University College, London. That's where all the clever people want to go now."

Alan Mott heard this last remark as he approached. "I like the sound of that, think of all the concerts you could go to, especially the operas. Oxford's a bit of a backwater from that point of view, don't you agree Phil?" he asked.

"Well, you're the cultured one, Alan. I leave all that sort of thing to you. Right, let's catch some fish shall we?" With that he stood up and pointed up stream and said, "Rather a good pool up there, what do you think young man?"

"Looks good to me, sir," Tat said cheerfully. He was enjoying himself.

They got back to the Tufton Arms just after six. Philip Mott caught two more fish, his brother and Tat one each. They stowed their gear away and struggled out of their waders.

"Now then," Alan Mott said, "I think a pint is called for."

They established themselves in the snug. Tat thought it was the most welcoming and cosy place he had ever been. The beer was delicious and went down surprisingly quickly. When Philip Mott came back from the bar with refills he deposited three large whiskies alongside the foaming pints of bitter.

"Now boys," he said with a mischievous grin, "I reckon we've earned these. Down the hatch." The two men took a generous gulp of liquor each. Tat hesitated and looked cautiously at Alan Mott.

"Go on my boy, you've earned it," he said encouragingly. "Don't worry; you don't have to be back until 8 o'clock, I've sorted it all out with Mr. Elliot. We'll walk back together."

Tat was delightfully merry when they left the Tufton Arms. Alan

Mott wasn't far behind. Tat found himself recounting the story of how he, Dick and Titch had met up at dawn to tickle fish with Liam and Pat. They both had hysterics when Tat described the confrontation with the gamekeeper and his dog. The detail of the baked hedgehogs finished them off.

They took the short cut across the playing field. The majority of the windows in the school seemed to be lit up. "Doesn't it look wonderful?" Alan Mott said, "Make the most of it, Tat my lad, not long to go now."

Halfway through the afternoon of 11th November 1918, prefects were dispatched to every classroom and study in the school. They had instructions to interrupt politely and announce the termination of hostilities in Europe. Germany had asked for peace. The war was over. Cheering broke out immediately and desk lids were rattled loudly. After ten minutes of pandemonium, the pupils and staff gathered in the school hall for a special assembly. The atmosphere was charged with excitement and it was with some difficulty that Mr Elliot led prayers of thanksgiving. He asked the school to sing 'Hills of the North Rejoice.' It had never been sung with such gusto. Tat couldn't resist singing out fully in his rich baritone. Several heads turned towards him, but he didn't care.

On the last weekend before the end of the Christmas term Alan and Joan Mott invited Tat and Dick to climb High Cup Nick. They piled into the Motts' Austin 7 and, with Joan driving, motored to Dufton. They left the car by the roadside and struck out across the fields. It was cold but would be much colder on the heights. They wore several layers of clothing with scarves, hats and gloves. High Cup Nick is a dramatic glacial feature, carved out by the ancient ice into a gigantic u-shaped gorge. Vertical cliffs of bare rock and scree flanked the cavernous space. Huge boulders lay strewn across its boggy floor. During the summer, hikers and fossil hunters frequented the place, especially at weekends. Under the lowering winter skies it was deserted and eerily silent. There was a covering of snow above the tree line.

When they reached the entrance of the gorge they paused for a while to take in its bleak grandeur. High Cup Nick is almost a mile in length and a quarter of a mile wide. They decided to split up and climb to the rim on either side. The idea was to keep each other in sight and meet at a mid-point where the cliffs swept together at the very end, which was shrouded in mist. They waved across the dizzying space when they were in position. A few snowflakes drifted down on the light breeze; Alan Mott called across to the boys. "Right lads, let's start, see you at the far end, right in the middle." Echoes rebounded off the cliffs. Tat and Dick looked at each other in surprise. Alan Mott sounded as though he was only about twenty feet away from them. Something about the angle of the cliffs or the deep void between them created a special acoustic quality. The sky had the strange livid look which the boys knew would result in a snow fall sooner or later.

Dick was all for making a race out of it, but Tat pointed out that they had been asked along as a special favour and were dependent upon the Motts for the drive back. They looked across at the distant couple on the far side and waved from time to time. Tat and Dick had never been on the heights above High Cup Nick. They had explored a short distance amongst the rocks at the entrance to the gorge once or twice on Sunday walks. They were thrilled by the sheer drama of it all. The snow-dusted fells swept away to their left. To their right snowflakes spiralled about the edge of the cliffs buoyed up by some unseen vortex of air. It was as though the snow was rising upwards out of the abyss, rather than falling from the sky.

Tat felt elated and couldn't wipe the smile off his face. He turned to Dick and said, "Bloody hell, Dick, this is grand. It's like being on the roof of the world."

Dick ran ahead and attempted a cartwheel. His thick clothing and heavy boots hampered him, however and he collapsed in a heap, laughing. He scrambled to his feet and threw a badly made snowball at Tat. It disintegrated almost immediately, which got Tat going. They doubled up and laughed hysterically, ending up on their hands and knees, with their heads hanging down. Dick finished them off when he produced a series of stuttering farts. They rolled around, completely helpless. After five minutes or so they subsided into silence. Dick raised himself onto one elbow and said, "Tat sing us a song."

"Don't be daft," Tat said.

"Go on sing us that hymn, you know, 'Hills of the North Rejoice', the one we did in assembly, the day the war ended; we all heard you," Dick said, with a knowing wink.

Tat looked at Dick and stood up, snow sticking to him. "You silly bugger, are you serious?"

"We're on the bloody hills of the north. Go on Tat, just for me."

It suddenly seemed right. Tat walked over to the edge of the cliff. He looked down into the gorge and all along its length from right to left. He cleared his throat and steadied his breathing. Looking straight ahead he lowered his chin slightly and sang. He was surprised at the increasing richness of his voice and the power of it. Within a few seconds echoes began to reverberate back to him from the cliffs opposite. By turning his head at intervals he was able to set up more echoes. It was as though ten or more singers were placed around the chasm, all singing the same tune. As Tat approached the last note, quite spontaneously, he converted it into a top G. He stood absolutely still and listened to the echoes merging with each other, and then separating. The last throbbing note floated off into infinity somewhere towards the entrance of High Cup Nick at least twenty seconds after Tat had stopped singing. Dick had joined Tat on the cliff's edge. "Tat, that was fantastic."

Tat suddenly thought of Alan and Joan Mott who must have drawn well ahead of them by now on the opposite side. He saw them, after peering through the lightly swirling snow.

"Look," he said, "over there. They'll be at the end in five minutes. Come on, Dick, let's beat them to it."

They panted to a stop at the appointed meeting place to find the Motts leaning against an enormous basalt rock. Alan struggled to his feet and held his arms out wide and said, "Tat my boy, I had no idea. That was marvellous, in fact it was more than that. It, it was the finest thing I've ever heard in the whole of my life."

Joan Mott joined them, "Thank you, Tat, thank you so much."

Tat gave Dick a shove and said, "It was his idea."

Then he looked away and felt the blush heating his cheeks. Dick said, "It was grand wasn't it? Tat's singing, I mean."

"It was inspirational," Alan Mott said. "Tat, what a voice you have. You've kept that to yourself, and the echoes, this place..." He flung his arms wide again, as though to embrace the gorge spread out before them. "It's magic that's what it is, sheer magic."

"Come on, you lot, let's shelter behind this rock," Joan Mott said pulling at her husband's sleeve.

"Right, this calls for a celebration," Alan Mott said, rummaging about in the knapsack he'd been carrying and pulling out a silver flask half-bound in black leather.

"Best single malt, what could be better, here you first, darling," he said passing the flask to his wife. They managed to squeeze three good mouthfuls each from the flask. The liquor immediately warmed them and made their spirits soar.

After ten minutes or so the first hints of dusk began to creep across the landscape. They could see the lights appearing in the villages and farmsteads down in the valley.

"I reckon it'll take about half an hour to reach the car from here. Come on we'd best get started."

They decided to swap sides for the return journey. Just as they were ready to start, Alan Mott put a hand on Tat's shoulder and said, "Tat my boy, just for Joan and myself, sing another song for us, when we get about half way along. We would appreciate it so very much."

Tat mumbled something indistinctly but Dick thumped his friend's shoulder and said, "Course he will, sir. After all we owe you for that dram."

They all laughed and set off. It was snowing steadily and still more houses were lit up below them. It was, as Dick said, like the best Christmas card anyone had ever seen. "What are you going to sing this time then?" he asked Tat as they reached the half way point.

"Dick you've really started something, you daft sod."

"Come on, Tat, you love it, you know you do. You sound just like those opera singers on Motty's records. Go on do us some opera."

Tat walked on for a few paces running over the Italian he had learned for 'Una Fatale' in his head. Yes, he could remember it, all of it. He positioned himself at the cliff's edge and called across the gorge to the Motts, "For your exclusive entertainment I will now perform' Una Fatale' from 'La Forza del Destino' by Giuseppe Verdi."

Tat drew in his breath and closed his eyes and after a moment's pause he began the aria. A newfound confidence suffused him. He knew it would be note-perfect with everything under his control. He had thought that his new voice might prove to be a transient thing, but now he knew it was there forever. He built the slow measured phrases of the aria and felt his powerful vibrato pulsing through his body. Soon his voice began to resound from every part of High Cup Nick. As the last echo faded, Tat felt that he would never be so happy and proud again. Tears of pure joy brimmed in his eyes.

After a few seconds of eerie silence, Alan and Joan Mott cheered and clapped, creating a fresh wave of echoes. Dick grabbed Tat's hands and whirled him round in dizzying circles, dangerously close to the cliff's edge.

"Tat, you're a genius," Dick shouted over and over again.

UNIVERSITY COLLEGE LONDON

When he had attended his interview in the Faculty of Law at University College, Tat had been shocked by the crowded complication of the metropolis. The crush of people milling about King's Cross Station had almost overwhelmed him. With gritted teeth he had found the taxi rank and been taken to Gower Street through a density of traffic he hardly believed possible.

University College, with its columned portico set back in the main quadrangle, had the same effect upon Tat as when he had first seen Appleby Grammar School at the age of ten. He had shown his letter of introduction to one of the beadles at the main entrance. These imposing, tough looking men wore maroon livery with frock coats and top hats. He was instructed to join a group of about twenty young men gathered nervously behind one of the stone lodges which flanked the main entrance. Eventually, one of the beadles asked them to follow him into the college itself. They entered a huge echoing corridor that seemed to run the whole length of the central part of the building. The beadle delivered them to various reception points to await their interviews.

Tat was left in a panelled lobby with six other applicants. They sat in silence on leather bound chairs set against the walls, avoiding each others' glances. Tat's stomach churned with nerves, as he tried to recover from the effects of his overnight journey and the chaotic crowds at the station. He still couldn't believe that his taxi had not been crushed flat in the endless stream of traffic, when only a few inches separated one vehicle from the other.

Tat had shaved with some difficulty in one of the cramped toilets on the train and changed his shirt for a freshly ironed one, as instructed by his mother. Despite this, he was aware that his tweed jacket and grey flannel trousers were somewhat the worse for wear after eight hours on the train. He had slept only fitfully. Despite having brushed his teeth just before reaching the outskirts of London, his mouth felt dry and sticky.

Tat was the third applicant to be interviewed. Five members of the Law Faculty sat behind a highly polished table with papers scattered upon it. A secretary occupied a smaller table off to one side. Tat was requested to sit opposite the interviewing panel. The silver-haired, bespectacled man in the centre introduced himself as Professor Lewis. He indicated his colleagues and explained their positions within the Faculty. Their names deserted Tat's mind within seconds.

"Well, I hope your journey wasn't too harrowing, Mr Taylor," Professor Lewis, said with a genial smile. "It's one I've made myself many times. You come from my favourite part of the world. I'm a fisherman you see. The Eden, especially around Appleby, has in my opinion, the best trout fishing in the country. Do you fish at all?"

Tat never knew whether Professor Lewis created this line of small talk in order to put him at his ease. These simple opening remarks certainly helped to relax Tat, however, and brought back vividly that day in the beech woods up stream from Appleby with Alan Mott and his older brother. The day when Philip Mott had devoted several hours to explaining how the various branches of the law worked and interacted. The day when his ambition to read law at University College had been born. Philip Mott had mentioned on that same day that he'd been at Oxford with the current Head of the Law Faculty at UCL although he hadn't named him.

With a confidence that surprised even himself, Tat answered the various questions put to him throughout the interview with relative ease. After half an hour or so the bald man sitting to the right of Professor Lewis asked him why he had chosen to apply to read law at University College.

"After all," he said, consulting a sheet of typed paper, "your exam results could just as easily have gained you a place at an Oxbridge College."

"I met a lawyer who was the brother of my house master at school. He told me that the best law faculty in the country was currently at this college. He advised me to apply here," Tat replied.

Professor Lewis, who was writing notes on a pad, looked up at this. "Well, he sounds like a sensible chap. What do you think, gentlemen?" he said looking around at his colleagues who nodded and smiled in agreement.

Tat, emboldened by this, said, "I think he might have been at Oxford at the same time as you, sir. His name is Philip Mott. He's a fisherman too."

Professor Lewis paused, took off his spectacles and laid them on the table. "My goodness," he said, "it's a small world and no mistake! We were not only in the same year at Oxford but served together in the Legal Division in France, until Philip got ill." Tat sensed that the interview as such was concluded. However, Professor Lewis seemed keen to return to the subject of fishing. He had, it turned out, fished on several occasions with Philip Mott and his friends along various stretches of the Eden. He had even stayed at the Tufton Arms in Appleby and the Kings Arms in Kirkby Stephen. After fifteen minutes the secretary approached the professor and in a hushed voice informed him that they were running over schedule.

"Oh, are we? That will never do, will it? Well, Mr Taylor, will you tackle that journey again this afternoon?"

"No, sir," Tat replied, "I'm staying the night in the college hostel in Bedford Square. I'll return to Westmorland tomorrow, in daylight this time."

"Good, good!" the Professor replied smiling. "Thank you for coming. You will hear from us in about ten days. Have a safe journey and don't catch too many trout before I get my next opportunity up there, will you?"

It turned out that two of his fellow applicants were staying at the UCL hostel in Bedford Square. After leaving their bags in the room they were to share, they went in search of a fry-up in a café on Tottenham Court Road. They were so relieved to have their interviews over and done with that they behaved like schoolboys, which is in essence what they still were. John was from the King's School in Canterbury and Chris, the Magnus Grammar School in Newark. Any differences in their backgrounds or accents seemed completely irrelevant as they revelled in each others' company and began to enjoy the hustle and bustle of the West End. John knew his way around. They wandered along Oxford Street and then down the curving splendour of Regent Street into Piccadilly Circus. Here the traffic reached new heights of chaos, its grinding roar rendering conversation between them impossible.

Eventually, they found themselves in Trafalgar Square. On top of his soot-blackened column the statue of Nelson stood smothered in pigeon droppings. John persuaded Tat and Chris to spend an hour in the National Gallery, which dominated the northern flank of the square. He was familiar with the layout of the gallery and took them straight to the Dutch and Flemish collections.

"Keep your eyes down, boys and follow me. You don't want to confuse your vision until you see the Vermeers. Right," he said eventually, "round this corner and you will have the treat of a lifetime. Trust me, I mean it!"

He was right. They were confronted by several small paintings of exquisite beauty. They were mostly of one or two figures in simple rooms. One, in particular, held Tat transfixed. It depicted a woman in the ordinary clothes of the period pouring milk from a jug in the corner of a room. It could have been his mother in the dairy at home. Eventually, John and Chris had to drag Tat away as the gallery was about to close. Tat never forgot the Vermeers and visited them often over the years, getting to know them intimately.

At ten thirty the same night the three of them drained their final pints in the Wellington, which they had found by following enthusiastic groups of students along Gower Street at around opening time. They quelled their high spirits as they approached the student hostel. Whilst they prepared for bed, Tat told the other two about the tremendous stroke of luck he had experienced with Professor Lewis at his interview.

"Jammy bugger," Chris said, "fishing of all things!"

The final farewells to his family and taking leave of Fell End in order to set off for his first term at University College had been hard for everyone, especially his mother. Although she was immensely proud to see Tat finally spread his wings, she had come to dread his departure for London. She, of course, had never been there and didn't know anyone who had; she couldn't imagine how Tat would cope with it and tried not to think about what troubles might befall him and what temptations might lead him astray.

As he and his father drew away from the farm in the pony and trap, Tat looked back and waved to his mother and brothers who stood at the yard gate. He knew from the way that Michael had put his arm around his mother's shoulder, that she was in tears. A couple of farm dogs ran alongside the trap barking excitedly until Jack sent them back with a swish of his whip. Finally, Fell End faded from view. For the rest of the ride to the railway station at Kirkby Stephen, Tat sat hunched and silent.

The atmosphere was stilted between Tat and his father whilst they waited on the windswept platform. Tat was ashamed to find himself wishing that they had parted company at the station entrance. Jack shook Tat's hand after they had hoisted his two suitcases into his compartment. Steam billowed around the bustling passengers and porters. Tat was glad that the general hubbub almost drowned out their final, muttered farewells. At the last minute, whilst Tat clambered aboard the train, his father pressed an envelope into his hand. Tat watched the receding figure through the grimy window as the train pulled away from the platform. Fighting back the tears, he opened the envelope. It contained a ten-pound note.

On his final day at school Alan Mott had given Tat the following advice, "Waste no time in joining the rugby club at UCL. Then, when you've settled in, join the choral society as well. Before you know it you'll make lots of friends. Not many freshers will have the talent or opportunity to do either, believe me. Remember, get yourself to the opera as often as you can. I'm told that students get a whacking discount at Covent Garden. I want to hear all about it when we next meet. I'm seething with jealousy already."

There were twenty-three students in the first year group attending the Faculty of Law. During the first week they had an introductory lecture from the head of each subject. They were allocated a personal tutor and shown how to use the enormous central library. They received a timetable of lectures and tutorials and a daunting list of books they were expected to buy from the UCL bookshop in Gower Place.

Tat was glad to find that John and Chris were among his fellow freshmen. First year students were expected to live in the various college hostels and halls of residence for their first year at least. John, however, had decided to travel to and from Canterbury on a daily basis. When Tat and Chris had teased him for failing to cut his mother's apron strings, he had replied, "Well, I'll get two hours each morning and night undisturbed, to read those bloody books. Which is more than you two will!"

He had a point. They soon realized that ploughing their way through the book list, and writing up their notes for the fortnightly essays was immensely time-consuming and required discipline. Tat found it hard to concentrate in the sometimes rowdy atmosphere of his hostel. Eventually, he developed a routine of reading in the hushed, if somewhat oppressive, Central College Library. He secretly envied John his undisturbed train journeys.

At first Tat used a dictionary and a glossary of legal terminology to facilitate his studies. He and Chris regularly tested each other as though they were preparing for French vocabulary at school. They vowed to learn ten legal phrases a week and more or less achieved this. They often caught each other out, one ambushing the other whilst rushing about UCL's echoing corridors with questions such as 'Explain Enduring Power of Attorney' or 'What is a Deed of Variation?'

THE HOMESICK CHIMP

Tat had added his name to a list of those wishing to join the UCL rugby club on the second day after his arrival. Trials were scheduled for the following Saturday. A sketch map pinned on the notice board showed the college sports fields situated on the northern edge of Regent's Park. Tat made a quick copy and checked it against the map of London back in the hostel the same evening. The trials were to start at 10am.

Tat set off early. He wore his Cumberland and Westmorland Colts shirt. He had played for them a dozen times or so in his last two years at Appleby. He pulled a pair of old cord trousers over his navy blue shorts and wore his canvas running pumps. With his boots and his own rugby ball in a rucksack, he jogged through the unfamiliar streets towards Regent's Park. As he got closer to the park the streets became grander. Big, white stucco town houses formed elegant terraces and crescents. Some had liveried coachmen outside them coupling fine looking horses up to shiny carriages. Outside others chauffeurs were polishing impressive looking motorcars.

Tat headed diagonally across the park. It was almost empty except for gardeners sweeping up leaves and carting them away in big wooden barrows. Soon London Zoo came into view. As he skirted around it he caught glimpses of its exotic inmates and heard their strange cries and roaring. He had been told that the animals could be heard echoing across the playing fields depending upon the direction of the wind. So much so that UCL's first fifteen were nicknamed 'The Chimps', throughout the university league. Tat regarded it as a priority to become a 'Chimp' as soon as possible.

As he left the zoo behind him he soon saw three pairs of gleaming white rugby posts rising above a bank of chestnut trees beyond. His heartbeat quickened with excitement. Tat trotted through the chestnut trees on a broad pathway surfaced with fine chippings. He stopped, panting slightly. In front of him beyond a low perimeter fence were three perfectly flat rugby pitches. Two were freshly mown. The newly applied demarcation lines were startlingly white and crisp. The pitch furthest away bore the marks of recent activity. Tat vaulted the fence and headed for this.

To his far right he noticed a smartly painted sports pavilion with a veranda running along its full length. He pulled the old cords off and removed his running pumps. After lacing up his boots, he ran into the middle of the field carrying his ball under his right arm. When he reached the centre spot Tat looked around him to make sure he was alone. Facing away from the pavilion he began a fast zigzagging run towards the opposite goal posts. Just before he reached the twenty-two line he kicked a drop goal that sailed through the posts in a high spinning arch. Tat ran between the posts and retrieved his ball. He weaved his way towards the posts from several different angles dropping four goals out of six attempts.

"Try to develop an unexpected strategy," the Cumberland and Westmorland coach had said during a training session at Penrith. "You lad, you're a good hooker and loose forward. No one in their right mind would expect you to be able to drop goals. So I'm going to teach you how to, alright?"

He'd been right. During his last year at Appleby Tat had practiced drop goal kicking until he could do it in his sleep. He could deliver them from any angle with a high rate of success. The trick was to choose your moment when you were within range, find a gap, steady your breathing and let fly. Tat had used this secret weapon to great effect while playing his last season for Appleby and Cumberland and Westmorland Colts. For a hooker to do such a thing was considered to be outlandish. He had attracted a good deal of hard tackling as the various opposing teams recognized what was going on. Unable to stop Tat from pulling this rabbit out of his hat, they attempted to immobilize him instead. Tat had always been able to take the rough with the smooth, however, and simply endured the punishment whilst notching up the points.

Tat began kicking his ball high above him. He caught it and gathered it to his chest. On an instant he sprinted away for a few yards before kicking it skywards again. He began to angle the ball away from himself so that he could catch it on the run. He knew the value of taking the ball at speed.

He was so absorbed that he failed to notice the dozen or so players who were gathering around the steps leading up to the pavilion. Tat had gone back to practicing his drop goals taking them on the run. Three out of three. He looked around as somebody started clapping from the touchline. Slightly embarrassed, Tat retrieved his ball and could see no alternative to joining his audience. Tat presumed that he would be exchanging pleasantries with a student of his own age. This, however, turned out to be a tall man in his thirties. He was handsome with the odd fleck of grey in his black, curly hair. He wore rugger boots and a navy blue tracksuit.

"Now, my lad," he said, "just where did you learn to do that?"

"Oh, I picked it up here and there," Tat replied, blushing slightly.

"Did you indeed, and if I'm not mistaken that is a Cumberland and Westmorland shirt. Anyway, I'm Max Wesley the college coach." He held out his hand which Tat shook hesitantly. "And you are?" he added, raising an eyebrow.

"Oh, I'm Tat, sir. Or rather I'm Thomas Arthur Taylor, but everyone calls me Tat."

They turned and strolled towards the pavilion together.

"So, Tat," Wesley said, "what position do you play? From your build you could do just as well in the pack or among the backs."

"I'm a hooker, though I've played scrum half a bit."

"Well, I've never met a hooker who can drop goals before."

"This one can," Tat replied. He was unsure of many aspects of his life but as far as rugby was concerned he had no doubts. He knew he was good and was eager to prove it.

After a couple of trial games Tat became the hooker for the second fifteen. He flung himself wholeheartedly into every game, stretching himself to the limit. He sensed that his team mates were taken aback by the intensity of his playing. His ability to kick drop goals from unexpected angles disoriented the opposition, while he regularly gained possession for his team from scrums and line-outs.

After four games for the second team, Max Wesley informed him that he was needed in the first fifteen. The regular hooker had glandular fever and was going to be off the pitch for the rest of the season.

"Settle in for a couple of games, Tat, then I want you to lead the pack. Is that alright with you?" Wesley asked after a training session.

"Yes sir, I led the pack at school before I became captain."

"I thought you might have done," Wesley said. "Oh, and by the way call me Max." Then he added, "I've had a word with Charlie Bentley the first fifteen pack leader. He's playing his last season before he leaves the college and fully understands that I have to bring in a replacement. Charlie may look like a thug but he's a very reasonable lad. You'll have no trouble with him."

Of course, the standard of the rugby was of a higher order in the first fifteen. It was faster and more ferocious, just the way Tat liked it. Any resentment there might have been when he took over as pack leader soon disappeared when it became obvious how good he was at it. He led by example, and was invariably the first forward on the loose ball and kept the team's possession up from the scrums and line-outs. On the whole, hookers are not noted for their speed; Tat was very quick, however, and dazzlingly agile. When he got the ball and ran with it he became as slippery as an eel, dodging into gaps which other players would have considered impossible to manoeuvre. Then there were his unexpected drop goals which frequently left his opponents slack-jawed with frustration.

Suddenly, without any warning before he suspected anything was wrong, or going to go wrong, it happened. A vague feeling of unease descended into full-blown homesickness. It was particularly bad at night when, after completing his studies, he lay in bed trying to get to sleep. The hustle and bustle of London life, the teeming traffic and crowds of people made him feel small and insignificant. Tat felt as though he had no control over his noisy chaotic surroundings. He longed to be with his family and friends, to be back on the farm fussing the dogs and collecting eggs with his mother; above all he missed her. He bought a calendar which he hung up in his room and began crossing off the days before the

Christmas vacation. Tat hoped this would make the remaining period pass more quickly.

He wrote to his mother at least once a week, taking care to conceal his worries. The last thing he wanted was to generate anxiety in her. After all, it was largely because of his mother's efforts on his behalf that he was in his present situation. She replied promptly with news about the farm and local goings on. Her letters were several pages long and often very funny. She seemed to relish describing the antics of his brothers, in particular. Tat was shocked to find that sometimes he failed to get to the end of his mother's letters without a painful lump forming in his throat; more than once he shed actual tears.

He had hoped that by immersing himself in his studies and becoming more involved with the rugby club that these distressing symptoms would decrease. He never gave any hint of his inner feelings to his fellow students. However, he was aware that he might be gaining a reputation for seeming to be aloof and unwilling to socialize. Tat did the bare minimum in order to get along with Chris and John. When he wished to be alone he gave the excuse that he had masses of reading to catch up on.

The rugby crowd was a boozy, rowdy lot, and would invariably meet up in the Wellington after home games. Obviously, there was something deeply satisfying about drinking copious amounts of beer after a tough game, especially if your team had been victorious. The landlord of the Wellington reserved the back bar for the rugger crowd when they played up in the park on Saturdays. He tolerated their noisy behaviour, always aware of his profit margin. The back bar was for male customers only. Tat didn't have the confidence to join in the fun and invariably slipped away after a couple of pints. Alone in his room he would force himself to write up his reading notes or plough on with the latest essay. He developed a ritual of re-reading the most recent of his mother's letters before falling sadly asleep.

After Max Wesley had informed him that he had been chosen to replace the regular hooker in the first fifteen, Tat had written to his mother as soon as possible to tell her the news. She had replied by return saying how proud they all were of him. Apparently, his Gran had announced his success to a packed public bar in the Black Bull and treated the assembled company to a free round of drinks. His mother had run into Mary Hollis and told her all about it.

Before long Tat received a letter from Miss Hollis saying how thrilled she was for him. This was followed shortly afterwards by letters of congratulations from Alan Mott and Mr Davies, Appleby's headmaster. Mary Hollis had apparently rung the school to spread the news. Mr Davies had made a special announcement about Tat's success at a morning assembly.

Tat continued his routine of rising early on the Sunday morning after a game. No matter how stiff and painful his joints were, he knew that a two or three mile run would shake most of the discomfort off. He invariably chose Regents Park for this therapy. His spirits always rose when he approached the zoo. He was by now familiar with its layout and got used to catching glimpses of the various animals as he trotted by. As ever, the chimps were the most excitable and noisy.

"Well, I'm one of you now," Tat thought when he passed alongside their enclosure. Imperceptibly, the burden of homesickness and isolation had begun to lift from his shoulders.

Tat's second match for the first team was a friendly game against Imperial College. UCL gave them a thorough thrashing. Tat had scored one of their four tries and dropped a goal. On leaving the pavilion he passed the college full-back at the bottom of the steps. He was tall and lithe with floppy blond hair and was tucking his trousers into his socks prior to mounting a disreputable looking bicycle. They nodded at one another.

Tat was about halfway across the park heading towards Gower Street when the full-back rattled up beside him on his bike.

"Hello there," he said. "You had a bloody good game today, fancy little goal you dropped. Not exactly normal tactics for a hooker. Where did you pick that up?"

"Oh, at school mostly," Tat said diffidently.

"Oh, yes, and where was that? You don't hail from these southern climes by the sound of it. You're obviously from the frozen north like me," he said with a chuckle. He had a mild Yorkshire accent.

"You're right," Tat replied, "I went to Appleby Grammar; that's in Westmorland."

"Good God," the full-back said, "so that's it. We've shared a rugger pitch before. I went to Sedbergh; we had regular fixtures with Appleby. You were their captain surely?"

"Well, yes I was," Tat said. "I think I recognize you now. We didn't have much luck against you lot I remember."

"That's because they starved us before away games in the hope that we'd kill and eat the opposition. Anyway, I'm Oliver Sinclair, what should I call you?"

"Call me Tat, everybody does."

"Well, good to meet you, Tat; call me Olly." They shook hands. When they reached the main entrance to the park dusk was already gathering. "Right," Olly said, "Tat, my boy, we are going to have a foaming pint of ale in the George and Dragon over there."

Olly drained almost half his pint of bitter in one greedy gulp and belched breathily.

"Oh lovely, just the job," Olly said, wiping his mouth on his sleeve. "So, Tat are you from Appleby, then?"

They drank with gusto and talked their heads off. They were delighted to discover that they both came from farming backgrounds. Olly's father farmed in a big way near Pateley Bridge up in the Yorkshire Dales. They shared a love of the high country and fishing. Tat felt completely relaxed and comfortable for the first time since his arrival in London. He was genuinely surprised to discover that Olly was studying sculpture at the Slade. He was in his second year. Tat knew little about the place apart from its location along the left hand side of the College quadrangle. It was obvious that Olly was passionate about his studies and had risked a serious falling out with his father when he had secretly applied to the Slade. Olly's mother had eventually persuaded his father to relent but not with a good grace, apparently. When they parted company rather the worse for wear, Olly had said,

"Well, Tat, you're the first genuine mountain man I've met down here. Look, come and see me at the Slade next week. I'd love to show you my work."

"Yes, yes, I'd like that," Tat replied hesitantly.

"Good man," Olly said. "Let's say five o'clock next Wednesday."

Tat was slightly alarmed as he watched Olly weave unsteadily away into the traffic on his dreadful, old bike. As he made his way back to his hostel he felt a warm glow flooding through him; perhaps the tide was about to turn, he thought.

MEETING ARTISTS

Tat eventually found the cobbled lane half way along Gower Place which Olly had described to him. He could tell from the direction in which it led that he would reach the back of the Slade building sooner or later. Considering how grand the façade of University College was, Tat was surprised to find that the rear of it was downright shabby. He had explored the jumble of sheds and lean-tos mostly used for storage adjacent to Gordon Square a couple of times. Students with lodgings on that side of UCL cut through this seemingly unplanned hotchpotch of buildings, creating much-used shortcuts into the rear of the college proper.

As he reached the end of the lane, which must have been in a permanent state of twilight due to the height of the sooty buildings flanking it, he heard an almost bell-like rhythmic tapping sound. The lane led into a series of interconnected yards with the back of the Slade beyond. Tat followed the sound of the tapping to his right. Several blocks of stone were stacked in an orderly fashion on either side of a pair of wooden gates which were partly open.

Tat pushed the gates open a little further and looked into the yard. More blocks of stone stood about, some of them were placed upon sturdy wooden structures. Olly, with his back towards Tat, was laying into a sizeable piece of stone with a stumpy looking hammer and a pointed chisel. Tat recognized the bell-like sound which he had heard earlier. His feet crunched against the stone chippings, which littered the surface of the yard, and Olly turned and saw him.

"Ah, Tat, so you found us then?" Olly wore a faded blue boiler suit and a comical hat made from folded newspaper. He was covered in a generous layer of stone dust.

"Good Lord," Tat said, looking around him. "I had no idea this existed. What a fascinating set up."

"Oh yes, this is one of the UCL's best kept secrets; not many of you learned types find their way here, I can tell you. Anyway, what do you think of this?"

He turned back towards his carving and surprised Tat by turning it, apparently without effort, first one way then another. Tat realized that the top of the carving bench was a turntable running on well-oiled bearings. Although Olly's carving was only partly completed, Tat could easily see that it represented a craggy male head with a strong jutting jaw and bulging eyes. It was about three feet high and carved from pale, closely grained limestone.

"What a fearsome looking customer. How on earth do you know where to start such a thing?"

"This is my African," Olly said, patting the stone affectionately. "I'm taking it from this. He indicated a white plaster portrait which stood on another turntable nearby. "I modelled this in clay last week. We have the most fantastic African model posing for us at the moment. Everybody wants to work from him; I was lucky to get in early. Isn't he amazing?"

Tat looked at the plaster cast more closely. It was life-size and Tat could make out the odd fingerprint clearly amongst the textured surface. He was struck by the dignity and inner poise of the portrait. The features all sloped back from the proud chin and the very prominent eyes gazed mysteriously from beneath the hooded lids. The hair was close cropped.

"Yes, he certainly is. So you mean you made this in front of the man himself, your African, as you call him, and now you are carving a bigger version in stone?"

"You've got it in one, Tat, my friend. However," he explained, "I want the stone carving to be a development of the image, not just a copy. I want to make it stronger, more African, if that's possible. If I'd wanted to copy it I'd be using a pointing machine, I want to carve it directly, straight from the shoulder, so to speak."

"Now you've lost me. What on earth is a pointing machine anyway?"

"Oh sorry," Olly said with a chuckle, "don't let me complicate the issue. I'll tell you all about pointing machines some fine day. Anyway, do you want a look around, then we'll go to the

Wellington for a pint?"

Oliver led the way through a dingy passage into the basement of the Slade, where the sculpture department was situated. A long corridor with big double doors at intervals leading off it stretched ahead of them. Olly showed Tat into each sculpture studio. Only a few students were at work. Olly explained that the classes began at nine and ended at five thirty. As the models left at the same time, most students did also.

"Only the dedicated ones stay on after hours, like me," Olly smirked. He had taken Tat into a studio where strange figure-like frameworks stood about, made of metal and wood. "These are armatures," he said. "We make these to hold the clay up in space. You build up the clay bit by bit until the framework is completely covered. It takes about a week to make the armature and then at least a month to build the figure. The life-model poses there in the middle of the room on that turntable." Olly pushed it with his foot and it whizzed around noisily several times. "We turn it every ten minutes so everybody gets a good look at every angle," he explained.

In the neighbouring studio, clay portrait heads shrouded in damp cloths stood on chest-high turntables. Olly unwrapped the portrait he was working on. Tat was amazed by the half-formed model; pellets of clay loosely applied to the armature already resembled a female head. Splinters of wood stuck out of the clay at intervals. Olly explained that these represented the volumes of clay yet to be added to the model.

"It may look a bit chaotic at this stage," Olly said, "but I can assure you, Tat, that the model is an absolute corker. She's a French ballet student from Covent Garden. I hope to get her to join me for a drink before long. Honestly, Tat she's a real beauty."

Olly showed Tat the drawing studio. It was enormous. Plants growing from terracotta pots were dotted around the cavernous space. Strange benches with upright supports at one end and spindly easels stood all around. Oliver explained that over a hundred students were engaged in drawing from the life models everyday. Sometimes ten models posed at a time for different groups of students.

Finally, Olly said, "Look, I'll just show you the casting room, then we'll get off for a pint. Alright with you?"

The casting room was a chaotic mixture of positives and negatives. It was one of the messiest places Tat had ever seen. The overall colour was dingy white. Bewildering rough shapes were stacked on the floor and at different levels on shelves. Several figures stood in the centre of the space in various states of finish. Off to one side completed casts dazzled Tat with their realism. They were like frozen white humans, perfect in every detail.

"You see how it works?" Olly asked. "A clay model is covered with plaster, each section is designed to separate from the next. It takes ages to learn how to do it well. But eventually it makes sense. Sorry, Tat, it's another world really. Look, wait for me here for five minutes while I get cleaned up."

Tat and Olly crossed the quadrangle and said good night to the beadle at the main gate. Jack Proctor was the beadle on duty; his left arm hung stiffly at his side. In place of his hand a hard, shiny leather glove, formed into a permanent fist, protruded from his sleeve. He had lost his arm on the first day of the Somme. He stood erect in the doorway of the right-hand lodge. "Goodnight, gents," he said softly, then added, "Don't do anything I wouldn't do!"

They turned left into Gower Street which was teeming with early evening traffic. It was almost dark. The newly completed bulk of University College Hospital loomed high above them on the opposite side of the street. The brick and stonework were as yet free of the sooty grime which covered most of the adjoining buildings, including University College itself. It seemed that every part of the hospital blazed with light twenty-four hours a day.

The slow-moving traffic was about equally divided between horse-drawn and motor vehicles. It generated a continuous roar and a mixture of mechanical and animal smells. Tat had learned to keep alert so as to avoid the flurries of horse dung squirted from beneath the tyres of passing taxis and buses.

Dozens of students thronged the pavements making their way

towards Euston Square tube station. Many formed untidy queues at the various bus stops located along the length of Gower Street. As the friends passed the number fourteen bus stop, Olly suddenly spoke to a girl who was muffled up against the evening chill. "Hello Jane," he said, "how long have you been waiting?"

"Oh, hello, Olly. I've been here half an hour already. I've lost any sense of feeling in my feet. Damned fourteen buses. I'm sure they're the most unreliable in London."

"Oh, it's always like this until about 7.30 or so. Look, Tat and I are going to the Wellington for a drink; why not join us and get a bus after rush hour? Oh, this is my friend Tat, by the way." Turning to Tat he added, "Tat, this is Jane."

Tat took the gloved hand the girl offered him and shook it briefly. "I'd love to; anything to get away from this lot," Jane replied.

As they made their way to the Wellington Olly and Jane chatted easily. Tat took sidelong glances at the girl to try to gauge her appearance. Her hat and scarf concealed most of her face. However, he was able to ascertain that she was at least as tall as him and walked with a light, easy step.

The Wellington was filling up fast, even though it had only been open for half an hour or so. It was a favourite haunt for University College students. It was full every lunchtime and every night. In rather a bold move, the landlord had declared the largest bar to be for mixed company. Very few pubs provided such opportunities. Tat discovered later that several pubs adjacent to other London colleges had taken the same step. The various landlords had recognized that the young men and women could be trusted to mix with one another without creating mayhem.

Tat spotted a free table in a corner and suggested that Olly and Jane grab it whilst he got the drinks. He was surprised when Jane asked for a pint of bitter. By the time he delivered the drinks Jane had removed her coat, scarf and hat. She wore a tight fitting black jumper and brown, ankle length skirt. Her hair was dark chestnut and framed her oval, animated face with loose, tumbling curls.

"Lovely, just the job," Olly said rubbing his hands together, "I can't tell you how much I'm looking forward to this."

"Oh thanks," Jane said taking a good pull at her drink. Tat noticed that she had a dainty residue of froth on her top lip which she wiped away with the back of her hand.

"So, how did you two meet?" she asked, "or let me guess. I bet Tat plays rugby too, am I right?"

Tat took this opportunity to address her directly for the first time. "How on earth did you guess that?"

"Oh well, I know Olly plays for the college, and well you look like a rugger player. Both my brothers are rugger mad. You look a bit like Marcus, my middle brother. Same sort of build."

"Well, you're right as it happens," said Olly. "Tat is our new demon hooker. But don't be fooled by his brutal exterior. Tat is clever, my girl, he's doing law."

"Oh, I'm impressed," Jane replied, smiling broadly, showing her even, white teeth. "Actually, I've seen you crossing the quad occasionally and in the Refectory."

"I take it you are at the Slade. Are you studying sculpture like Olly?" Tat asked.

"No, I'm a painter; I'm in my second year," Jane replied.

"So will you do three years altogether same as Olly?" Tat enquired.

"Yes I will."

"Jane's a bit of a star actually," Olly commented. "She won the drawing medal last year. Knocked everyone else into a cocked-hat, including me. You should see her stuff, Tat, most impressive."

"Oh do shut up, Olly," Jane said giving him a playful push. "You'll have me blushing next."

They all laughed. Olly got up to get another round of drinks, threading his way through the considerable crush. Left alone with Jane, Tat felt a surge of nerves flutter in his stomach.

"I've seen some of Olly's work this evening," he said tentatively. "I think he's ever so good. I envy you lot, having such natural talent. It's the first time I've been into the Slade. We outsiders consider it to be a place of mystery." Tat stopped, realizing that he had begun to prattle on. He fumbled in his pockets for his cigarettes and offered one to Jane to cover up his confusion.

"Actually, I roll my own," she said. "Our gardener taught me how to do it and I've got used to the taste!" To Tat's amazement, she extracted a tobacco tin from her large shoulder bag and began rolling a cigarette there and then. She made a good job of it and accepted a light from Tat.

"I've shocked you haven't I?" she said after blowing out a plume of blue smoke. "I suppose you think it's not very lady-like. Certainly, that's the opinion of my parents."

Indeed, Tat was shocked. He couldn't remember ever seeing a female roll a cigarette before, let alone smoke it. Recovering his composure, he said, "Well, I did know a gypsy lass who smoked a pipe. She was a beauty as well, I can tell you." He felt his cheeks and ears turning hot as he realized he had implied that he considered Jane to be a beauty.

"Well," she said grinning broadly, "I'm not altogether sure if that was a compliment or not. Should I give you the benefit of the doubt I wonder?"

"I'm sorry I didn't mean…" Tat stuttered.

Jane touched his hand briefly and said, "It was a charming thing to say. Who was this mysterious gypsy beauty, anyway?"

Tat was relieved to be given an easy exit from his confusion. "Oh, it's a long story. I'll tell you some other time maybe," he muttered.

"I'll hold you to that, master Tat," she said, pulling on her cigarette.

Olly appeared with the drinks on a tin tray.

"What a crush," he said. "Come on Tat, give us a ciggy I'm gasping!"

Tat was glad to let Olly dominate the conversation again. He was confident and funny, full of gossipy stories about their fellow students at the Slade. He was relieved that Jane didn't refer to his clumsy remark. It pleased him vaguely that in an odd way he and Jane shared a sort of secret.

When they emerged into Gower Street the traffic had thinned out considerably. They left Jane at the fourteen bus stop. Apparently, she shared a basement flat with a girl friend in Fulham. Olly and Tat parted company at Euston Square underground station. Olly had digs in Earls Court somewhere.

As teenagers, when Tat, Dick and Titch spent their Saturday afternoons in Appleby they would watch out for girls and young women going about their business in the town. They would award points on the basis of bosoms, hips and pretty faces. They looked and looked but never even got to talk to a girl, let alone touch one. Since his arrival at UCL, apart from passing the time of day with one or two of the female law students, of whom there were precious few, Jane was the only girl Tat had actually talked to. He was aware that he hadn't made a very good job of it. Thank goodness, Olly had been there, he thought.

Jane was posh. Not only did she talk with what Tat easily recognized as an upper class accent, but also she had referred to 'the gardener' as the individual who had taught her to roll cigarettes. This hinted at a privileged household, probably in the country somewhere, otherwise why would she need accommodation in London? He would have expected a girl from such a background to be arrogant and dismissive, but she wasn't. In fact, she had an easy, friendly manner with a ready smile and was definitely pretty. Tat might even have described her as beautiful. Dick and Titch would have awarded ten out of ten on all counts more than likely.

JOINING THE CROWD

Tat gradually gained in confidence as his homesickness faded. Hesitantly, he joined in the revelry at the Wellington after home games, and grew to realize what fun it was. Olly was always in the thick of it and the sheer force of his enthusiasm drew Tat along. As the beer went down, they would tell jokes and outlandish stories. Olly recounted how, whilst at Sedbergh, he had discovered that he could imitate the neighing of a horse in the back of his throat without any outward signs occurring. He would choose his moment when, for example, walking along a corridor crowded with boys and masters hurrying along between classes. Then he would let rip with the loudest neigh he could muster, creating confusion and hilarity in more or less equal measures.

He carried on for almost a year, or so he claimed, neighing in unexpected circumstances, without being discovered. Eventually a cunning prefect, who had grown suspicious, finally nailed him during evening prep when Olly had taken a risk and neighed loudly, piercing the studious silence and reducing his fellow pupils to hysterics. Of course, he had received six of the best. Olly demonstrated his peculiar skill before the assembled crowd in the back bar of the Wellington and brought the house down. It turned out that he could low like a cow and grunt like a pig just as well, all impressively loud and with no outward sign.

Big Charlie Bentley, the second row forward whom Tat had replaced as pack leader had a surprisingly delicate trick up his sleeve. Apparently, a prefect at his school in Taunton had taught it to him. Charlie seemingly felt impelled to share it with the world. Apparently, the prefect had been disgusted when Charlie had farted and managed to drag the noxious fumes around with him trapped in the folds of his clothing. "Trouble with you, Bentley," he had sneered, "is that you are a slow-release fartbag."

The prefect then gave Charlie a master class in stench avoidance and detection. He demonstrated the technique to Charlie. As the prefect was unable to fart to order he told Charlie to imagine that he had done so. "Choose your location carefully," he advised. "Produce your fart, then agitate your clothing vigorously in and around the area of your backside, slap, shake and flap the clothing with enthusiasm; make sure you cannot be observed. Then walk away confident in the knowledge that your stench is left behind, isolated and forgotten."

Charlie, who could fart to order, had a space cleared in the middle of the crowded bar, in order to demonstrate the technique. He did the deadly deed loudly on one side of the cleared space, agitated the clothing around his posterior, stepped briskly across the space and invited volunteers to test the practicality of the demonstration. True enough the particularly pungent aroma did remain isolated, whilst he remained as pure as the driven snow. This demonstration launched at least thirty secret, trouser-slapping young men upon the world.

Several more first fifteen players did a turn, some recited rather off-colour verse monologues, others told long, seemingly endless jokes, apparently called 'shaggy dog stories,' a term which Tat could make little or no sense of. Then Leon Kussoff, the very swift right-winger in the team, stepped forward. Yet another and rather larger space was cleared and amidst cheering and rhythmic clapping he began the dance for which he was renowned. His father had been a major in a Cossack regiment during the war and, having been separated from his unit on the Polish border in 1917, had joined up with the London Irish Brigade. Eventually, the whole Kussoff family had ended up as émigrés in London. Leon had finished off his schooling at St Paul's and was currently in his second year at UCL, studying political history. He had learned to dance in the manner of Cossack soldiers from his father and uncles.

Leon leaped into the cleared space and spun round in circles with his arms folded across his chest and his chin held high. Suddenly, he squatted on his haunches and seemingly without effort kicked his legs out at various angles, first one then the other. All the while the crowd clapped in unison and yelled encouragement. Leon rose up spinning like a top, before launching into a high stepping foot stamping dance with his hands on his hips. He yelled out at intervals, half singing and half shouting staccato phrases in what Tat presumed to be Cossack dialect. Then, without warning, he executed a backwards somersault and landed on his left foot. The crowd cheered and clapped uproariously for a full two minutes.

The singing started next, one rugby song followed another, each one cruder than the last. Tat already knew most of them from his school days and encouraged by the general bonhomie and copious amounts of beer, sang out in his full baritone. Several individuals were called upon to sing solos and Olly, who had noticed Tat's impressive voice, dug him in the ribs and hissed into his ear, "Go on Tat, sing us a proper northern song, they'll love it."

Tat refused at first, but when Olly pushed him forward the crowd began to chant his name over and over again, he saw that he had little choice in the matter. Do ye ken John Peel, he decided that should fit the bill. Olly grabbed a nearby chair and half lifted Tat up to stand upon it. So placed and with the flushed, beaming faces of his team mates all around him, all his inhibitions seemed to fall away.

Tat set his shoulders back and took a deep breath. He had grown up with the song although he couldn't remember the last time he had sung it. As was often the way when he hadn't used his voice for weeks at a time, it seemed bigger and richer than ever. Revelling in its power, Tat sang the old hunting song as never before. He noticed the expressions on the faces of the crowd change from careless abandon to surprise and delight. Olly, clearly thrilled, began to join in the refrain and soon the rest followed. Tat converted the final note into a top G rising majestically above the raucous chorus. Thunderous applause broke out and Tat was thumped on the back so enthusiastically that he slopped half the pint Olly pushed into his hand down his shirt front. He felt deliriously happy and had to swallow several times to prevent tears of joy from brimming in his eyes.

After a further half hour or so, the landlord called last orders and rang the old brass bell that hung over the bar. A chorus of regret and denial was followed by a general stampede to the bar to secure the last pints of the night. Charlie Bentley insisted upon treating

Tat and took the opportunity to say, "Tat my boy, you've got one hell of a voice there, you sly dog. Give us another, one to make me cry." He pulled a grief stricken face and pretended to sob. Others, who overheard this exchange, took up the job of encouraging Tat.

"Come on, Tat, send us home with a sad one," Leon yelled. "Russians love to have their hearts broken." Tat was hustled into the centre of the crowd and hoisted up on the chair again.

"Right, you lot," he shouted, "let's have some hush." After a slight pause, Tat launched into 'My Love is Like a Red, Red Rose.' After the first verse the crowd fell completely silent. The sea of sweaty, grinning faces became composed and wistful. Even the landlord paused from gathering the empties and leaned over the bar so as to catch every phrase of the song. Once more Tat was cheered to the rafters and found that he had two more pints to consume in the remaining ten minutes or so before the bar was emptied. Outside in the courtyard there was a good deal of intoxicated horseplay before they all began to address the sobering business of finding their way home to their digs and hostels.

Tat and Olly weaved unsteadily along Gower Street linking arms. As they passed the gates of the college, Nathan Steadman, the senior beadle, known to all as 'the Boss' stood implacably in the doorway of the left-hand lodge. He had, in a former life, been a sergeant major in the Grenadier Guards and served the full four years with them in France and Belgium. He always wore his medals on the lapel of his maroon frock coat and was never seen without his top hat. As Tat and Olly reeled past he stepped forward and said, "Keep it down, gents, there's a couple of coppers down at Euston Square station."

Tat and Olly made a great show of composing themselves, shushing each other theatrically. As they tiptoed off the Boss smiled and shook his head. Tat left Olly a hundred yards or so from the tube station at the entrance to Gower Place, relieved that he only had a short distance to go to his hostel. Olly took Tat's sweaty face in both hands and looked into his eyes. With an effort he said with what seemed like great sincerity, "Tat, you sing like a bloody angel, you should drop the law and sing for a living. Remember,

Tat I'm an artist and I know about these things."

"Don't be daft, Olly. Go on, bugger off home before you miss the last train."

Olly looked even harder into Tat's eyes and went on, "Tat, I'm an artist and you are too. Think on lad, I know about these things." Then Olly thumped Tat on the shoulder and walked away, not altogether convincingly, in the direction of Euston Square.

"Watch out for the cops, Olly," Tat called in a hoarse stage whisper. Olly raised his hand to show that he'd heard, without turning round.

Tat was within sight of the student hostel when without warning he vomited spectacularly into the gutter. The experience was deeply unpleasant and went some way towards sobering him up without clouding his happiness.

Olly eventually succeeded in persuading the young ballerina, who had posed for the portrait class at the Slade, to join him for a drink on a couple of occasions. Tat had spotted the pair of them in the mixed bar at the Wellington one evening when he had called in for a quick pint with John and Chris. Olly had seen him over the shoulder of the ballerina and given him a sly wink.

At a Saturday morning training session a couple of weeks later Olly told Tat with some excitement that he'd fallen head over heels for his ballerina.

"Honestly, Tat she's so gorgeous and sweet. You've got to meet her, and then you'll see for yourself. She loves my portrait of her and wants a cast of it." He went on to explain that he was meeting her that same evening at the Nags Head in Covent Garden. He was insistent that Tat drop everything and join them.

"I've told her all about you; there'll be quite a gang, some of her friends from the ballet school and a few from the Slade. Pop in around seven thirty, don't let me down." Tat explained that he intended to complete an essay on criminal law reform that evening to which Olly retorted, "Sod that for a game of soldiers, Tat. Be there or I will take it as a personal insult."

Tat followed Olly's instructions, rather against his better judgment, and eventually found the Nag's Head on the corner of Floral Lane. It was a large pub with several rooms. Tat soon found the mixed bar which was full of well-dressed folk, many of whom were in evening dress, presumably pausing for a quick drink prior to attending a performance at the Opera House. Eventually, he spotted Olly and his group tucked in a corner well away from the main door. Olly saw Tat as he worked his way through the crush.

"Tat, my boy," he yelled, "over here, I've saved a seat for you."

Tat signalled that he was going to get a pint at the bar. He suddenly realized that he was quite nervous about joining this group of strangers. Ordering his drink would give him a few minutes to compose himself and a good gulp or two might provide him with some much needed Dutch courage. Somewhat reluctantly he made his way over to the by now animated group.

"Ah Tat," Olly said, his face flushed with good spirits and excitement. "Everybody, this is my good friend, Tat." He started to introduce everybody in turn, then said, "Oh sod it, just come and sit here; you'll never remember everybody's name anyway."

Tat squeezed in and occupied a tight space on the leather banquette next to Olly, taking care not to jostle the central table. Olly took a huge gulp of his pint and only just suppressed a beery belch. Wiping the froth from his lips, he put his arm around Tat's shoulders and pulled him round to face the extremely pretty girl sitting on his other side.

"Annette," he said, "meet Tat, lawyer, rugger hero and singer, not necessarily in that order of precedence.

"Hello," the girl said, "pleased to meet you. Olly never stops talking about you. In fact, let's face it Olly never stops talking full stop."

She spoke with a strong French accent. Tat mumbled indistinctly in reply, realizing uncomfortably that he, as the latecomer, was the centre of attention. He was relieved, however, when everybody laughed heartily at Annette's joke at Olly's expense.

"Oh no, that's too cruel," Olly cried in mock self-righteousness. Annette feigned remorse and gave Olly an affectionate peck on the cheek. More laughter followed. Tat took advantage of the general hubbub and snatched a quick look around the group. He guessed that there were four ballet dancers present, three girls who shared the same hairstyle and had similar physiques. Their hair was pulled back from their faces and tied in a tight bun at the back. They sat upright in their chairs and handled their drinks in a delicate, almost prim fashion. The male dancer was lithe and cat-like in his movements and so far hadn't shown much enthusiasm for joining in the general high spirits. Suddenly, Tat saw that Jane was sitting three places to his right with a couple of Slade students he had seen from time to time in her company around UCL. She looked across at Tat and mouthed, "Hello, Tat," to him. Tat nodded and smiled at her and realized how pleased he was to see her there. He noted how much bigger she seemed in comparison to the dancers.

It turned out that Annette was from Paris. She was extremely bubbly and kept up a stream of lively banter, especially with her friends.

"What do you think?" Olly hissed into Tat's ear, "isn't she wonderful?"

"She certainly is," Tat whispered. "I see now what all the fuss is about. What a lovely voice she has."

Olly in his typical blustering way turned to Annette and said, "There you are Annette, you have another admirer. Tat's just told me that he thinks you have a lovely voice, isn't that right, Tat?"

Tat felt himself blush as Annette inclined her head towards him saying, "Thank you kind sir, and you have the same accent as Oliver, n'est ce pas?"

"The same but different, Annette," Olly said, "Tat is from the north alright, but he's a genuine mountain man. He's from the frozen wastes of Westmorland, aren't you, Tat my boy?"

Tat covered his confusion by draining his pint and making as if to revisit the bar for a refill.

"No, no," Olly snorted, "we have a kitty going." He indicated a large glass ashtray in the centre of the table brimming with coins.

"Shove half a crown in there, Tat, and we'll all have another."

Tat did as he was asked and, standing up, offered to get the round in. The lad from the Slade sitting next to Jane volunteered to jot down the complicated order on a page torn from a small sketchbook he took from his jacket pocket. Clutching this, Tat took a fist full of coins from the ashtray and struggled towards the bar. Whilst he waited for the barmaid to make up the drinks, he lit a cigarette and inhaled deeply. He was finding it all heavy going and more than half wished he'd stuck with his intention to finish his essay.

"Let me help you with this lot, Tat; it'll take at least three trips to and fro through the crowd." Tat started slightly and looked up to discover Jane standing behind him.

"Oh, Jane," he said, "I didn't see you there. Thanks, that would be a great help."

"Give me a light, Tat," she said holding up one of her hand - rolled cigarettes.

"Oh yes, of course," Tat said patting his jacket pockets to locate his matches. He struck a match and offered it to Jane. His hand shook despite his efforts to steady it.

"So, how are you, Tat? I haven't seen you to speak to for ages."

"Oh I'm fine," Tat replied. "It's busy isn't it? I've never been here before."

"Well, I suppose it's the closest pub to the Opera House," Jane said. "Annette says that it will half empty in a couple of minutes as they all rush off to take their seats."

"Oh, I see." He glanced around the bar and could already discern a flow of people collecting their coats and hats making for the door. "In fact, they've already started. Look!" he said.

"At least it will make it easier to cart the drinks over, that's something," Jane said blowing smoke through her nostrils.

"Well, Olly seems to have fallen on his feet," Tat said.

"Indeed he does, maybe this one will last more than the usual fortnight," Jane replied, rolling her eyes slightly. "He does rather love them and leave them, our Olly."

"Oh really," Tat said. "I didn't know. I've only known him a few weeks."

"She certainly is a beauty, though, and seemingly that Parisian accent has captivated you as well, eh Tat?"

"Oh no, I wouldn't say that," Tat stammered, "It's just Olly…"

Jane gave a low, throaty chuckle and added, "It's alright Tat, I'm only teasing you. Ah, that's the drinks all done. Have you got a couple of trays, please?" she asked the barmaid, whilst Tat fumbled his way through the coins.

When the drinks had been distributed, Tat ended up sitting next to Jane after the others shunted along the banquette to make way for them. He noticed that Jane was wearing a fitted white shirt which was tucked tightly into a broad black belt. He smelled what he thought was rose water drift across to him as she settled into her seat.

She chatted easily to the male ballet dancer who sat on her other side. It transpired that he was Polish and spoke very little English. Jane seemed completely at her ease, however, and eventually they decided that they both knew enough German to carry on a conversation. Suddenly the dancer leant across Jane and addressed Tat.

"You are artist also?"

Taken aback, Tat replied, "No, no, I'm studying law." He looked confused and asked Jane to translate.

Then he said, "I think you are artist anyway, not advocate."

"So there, Tat, that's put you in your place," Jane said raising a quizzical eyebrow.

Before long several members of the group made preparations to leave. They sorted through coats, scarves and hats and began to make their farewells. The ballet dancers left together with Olly in tow. He stole a glance at Tat on his way out and winked as he held the door open.

"Walk me to the bus, Tat?" Jane asked.

"Oh yes, of course," Tat said. They said goodnight to the male dancer on the pavement. He bowed slightly as he shook each by the hand in turn, brushing Jane's hand with his lips. Before he turned to walk on his way he looked at Tat again and said, "Artist!" Then he was gone.

Tat was confused and embarrassed by this strange reaction to him.

"What on earth did he mean by that," Tat asked as they made their way towards Shaftsbury Avenue. "Did you catch his name? I didn't."

Jane laughed and said, "Well no, I didn't actually. I think he was rather impressed with you, Tat." Then imitating a Polish accent she added, "I think you are artist."

"I still don't get it," Tat said frowning. "What did he mean? I'm not an artist, and never will be."

"Let's just say that it might have been his way of telling you he thought you were special," Jane said in a studied sort of way. She took his arm.

"How do you mean?" Tat said becoming more confused than ever.

"Well, I have a nose for these things, Tat. I think our Polish dancer friend prefers boys to girls," Jane said chuckling slightly. Tat stopped in his tracks and stared at Jane in shock and horror and said, "You mean, oh no, you mean he's a...a."

"Yes, Tat?" Jane said encouragingly.

"You mean he's a Mary Jane," Tat spluttered. Jane laughed out loud at this and squeezed Tat's arm.

"Oh Tat, you're so sweet, you really are. Come on, there's my bus, number fourteen; it's a miracle. See you soon, Tat, and please don't look so worried."

She waved to him from the boarding platform of the bus until it was engulfed by the jostling traffic.

THE FIRST OPERA

Tat handed in his completed essay the following Wednesday, after the mid-week lecture in the hall with the raked seating. He had been amazed at the density of the winter fogs which smothered the city for days at a time. Under these conditions it was impossible to see from one side of Gower Street to the other. The traffic crawled along at a snail's pace. The constantly lit mass of University College Hospital seemed to hang in the choked air like a huge ghostly spectre. The fog often entered the buildings and on such days the bigger spaces, including the lecture hall, became grey and clammy with the soot-laden air. The lecturer down below the high seats was lit by a single shaded bulb above the lectern and appeared to float above the podium. His voice like all the other sounds became slightly muffled and indistinct. Tat rather enjoyed the strange effects the London fogs brought with them, though he was aware, and becoming more so, that Londoners dreaded and even feared them.

Olly waylaid Tat as he left the law faculty and was about to strike out across the quadrangle.

"Tat," he called through the gloom. "I'm glad I caught you. Come for a quick pint at the Wellington. I've got something to tell you."

As they pushed their way through the fog, Olly quizzed Tat about Annette, shouting above the grinding din of the slow moving traffic.

"Well, what do you make of Annette then, isn't she the bee's knees?"

"She's that, alright Olly," Tat replied. "Where does she live?"

"That's a bit of a bugger actually, she lives in Barnes of all places. The ballet school is over there and she shares a place with the other lasses you met in the Nag's Head. I've walked miles getting to and fro over the last few weeks. Mind you, it's keeping me fit. Come on, I'll race you to the boozer." With that he was gone, disappearing into the fog at a fast trot. Tat half-heartedly gave chase but kept having to check his pace to avoid crashing into other pedestrians, so dense was the fog.

Olly was seated at a table with two pints in front of him. His was already half empty when Tat entered the back bar. Olly had just lit a cigarette and offered one to Tat.

"See the fog's got in here as well," Tat said.

Olly looked around and said, "Yes I suppose it has, you get used to it after a bit. It's in the sculpture studios; smells like somebody's lit a fire with damp coal. The models hate it, they get smuts all over them."

"Anyway, what do you want to tell me?" Tat asked after he'd taken a good swig at his pint.

"Well, it's two things actually," Olly replied. "I want you to sit for me, I want to make your portrait."

"What me? What on earth for?" Tat said, somewhat taken aback.

"Well, I like your ugly mug," Olly smirked. "No really, you've got good strong features and I want to keep a portrait on the go all the time if possible. Go on, Tat, say you'll do it!"

"Well, I don't know if I can spare the time, Olly, there's so much reading to do, never mind the essays," Tat said. Inwardly he was flattered, however, and couldn't deny he was interested in the proposition.

"What would it involve, anyway?"

"It would involve you sitting still and keeping your trap shut. I'm the one who would do the work. Please, Tat, say yes," Olly said.

Tat could see that Olly was sincere and after playing hard-to-get in order to tease him, he eventually agreed.

"We'll do it in the sculpture department, say two sessions a week until it's finished. It won't take long, at least it shouldn't do, you can have a cast, if you like it. So that's settled then. Right, you can get the pints in to seal the deal." When Tat returned with the beers Olly gulped half of his down greedily as usual.

"Tat," he said, "with that booming singing voice of yours, would I be right in thinking that you like opera?"

Tat was genuinely surprised; opera had never been mentioned between them. "Well, actually, I do like opera. At least I like the sound of it. We had a housemaster at school, Alan Mott; he was crazy about it and had this huge record collection, mostly opera. He often played them to me and some of my mates. I just loved it, immediately I mean. Somehow it just touched the spot straight away."

Tat took another swig of his beer and lit a cigarette, offering one to Olly. "I was in the choir at school," he went on, "that is until my voice broke. Then somehow this big voice landed in my lap. Mind you, I didn't let on to anybody, really. I was sort of embarrassed about it."

"You mean nobody knows you've got it, the voice I mean," Olly said genuinely surprised.

"Well, yes and no." Then he told Olly about the day on High Cup Nick in the snow. "So Dick Machin and Alan Mott and his wife, they know about it and now you and the rugger crowd know. That's about all," Tat said reflectively. "I suppose I'm still a bit embarrassed by it. I get confused when I think about it."

"I see," said Olly. "Anyway I had a feeling you would like opera. My mother is an opera lover and like your Alan Mott she has tons of records. I was brought up with it really. Anyway I told Annette about your voice and she said you shouldn't ignore it."

"Oh hell, Olly," Tat groaned, "why not tell the whole pub as well?"

"No need, Tat old lad," Olly replied. "This after all was the setting of your last public performance, remember?"

Tat shrugged and shook his head smiling. "Yes, so it was..."

"Anyway, this is the point; Annette has got four tickets for La Traviata this Saturday at Covent Garden. Tat, it's the real thing with Italian singers. Do you want to go?"

"You bet I do. La Traviata, I know it quite well. At least I know the recordings Alan had of it well. Thanks Olly, I'd love to go."

"Good man," Olly said smiling broadly. "I've asked Jane as well. Apparently she's seen quite a bit of opera on trips to Europe with her parents. She's been to Covent Garden quite often too, apparently."

Tat was glad that Jane would be there, although he didn't show it. It made him pleased and nervous in about equal measures.

They met in the Nags Head. Olly and Annette were already there. Whilst Tat found a spare peg for his coat and scarf, he spied on them briefly. They were being rather lovey-dovey, to Tat's way of thinking. He braced himself and called out to Olly from some distance so as to break up their intimacy. Olly looked up and waved Tat over. Tat made a gesture to show that he was going to the bar. Olly sprang to his feet and joined him.

"Tat," he hissed, "let's have whiskies; all that beer, I'm telling you my bladder will never hold out."

"Alright Olly, its probably a good idea. What about Annette?" Tat smiled and waved to her over Olly's shoulder.

"Oh, she'll have a dry sherry. Is that OK?"

When Tat weaved his way through the well-turned-out opera-goers he almost collided with Jane.

"Hello, Tat," she said, then added mischievously, "you are artist!" in a gruff imitation of a Polish accent. "Lovely to see you," she added, giving Tat a peck on the cheek.

"Hello, Jane," Tat said, as his tray with the double whiskies and the schooner of sherry wobbled. They both got the giggles and Tat came close to spilling the drinks. "Look," he said, "hold on, I'll get yours. What will you have?"

"Don't worry, Tat, I'll get my own and follow you, otherwise it will just hold everything up. Go on, I mean it," she said in a mocking school-ma'am sort of way.

"Yes miss, as you wish."

"Tat, my lovely lad, let's get stuck into these; we should have time for a couple more before we go." Tat noticed the empty whisky and sherry glasses on the table which made him keen to catch up.

"Let's have some water with them," Olly said, indicating the carafe of water near Tat's elbow.

"Hello, monsieur Tat," Annette said, "you boys both look very elegant." She half stood up and offered her cheek to Tat. He kissed it lightly and to his surprise she turned her head to enable him to kiss the other. This seemed terribly foreign to Tat and he fumbled about in his pockets for his cigarettes to cover his embarrassment.

"Relax Tat, my boy," Olly drawled, "it's the Parisian way. I must say I rather like it."

"Oh you, yes you would do," Annette said giving Olly a playful shove.

Tat realized that Annette's remark about their supposed elegance was all down to the fact that they had observed her instructions and worn clean collars and sober ties. Apart from this, their jackets and trousers were edging towards the shabby side of things. Jane arrived and Tat noticed that she was carrying a double whisky. She kissed Annette on both cheeks and gave Olly a brief peck. She swept off her topcoat and revealed a crimson dress in the latest fashion, with ankles on show, and a broad rust-coloured sash.

"Oh là là," Annette trilled, "you look like a Parisian model, how becoming, how chic."

Tat and Olly took a second or two to recover, then they both stammered clumsy compliments about Jane's outfit. In truth they were shocked, neither had the remotest idea that Jane had access to a wardrobe which could possibly contain such a dress. She looked wonderful. The whole effect was topped off by her dark red hair, expertly piled up and pinned, making her seem unreasonably tall, Tat thought. A black choker with a single pearl hanging from it drew discreet attention to the daringly low-cut scooped neckline of the dress.

"Don't worry, you lot," she said in a matter-of-fact voice, "I borrowed it from my mother. There's no way I could even remotely afford such a thing. Anyway, I'm glad you like it." She fluttered her eyelids and she and Annette burst out laughing. She then proceeded to ruin her dramatic entrance by taking out her tobacco tin and rolling a fag as she insisted upon calling her roll-ups. Several bystanders in evening dress looked on disapprovingly at this performance, much to Tat and Olly's amusement. Tat gave her a light and Jane haughtily stared at her audience and blew a plume of blue smoke in their direction.

"Jane, honestly you're incorrigible," Olly spluttered through his laughter.

"We aim to please," Jane said in the most cut-glass accent she could muster. She inclined her head demurely, which set them going again.

Suddenly, Annette leaned towards Tat and said, "So Tat, I hear you have a wonderful voice. Olly says it is positively operatic."

"Oh no, Olly," Tat groaned, momentarily rolling his eyes.

"I spoke nothing but the truth," Olly said with a wave of his hand.

"So what is this all about?" Jane asked. Then turning to Tat she said, "Well, Tat, have you been keeping something from me? I can't have that now, can I? Come then do tell, master Taylor."

"Oh no, it's just Olly, he's got the wrong end of the stick as usual."

"I have bloody not, you devious swine," Olly protested. He then launched into a full description of the booze-up in the back bar of the Wellington.

"Everybody did a turn, or at least those who were capable of it, and some who weren't. Then my friend here lets fly with 'Do Ye Ken John Peel'..."

"Only because you forced me to, remember that, if you please."

"Nonsense," said Olly, "anyway, Tat then proceeds to take the roof off the boozer with this gigantic bass voice..."

"Baritone actually," Tat said in a weary tone.

"Fairly rattles the timbers, he does, then, as though that's not enough, he breaks all our hearts with this encore, something about hearts and roses for God's sake."

"My Love is Like a Red Red Rose," Tat said.

Jane by this time is looking at Tat in open astonishment. "Is this true Tat?"

"No, it's just Olly exaggerating," Tat explained.

"Listen to me, Jane, ignore the young farmer. I'm telling you exactly like it was, scout's honour," Olly put his right hand over his heart, "see, I swear."

"It must be true," Annette said. "Olly hasn't stopped talking about it, and I say this, monsieur Tat, if you have this gift, this voice, you must do something with it. If not, it would be like me keeping my dancing a secret, n'est-ce pas?"

"Well, I will have to give this some thought; that's clear to me," Jane said, stubbing out her fag. "Now then, we have quarter of an hour before we should leave this beautiful place, so I am going to get the drinks. My mother gave me a tenner along with the dress. Come on Tat, you can help me."

When they were at the bar, she turned to him and said, "I've always thought you might have hidden depths, but I had no idea it would take this form. You are full of surprises aren't you?"

As they left the pub Olly nudged Tat and whispered, "Tat, I feel wonderful. Those whiskies certainly hit the spot don't they?"

"I know," Tat replied, "talk about a warm inner glow."

Floral Lane was packed with opera-goers all making their way to the main entrance of the theatre. When they were about halfway along, Tat began to notice the street beggars. They muttered from the shadows, many displayed their wounds, amputations mostly; hands, feet, whole limbs in some cases. Some had parts of their faces missing, others the puckered, livid skin of burns. They wore the dirty remnants of military uniforms. Discoloured medals hanging from ragged ribbons clinked dully as they held out their begging bowls. Crudely-made signs fixed to lengths of string hung from their scrawny necks displaying their regiments, ranks and numbers and brief explanations of their current status. Tat noticed several examples, 'wife three nippers homeless' and 'we fought for you,' or just 'HUNGRY please give.'

Without drawing attention to herself Jane deposited coins into the bowls or hats of as many as she could reach. When they got to the main entrance she had tears swimming in her eyes which she dabbed at with a tiny lace hankie. Annette put her arm around

Jane's waist and said, "It is even worse in Paris you know, poor devils."

The sheer size and grandeur of the main lobby left Tat and Olly speechless. They stared at the soaring columns and crimson hangings and carpets and couldn't help wishing that their dowdy clothes were more up to the mark. Annette and Jane went off to powder their noses. They still had ten minutes to find their seats. Elegant people milled around depositing their hats and coats and buying programmes.

Tat said, "You always see the poor sods outside the posh theatres and restaurants, have you noticed? And the railway stations, I suppose the pickings are better where people congregate."

"I know," replied Olly. "Brings you up short doesn't it?"

Through the crowd beyond the wide open doors they both saw several policemen moving the ex-servicemen on. They were none too gentle about it either. "Strange, isn't it?" Olly said. "They look like old men but if you think about it they only got back a couple of years ago. They're probably only in their late twenties or early thirties, most of them. I sometimes wonder if I'll see somebody I was at school with. I know of several lads who got through it but never came home. They say thousands are left unaccounted for, mostly in the big cities."

Annette and Jane returned. As they came towards them through the crush Tat found himself comparing them. Annette with the so correct posture, petite and almost boy-like and Jane, tall and curvaceous. The spectacular scarlet dress seemed to radiate heat. Many heads turned to watch them as they passed by. Jane was referring to a programme which she had bought for them to share.

"Now then," Annette said, "we have many stairs to climb. This way."

The wide, grand stairs were crowded. They edged their way onwards and upwards, the girls leading the way. Tat found himself gazing straight at Jane's curvaceous behind swaying from side to side ahead of him.

"Now then, boys, just take a peek through here," Jane said

suddenly. "It's the Crush Bar, only those with the most expensive seats get to drink in there. I've been there a couple of times with my parents."

Olly and Tat stared goggle eyed at the opulent scene before them. Scores of beautifully turned-out people in full evening dress were milling about. A generous hum of conversation and well-bred laughter floated through the handsome pillars towards them.

"Wait till I tell my mum about this; she won't believe it," said Tat.

Annette had secured seats for them on the front row of the upper circle. The staircase became narrower and shabbier as they approached their destination. The attendant, who was one of the dancers they had met previously in the Nag's Head, greeted Annette with the by now familiar kisses on alternate cheeks.

"You remember my friends, don't you, Becky," Annette said. "This is Olly and Tat's first visit. Poor things, they are simple North Country boys."

"Not so much of that, if you don't mind," Olly said. "Hello, Becky, you earning a few extra bob then?"

The girl shrugged and said, "Well, it's nice and warm anyway. It's good to see some friendly faces." Then she added pointing, "Down there in the middle at the front, watch out for the steps; they're ever so steep."

Tat couldn't believe how steep. He felt a wave of vertigo pass through him. As they descended towards their seats the full vista of the interior of the theatre came into view. It was fabulous. Tat in his wildest dreams could not have imagined how vast and ornate it was. Tiers of white and gold boxes curved along the sides and huge chandeliers hung from the moulded ceiling. As they took their places Tat and Olly craned forwards to look down on the crowded dress circle and below that the stalls. At the centre of it all, down at the front, was the orchestra pit already packed with musicians holding their instruments at the ready. Above them hung the biggest velvet curtains in the world, Tat thought. They were a rich luminous blue, embellished with gold. The din of excited chatter was almost deafening.

"Now, boys, let me tell you the story." Jane said in her schoolteacher voice. She was too late however, as just then the conductor strode up to his podium in front of the orchestra. A powerful burst of applause greeted him as he bowed deeply several times to the packed audience. Complete silence followed as the lights faded abruptly and the conductor turned to face the orchestra his baton held high in his right hand. Just before he cued the players in Tat thought how excited Alan Mott would be if he knew what was about to happen.

The first breathless violin chords took him by the throat and he knew he was lost. The fragrant scent exuding from Jane sitting next to him, the prelude soaring across the huge void from the orchestra pit caused a strange weightlessness deep within him. My God, he thought, this is as near to paradise as it gets.

THE EIGHTH SITTING

"Ouch!" Tat exclaimed, "Watch what you're doing with those things Olly."

"Sorry, I really am doing my best, Tat." Olly said.

He put the callipers aside and added a small quantity of clay to each side of the forehead of the portrait. Stepping back three or four paces Olly squinted through his half-closed eyes for several minutes.

"Yes," he said, "It's going well. Run your fingers through your hair will you Tat. I don't want the portrait to look too neat and tidy. Get rid of your parting for a start."

This was the eighth sitting so far and Tat had more or less got used to the situation. Olly continued to take frequent measurements of every conceivable part of Tat's head, cross-referencing the relationships between them. He often marked points he regarded as the most important by sticking matchsticks into the clay. By now there were twenty or more protruding out of the surface, giving the portrait a bizarre, other-worldly appearance. The callipers Olly used to transfer his measurements were surprisingly sharp and now and then he accidentally caught Tat's skin with one or other of the two points. Tat found this particularly daunting when Olly took measurements from around his eyes, nose and mouth.

"I need a fag. Let's have a break for five minutes." He offered Tat a cigarette and they both lit up. Olly had decided to model Tat's head turned as though looking over his left shoulder. It was surprisingly difficult to maintain the pose for more than half an hour or so without it becoming painful. Tat rubbed his neck and shoulder and turned his head from left to right to ease the discomfort. They stood together in front of the portrait inhaling on their cigarettes.

"Come on then, Tat, what do you think of it? It's about half way."

Tat walked around the model in order to view it from every angle. The surface of the clay was rough and textured with the marks left by Olly's fingers and modeling tools. The volumes were built up with hundreds of pellets of clay and, as yet, these were still clearly visible. Matchsticks bristled all over the surface. It had been agreed that Tat would sit for two hours every Friday evening until the job was done. The sculpture studios were more or less deserted in the evenings, especially on a Friday.

Tat was genuinely impressed by the speed and efficiency with which Olly tackled the project. Despite the unfinished rough state of the portrait, Tat had gradually seen his own likeness appear at least from the front view. Like most of us he had little or no idea what he looked like from the side or back.

"Well, I must admit I'm impressed, Olly," Tat said eventually. "I can see myself emerging bit by bit. It's kind of spooky, like sorcery or something."

"I tell you what," Olly said, stubbing out his cigarette, "let me take the matchsticks out, it will only take a few minutes to put them back in their relevant holes. You'll be able to see the form better."

When Olly had removed the matchsticks they both stood a few feet back from the portrait. "Yes, you're right, it's terrific, really Olly, it's remarkable." Tat felt slightly breathless for a moment and quickly became embarrassed as he realised that he was genuinely moved by the experience.

"Thank you, Tat, that is praise indeed. Go and stand next to it for a minute will you. Remember, take up the pose." When Tat was correctly positioned, Olly asked him to fold his arms across his chest.

"That's wonderful," Olly said walking quickly around Tat and the clay model. "No, no, don't move Tat, just stay put." Eventually he said, "Look Tat I've got an idea. Take your shirt off and fold your arms again just like before."

"Oh no, Olly," Tat said. "You'll want me stark bloody naked next."

"Go on, remember this is art my lad, it's more important than anything else in the world," Olly said excitedly.

"I'll freeze for a start. Is it really necessary, Olly?"

"Don't worry, I'll light the paraffin heater if you want. Anyway,

I just need a quick look at this stage. Come on Tat," Olly pleaded. Tat reluctantly took off his shirt and struck the pose again.

"Fantastic, just the job. Right, my lad, this is going to be a portrait including the full torso and folded arms."

"But won't that take twice as long to do?" Tat said suspiciously.

"No, not really. I'll promise to work twice as fast. Now let me take a few measurements so that I can add the armature to support the extra clay. I'll have it all set up for the next sitting and I'll have a heater, or perhaps even two, to keep you warm."

Inevitably they ended up at the Wellington after Olly was satisfied he had achieved everything necessary to enable him to enlarge the portrait to his satisfaction. As they got stuck into their first pint, Tat continued to grumble about this new development. Inwardly he was rather excited, however. He was proud of his muscular physique and felt flattered by the prospect of it being captured in clay. Anyway, Olly's enthusiasm was infectious and Tat allowed himself to be pulled along by it.

DAVID THOMPSON

THE CHRISTMAS VACATION

The Christmas holiday which Tat had so looked forward to was everything that he had hoped it would be. Michael met him at the station in Kirkby Stephen with the pony and trap. Dusk was gathering as they made their way through the lanes beyond the town. They talked nineteen to the dozen, both eager to catch up with the other's news and gossip. They dismounted as they began the climb up the lane towards Fell End, to give the pony a rest. Tat was surprised to find himself comparing his appearance to that of his brother. Michael was wearing rough working clothes. Tat recognized his overcoat as an old one of his father's, tied around the waist with a length of cord. His hobnailed boots crunched heavily on the stony track as he led the pony by its bridle.

Tat, in his brown brogues and Harris Tweed coat, felt positively over dressed and slightly embarrassed. It was almost dark by the time they climbed into the trap again at the top of the hill. The lights showing through the ground floor windows of Fell End twinkled suddenly ahead of them. In the dark they seemed to float, whilst above, stars filled the huge winter sky.

"There'll be a frost tomorrow," Michael said sniffing the still cold air. "It might even snow."

As they rattled into the yard, the side door of the farm house opened wide and Ivy Taylor stood silhouetted against the lamp light from the passage. Before Michael reined the pony to a halt Tat leapt from the trap and ran to embrace his mother. They hugged tightly for several seconds before Ivy held him at arm's length and with tears glinting in her eyes said,

"Eh, our Tat, you look grand, quite the city gent in that posh top coat. It must have cost a fortune."

"I got it half price in a sale at the Army and Navy Store, our Mam, don't you worry," said Tat. He felt a lump forming in his throat and knew he would weep if he weren't careful. Luckily, his father and John came through from the kitchen and shook his hand vigorously, lightening the atmosphere by teasing him mercilessly about his appearance.

"I thought you must be some toff lost his way in the dark, our Tat," his father said mockingly, whilst grinning from ear to ear.

"You won't get far mucking out the beasts in that get-up and no mistake," John added.

Tat took everything they could throw at him as they made their way through to the kitchen. The place was exactly as he had so often remembered, softly lit by oil lamps.

"Now then," said his mother. "You said in your last letter that you wanted ham and eggs for your first supper, so that's what you're going to get."

"That would be wonderful," said Tat. He instantly realised that he was using the kind of expression he had got used to amongst his college friends. He was aware that even his accent was already partly ironed out. He also knew he would be mocked for this, especially by his brothers.

"Oh would it now," Michael said as he came into the kitchen carrying Tat's suitcase. "And where would his lordship like his luggage putting?"

"Now then, our Michael," Ivy said good-naturedly. "Leave the poor lad alone, remember he's had eight hours on the train."

Michael threw a mock punch at Tat as he made his way to the sink to wash his hands. Tat ducked just as he'd always done, before hanging his coat up in the passage. There was much fingering of his blue and black UCL scarf and rugby club tie. Ivy disappeared into the pantry and emerged with an unopened bottle of whisky her mother had given her some weeks before.

"Where have you been hiding that, our Ivy?" Jack asked.

"Never you mind," Ivy replied. "I've been saving it for tonight, so there. Get some glasses, our John, quick sharp."

They sipped whisky and hot water seated around the big kitchen table whilst Ivy bustled to and fro, preparing the supper. After a couple of glasses apiece the atmosphere became even more animated and boisterous. Ivy called them to order as she served up the ham and eggs. Tat noticed that, as ever, they all did exactly as she told them, including himself.

"Cut some bread, our Tat, if you please," she said and ruffled his hair just as though he were a schoolboy. As they set about their supper, Tat said, "This is just the job, our Mam. You know I haven't had ham and eggs since the last night I was here."

"I dare say there's nobody in London knows how to cook it," Tat's father said, "Not like this anyhow."

"I never thought of that. I dare say you're right Dad."

After the pots had been cleared away Michael began to roll a cigarette whilst his father filled his pipe. Tat offered Michael one of his cigarettes.

"No thanks, our lad," Michael said. "I've got used to these over the years."

"I know a lass in London who rolls her own," Tat said.

"No never, our Tat," his mother said sitting down at the table again. "I've never heard of a lass doing owt like that before. She can't be much of a lady, playing that game."

"She's quite posh actually," Tat replied, "and she drinks pints as well."

"Well, I never did!" Ivy said shaking her head in bewilderment, "Whatever next?"

Tat told them about the Slade being right in the middle of UCL and how he had met quite a number of art students through Olly.

"Is that the Sedbergh lad you played rugby against when you were at Appleby?" his father asked. "Isn't he a farmer's lad an' all?"

"That's him, over near Pateley Bridge." Tat told them about the portrait Olly had begun to model of him. By this time they had almost stopped teasing him about his appearance and his modified accent. They had accepted him home again and were prepared to listen attentively as he filled out the details of his new way of life. He told them all about his studies, his new friends and rugby matches, the great London fogs and the opera at Covent Garden. Tat knew some kind of corner had been turned. Although the youngest, he no longer felt as though they regarded him as the baby of the family. He had seen and done things that they never would and they were keen to hear all about it.

Later, climbing the creaking stairs to bed, carrying his flickering candle, he felt as if time had stood still and he had never been away. Michael was already asleep. Tat drew in his breath as he stripped and hurriedly pulled on his pyjamas. The room was freezing cold. He gritted his teeth as he wriggled down into his bed which he judged to be several degrees colder than the room itself. Tomorrow, he thought, I'll dig out some of my old farm togs and get stuck in helping Dad and the lads with whatever they wanted him to do.

Next morning he was ashamed to find that they had let him sleep in as though he was deserving of special attention. Feeling rather ashamed he made his way down to the kitchen, still in his pyjamas, to get some hot water to wash with.

"There you are, our Tat," his mother said looking up from the washtub over which she was wringing out some fresh washing. "I'm just about ready to put this lot through the mangle in the wash house. Do you want some hot water? There's plenty in the big kettle over on the range."

"Oh, thanks," Tat said, "Mam, you shouldn't have let me sleep in. I wanted to get out on the farm with the others."

"Don't be daft, our Tat. You need a good sleep after that journey yesterday. You've got the next two weeks to get up at the crack of dawn if you want to." As she bundled up the washing and headed for the passage door she called back over her shoulder, "We can have a bite of something together when I've done with this lot."

Tat had ferreted about upstairs looking through various drawers and cupboards until he'd found some work clothes that still fitted him. They felt strange at first as he'd got used to his sports jacket and flannels. He found his old work boots tucked away in a corner at the back of the scullery.

"Well Tat, you look ready for action," his mother said as she came back into the kitchen. "Let's have some bread and jam. You cut a couple of slices while I mash us a pot of tea."

"Can I have dripping, Mam? That's another thing I haven't had since I was last here."

"Aye, course you can love; happen I'll join you. I've got a new pot in the pantry."

As they ate together Tat felt completely at ease. Just me and Mam, he thought, in this lovely warm kitchen. Exactly what he'd longed for during the time he'd felt so homesick.

"Your Dad and the lads are mending some walls up in the top field near the railway."

"Good, I'll get up there shortly. No doubt they'll tease me to death for sleeping in."

"Aye they don't change, bless 'em. Mind you, you'll have to make time to visit your Gran now and again, and Mary Hollis wants to see you. She told me so the other day when I ran into her in Winton. So think on Tat you've got a lot to fit in while you're here."

"I know Mam. I won't let you down, but I really want to get stuck into some graft on the farm for a day or two."

Ivy laid her hand over Tat's, "I know lad, you'll do your best. Your Gran and me are real proud of you Tat, we all are." Her lower lip quivered slightly as she spoke and tears swam briefly in her eyes.

"Now, now, Mam. Don't you start." He leaned forward and gave her a hug and kissed her cheek. "Right, I'm going to get cracking up to the top field."

Out in the yard Tat got his first sight of the stone walled fields sweeping up and away to the fells beyond. The huge span of the sky was a strange milky blue with the odd ragged cloud here and there. What a contrast this silent empty place was to the hustle and bustle of London with its constant noise of traffic and people always on the move. How he had missed it.

"Thomas, how well you look," Mary Hollis said warmly, shaking his hand. "Come in, come in do, let me take your coat." She led the way through to her sitting room. Mary's mother had died two years previously so she'd lived entirely alone since.

"So what is it like being home again after, what is it, three months Thomas?" Mary asked, after they had settled in the two arm chairs flanking the fire.

"Oh it's just wonderful," Tat said eagerly. "I'd kind of lost track of how beautiful it is and how peaceful. I've been helping my Dad and my brothers most days."

"You never know, after a couple of weeks, you'll probably start to miss London."

"Well there are some things I do miss, I suppose. The rugby and my friends, for instance." He went on to explain how through the rugby club he'd been drawn into the midst of an extremely lively sociable crowd and how Olly fitted into the picture.

"How extraordinary that he recognized you from your Appleby days. So is he studying law as well?"

"No, that's the interesting part really. Olly's studying sculpture at the Slade."

"The Slade!" Miss Hollis exclaimed, "Well he must be good, they only take the crème de la crème there.

Tat told Mary about Olly persuading him to pose for his portrait. "It will be a proper sculpture, Miss, not a sketch or drawing."

"How exciting," Miss Hollis said. "There now, I told you that you would begin to experience totally different things from what you are used to, once you found your feet."

"Actually, I knock about with several Slade students, mostly through knowing Olly. On the whole they're more interesting than your average law student. Don't get me wrong, the people in the Law Faculty are friendly enough, but a bit predictable, if you get my meaning." After a while Miss Hollis disappeared into her kitchen to get some tea and cake organized. As she poured the tea she asked, "Well Thomas, are any of your Slade friends of the female variety?"

Tat blushed deeply and set about gulping his tea which was fearfully hot, hoping the flush in his cheeks would subside. If anything, it increased. Miss Hollis noticed all this but was far too discreet to draw attention to it. Instead she said, "Have some sponge cake, Thomas. I only made it yesterday. Even though I say it myself, my cakes have been turning out very well recently."

"Oh yes Miss, it's lovely," Tat said still playing for time. He took several healthy mouthfuls and washed them down with more tea, which was by now slightly cooler. He knew it was considered rude to seem to avoid a reasonable question so he said, "Well, Olly has a French girlfriend, Annette. She's at the Covent Garden ballet school in Barnes. I've met a couple of her friends.

"Well Thomas, you're mixing with artists and ballet dancers already after only one term."

"Yes I suppose so," said Tat who was feeling calmer now. "Oh yes, and I've met Jane who's studying painting at the Slade; that was through Olly too really."

"What a lovely name, Jane. Is the girl as lovely as the name then?"

"Well yes, she is really," Tat said feeling the threat of his blushes returning. Then to lighten the moment he said, "She rolls her own cigarettes, and drinks pints of bitter."

"Well, well, she sounds like quite a character, does our Jane. So would you describe her as just a friend or a bit more, eh Thomas?"

Tat trusted Miss Hollis, he always had, so he took the plunge knowing what he said would go no further.

"Actually Miss, I do like her a lot but she comes from such a different world to me. She's so posh for a start off. She's not snooty or anything but I get the impression that her family is ever so rich and have a big place in Kent somewhere."

"Surely those things are irrelevant if you get on well together," Miss Hollis said encouragingly.

"Oh we do get on well, for a start we make each other laugh. I've never met a really funny girl before, she's hilarious actually... Let's face it I've never known any girls at all have I, not really Miss?"

"Oh there's plenty of time Thomas; all kinds of experiences lie in wait for you. If you are fond of Jane just take it gradually and let the friendship develop naturally over time. Have you been anywhere special with her, just the two of you, I mean?"

"No worse luck," Tat said ruefully. "I just can't seem to pluck up the courage to ask her. Not so far anyway."

Then Tat told Mary Hollis about La Traviata at Covent Garden. He tried to do justice to what to him had been the absolute high point of his first term at UCL. He explained that through Alan Mott's enthusiasm he had already developed a love of opera while still at school. He said that knowing the recordings made operas more accessible, like knowing Shakespeare's plays before seeing them in performance. Jane had looked stunning, he told her, she could easily have been one of the cast of the opera in her dramatic red dress and piled up hair. Tat ran out of steam eventually and ended by saying, "It was all so beautiful, Miss, I just loved every minute of it."

"I envy you, Thomas, I really do. Kendal Operatic Society is as near as I get to such a thing; hardly a valid comparison is it? Do you think you'll get the chance to go to other operas or perhaps the ballet?"

"Oh yes, in fact I see it as a priority. As London based students we get in for a third of the price. That goes for some of the theatres and, believe it or not, London Zoo. All you have to do is show your student identification. Oh yes, Kew Gardens is on the list as well!"

"Now there you have it Thomas. What a list of places to go, some indoors, others outdoors, some during the day, some in the evening, Jane could surely be tempted to accompany you to something on that list."

"I suppose you're right Miss. It's just getting the courage to ask. I'm not sure I can. Pathetic isn't it?"

"Don't force the issue, that's my advice. Let it come about at its own pace. You might be surprised. The initiative may be taken out of your hands."

"How do you mean, Miss?"

"She may ask you first, have you ever thought of that? Don't despair Thomas, you're just starting out on your journey. Look what's happened in your first term. You've got three years at university. Then some would say you will have the real world to face up to."

Tat felt grateful to Mary Hollis for clarifying some of the things he felt confused about. Suddenly he realised he'd been in her cottage for almost four hours. "Miss, I'm sorry, I hadn't a clue that I'd been with you for so long, you must be sick of the sight of me, and probably the sound of me."

"Not at all, Thomas. It's been fascinating, every bit of it."

As she helped Tat into his overcoat she felt the soft green tweed and remarked, "I say Thomas, this is rather beautiful, where did you get it?"

"Oh, I was telling my mother the other day that I got it for half its original price at the Army and Navy Store in Victoria Street. They had a sale going, so I got some family Christmas presents there as well."

"Mmm, I predict that another interest of yours might be beautiful clothing, I wonder."

"Oh, I don't know about that," Tat said, blushing slightly again. "Thank you Miss. It's been good to see you again. I'm sorry to have stayed so long."

"Nonsense, do try to come again before you go back to college. Oh, and Thomas, you must start calling me Mary. Now off you go before it gets dark." Tat was amazed when instead of shaking his hand Mary hugged him briefly and kissed his left cheek.

As he left Winton and started the climb towards Fell End a few flakes of snow began to float silently across the fields. When he reached the Scotts Pine, Tat paused before he tackled the now somewhat neglected stile in the stone wall. He looked up at the horizontal branch by which he, Dick, Allen and Brian had gauged poor Bill Fletcher's height. In the gathering gloom he looked back and forth along the lane where they had encountered Bill on so many occasions. Tat wondered whether the giant's spirit haunted the lanes around Winton. The thought caused him to shiver and pull his coat collar up around his chin. Tat jumped down from the stile and struck out across the field as the snowfall gradually increased. It would be Christmas in four days and he had arranged to meet Dick in the Kings Arms in Kirkby Stephen in the mean time.

Tat trudged through the snow. He'd borrowed one of his father's shepherd's crooks to stop himself sliding about on the downward slopes. He had no intention of ruining his precious brogues and instead had worn his work boots and a pair of Michael's leather leggings and his brown moleskin knee-britches.

"Now remember, our Tat, them's me Sunday britches so don't go falling over in the snow or you'll answer to me," Michael had said ominously.

The view down the Eden Valley was breath-taking in the late afternoon light. The patchwork of fields stretched as far as the eye could see. Here and there the Eden glinted like polished pewter, snaking its way towards Appleby. The blanket of snow made the stone walls and thick woods seem inky black by contrast. The sky had that strange livid look that often presaged further snow falls. Off to Tat's left and right the fells rose up to meet the more distant crags where the snow might be five or six feet deep. Apart from the crunching of his boots in the snow it was absolutely silent.

It had always amazed Tat that, once he began the descent, it seemed only to take minutes to reach the valley floor. In such a short time he was part of the vast panorama which he had just observed from above, swallowed up in it almost. He avoided approaching Kirkby via Silver Street, which still kept its fearsome reputation after all these years. He entered the town over Frank's Bridge remembering his ride across it eight years before on Sergeant Crowther's shoulders.

He had at least half an hour to spare before he was due to meet Dick so he decided to walk up the High Street to see if anything had changed in the town. He wondered if he should call at the Black Bull to see his Gran but decided against it. One reason he and Dick had chosen the Kings Arms in which to meet was because Tat knew that his Gran would monopolise them all evening otherwise. Indeed she would have probably insisted upon he and Dick spending much, if not all of their time, with her in her private parlour, drinking tea. He had already spent a couple of afternoons with his Gran and in two days time the whole family was to gather at the Black Bull for Christmas dinner. Mrs Watson closed the pub for the whole of Christmas Day.

Much of the snow had been cleared from the pavements by the various shopkeepers and householders. This had left piles of snow in the gutters and up against walls. The town was almost deserted due to the weather. There were no vehicles about and only one horse and trap passed by on the way to the station presumably. The horse's shod feet rang out on the frost-hardened road. The occupants of the trap were muffled up against the weather and completely unrecognizable, although one of them nodded at Tat. Tat strolled past the Masonic Hall where he and Dick had sat their entrance exam for Appleby. He smiled to himself remembering how exciting they had found it all and how Dick had nearly got him into trouble for giggling. Glancing at his pocket watch he decided it was about time to make his way to the Kings Arms. He paused outside Longdon's, the butchers near the Market Square. The shop window was hung from top to bottom with plucked turkeys and game.

As he crossed the square he stopped suddenly and tried to work out what was different. At the top of the cobbled slope stood a large granite cross on a hexagonal sandstone base. Tat approached the structure which was obviously newly installed and realised that lists of names were cut into the sandstone and inlaid with lead. Above, similar lettering etched into the shaft of the granite cross caught his eye. It read as follows: To our Glorious Dead who gave their lives in The Great War 1914-1918.

Tat began to work his way through the lists of names. He recognized every one of them as the father, brother or cousin of boys he had known since his childhood. Tears prickled behind his eyelids. When he had read every name he shook his head in disbelief. "I need a drink sharpish," he muttered.

There were two bars in the hotel, the public bar which was a large spit and sawdust affair much the same as his Gran's across the street, and the snug, which was a cosy panelled room with a crackling log fire. He had agreed to meet Dick at six o'clock in the latter.

Tat used the scraper outside the main entrance to clean his snow caked boots. The passageway inside was hung with brightly coloured Christmas decorations and lights. Tat's heart lifted at the sight. He opened the door to the snug and was gratified to feel the warmth of the fire immediately. There was only one customer at the bar, it was Ben Longdon, the son of the butcher. Tat had known him off and on all his life.

"How do, Tat," Ben called to him, "bloody cold out there isn't it? I'm just having a hot whisky before I get off home."

"Hello, Ben. Aye, I don't blame you. In fact I'll do exactly the same."

"I'll get it for you, lad," Ben said. "Call it a Christmas treat."

"Thanks Ben, that's good of you," Tat said removing his coat.

"Aye well, I heard you were studying, where is it London?" Ben asked. "I dare say you're on limited funds." They sat nearer the fire with their tumblers of whisky and hot water.

"What's it like down there then, Tat?" Ben asked after they had both lit a cigarette.

"Well, it took a bit of getting used to, that's a fact. But I've got the hang of it now I think."

"I'll get there one day. I've always fancied the Smithfield Show."

"I've just been looking at your shop window, quite a display you've got there," Tat remarked.

"Aye, all that lot'll be gone tomorrow, it's a good time for the butchering trade. The next busy patch is when the gypsies come in the summer. They always spend on meat."

"Aye, so I've heard," said Tat, then added, "I've just seen the cross in the Market Square. I spotted your cousin on it. Quite knocked me back actually. When did that go up?"

"About a couple of months ago. They've been raising money for it for the last two years. Aye young Charlie, he was only seventeen. Lied about his age and joined up without his Mam and Dad knowing owt about it. Poor young bugger," Ben said.

"Terrible, I suppose we were lucky to be just that bit too young. All those lads, on both sides, terrible!"

"Aye well," Ben said. "What's done is done, nowt we can do about it now. I tell you what though Tat you look more like a farmer than your Dad, what with your leggings and britches. They don't wear that kind of stuff in London surely?"

Tat laughed out loud, he had completely forgotten about his outfit.

"I see what you mean Ben. No, I couldn't get away with this at college! No, no, I borrowed the bottom half from our Michael, he says he'll kick my arse if I muck his best moleskins up. The top half's my own," he said, indicating his black roll-necked sweater and sports jacket.

"Well lad," Ben smiled, "it all goes together, I might dig out something of the sort myself one day!"

DICK'S REVELATION

Dick blustered through the snug door bringing a cold blast of air in with him. His face was almost crimson, at least what you could see of it above his scarf and below his cap. He had on a battered brown leather coat which reached almost to the floor and seemed to be at least two sizes above his own.

"Tat, lad," he said breathlessly, "there you are! Get me a whisky, quick sharp! How do Ben, long time no see!"

Tat thumped Dick on the back and shook his leather gloved hand, "Dick, it's good to see you."

"Mind my hand, it's that frozen it might drop off," Dick gasped, quickly moving closer to the fire.

Tat went to the bar and called over his shoulder, "Ben will you have another?"

"Nay, Tat lad, I'm late already thanks all the same." He began struggling into his top coat and wound a big woollen scarf around his neck. "Anyway lads, if I don't see you before, Merry Christmas to you both!"

Tat returned from the bar with two whiskies and a jug of hot water. Dick had removed his gloves and was rubbing his hands together over the fire.

"Oh thanks, Tat, by God do I need that. Cheers, lad." He took a good slug of his whisky and said, "Just the job, eh?"

Dick eventually removed his disreputable coat and hung it next to Tat's. He was wearing a long sleeved Fair Isle sweater and corduroy trousers tucked into thick woollen socks. Tat thought Dick might have grown an inch or two but other than that he was still the same wiry, little fellow. Having warmed his hands through, Dick held his feet out towards the fire. Like Tat, he was wearing hob-nailed boots.

"Don't set your boots on fire, Dick."

"They're too wet to catch fire," Dick replied. "The snow's that deep up around our place. I almost turned back but I knew I'd never hear the last of it. Tat, you look more like a farmer than I do!"

"That's more or less what Ben said. I promise you it's not deliberate. I just want to keep the snow out."

"Anyway, it's quite stylish," Dick said. "Then you always did have an eye for clothes." They went on to pints of bitter after one more whisky apiece. Meanwhile, a few more customers had entered the bar. Dick, now thoroughly warmed through, suggested that they move into a secluded corner in order to talk more freely.

Dick chatted about life at Newton Rigg. He'd never played another game of rugby after leaving Appleby. "Too dangerous for my liking. You said in your letters that you'd wangled your way into your college first team. Will you never give it up, Tat?"

Tat had written three letters to Dick since they'd parted company and received one postcard from him in return. "Yes you little sod, a measly postcard. If you don't do better than that I'll give up writing to you altogether."

"Oh you know me, Tat, I've never been much good in that department. You write a good letter, please keep it up. I've enjoyed them a lot." Dick adopted one of his mock-pleading faces Tat remembered from school.

"You don't change, Dick. Go on, get the next round in."

They left the King's Arms at nine thirty, conscious of the climb through the snow they had ahead of them. They were decidedly merry and, muffled up as they were, they didn't really feel the cold initially.

"I'll tell you what," Dick said. "Let's go the short way through Podgill and along the railway."

After they had started boarding at Appleby they hardly ever returned to Podgill or the railway cuttings and certainly not the viaduct. The tragedy of Bill Fletcher's death had cast a pall over the place.

"Are you sure, Dick? We might run into Bill's ghost." Dick stopped and looked hard at Tat for a moment.

"Come on, our Tat, you don't believe in ghosts do you? Surely not!" he said, mockingly. "Not the hero of the rugby field."

"Right," Tat said. "I'm going to kick your arse, you little sod."

Dick sprinted off immediately with Tat in hot pursuit. Dick was quick, always had been. By the time Tat caught up with him he was standing his ground on Frank's Bridge with half a dozen snowballs at the ready.

Tat skidded to a halt as the first burst on his chest. He gritted his teeth and began to gather up snow with which to return Dick's fire. The two friends pelted each other with snowballs at a distance of ten feet or so. Most of them fell harmlessly into the river, which slid darkly beneath the bridge. They were laughing hysterically and making an awful racket. Suddenly a window crashed open in one of the river side cottages and a woman's voice yelled angrily.

"Shut that noise up. I've bairns asleep in here. Sod off home quick sharp."

Dick and Tat ran for it and after twenty yards or so collapsed into the snow, wheezing with laughter. Still panting, Dick said, 'Tat, have you done it yet?'

Mystified, Tat raised himself on one elbow and said. "Done what?"

"You know," Dick said, "have you had your leg over a lass yet? There must be plenty of choice in London, for Christ's sake."

"Well, no, I haven't as it happens," Tat said at last.

"Well, it looks as though I'm going to beat you to the draw on that score." Dick said with a smirk.

"What do you mean? Come on spill the beans, as if I could stop you."

"There's a barmaid at our local just down the road from the college. Some of the lads say she's up for it. Anyway, she's been giving me the eye for a week or two, so I intend to try my luck when I get back in the New Year." Dick said, obviously warming to his subject.

"You sound pretty sure of yourself. She might tell you to get lost; let's face it you're not exactly God's gift."

"You cheeky sod," Dick snorted. "Hold on a minute, I've just remembered something."

He rummaged through the pockets in the voluminous folds of his topcoat.

"Ah here we are," he said grinning broadly. " One hip-flask full of single malt, it's a Christmas present to me, from me." Dick took a gulp and coughed two or three times. "Just the job. Here you are, Tat, lad."

"Christ, Dick," Tat said." You're cleverer than you look, thanks."

After the liquor burned its way down his throat, he added. "Come on then, tell me why you're so cocky about having your filthy way with this bar-maid."

"She's been obliging some of my mates regularly for the last few weeks, so I don't reckon I will have any trouble." Dick paused and lit a cigarette.

"Good God, Dick, What sort of a lass is she?"

"Well, seeing as how you ask; she's married to a sailor who's away for months at a time. I suppose she gets lonely."

"What you're really saying is that she's a common tart."

"Yes, I suppose she is, but I'm assured that she is a very enthusiastic one. Come on, lad, we'd better get going."

As they trudged through the snow, the trees of Podgill loomed up ahead of them inky black.

"I still don't see why this lass would choose a little squirt like you though, whether she's a scrubber, or not," Tat said at last.

"Oh I see," Dick said, smirking. "I forgot to mention her terms and conditions, as no doubt you legal types would put it."

"What the hell do you mean, 'terms and conditions'?"

"Well, Tat lad. What I mean is that she gets five bob every time and I reckon my money is as good as anybody's."

"You mean you are actually going to pay for it, for Christ's sake?"

"Spot on, old son," Dick said grinning from ear to ear."When I can afford it anyway."

"For God's sake, Dick," Tat said in exasperation. "What would your Mum and Dad say?"

"Well, I'm not planning on telling them. Honestly, you should see yourself Tat, are you sure it's a lawyer you are going to be and not a bloody vicar?"

Tat hadn't ever been able to remain angry with Dick for long. He suddenly saw the outrageous, hilarious side of it all and his shoulders began to shake with laughter.

"You horrible, little sod," he sniggered.

"So I am," Dick chortled back. "Have a drink, old cock," offering Tat the hip-flask.

They stifled the fit of giggles that threatened to overwhelm them, for they had entered Podgill. The thick blanket of snow and profusion of trees combined to create an overwhelming silence, which it seemed a violation to break.

Soon enough, as they picked their way through the dense wood, the viaduct loomed up ahead, jet black against the star-filled, winter sky. Their panting, plumed breaths and the crunching of the frost-hardened snow under their boots were the only sounds. Eventually, they reached the stream which was more than half frozen over. The ice wedged between the pebbles and boulders along its flanks squeaked eerily as they tiptoed across. Then on and up the steep embankment they climbed, slipping and sliding, hanging on to the roots and overhanging branches until they reached the gate which led onto the track. They stood, out of breath and, despite the cold, sweating profusely, and stared along the viaduct which stretched ahead of them for two hundred yards or more. A snow plough must have swept the track clean of snow within the last two hours as the rails glinted brightly in the starlight.

Dick was the first to start across, beckoning Tat to follow him. Tat hurried to catch up, his heart hammering in his throat. They were level with the topmost branches of the trees, their skeletal forms absolutely still in the frosty air. Half way across Dick put his hand on Tat's arm. He leant towards him and whispered, "This is where old Bill jumped off, let's have a tot and a fag to pay our respects."

Tat nodded reluctantly in agreement. All he wanted was to be off the viaduct and get home to bed. They each took a swig from the hip flask which by this time only contained a mouthful each. Dick found his cigarettes and matches. As he struck the match a tawny owl screeched piercingly only a few feet away and clattered off its perch passing between Tat and Dick's faces. Without a second's hesitation, they dropped their unlit cigarettes and sprinted across the remaining length of the viaduct as fast as the slippery sleepers would allow them. They didn't stop until they had put half a mile at least behind them.

They collapsed into the snow piled up by the plough, their breath rasping in their throats, shaking partly in panic and partly through exhaustion. After a minute, Dick gasped, "I suppose you're going to say that owl was old Bill's spirit or something equally daft."

"I didn't notice you stopping long enough to find out," Tat wheezed in reply.

After discovering that Dick had dropped his cigarettes, they smoked Tat's last two between shaking fingers. Eventually, they parted company at the point where Tat would cut across the fields towards Fell End. Dick still had a way to go up the track. They arranged to meet again the day after Boxing Day. When Tat was half way across the first field he heard Dick begin to whistle tunelessly some way off. It carried a slight echo with it suggesting that he had entered a deep cutting. Tat grinned to himself guessing that, despite his bravado, Dick was whistling to keep his spirits up now that he was all alone.

Tat took his boots off outside the back door of the farm house and, carrying them, tiptoed along the passage into the kitchen. His mother, knowing he was likely to be late, had left a single oil lamp burning low. She had also left two slices of bread on a plate with the pot of beef dripping and a knife beside them.

Smiling, he spread the creamy dripping generously on each slice and sat down. "Trust our Mam," he said to himself. As he ate he thought of Dick, and his plans for the barmaid in Penrith. He only just managed not to laugh out loud. Ruefully, Tat thought, "Mind you, at least Dick will be over that hurdle, even if it does cost him five bob to get there." He stripped to his underwear downstairs, cursing as he saw the state of Michael's moleskin britches. He cringed at the thought of having to take a tongue lashing from his older brother the following day. Perhaps he would be able to persuade his mother to give them a going-over before Michael enquired after their condition. Tat glanced at the grandfather clock ticking away loudly in the corner. He hung his head upon discovering that it was twenty past midnight. He had got his father to promise to wake him in the morning at the same time as his brothers. That would be in just over five hours and he would be nursing a nasty hangover.

Ivy had been thinking about Mary Hollis living completely alone since her mother died. She found it hard to imagine what it would be like, as her own life was so full. In fact, she never had a moment to herself, whereas poor Mary probably had far too many. She had visited her mother at the Black Bull the day before to discuss the arrangements for Christmas day. On an instinct she had asked her mother what she thought about the idea of inviting Mary to join them for Christmas dinner.

"Poor lass," she had said, "she'll be all by herself most likely and she's done such a lot for our Tat."

"Well, Ivy, one more won't make any difference. She's a good lass is Mary, she shouldn't be on her own for Christmas."

"I happen to know she's got the telephone in," Ivy said. "Can I use yours, mother, to ask her what she thinks?" Mrs Watson had been amongst the first people to have a telephone installed in Kirkby Stephen.

"What a kind idea," Mary said. "I have been rather dreading Christmas Day; it hasn't been the same since poor mother died. Please tell Mrs Watson I'd love to join you all."

CHRISTMAS DAY

Jack took Ivy and all the provisions down to Kirkby in the pony and trap. Michael, John and Tat walked. Thanks to his mother's prompt attention, Michael never did discover the sorry state of his best moleskin britches after Tat had borrowed them. So much so that he had loaned Tat another pair, which he'd never liked, in charcoal grey Derby tweed. Indeed, these proved to be so scratchy that Tat had opted to wear long johns underneath them. He carried his brogues and flannels in a knapsack, along with the various presents he would give his family after Christmas dinner. His mother had suggested that he could change at the Black Bull, as otherwise he might get seriously overheated. Mrs Watson could be guaranteed to have a roaring log fire going in her dining room.

The brothers behaved like schoolboys on the two-mile hike to Kirkby Stephen. They engaged in a running snowball fight practically the whole way. This resulted in frequent slipping and sliding and it wasn't long before they all had a generous powdering of snow on their Sunday best. With no parent present to curb their high spirits, it never occurred to them to restrain themselves. They even found the time to make a giant snowball at the top of one particularly steep incline. By the time they were ready to let it go downhill it must have weighed over two hundredweight. As the snow ball gained speed it continued growing in size. The brothers slithered after the monster, yelling their heads off with excitement. They cheered madly when, fifty yards ahead of them, the missile exploded impressively against a dry stone wall.

As they reached the outskirts of the town the church bells were going at it hammer and tongs. They would be attending Evensong in St. Stephen's later. When the brothers entered the Market Square they did their best to brush off the snow from each other. Satisfied that they looked fairly neat and tidy, they presented themselves at the back door of the Black Bull.

Michael suddenly said, "Let's sing a carol, 'Good King Wenceslas', maybe our Gran'll give us a tanner each. Tat, you set it off and we'll join in."

Tat sang out with his full baritone and his brothers joined him on the second line. Although they were not in his league, they could sing in tune; John was a decent tenor and Michael, a baritone like himself. They made a powerful sound between them and were tackling the third verse with increased gusto when their Gran opened the door. She was beaming broadly and had on a red paper hat with a gold star at the front. Their mother and father stood in the passage behind, chuckling. Mrs Watson began to conduct the brothers, insisting that they complete the carol before allowing them in.

"That was grand, lads," she said, as they bustled about hanging up their coats. "How much should I give them Ivy?"

"Oh a pint from the bar is probably what they're expecting, mother!"

"Go on through, lads. Ivy, pull 'em a pint apiece. You can stay in the bar for a bit, have a game of darts or summat, and stop you getting under our feet."

Jack joined his sons in the bar, which seemed huge without the usual clientele milling about in it. There was a big log fire going in the ingle-nook and multi-coloured Christmas streamers and bunches of holly hung from every available vantage point. Ivy got them a pint each and then retired to the kitchen at the back of the pub to help her mother and Clarrie with the dinner. They were having roast turkey and a couple of roast chickens with all the trimmings. Ivy had made two very handsome Christmas puddings which they would have at teatime with brandy butter. Eventually, Ivy and her mother were sufficiently satisfied with the progress of the cooking to leave it to Clarrie for the next hour or so. They called the boys through to rearrange the tables and chairs in the main dining room where Mrs Watson's regulars normally ate. They pulled four tables together with chairs to seat them all. Mrs Watson and Ivy spread a red gingham tablecloth which had the effect of making them seem like one big table. They laid out the best cutlery and mats, remembering to put a place for Mary who was walking the back way from Winton.

Ivy went through to pour the men folk another pint and found them engrossed in a game of darts. On her way through to her mother's sitting room, she heard a knock at the back door. It was Mary Hollis all muffled up against the cold. She was wearing shiny black wellingtons and carried a large Gladstone bag.

"Now then, Mary, come away in and get warmed up; you must be perished," Ivy said.

"Thank you, Ivy. Do you mind if I leave these top boots by the door here and slip on my shoes? I have them in my bag."

"No, not at all, look use the bootjack just behind you there in the corner." They joined Ivy's mother in her sitting room.

"Merry Christmas, Mary, come in lass and sit you down by the fire," Mrs Watson said, getting up to shake hands. "We're just about to have a glass of amontillado; you'll join us, won't you?"

"Merry Christmas to you both," Mary said rubbing her hands together. "Oh yes please, that would be lovely."

Ivy poured a glass of sherry each. "Take one for Clarrie, Ivy, there's a good lass," Mrs Watson said. They gathered round the fire and sipped their drinks.

"Where are all the men folk then?" Mary asked looking around as though they might be hiding behind the furniture.

"Oh, in the bar playing darts," Ivy said. "They never seem to quite grow up, do they? It saves them getting under our feet doesn't it, mother?"

"Aye right enough. The boys sang us a carol when they arrived today, 'Good King Wenceslas, it was grand. Our Tat led the way of course. He's got a beautiful voice has the lad."

"You know I often think Thomas could have a real future as a professional singer, in opera especially," Mary said.

"Aye I remember you saying so," Ivy said. "But there'd be a lot of risk involved. Tat made up his own mind to get into a proper profession. After all, he can still sing as a hobby, can't he?"

"Oh yes, I hope he does. He told me when he came to visit that he's thinking of joining the college choral society when he goes back." Mary said.

"Mind you," Mrs Watson said, "what with his studies and rugby he'll be lucky to find the time for owt else."

"Oh he'll manage, I dare say," Ivy said refilling their glasses, then added. "Did he tell you about this portrait idea?"

"What's this about a portrait?" Mrs Watson asked.

"Well, mother, some young chap who's in the college rugby team is making a sculpture of Tat. There's part of the college where budding young artists go to study. It's called the Slade School of Fine Art, Tat says. What a mouthful, eh mother?" Ivy chuckled.

"Well, I never did, so it's not going to be a painting then?"

"No this lad, Olly they call him, is studying to be a professional sculptor. Believe it or not, he went to Sedbergh School up the road and he recognized our Tat from when they played Appleby at rugby. He's a farmer's lad an' all from over the Dales somewhere."

"By Jove, it's a small world and no mistake," Mrs Watson said shaking her head.

"Yes, it's fascinating isn't it?" Mary said. "Olly must be very talented; I understand that they only take the very best at the Slade."

"Funny isn't it?" Ivy said. "I doubt whether this Olly lad can sing like our Tat and I know Tat can't draw to save his life." They all laughed.

Clarrie, red-faced from the heat of the kitchen, appeared in the doorway. "Pardon me, Mrs Watson, but you said you wanted to make the gravy yourself. Everything else is more or less done."

"Right you are, Clarrie. Ivy get them lads through and Jack can start carving," Mrs Watson said, then added, "Mary, do you fancy stirring some gravy for us?"

Mary was eager to help and offered to take the various dishes through, piled high with roast potatoes and sprouts. She ladled the bread sauce and sage and onion stuffing into serving dishes and placed them strategically on the gingham cloth.

Mrs Watson said, "You know, Mary, if you ever pack up teaching, you can have a job here!"

When Jack had finished carving, Ivy and Clarrie began to bring the heated plates through with succulent slices of turkey and chicken on them. The boys and Jack had refreshed their pints from the bar and Mrs Watson opened a bottle of claret she had kept aside especially for the women.

"Now then we don't want all the lads in a bunch," Mrs Watson called out above the gathering hubbub, taking charge as usual. She more or less satisfied herself that everybody was seated appropriately.

Jack was expected to say grace which he hated doing. Mrs Watson was not a particularly religious woman but she insisted upon a grace being said on Christmas Day. However, he was reprieved unexpectedly when his mother-in-law said, "Now then Mary, would you be so kind as to say grace for us."

"I'd be honoured, Mrs Watson," Mary said smiling. Everyone lowered their heads whilst Mary stood. "For what we are about to receive may the Lord make us truly thankful."

Everyone chimed in with a hearty "Amen." Then the loading of plates began, which necessitated much passing to and fro and pouring and ladling. Mrs Watson insisted that Clarrie join the party. She had placed her between Michael and John and poured her the first glass of claret saying, "Now, Clarrie lass, get that down you, you deserve it. You two," she said to John and Michael, "see Clarrie wants for nowt." There was a brief lowering of the noise level as everyone started eating.

Mary was the first to speak, "You know I don't think I've tasted a Christmas dinner anywhere near as good as this in all my life. It's delicious."

Affirmations from all round the table followed. Then Mrs Watson raised her glass and looking straight at Clarrie said, "The lion's share of this is all down to our Clarrie; let's drink a toast to her."

Everybody raised their glasses and with rather more enthusiasm than was necessary called out, "To Clarrie."

Poor Clarrie was so taken aback that she became redder in the cheeks than she already was and lowered her head to hide her confusion. She was a tubby lass with a tolerably pretty face. John, emboldened by the four pints under his belt, gave her a hug and kissed her cheek whilst everyone clapped and cheered. It took at least ten minutes before Clarrie could look up and meet anyone's eye.

As time went on the conversations around the table got noisier and more animated. Christmas crackers were pulled and soon everybody was sporting a brightly coloured paper hat and childish jokes and riddles were read out. Mrs Watson brought another bottle of claret from her secret store and refilled the wine glasses. Ivy was dispatched to the bar for more beer. As she expected, her husband and three sons leapt at the chance of second helpings. "Where do they put it all?" she thought.

Clarrie, Ivy and Mary began to clear the pots away. It was almost two hours since they had sat down. When they had boiled sufficient water for the mammoth washing up, Tat said to his brothers, "Come on you two, let's do the pots." It took several changes of hot water, soap suds and five tea towels to complete the task. As the last saucepan was put on the rack above the range Ivy asked, "Do you fancy playing the piano, Mary? There's one in the bar and I happen to know my mother had it tuned last week. She's very particular about it."

"Do you know, Ivy, I brought some music with me on the off chance. I've got a dozen carols or so and some of the songs Thomas used to practice with me. Do you think he'll sing for us?"

"I wouldn't be at all surprised. I'll get my mother to ask him; he'll do owt for his Gran."

Once the kitchen chores were completed Clarrie took her leave with a generous Christmas box from Mrs Watson and the thanks of everyone. The whole party made its way through to the bar. Mary, who had only rarely been in a public house, found it all fascinating. It was after all, under normal circumstances, a totally male preserve. Mrs Watson unlocked the piano and gestured to Mary to try it out.

"It's freshly tuned, Mary, so I think you'll find it acceptable."

"Yes, Ivy told me," Mary replied.

Jack put another couple of logs on the fire and began to fill his pipe. Ivy pulled more beer, though in truth, the men folk were almost too full to drink it, but that didn't stop them trying.

Mary struck a few chords and rippled melodically up and down the keys. "Yes, that is very nicely tuned," she said. Then she played a few bars of 'Greensleeves' followed by a snatch of 'Abide with Me'.

"Come on then, lads," Mrs Watson said, "Do us Good King Wenceslas again to get us going. You'll have a proper accompaniment this time."

Mary had brought her bag through and delved into it to find her music. "Ah here it is, good. I also have 'Silent Night' and 'In the Bleak Mid-Winter', oh, and most of the old favourites."

They sang lustily for almost an hour. Tat held back to some extent so as not to drown the others out. Also, he mostly sang in counterpoint to widen the sound. Mary, who had only heard him sing alone since his voice had broken, was impressed by his ability to do this. She noticed the look of sheer pride on his grandmother's face. Eventually, they had worked their way through Mary's supply of carols.

Mrs Watson brought a glass of claret through for Mary. "By, you play well lass, that piano has never sounded so good, has it Ivy?"

"You're right there, Mother," Ivy said amidst a general murmur of approval.

"Now then, our Tat, sing us Silent Night again, on your own this time, just for your old Gran," Mrs Watson said persuasively.

"I'd love to," Tat said, feeling particularly full of Christmas cheer and after kissing his Gran firmly on both cheeks took his place by the piano.

"Do you want to see the words at all, Thomas?" Mary asked.

"No thanks, I'm pretty sure I can remember."

They knew each other's methods well enough and Mary nodded when she was about to begin. Nobody in the room had heard Tat sing alone for many months and then it had only been the odd snatch of a tune as he busied himself about the farm. Whilst he had sung along with the carols, Ivy had noticed a new resonance in his voice and a sense of its power being held back. She was positively excited at the prospect of hearing him sing alone with a proper accompaniment. As he and Mary launched into the carol, Tat decided he would start the piece softly and gradually build up to full volume, verse by verse. Ivy and her mother exchanged glances as each verse increased in power and expression. Tat was pleased to feel the voice flowing effortlessly through his chest and throat. He felt that his impressive vibrato had developed even more since he had last sung.

Everybody clapped and cheered wildly when the carol finished. His brothers and his father slapped him on the back.

"Oh Tat, you get better and better," Ivy said kissing him warmly.

"He does, doesn't he?" Mary added.

Tat beamed with pleasure. "Does that mean I can have another pint, Gran?" he asked.

"Aye, 'course you can, lad, you all can," Mrs Watson said. "In fact, I'll draw them myself."

"What else have you got Miss?" Tat asked Mary.

"Now then, not so much of the miss. It's Mary and that goes for Michael and John as well," she added.

The brothers looked confused. How could they possibly call their primary school teacher by her first name? Tat still hadn't tried, so he steeled himself and said, "Well, Mary, what other music have you got with you?"

"Thank you and I shall call you Tat from now on," Mary said graciously. Tat's embarrassment was suitably covered as he and Mary made a selection of songs. John and Michael nudged each other and would have started giggling if they had not caught the warning look from their mother. Eventually, Mary and Tat proposed half a dozen songs which included, 'Bless This House', 'The Skye Boat Song', 'Barbara Allen' and, Jack's old favourite, 'My Love is Like a Red, Red Rose.'

Tat's voice seemed to grow in strength and expression. His family sat transfixed throughout the recital and applauded ever more enthusiastically at the end of each song. Ivy and Mrs Watson had tears in their eyes and when Tat had finished the Scottish ballad, so had his father. They all thought they knew the voice, having grown used to it across the years but they had never expected it to blossom into its present splendour.

Tat himself, who had never sung such a sustained amount in one go, with a proper accompaniment, was almost as surprised as everybody else. He felt exhilarated and was delighted by the response he received. Mary, perhaps more than anybody, was moved deeply by the experience. She knew about music and had a well-selected record collection which included opera and oratorio. She recognized how Tat's voice had matured into the equal of any baritone she had ever heard, despite the fact that he was not yet nineteen years of age.

"Eh, our Tat," Mrs Watson said, "that was grand. You get better and better, damned if you don't. Now then Ivy, it's about time we sampled your Christmas puddings. Come on, lass, we'll make some tea as well."

Whilst Ivy and Mrs Watson bustled about in the kitchen, Mary took the opportunity to have a quiet word to Tat. "I had no idea you had come on so far. Have you been practicing down in London?"

"No," Tat replied, "in fact I've got no opportunity to do so. The only bit of singing I ever do is in the pub after rugby matches. Then it's not exactly ideal obviously."

"Well, it's a sort of miracle then. Tat, you really must join the college choral society next term. They'll have you singing solos in no time at all."

"I'll certainly do my best Miss, I mean Mary," Tat said blushing slightly. He had his own theory regarding his singing. The longer his voice remained dormant, simply residing, unused, within his chest, the more powerful it seemed to become and the greater its range. It was as though when it was released, as it had just been, it was demonstrating how it was secretly growing and maturing. Tat knew this was a rare thing, only experienced by very few individuals. It was, he felt, as though his voice was a living creature which resided within him and could only be released at his bidding.

"Do you know Tat, since you told me about La Traviata at Covent Garden I've found the sheet music for several arias from it including 'Di Provenza'. Do you know it?"

"Yes I do, as it happens. I got to know it very well at school. Alan Mott had a recording of it by Tito Ruffo. I've always loved it."

"Look," Mary said, holding up her sheet music. "The words are here as well, in Italian of course."

Tat glanced at the music and found that the Italian he had picked up phonetically all those years ago coincided with the score.

"Well, well, can you play it, Miss?" Mary ignored the 'miss,' realizing it would take time for Tat to settle down fully to calling her Mary.

"Yes, I thought it would be worth bringing on the off chance. Would you like to give it a try?"

Tat looked around him and seeing that his father and brothers were on their way through to Mrs Watson's parlour for tea and Christmas pudding, thought now would be as good a time as any to try a bit of opera.

"Come on then Miss, Mary I mean, sorry, let's give it a go," he said urgently. Mary played the soft introduction and nodded to Tat to indicate where he should come in. He needed no prompting, however. The aria, which he had loved so much as a schoolboy, had reduced him to tears when sung so beautifully at Covent Garden by Matia Battistini. He knew that it was dedicated to the beauty and serenity of Provence in southern France and was sung tenderly with a rising strength at the end of each verse.

By this time, Tat had no inhibitions left. He had sung carols with his family and a complicated selection of folk songs and ballads. He was relaxed and confident. Effortlessly, he almost crooned the opening lines and sang out fully for the closing bars of each verse. It all floated through to the parlour where Ivy and Mrs Watson were pouring cups of tea. They paused and let the aria wash over them.

Tat's distant voice throbbing with emotion filtered mysteriously along the passages which added an extra layer of poignancy to the aria. Neither of them would ever forget it.

After they had all eaten as much as they could manage of the succulent Christmas pudding and brandy butter sauce, it was time to exchange gifts. Ivy had made it clear in her original telephone conversation inviting Mary to join them that she wasn't to think of providing presents for any of them. It was, she had explained, just too lopsided, what with there being six of them, including Mrs Watson. Mary, of course, had her own ideas on the subject. She had selected beautiful leather bound editions of three of her favourite novels; 'Kidnapped' for John, 'Rob Roy' for Michael and 'The Bride of Lammermoor' for Tat. This she knew had been adapted as a highly charged opera by Donizetti and would serve him well when he came across it. She had baked a victoria sponge for Jack and Ivy and another for Mrs Watson. To avoid any awkwardness, Mary had made the first move saying, "I know what you said Ivy but I'm so grateful to you all for asking me to join you today that I want you to have these small tokens of my gratitude, just to set the ball rolling."

"Oh Mary lass, you shouldn't have really," Ivy said, "There's so many of us."

"Nonsense," Mary said. "It's a great pleasure to have such a jolly bunch of individuals to give presents to at Christmas."

They opened Mary's gifts, which were attractively wrapped, and they were all genuinely moved, remembering that Mary's only other real alternative would have been to spend Christmas alone in her cottage. Mary put on her schoolteacher voice and said, "Now boys I will be setting you some questions on your books next month, so buckle to and remember to make some notes!"

They all laughed and Ivy leaned across and briefly hugged Mary and whispered, "Thank you, Mary, and for playing the piano so beautifully." Then added, "here let me fold up the wrapping paper. I'm sure I can find a use for it again." More laughter followed. To Mary's delight, Mrs. Watson handed her a bottle shaped package.

"There you are Mary lass, a bottle of amontillado; it'll keep the chill out come the really bad weather."

"Aye so will this," Ivy chimed in. She had decided not to wrap her and Jack's present and instead placed a beautifully crocheted shawl made up of richly coloured individual squares around Mary's shoulders.

"Oh how lovely," Mary said, her eyes bright with excitement and perhaps a tear or two. "You are so kind, thank you so very much."

Mary was happy to take a back seat as the present giving continued. Michael and John had clubbed together to get Tat a splendid new rugger ball in the knowledge that his old one had long since fallen to pieces. Tat presented his brothers and his father with splendid Oxford check shirts he had spotted in the sale at the Army and Navy stores and his mother and Gran with a bottle of rosewater each, from Harrods, of all places.

In great secrecy Mrs Watson had joined forces with Jack and Ivy to obtain a UCL rugby club blazer for Tat. It had been ordered by letter from the college outfitters in Bedford Square a month previously and hidden in a wardrobe at Mrs Watson's in order for the packaging creases to hang out of it. It was a splendidly gaudy affair in black and blue vertical stripes with the club insignia on the breast pocket. Tat was astonished at the originality of this gift. He was, of course, required to put it on there and then and pace around the room so that everybody could appreciate it.

There was some teasing to withstand of course, regarding the somewhat bizarre combination of the blazer and his britches and leggings. He had, after all, never got around to changing. Michael and John were not allowed to get off scot free, however, as their mother and gran had knitted them both richly patterned Fair Isle sweaters which they were also expected to put on. They had both dropped enough hints over the preceding months as several of their friends had already acquired such sweaters.

Mrs Watson had checked to make sure that the main road had been ploughed clear of snow. She had asked her stable lad and driver, now a married man with two small children, to drive Mary home that evening. Luckily, he was a strict teetotaller and knew he would receive a generous Christmas box from Mrs Watson. Mary collected her belongings, and muffled up against the cold, was installed amidst much jollity in the back of Mrs Watson's Rover.

"Thank you all so much. I've had a wonderful time. I'll never forget it," Mary said through the passenger window.

"Nay lass, it's been a pleasure," Mrs Watson said. "I've never heard the piano played so well. Now George, take it nice and steady. I dare say there'll be ice about." They remained on the pavement waving until the car's lights disappeared, swallowed up by the winter night.

They went back into the Black Bull just long enough to get their coats and scarves. It was time for Evensong at St. Stephen's. The bells had been sounding for a good twenty minutes. It seemed as though half the population of the town were making their way to the church. They were lucky to find a pew which would seat them all together. The atmosphere was decidedly jolly with people calling out the compliments of the season to each other. It was noticeable to the vicar, who was donning his robes in the vestry, that his congregation had participated in a good Christmas dinner that day washed down with a deal of liquor. He looked forward to this service as the feeling of good will and good humour flowing through his church was infectious.

Many years later, after Tat had begun to go to the opera at Glyndebourne, he would remember this. Apparently, he was told, the second half at Glyndebourne went much better than the first owing to the amount of champagne consumed with supper during the interval. The carols were sung with gusto and the prayers and responses called out with great enthusiasm. After the service, the vicar stood at the church doorway wishing his congregation a merry Christmas. His hand was shaken ferociously dozens of times and the only thought that marred his uplifted spirits was that it would ache for days afterwards.

It was a tradition now that the Taylor boys were grown men, that Jack and Ivy would stay the night at the Black Bull. To have attempted the drive back to Fell End in the pony and trap after dark in winter weather was considered too dangerous. They would undertake the journey the following morning. The boys, however, would walk back and check the beasts before bed time. Mrs Watson poured them a strong short apiece to help keep the cold out.

It was close to midnight when the brothers took their leave. As they left the outskirts of the by now deserted town, the snow covered fields were flooded with moonlight. Tat was relieved that neither Michael nor John suggested they take the route home through Podgill and across the viaduct. He made them laugh with the story of the tawny owl scaring Dick and himself half to death a couple of nights previously. They threw a few badly made snowballs at each other but by now the rich food and drink consumed throughout the long day took its toll. They were content to trudge up the steep track towards Fell End in quiet conversation. They didn't even have the energy, when they crested the last rise, to turn and look at the breathtaking spectacle behind them. The Eden Valley shrouded in snow and bathed in moonlight stretched away for miles towards the black Lake District fells beyond.

THE SITTINGS CONTINUE

"Right, Tat," Olly said cheerfully, "I hope you appreciate the trouble I've gone to." He indicated the two paraffin heaters he had lit half an hour previously and the folding screen he had placed across the corner of the sculpture studio. "To prevent you being spied on by prying eyes."

He had constructed the armature to support the torso and arms out of wood and wire and blocked in the centre of this with clay. "I've put the whole thing on a stronger turntable. It'll weigh several hundredweight by the time I get it up to size. Right, get your shirt off, old son and let's have a look at you."

Olly spent at least ten minutes walking around Tat and pacing back and forth checking that the pose was exactly how he wanted it.

"That's marvellous," Olly said at last. He worked hard loading the armature with clay and only allowed Tat two five-minute rests in the first hour. He bashed the clay into place with a baulk of timber.

"That sounds disturbingly like getting the cane through your pyjamas at school," Tat joked, his shoulders shaking slightly.

"Keep still Tat, I know what you mean. Take that, boy," he went on, "This is hurting me more than it's hurting you." That did it; they both got the giggles.

"Oh, all right then," Olly said recovering slightly. "We've probably got far enough for now. You get your togs on while I cover this lot up. Oh, turn the fires off, Tat there's a good lad."

In the Wellington they discussed each other's Christmas. Tat recalled with enthusiasm how much he'd enjoyed it all, seeing his family and old friends. He told the story of how he and Dick had braved the walk across the viaduct and been scared stiff by the tawny owl. Olly had not had as good a time by all accounts; he had encountered further opposition from his father regarding continuing at the Slade. His mother had interceded on his behalf, as usual. But, all in all, Olly was happy to be back doing what he loved most.

A few days later Tat had encountered Jane crossing the main quadrangle. She had kissed him briefly on the cheek and seemed genuinely pleased to see him. She asked Tat to walk her to the fourteen bus stop in Gower Street. Whilst waiting for her bus which, as usual, took forever to arrive, Jane said, "Olly has told me about the portrait he's making of you, Tat. I asked him if he'd mind if I came along and did some drawing. I promised him I wouldn't get in the way. Anyway, he's fine about it but said I'd have to ask you first. Do say yes Tat, it will be such a good opportunity to draw something different, other than the same old models in the life room time after time. What do you think?"

While she talked Tat found that inwardly he went into a flat spin. What Jane was suggesting was, to her, a straightforward proposition. To Tat however, the very idea of having Jane inspect his naked torso across a period of at least two hours whilst he stood silent and motionless filled him with panic. Suddenly, he realised that she expected an answer and that he was failing to provide one. He saw a fourteen bus approaching the stop and forced himself to say, "Of course, Jane, of course I don't mind."

DAVID THOMPSON

A SURPRISE OUTING

Tat had taken a battering during the first game of the new term. To make things worse, UCL had been beaten decisively by Durham. Many players had thought the match should never have taken place, as the pitch was frozen solid. The hard ground seemed to favour the opposition which led to a certain amount of ironic banter about Durham existing in almost Polar latitudes. There were many injuries on the day, most of which were sustained through sliding along the concrete hard surface after tackles or players simply losing their balance. Tat was bruised and lacerated down the left hand side of his torso and the college doctor later informed him that he had cracked three ribs. He would be off the rugby pitch for a month or more and unable to pose for Olly for at least as long.

Life was painful. Ordinary things like getting dressed and getting in and out of the bath seemed to take twice as long as usual. Even shaving became arduous. Tat was thoroughly fed up, but drew some comfort from the fact that he was excused the ordeal of posing for Olly in Jane's presence. He had been dreading this prospect and counted himself lucky to be off the hook for the time being, although he would have chosen a less brutal solution if he'd had a say in the matter. Most of his friends mocked his discomfort, especially his team mates, many of whom had black eyes and scraped elbows and knees to put up with themselves. They accused Tat of playing up his injury and gave him a hard time if they caught him cautiously hauling himself up and down stairways, anxiously gripping the handrail, or hobbling slowly across the quadrangle. Eventually, Tat took to using a walking stick to ease the sheer discomfort of getting around the college. This attracted even more mockery but Tat took it all in good part. At least he was able to threaten his tormentors with the stick if they got too cheeky.

Crossing the quadrangle opposite the main entrance to the Slade on a gloomy Friday afternoon, Tat was intercepted by Jane. She was sporting a long striped butcher's apron liberally spattered with oil paint; her hair was escaping from the various pins and combs which usually kept it in place.

"Oh, Tat, I'm glad I've caught you. I know you lawyers usually make your way over to your last lecture about now, so I was keeping a look out. How are you feeling? Still walking on eggshells by the look of it. Poor you." Jane laid a rather grubby hand on his arm. Tat was very pleased to see her, and despite his aches and pains found he was grinning broadly.

"Oh, I'm still alive. Everything takes twice as long as it should. I've even sunk to this," Tat held up his walking stick.

"I think it adds a certain distinction, anyway, Tat," she went on, "I've got a surprise for you. Be ready at 1pm tomorrow, dressed for the outdoors."

"What do you mean?" Tat said genuinely puzzled.

"Just trust me," Jane said breezily. "Be ready, dressed warmly remember. Wait at the front door of your hostel." She kissed him lightly on his less bruised cheek and walked quickly back into the Slade. Tat trudged off slowly and painfully to his lecture. He couldn't imagine what Jane had in mind but he was thrilled at the prospect of seeing her, presumably by herself, the following day.

Jane had arranged to borrow the wheelchair through her former school friend and flat mate, Nicola. They had attended Benenden together and Nicola was a junior nurse at University College Hospital. A porter had the wheelchair waiting for her; it was the very latest model and the porter assured her it had never been used before. Having signed for the chair, she wheeled it the short distance across Gower Street and into Gower Place. She was pleased with the chair's smooth action and ease of manoeuvre. Although chilly, the sky was pale blue with a watery sun. As she approached the hostel she spotted Tat leaning against the railings, smoking. He waved and limped towards her leaning heavily upon his stick. She noticed he had on his long green overcoat and was suitably muffled up by his college scarf.

As she drew up to him, Tat said, "What on earth is this then?" indicating the wheel chair with his stick. "Where's the invalid?"

Jane pecked Tat on the cheek and said bossily, "Now my lad, we are going to watch the rugger match. In you get and no arguments. I think I know the quickest route."

"But I can't possibly turn up at a match in a wheelchair, honestly Jane, especially being pushed about by a lass. There'll be a riot or something." He was truly shaken by the prospect.

"Excuse me, my lad," Jane replied, placing her hands on her hips to emphasise her determination. "I've been to a great deal of trouble to obtain this very swish wheelchair and so has my best friend Nicola at the hospital. So I would appreciate your co-operation if you don't mind." Jane was having a deal of trouble keeping her face straight while delivering this speech. "Now in you get please."

Tat could see he was beaten and very reluctantly eased himself onto the luxuriously padded leather seat. Jane moved around to the rear of the wheelchair and grinning broadly, extricated the plaid rug stowed away in a pocket at the back. Forcing her face into its former severity, she arranged the rug around Tat's knees. She stood back a little and said, "Very nice too, so let's be off then." She soon got the hang of steering the chair efficiently and found it was surprisingly easy to manipulate over the edges of pavements and back up again. She chatted continuously to Tat, trying her hardest to put him at his ease.

After a while, Tat began to relax a little and was surprised to find he was enjoying this painless and novel means of locomotion. Jane stopped at the gates of Regent's Park saying, "Time for a fag I think don't you?" She rummaged in her shoulder bag and found her tobacco tin. "I tell you what, let's pull up to that bench over there. I never have got the knack of rolling these things standing up."

Jane steered Tat across the broad path and pulled up next to one of the wooden benches at its edge. She sat down and began rolling her cigarette. Tat took out his own packet and matches. He took a long look at Jane and noticed that her cheeks were slightly flushed, presumably from the exertion of pushing him along. She had on a very expensive looking top coat of soft crimson material with a black fur collar and cuffs. Her red-brown hair glinted in the winter sun. Tat thought she looked lovely.

Seeing that she had completed the manufacture of her roll-up, he placed a cigarette between his lips and leant forward striking a match between his cupped hands. Once Jane got her ciggy going, he lit his own. They both exhaled plumes of blue smoke which slowly drifted off in the light breeze. Jane looked at Tat and smiled a slow smile, "Well, Tat, I can tell by your demeanour that you don't find being pushed around by a lass, as you put it, quite as distasteful as you first thought." Raising an eyebrow and inclining her head to the side slightly, she asked, "Am I right?"

Tat felt abashed and said, "Sorry, Jane, I wasn't thinking straight. It's great fun actually and so comfortable. Thank you for taking such trouble."

"That's more like it," Jane smiled and patted Tat's hand, then added, "Tat I have no intention of parking us both on the touch line. My plan is to leave the chair where the bikes are left behind the pavilion and then to watch the game from the comfort of one of the benches on the verandah. That alright with you?"

Relief flooded through Tat. He had dreaded being paraded around in the wheelchair in front of his team mates. He knew they would mock him mercilessly and he would never hear the last of it.

"That'll be wonderful, thanks, Jane."

"Honestly, Tat," Jane said crushing her roll-up under her foot. "I thought you would trust me a little by now." She stood up straightened her coat, pulled her gloves on and said, "Right then, let's get to it. For your further information, I've timed this outing so that we reach our destination ten minutes after the game has started, so we can sneak round the back of the pavilion without being seen and take our seats unobserved. We can leave five minutes before the end if you like."

"I'll go along with anything you say Jane, you're in charge."

"I should think so too," Jane said smiling and ruffling Tat's hair lightly.

UCL's opponents were Jesus College, Cambridge. The going was quite soft in contrast to Tat's last outing two weeks previously and the teams were quite equally matched. Tat realised with some surprise that he hadn't watched a game from the outside, so to speak, for as long as he could remember. He was always in the middle of everything. Olly and some of the others had spotted Tat and Jane on the verandah and waved good naturedly from the pitch. He thoroughly enjoyed working out which moves looked as though they might bear fruit and lead to an advantage one way or the other. Jane took his enthusiastic comments in good part and stood to cheer and shout out encouragement to UCL from time to time. Tat found that he had more than enough opportunities to inspect Jane from many different angles without her knowing it. She was a real beauty and no mistake and had a special air about her. He liked the bossy act she put on in order to get her way, especially as it was obvious that just beneath the surface she was fighting off fits of giggles.

At half time the teams milled around chatting and joking with each other. Steam rose from their sweaty bodies in the thin air. A reserve, muffled up against the cold, took heaps of half oranges out to both teams on a large tray. These were devoured within minutes. Jane suddenly delved into her bag and said, "Crikey! I almost forgot; I've got something to keep out the cold in here. Right you are, Tat, have a nip of this, it's best Navy rum."

"Goodness, Jane," Tat said grinning. "Now you're talking. You think of everything." He took a swig and luxuriated in the fiery taste of the liquor as it slid down his throat.

"We aim to please," Jane said as she took the flask from Tat. "Down the hatch." She took a good swig of rum and made a face. "Just the job, eh!" she said, rather wheezily.

As the second half proceeded, Tat was relieved to see that UCL were pulling ahead. A very decisive try was converted by Olly who actually had the cheek to turn towards them and execute a theatrical bow. Tat put two fingers in his mouth and whistled very loudly three or four times. He immediately regretted this as the effort sent a spasm of pain through his cuts and bruises. He winced and groaned out loud.

"Oh poor you," Jane said anxiously patting his arm, then added, "Where on earth did you learn how to do that?"

"Sheep dogs," Tat panted in reply. It was all he could manage. He gestured to Jane to hand him the flask.

"Of course, you poor love," Jane said anxiously, "here, have a good belt, you've gone quite pale."

As the game drew towards its end, UCL were fourteen points clear and dominating the play, with fluid running moves and clever kicking. Jane reminded Tat that if their exit was to go unnoticed it was time to make a move. She helped Tat to his feet, got him loaded into the wheelchair behind the pavilion and tucked the rug around his legs. She made sure that the pavilion masked their initial progress before taking the main path beyond the trees past the zoo.

"Well, I think we got away with that all right," she said cheerfully. "Did you enjoy it, Tat?"

The rum had done its work. Tat's aches and pains had almost disappeared and he felt positively euphoric.

"Oh yes, I certainly did; it was wonderful to watch a match like that, especially as we played so well. I can't wait to get back on the pitch," Tat said grinning broadly.

Jane stopped the wheelchair and put her arms lightly around his shoulders from behind and planted a soft kiss on his left ear. "Oh Tat, you really are the sweetest boy."

As they proceeded through the main gates of the park Tat wondered if it was possible to be any happier than he felt at that moment.

Jane gave herself the luxury of hailing a taxi outside the main gates of UCL once she had delivered Tat back to his hostel and returned the wheelchair, and signed for it once more. She had gone to the ladies' toilet in the hospital and brushed out her hair before re-pinning it and freshened her lipstick. She applied a little powder to her flushed cheeks and dabbed perfume on her neck.

In the taxi she realised she was quite light headed from the rum. She smiled as she thought back on the day. Tat was so innocent and charming, quite unlike the other young men she knew. There was a beauty about him, which she found all the more appealing because he was clearly unaware of it. She knew that he had been looking at her throughout the afternoon, when he thought she wouldn't notice. She could have teased him for this in her usual pretence at bossiness but, in truth, she had enjoyed it.

She alighted at the top of Shaftesbury Avenue and made her way into Neal Street. It was almost dark and slightly foggy. About half way towards Covent Garden she stopped at a dark blue door, number twenty-three, and inserted a key into the lock. She realised that she had been gripping the key tightly ever since leaving the taxi. It had left its impression on her black leather glove. A bare staircase led on and up from the tiled hallway. She climbed five flights to the top floor; each landing was dimly lit by a single gaslight. As ever Jane didn't encounter anybody on her way up; the building seemed deserted, although she knew that such a large place must have occupants of one sort or another. Her heart was beating loudly against her ribs, partly from the climb and partly from intense desire for the man who was waiting for her on the other side of the door in front of her.

AN ARTIST WITH A SUITABLY IMPRESSIVE REPUTATION

It had all started early in her second year at the Slade. The students organized a termly exhibition of their work in all categories, which they called the Sketch Club. The work was hung in a rough and ready manner in the large life-drawing studio. The easels, drawing-donkeys and potted plants were stacked in a corner to make as much room for the students' work as possible.

An artist with a suitably impressive reputation was invited to attend and give a criticism of the exhibition and take part in a question and answer session. A senior student was given the task of writing a letter to the chosen artist explaining the nature of the event and asking them to be so good as to give up an afternoon of their time. A first, second and third prize of five pounds, three pounds and one pound respectively, were to be awarded on the chosen day. The students were encouraged to put in four pieces of work each and got more and more excited as the event approached. Jane put in two life paintings and two landscapes, done outdoors near her home in Kent. The highly regarded painter who had accepted the most recent invitation was Giles Clinton RA.

He turned out to be very impressive. As he was ushered into the crowded life room by a senior tutor, the assembled students broke into a round of spontaneous applause. He was about forty-five or so with floppy black hair going grey at the temples. He had the good looks of a leading actor and was over six feet tall with a lithe athletic physique, beautifully dressed in a handmade, dark flannel suit with a sparkling white shirt. He wore a silk crimson cravat tied in a loose bow at his neck. He was just too good to be true. As if all this wasn't enough when he spoke, his voice turned out to be deep and slightly husky, with a silky southern Irish accent.

He had the assembled students captivated for three hours or so, moving on assiduously from one student's work to the next, taking care not to miss anybody out. Everybody felt as though they had learnt something of value that day. When he announced the three winners, Jane was astounded when she got the first prize, because, although he had spoken highly about her exhibits, he hadn't hinted in anyway that she was to win. When she walked up to Giles Clinton to collect her winnings, which turned out to be five gold sovereigns, she knew she was blushing like a school girl and that she looked a mess in her paint spattered apron with her hair all over the place. The applause from her fellow students had been deafening.

Three days later Jane found an envelope in her cubby-hole which just had Jane, written in a beautiful flowing hand upon it. It turned out to be a note from Giles Clinton inviting her to lunch at an Italian restaurant in Neal Street that coming Friday at 1pm. She thought long and hard as to whether she should ignore the offer or just turn up. After all, if she did the former, she would almost certainly never run into Giles Clinton again, so there would be no embarrassing outcome.

As she walked down Neal Street looking for the restaurant her stomach churned with anxiety; in fact she felt thoroughly nauseous. She was five minutes late and as she entered the restaurant she saw Giles straightaway as he stood up at a table near the back. He was smiling broadly and beckoned her over to join him. He took her hand and bent down to kiss it lightly. A waiter came over to take her coat and Giles ordered a bottle of Chianti and gestured for her to sit down. He was so warm and welcoming that Jane began to feel much more at ease than she expected.

"Well, now, Jane," he said raising an eyebrow, "have you spent the five quid yet?"

"Well, I've spent one. I stood my friends a few drinks at the Wellington after your visit. It was fun."

"I'm sure it was, if I'd known I would have joined you," Giles said smiling.

"I'm sorry, I should have thought..." Jane said blushing slightly. Luckily, the waiter arrived just then with a straw covered bottle of Chianti and two glasses.

"Alright, Luca," Giles said, "I'll pour."

The wine just slipped down as they chatted and Giles signalled to the waiter to bring another bottle. They ate mussels in a fresh tomato sauce and delicious spaghetti cooked with herbs. Giles told her how highly he thought of her work and that he had quickly singled her exhibits out as the best by a long way.

"You have the gift of making your painting seem effortless, whilst solid and accomplished at the same time and what a colourist you are, my dear. I really do think you will go far."

"Gosh, do you think so? I didn't realise my work was that special. I mean the tutors are very encouraging at the college, but nobody has ever said anything like that before," Jane lowered her eyes, when it suddenly dawned on her that the wine had loosened her tongue.

"Listen, trust me, I've looked at paintings all over the world; I know what I'm talking about," Giles said seriously, leaning forward slightly. "I'd like to see more of your work. Would you bring some for me to see? My studio is just three doors along from here."

"Gosh..." Jane said, she was determined not to make a fool of herself. "I would hate to put you to such trouble, really I would."

"Not at all, my dear. I never put myself out if I don't think it's worthwhile. I mean what I say. Look here's five quid; bring me a selection of your drawing and painting this evening. Take a taxi; get the driver to help you up to my studio. It's on the top floor I'm afraid. The end door on the top landing. Give the bloke a couple of bob for his trouble."

"Gosh," Jane said and cursed herself for saying it so often, "I don't know really, I'm not sure. I mean are you serious?"

"I'm never anything else, Jane, so let's say six thirty this evening. Come on now I'll show you the door." They retrieved their coats and Giles paid the bill. He was obviously a regular customer.

"Now then, Jane," Giles said, once they were out on the street. "Here we are, number 23, wait a moment. I'll get you a key. Giles opened the door and unlocked a tatty looking cupboard high up on the wall. He selected a key from within it and gave it to Jane.

"There you are, my dear. This is the key for the main door here, up to the top, remember, tip the cab driver to help you, furthest door back on the top landing. Six thirty or thereabouts. I'm looking forward to it."

Jane got Olly to help her take the six canvases she had selected down to the main gate, plus a folio containing twenty drawings. She told Olly that she was taking it all to her flat in Fulham in order to free up her painting space. To her relief, Olly didn't pester her with questions. He was his usual good-humoured self and insisted that she owed him a couple of pints for his labour. When he had commented upon her outfit as being rather grand she had told him that she was meeting her mother later on for supper.

The beadle on duty had hailed her a taxi and helped her load up her work. She gave him a shilling and suggested he get himself a drink when he finished his shift. She had indeed dressed with special care, attempting to strike a balance between good taste and attractiveness. Beneath her crimson topcoat she wore a black silk blouse with a low-scooped neckline.

Luckily, with the taxi driver's help, between them they managed to get all her work up to the top landing in one trip. As Giles Clinton had suggested, she gave the driver a generous tip for which he was very grateful. Jane gave herself a minute or so to calm her breathing and compose herself. She arranged the folio and canvases against the wall next to the end door on the landing, and after straightening her back and shaking her head slightly, knocked firmly on the door.

After a few seconds, Giles opened it. He smiled broadly and said, "Ah Jane, you made it then. Let me help you with these, my dear." He took the bundle of canvases whilst Jane took care of the folio.

"There now, how nice to see you, let me take your coat and scarf." As he took her coat from her shoulders Jane glanced down at her blouse and knew instinctively how careful she would have to be regarding her posture. A screen was arranged about four feet or so from the doorway masking the rest of the room from her view.

"There now, come in, come in and get warm." Jane followed Giles into the room and before she could stop herself said, "How utterly marvellous."

Jane shared a studio at the Slade with five other painting students; her space within this was about fifteen square feet. Never having experienced anything else, she took her cramped working conditions for granted.

"I never dreamed I'd see anything like this," Jane gasped, trying to take it all in. She guessed that the huge space stretching out in all directions before her must occupy the whole top floor of the building. It was enormous. On one side, floor to ceiling windows with canvas blinds pulled down at various levels, looked out across the rooftops towards Covent Garden. At least half a dozen heavy dark wood easels with brass winding mechanisms supported large half painted canvasses. Racks full of paintings stretched down one wall. All over the opposite wall dozens of drawings and watercolour sketches were pinned in groups according to their subject matter. The place was softly lit by a dozen oil and gas lamps. Jane breathed in the rich heady smell of oil paint, linseed oil and turpentine, her favourite smell in all the world.

"I take it you approve?" Giles said.

"Oh yes. It's magnificent, I never knew, I mean I've imagined often but I never knew, gosh! It's enormous and so much work! Oh Lord, look at this one!" She had stopped in front of a large vertical canvas depicting a life size nude. It was of a statuesque African woman with velvety almost purple skin, ornate drapery cascaded down behind the figure filling the whole background.

"Oh, it's exquisite," Jane said almost in tears.

"Oh the lovely Efua," Giles said standing next to her in front of the painting.

"I found her posing for the students at the Royal Academy Schools. I do a bit of teaching there now and again. I've about three more days to go on this one. See the drapery is over there, she'll be here tomorrow, bless her."

Giles let Jane wander through the studio whilst he busied himself in the kitchen which was portioned off in a corner. After a while he emerged with a pot of coffee and cups on a tray which he placed upon a small brass topped table next to an iron stove.

"This thing eats coke at this time of year," he said, "but it keeps the place cosy and the models appreciate it, of course. Now then this is Moroccan Mocha, thick and strong. You take it black with one spoonful of brown sugar," Giles said pouring them each a cup.

Jane had noticed that all manner of things scattered throughout the studio were from exotic locations. Turkish carpets, ceramic vases, textiles of every description and bronze and stone sculptures half hidden beneath pot plants, seemed to fill every space not taken up by the work in progress.

Jane took a sip of coffee and within seconds felt her heart thumping. "Phew, that's strong."

"Aye, it takes getting used to. I got to like it on my travels in North Africa. It'll do you the world of good, believe me."

"I suppose you've picked up all these beautiful things abroad, then?"

"I have indeed, I can't resist them. Mind you, I'm attempting to kick the habit, as you can see there's not much space left. I use the bits and pieces in my work of course."

"Forgive me, but I know your work mostly through your landscapes. All the paintings here are figures or still lifes."

"I know, I know, for the last two years I've divided my time up rather. I spend six months or so in here working with various models and my 'props' as I call them. The rest of the time I'm abroad usually working outdoors. I love the sun and the heat." He drained his cup and waved his hand towards the racks opposite.

"These are full of landscapes. But now then my girl, let's have a look at your work. That's what we are here for."

Jane was astonished to find that over an hour had passed whilst Giles painstakingly went through her work. He was very taken with her drawings both from the figure and the landscape. "I envy your facility, my dear. I can see I'll have to raise my game. There's nothing I can teach you about drawing, especially the figure, but I would advise you to relate the models to their surroundings more."

"I know you're right," Jane said grimacing slightly. "The trouble is at college all you see beyond the model is more students doing what you are doing. It's so cluttered and chaotic and well, uninspiring really."

"Oh yes, I can appreciate that," Giles said rubbing his chin. "Now then, what are you doing tomorrow?"

"What day is it, Saturday? Nothing much, catching up on my domestic chores probably."

"Come and draw Efua," Giles nodded towards the painting of the African model. "You can use that drawing easel over there and I've got all the materials you are used to."

"Oh no, I couldn't possibly. Surely I'd distract you?"

"Nonsense, I'd be honoured, really I would. You'll be welcome company anyway, Efua hardly speaks a word of English."

"Well in that case I'd love to."

Giles stacked her things into an empty rack and suggested she collect them at her leisure. As he helped her on with her coat Jane sensed that he leaned forward slightly and stole a look down her blouse. As he saw her out he said, "My goodness, it's quite late, can I give you something for a taxi home?"

"No really it's alright I've got enough left from the trip here earlier. Oh how embarrassing, I should have given you the change."

"Nonsense, nonsense," Giles said taking her hand and kissing it lightly. "Let's say 10am or thereabouts tomorrow?"

Jane drew from the lovely African model for four or five hours over the Saturday and Sunday of that weekend. She did seven drawings and loved every minute of it. Giles took time away from his canvas to talk Jane through each drawing at various stages. He was impressed and she knew the drawings were amongst the best she had ever done. She had revelled in the opportunity to place the figure in the inspiring setting of the studio.

THE SEDUCTION

Jane knew that Giles was attracted to her as early as the lunch they had shared in the Italian restaurant. He was handsome, charming and successful. As they spent the weekend both working from Efua, Jane knew deep down that Giles wanted to make love to her. As he talked to her about her drawings he stood close, so much so, that she could feel his physical warmth. His deep, husky voice had an almost hypnotic effect on her. The fact that the voluptuous Efua stood before them naked charged the atmosphere with subliminal eroticism. Now and again Efua caught Jane's eye and a faint smile played across her lips. It was as if the model knew how she felt. It occurred to Jane that Giles and Efua might be lovers. The model was still wandering about the studio clothed only in a silk Chinese shift on both the Saturday and the Sunday when Jane left.

At nineteen Jane was a virgin. At Benenden virtually the only males she encountered were gardeners or tradesmen. As a teenager at boarding school she had discussed the prospect of falling in love and becoming sexually active in intimate conversations with her closest friends. Several of them had succeeded in arousing themselves and encouraged her to do the same. She had found this to be surprisingly easy and longed to share this experience with the man of her choice. She had gone straight from school to the Slade two years previously, and although she enjoyed the company of the male students she had not, so far, found any of them particularly appealing. If anything she found older men more attractive and enjoyed their company.

On the Monday following the drawing sessions at Giles's studio, Jane had visited the lady doctor who saw UCL female students about their various ailments. Jane knew that Dr Groves was a progressive feminist, who had been involved in the suffragette movement up to and throughout the war. It was well known that she would assist in matters of contraception if her patient could put forward a convincing case for such measures. She examined Jane and explained that a diaphragm was the best solution for her.

Jane readily agreed and was surprised that the fitting procedure was quick and relatively painless.

"So," Dr Groves said, as Jane prepared to leave. "Technically, you are no longer a virgin. This should mean that you will not experience the discomfort and blood loss associated with having intercourse for the first time. Let's hope you enjoy your new opportunity, but don't, I repeat don't, come back to me carrying a baby, as that, rather uniquely, will be your fault."

Giles had invited Jane to visit the studio on the following Wednesday evening. She had taken her black low-necked blouse and a rather lovely woollen skirt, full length and flared on the bias, to the Slade, to change into after a day's painting. She had bought a fitted black camisole with whalebone supports subtly tailored into its structure, also in black. This created a deep cleavage. She did her hair, carefully pinning it up and applied perfume to her neck and breasts. She carefully inserted her diaphragm.

Giles had invited her expressly to see the now finished painting of Efua. Jane hoped that the model would have left by the time she arrived. She wanted Giles to herself. Finally, she pulled on black silk stockings and high heeled black patent-leather ankle boots. Jane let herself into twenty-three Neale Street with the key Giles had insisted she kept, just after seven pm. She knocked at the studio door and Giles greeted her effusively a second or two later.

"My dear Jane, how good to see you," Giles said beaming broadly. "Come in now, let me take your coat".

Jane knew he would steal a glimpse over her shoulder as he often did, depending upon which top she was wearing. She arched her back slightly pushing her thorax forward as he drew her coat off her shoulders. She knew from the intake of breath and slight cough that Giles enjoyed what he saw. She smelt whisky on his breath.

"Jane, you look wonderful, in fact, I'd like to paint you just as you are." He had moved across the studio to face her. He openly looked her up and down his gaze lingering on her daring décolletage.

"Well, what do you say, would you agree?" Giles went on.

"I'd be honoured," Jane said, inclining her head demurely.

"Wonderful, bloody wonderful." Now come on, I've got a couple of bottles of champagne in the ice bucket over there. We'll celebrate the finishing of Efua's picture, and possibly the start of yours."

Giles led Jane over to the table by the stove.

"Now, let's have a glass of bubbly each and inspect the latest Giles Clinton painting." He laughed in self-mockery as he uncorked the first bottle and expertly poured two glasses.

"Now, my dear, take my advice. Gulp the first down quickly to get the full effect." Without hesitating he downed his champagne in three good mouthfuls. "Come on now, follow suit Jane, no arguments."

Jane rather liked to be bossed about by Giles. Most often it was she who took that role, in her habitual teasing way, with her friends at the Slade. To prove the point she downed her glass in one, and burped lustily as though to underline her enjoyment. Giles laughed, and said, "Right Jane, let's pour another before the great unveiling."

Jane felt the champagne immediately. Giles hurried over with two refills and ushered her towards the big vertical canvas over which he had thrown an oriental cloth. "Now stand back at least ten feet. No, no, further back, now stand there."

Giles stood next to the covered canvas and raising his glass, shouted, "I give you a toast, go on girl, drink now." He took a deep draft from his glass, "To the lovely Efua." He whisked the cloth to one side and stood with his arm outstretched towards his painting, " Now Jane tell me what you think?"

The finished painting was breathtaking, "Oh Giles it's beautiful, you must be so pleased." Jane said, genuinely moved.

"Oh yes, you are right there my dear girl, I am pleased alright."

They stood close together in front of the huge painting, talking it through inch by inch. Since Jane had last seen it Giles had added a series of luminous highlights to the figure. These had the effect of creating a kind of inner glow. Giles had retouched the model's eyes and mouth so that Efua looked straight out of the canvas at the viewer, in an almost confrontational manner. The folds in the cascading backdrop were darker and more dramatic. It was beautifully executed. Some parts were left in a rough sketchy condition whist others were extremely refined and almost sculptural.

As Jane gazed in awe at the canvas, Giles explained how and why he had treated various parts of the image differently. As often happened, the sound of his deep lilting voice set up a kind of vibration behind Jane's forehead. The voluptuous Efua with her frank gaze and confident nakedness held Jane transfixed. She felt even surer that Giles had made love to the beautiful African.

"Anyway, I intend to submit it to the Royal Academy next summer." Giles said eventually, emptying the champagne bottle into his glass. "I'll have to get my little man in to put a suitable frame round it. It'll cost a bloody fortune, but so what eh?"

"What sort of response do you think it will get?" Jane said, making a serious effort to concentrate.

"Oh, it'll put the cat among the pigeons I daresay." Giles laughed. "You know, respected R.A. submits life size painting of erotic young African woman, that sort of thing."

"Well, she certainly is that alright," Jane replied wistfully.

"And so will you be, my dear. Come on now, I'm going to hold you to your promise. I need to make some drawings of you, just as you are, agreed?"

Giles busied himself setting up a high stool for Jane to sit on along with some pot plants and textiles for a background. He called across to Jane.

"Now, my dear, are you any good at opening champagne bottles?"

"Oh yes, that's one thing my father made sure of."

"He sounds like a sensible chap. So be a love and do the honours will you, over there in the ice bucket."

Jane fulfilled the task without losing a drop. She remembered her father's instructions, turning the bottle not the cork. She filled the glasses and joined Giles amongst his props.

"Oh, lovely, just the job," Giles said, taking his glass. Jane noticed that his gaze lingered on her neckline once more. She smiled a slow smile. He held her look and drank.

"Right," he said, shaking his head slightly. "I want you sat here; let me help you." He took her arm and helped her settle on the stool.

"I'll just get a light up here," he said, and placing an oil lamp upon a carved wooden pedestal, stood back and added, "Wonderful, deep shadows. Lean forward slightly fold your hands and rest them on your lap. Head slightly to the left."

Giles paced around Jane for a silent minute or so assessing where to set up his drawing easel. Whilst he prepared his materials Jane felt the straps of her blouse and camisole slip off her right shoulder. Giles was ready to draw. Jane said, "Should I replace this?" indicating her exposed shoulder with a slight shrug. The strap slipped down further.

"No, certainly not, it looks terrific. I'll just move the lamp back a bit." Before returning to his easel, he stood in front of Jane looking down at her cleavage deep in shadow. "Do you mind if we make this symmetrical?"

"What do you mean?" Jane asked, knowing very well what he wanted.

"This," he reached his hand across the short distance between them and slid the straps off her left shoulder.

"No, not at all."

Giles rummaged noisily in his charcoal box and selected a heavy soft stick. He drew swiftly, the charcoal made scuffing sounds as it impacted the rough paper. Every so often he stood aside from his easel and stared long and hard at Jane. After twenty minutes or so he grunted, and said, "Lovely, gorgeous, lovely." He removed the drawing and clipped a fresh sheet onto his board.

"Now, look straight at me, put your arms behind you, link your fingers together. Good, that's very good." Jane arched her back to ease a slight ache and moved her head from side to side, she felt a hairpin slide out and clatter to the floor. Several locks of her hair broke free and fell down around her bare shoulders.

"Oh sorry, should I...?" she said blushing.

"No, leave it, it's beautiful as it is. In fact, let your hair down would you? Leave it just as it falls."

Jane reached up and removed the pins from her hair, letting it fall at will. As she replaced her hands behind her back again she felt her blouse and camisole slip down further. She resisted the urge to adjust them and looking straight at Giles said, "Is that what you want?"

"It is, indeed it is, you look wonderful."

He chose a fresh stick of charcoal and drew with even greater energy, occasionally rubbing the charcoal with his fingers before drawing through it again. Suddenly, he stepped back and stared at his work. Eventually saying, "Right, enough is enough. It's fresh and jumpy, just how I like it. Another glass I think." He refilled the glasses and walked towards Jane, "Let's drink, to you my dear, you make a lovely model."

Jane took her glass and drank deeply. She stood up and made as if to adjust her fallen straps.

"No, not just yet." He took Jane's glass and put it with his own on the tray, placing his hands on her bare shoulders. He bent down and kissed her on the lips. She shifted her weight and pushed against him.

"You lovely girl," Giles whispered, gently stroking her hair.

He led her to a nearby couch where they lay together. To Jane's delight he showed great consideration, taking his time kissing and caressing her until she seemed to drift into a cloud like state of anticipation. It was the hot pulsing weight of him as she gave herself completely to Giles, which tipped the balance when she was engulfed by repeated waves of rapturous ecstasy. Later, as she washed in the little bathroom next to the kitchen and re-applied her make-up and perfume, she was amused to see that her breasts were streaked with charcoal. She knew that her life had changed forever.

From that moment on, over the next six months or so, Jane lived a secretive double life. To her friends at the Slade and those she had met through Nicola, she remained the same confident and amusing girl. With her family, when she spent the odd weekend and time during the college holidays at their affluent home near Groombridge in Kent, she gave nothing away. She had of course mentioned winning first prize at the Sketch Club but had avoided mentioning the prize giver. In fact she never so much as uttered Giles Clinton's name to anyone, in case it stimulated even the vaguest curiosity. Each week she visited the Neale Street studio two or three times and sometimes spent Saturday or Sunday there as well. She drew there alongside Giles and eventually started a series of paintings, mostly still-lifes and a self-portrait.

Giles made love to her at every opportunity. She revelled in this new experience, fed by lust and creativity. Not for her the prospect of postponing everything until her wedding night, when she would submit herself to the immature fumbling of some young man who might well be as inexperienced as herself. She was aware that she could occupy only a part of Giles Clinton's life, but it was the part she wanted. Perhaps, despite his appetite for making love to her and his charm and sensitivity, he was simply using her. If so, she grew to realize, she was just as guilty of the same thing.

Jane wondered whether Giles had other lovers. The models he used were mostly pretty young women, often of different nationalities, speaking very little English. Nobody, Jane thought, could be so good a lover without having had a world of experience. She made up her mind never to question him on the subject. For now, she was satisfied with her lot and felt instinctively that she could ruin everything by prying into parts of his life she didn't share. She surprised herself, realizing that she could achieve this equilibrium without losing control. She loved her secret life, but as yet, was not in love.

SHOCKING NAIVETY

Jane was shaken by an incident which occurred at the National Gallery one Sunday afternoon, some months after the affair with Giles had started. She was with Nicola and a couple of her friends looking at the French Impressionist collection. She was showing off rather, explaining the complex layering of colour and textures and how important the different qualities of light were to the French painters, when she heard Giles Clinton's distinctive Irish brogue, some way off at the far end of the huge room. Jane felt a rush of panic in her stomach and brought her informal lecture to a close. She glanced over her shoulder and saw Giles walking towards her and her friends. He was accompanied by an expensively dressed woman of about his age and two beautiful children: a tall teenage girl and a younger boy aged about seven or eight.

Jane couldn't leave the scene without causing confusion to her friends. As it was, her sudden silence had already baffled them. She stammered something about finding the Rembrandt room. Whilst encouraging Nicola and her friends to move on, she stole another glance at Giles, who by now was only a few feet away; to her dismay she locked eyes with him momentarily. Giles was impassive and briefly shook his head as a warning to her not to make contact. The woman, who Jane noticed was very attractive, and the two children remained oblivious.

The next time she visited Neale Street, Giles sat her down in the little kitchen while he made coffee. She was surprised at how hesitant and contrite he was when he explained that the woman she had seen him with on Sunday was his wife, accompanied by his two children. Although she had wondered as to whether Giles had other lovers in his life, it had never occurred to her that he might be married with a family. How could she have omitted that possibility from the equation? She was shocked at her naivety and even more shocked at her response to what should have been obvious. Giles was struggling; the shine had gone out of him.

As time went on she found herself imagining Giles at home with his family; she became increasingly conscious of the quagmire of complications she might get sucked into. Giles was living a double life like herself, but for him the stakes were enormous. The lies he must have to tell to cover his tracks. Did he carry the scent of her back to the home he shared with his wife? Perhaps he had clean clothes he changed into after she had left.

The notion, which tilted her emotions off kilter most, was of the horror and disgust she would feel if her own father had been engaged in similar subterfuge. Her family home was a happy place full of playfulness and decency. Jane's father was a successful stockbroker, a tall handsome man with a good sense of humour. He was devoted to her mother, even more so since the War, when he had been in France for so long with his regiment. His surviving that without serious injury seemed to have brought her parents closer together. What if her father, who was only ten years older than Giles, had a mistress? What if she was the same age as her, a secretary say, at his firm in the city? What if they engaged in the same sort of sex as she and Giles? Had he been seduced by her as the champagne flowed, or had he forced himself on her? Tears gathered in her eyes as the images became more and more graphic.

When alone, Jane's mind whirled continuously around the position in which she found herself. She had taken the nude self-portrait back to her flat in Fawcett Street. The idea of continuing it in Giles' studio was impossible. She leant it against the back wall of her bedroom. When she looked at it she was only too aware of the erotic charge the painting carried. Throughout the various stages of the portrait Giles had made love to her. The image she had made of herself was that of a voluptuous young woman; she turned the painting to the wall. Jane knew that she had to extricate herself from Giles' world. She returned to Neale Street just once more to say goodbye; they kissed and embraced. Eventually, Giles told her he was due to go off on his travels, first to southern Italy and then to Egypt. Over coffee Jane thought Giles was about to ask her to accompany him; thank goodness, however, he didn't but he promised to bring her something special back with him. She kissed him goodbye as she left and he suggested that she should carry on using his studio whilst he was away.

TAT'S INJURIES HEAL

Eventually, Tat was sufficiently healed to attend practice sessions with the rugger squad. It was a relief to hold the ball again and run with it. Inevitably however, Olly saw this as the signal for Tat to resume sitting for him. He made a fuss about it of course, but realised that he couldn't put it off forever. He had promised Olly his co-operation and after all, the sculpture was already partly established. Unfortunately, Tat recalled he had also promised Jane that she could attend the sittings and make drawings from him, stripped to the waist. Perhaps, after the delay caused by his injuries, she would have forgotten all about it.

"I've kept the clay au-point, as the French say," Olly told him as he lit the two paraffin heaters in the sculpture studio. He placed them as close as he could to where Tat would stand, but not so close so as to dry out his clay.

"Believe it or not, I've had to chuck the cloths away and replace them with fresh ones a couple of times. They develop mould and even weird little fungi if left for too long. As if that wasn't enough, they stink to high heaven into the bargain. There we are, let's have a look," Olly said, standing back to familiarize himself with the piece.

"Right Tat, my lad," he said at last, "let's get you sorted out. Come on, pullover, shirt and vest, if you're wearing one, off. Put them on that stool over there." Tat did as he was told, knowing that he would appear ridiculous if he complained, having already agreed to this aspect of the project.

"Good man," Olly said, "Right, stand there on that turntable, I'll hold it steady whilst you get on. Good, good."

Olly paced around Tat and his model to reacquaint himself with how to arrange Tat's posture. "Now then, Tat, fold yours arms, turn your head to the left and stand with your weight on your right leg. Oh yes, marvellous, just the job. We'll go for half an hour at a time with a five minute break before setting up again, alright?"

"Anything you say, oh master," Tat said sarcastically.

Grinning broadly, Olly set to work. They had just lit cigarettes at the start of the second five-minute rest when Jane bustled into the room with her drawing board and materials clattering against the door frame. Tat was taken by surprise. For some reason he had assumed that when, and if, Jane showed up, he would be safely posing, still as a statue, on the turntable. Here he was, however, half-naked, smoking and chatting with Olly as though he did it every day.

"Hello, you two," Jane said, putting her drawing equipment down noisily. "Sorry, I'm a bit late, I had a corner of a landscape to finish off. The paint was just dry enough, you know."

"Oh hello, Jane," Olly said, "I wondered if you'd show up. Set up over there I'll be turning our boy every so often so it'll have to be quick sketches, I suppose. Is that alright?" Tat felt himself blushing and made a move to put at least his pullover on to cover himself.

"Don't bother with that, Tat. We'll be starting again in a minute. Jane's seen plenty of life models; don't flatter yourself that you are anything special."

Olly's dismissive remark made Tat feel even worse than he did already. He just stood there not knowing what to do or where to look.

"Don't worry about me, Tat," Jane said kindly. "Olly's right. We draw and paint life models all the time. Please finish your fag... only a little bit of bruising left I see. You must be relieved to be back in the land of the living. I'm so glad for you."

Tat strained to feel more at ease and to prove it crushed out his cigarette, put his hands in his pockets and attempted what he hoped was a nonchalant smile. Still blushing he said, "Sorry, I'm just not used to it. Ignore me, I'm being daft."

"Well we won't ignore you Tat, that won't bring home the bacon, will it?" Olly said grinning, then added, "Up you get."

Jane found a stool and elected to draw in her sketchbook using a soft pencil. She changed her position from time to time depending upon the view of Tat offered to her after Olly had moved the turntable.

Tat's anxiety gradually faded away as he got used to the situation. He soon saw that he was being viewed as an object. His figure represented no more than a series of shapes and contours to be interpreted by Olly and Jane in whatever way they thought fit. He became fascinated by the concentration and energy that Olly put into his work. He frequently prowled around his sculpture muttering to himself, adding clay to one area whilst cutting it away in others. By contrast Jane was silent, sometimes holding her pencil up and squinting along it as though measuring his proportions. Eventually, she moved her drawing position entirely, to some point behind Tat a good ten feet away. Despite the fact that Olly turned him frequently, Tat was unable to make out what Jane could possibly achieve from such a distance. After two hours of intensive activity, Tat was much more aware of his aches and pains from holding the pose, than any feelings of embarrassment. He wondered how standing still could possibly turn out to be such hard work.

"Right then," Olly announced. "That'll do nicely thank you. They'll begin shutting the place soon so let's clear up and get a couple of pints inside us."

Tat got down from the turntable and clasped his hands high above his head and moved his torso from side to side in an attempt to ease his discomfort. Briefly, he caught a glimpse of Jane watching him and quickly dressed himself. He was all fingers and thumbs and took two attempts at buttoning up his shirt correctly.

Once dressed satisfactorily, he went across to look at the progress Olly had made. Olly was over at the sink re-soaking his cloths, wringing the excess water out of them. Jane joined him and said, "There's no mistaking who this is, is there? Just look at the back here, the strength across the shoulders. It's wonderful don't you think?"

"I can't believe it's possible," Tat replied genuinely impressed. "I suppose it is like me, I had no idea I looked so..."

"Tough?" Olly said carrying his dripping cloths over. "Strong, athletic, that kind of thing?"

"Well, I don't know about that," Tat mumbled, blushing again.

"Well I do," Olly said draping the wet cloths over the sculpture. "I chose you my lad because of that rippling physique of yours, you mountain man. What do you think, Jane?" he asked laughing.

"Now Olly, stop teasing or you'll lose your model. Take no notice of him, Tat. Remember there aren't many chaps around who have had their portrait made so beautifully. Especially in the peak of condition. Olly's right Tat; tough, strong, athletic is exactly what you are. You ought to be proud of yourself." Whilst Jane spoke Tat saw that she was serious and meant what she said.

"Blimey," Olly said, "don't turn his head, Jane; he'll want paying next."

They looked at Jane's sketches. They were amazingly fluent. Even though they had been executed at great speed, she had captured the essence of the pose underlining Tat's stocky muscularity, with blocks of shadow. Tat was most surprised by the drawing she had done whilst furthest away. In not more than twenty minutes she had drawn the whole scene filling the page. There was Olly working on the sculpture, clay in one hand and a modeling tool in the other, leaning forward slightly. Tat was depicted as a dark opaque silhouette seen from behind. Jane had sketched in much of the paraphernalia of the studio, the covered models by other students on turntables of various kinds, the paraffin heaters and the vaulted ceiling fading away into the gloom. The drawing summed up the cluttered place with Olly and Tat at its centre. Tat thought that, despite having been achieved at great speed, the drawing was more like a picture, rather than a sketch.

"My goodness, Jane," Olly said. "These are terrific, especially this one done at a distance. I could tell exactly where this is and exactly what is going on if it was shown to me fifty years from now."

"Oh good, I think I can develop a painting from it actually, I might start it next week with any luck."

"Excellent idea," Olly said and added, "Well Tat it wasn't so bad being the centre of attention for a few hours?"

"Well, no, I suppose not," Tat said smiling. "I enjoyed it in a manner of speaking. It just takes getting used to; it's not exactly comfortable mind you." Tat rolled his shoulders up and down to emphasise the point.

"Oh poor you," Jane said, laying a hand on his arm. "Would you like to choose a drawing to keep, Tat? You can have any you like except the bigger one."

"Have this one, Tat," Olly said urgently, holding a drawing out towards him. It showed Tat from the front, arms solidly folded, his head and neck turning away slightly in shadow. "It's terrific and one day will probably make you rich; go on, don't hesitate."

"Really, do you mean it, Jane? Can I really have it?"

"Of course I mean it. It's yours, you deserve it after all and Olly has made a good choice. Here let me roll it for you and tie some tape around it; far the best way of keeping it safe for now."

Jane saw that a fourteen bus was on its way whilst they walked along Gower Street. She made her excuses and waited at the bus stop whilst they continued to the Wellington.

Tat was thankful that the whole thing had gone well. He had been nervous for days beforehand, particularly about appearing half naked in front of Jane. Now that he'd done it he realised he had been stupid for displaying such naivety. Anyway, he consoled himself by regarding it as yet another hurdle he had got over without serious harm. He actually found himself looking forward to the next session in a week's time. Tat wrote a long letter home that night describing what had happened and what a thrill it turned out to be. He didn't mention that he'd been stripped to the waist, however. That would have to remain a secret for now. As he drifted off to sleep he found himself regretting that Jane had chosen not to join them in the pub. He recalled what Miss Hollis had said to him just before Christmas. Would he ever gather the courage to ask Jane out? Up to a point she had been right in her assumption that Jane might take the initiative. After all she had carted him off to the rugger match in the wheelchair. Most likely she had just felt sorry for him.

DAVID THOMPSON

AN UNFORSEEN INVITATION

Tat had become well acquainted with the faculty's lecturer in criminal law. Jack Douthwaite was a good looking, fair-haired man in his mid thirties. Unlike many of the law tutors, Jack was friendly and approachable. Occasionally, he joined Tat and various other law students for a few pints at the Wellington. Jack's passion was jazz; he talked enthusiastically about it at any given opportunity. Tat had barely heard of it but was aware that it was hugely popular in America.

"It's the musicians, especially in New Orleans and Chicago, who are the kingpins of jazz," Jack explained, "It's thought of as a bit disreputable, mind you, on account of it being played in brothels and the like."

One evening after a couple of pints, Jack invited Tat, John and Chris back to his flat in Museum Street, just off Russell Square. He was a bachelor and shared the flat with a couple of barristers from his chambers. He was keen to play some of his records to them.

"You chaps have just got to know what I'm talking about; you can describe it as much as you want but there's no substitute for the real thing." The flat was surprisingly elegant with dark panelled walls and antique furniture. Jack made a large pot of coffee and introduced his flat mates.

"I'm going to play these chaps some jazz," he announced.

"Well, there's a surprise," the taller of the two replied. "I warn you boys, Jack is an absolute fanatic, but to give him credit, he does know his stuff. Anyway, we are all converts here, not that we had a lot of choice."

Jack showed them his record collection which filled two long shelves in the sitting room.

"And this little beauty is my pride and joy," Jack said beaming. He indicated a gleaming record player with an impressive black lacquer horn towering over it.

"My spies assure me that jazz can only be properly appreciated on a player like this. It's electrically driven; this is the real McCoy for jazz."

"Where on earth did you get all these?" Tat asked glancing along the neatly labelled rows of records.

"Well, most of them have been brought over by my uncle George. He's first officer on a cargo boat. He sails back and forth to the States several times a year, particularly to New Orleans. So I give him a shopping list and he does the rest, bless him. You simply can't get them here, not yet anyway."

Jack played them a selection of his favourite bands. It took Tat a while to come to grips with the jaunty, hollow sound. But as Jack pointed out the role of each instrument and the interplay between them, it began to make sense. Jack was most excited by a very young cornet player called Louis Armstrong who had, at the age of seventeen, joined the King Oliver Band. Jack played a recording of the Oliver Band before the arrival of Armstrong, followed by another which included him. Two cornets played in counterpoint.

"There you see, the younger player seems to be pushing the older along don't you see? Armstrong is the coming man, believe me."

Over the next hour Jack introduced them to Jelly Roll Morton, Sidney Bechet and the most extraordinary singer called Bessy Smith. Jack brought out a bottle of whisky and poured them a generous tot to go with the coffee. Tat closed his eyes and tried to imagine the exotic world in which this music was being played. The record covers bore illustrations of musicians dressed in evening clothes holding their instruments. They were very formally posed and looked prosperous. Bessy Smith was a big, voluptuous young woman in a fashionable evening dress with a glittering fringed headdress. Tat couldn't imagine such well-turned out musicians playing in brothels.

"They look so successful and well dressed on the record covers. But you say they play in pretty suspect places," Tat said somewhat confused.

"Yes, well I would guess that the record companies make sure they dress up like this for commercial reasons. My uncle George could tell you a thing or two about the dives they play in. It's another world, believe me. Mind you, these blokes are the crème de la crème and lead a high old life by all accounts. I suppose it's a bit like boxers and say bullfighters in Spain. Their talent makes them special." Jack did his best to explain the segregation between blacks and whites in America.

"These chaps are the children of African slaves after all. In fact, jazz music has its origins in African tribal songs and rhythms. Especially in New Orleans where it got all mixed up with European music. It became melted together really. There are white jazz players too of course. Here listen to this one. This is the Original Dixieland Jazz Band. It's called 'Livery Stable Blues'."

By now Tat, John and Chris were getting the feel for the music. They tapped their feet in time to the tune and couldn't help smiling at the sheer exuberance of it. "Good, isn't it? Even I can't tell that the band is made up of white chaps; damned clever really."

The music went round in Tat's head as he walked back to his hostel. Somehow he decided it was light and heavy at the same time. A couple of weeks later Jack Douthwaite signalled to Tat to stay behind after his fortnightly lecture. Tat stood to one side as Jack chatted to a small group of students.

"Tat, hello there, sorry to keep you waiting but I've got something to tell you which you might find interesting. Well, I hope so, anyway. Let's go to my study. I'll make a pot of tea. You remember the last record I played to you chaps the other night?" Jack asked.

"You mean the Original Dixieland Jazz Band?"

"Absolutely, well done for remembering the name - it's quite a mouthful. Apparently they spell jazz with two esses, goodness knows why. Well, they are here in London right now." Jack took an Evening Standard from his brief case with a photograph of the band on the third page, accompanied by an article.

"Look, here we are. Anyway, I went to see them at the Hippodrome last Saturday. They were part of a sort of variety show with acrobats and comedians all doing a turn. George Robey was the top of the bill. I've never been able to take to him, I'm afraid. In fact, we left before he came on." Jack refilled their cups and continued, "Well, anyway the band were marvellous, brought the house down. So different to their recordings, doing it right there in front of you, so to speak, clear as a bell. They were so funny as well."

Jack fiddled with the newspaper article again and said, "Now then where are we, oh here it is. Their pianist has collapsed with appendicitis and is being replaced by the English pianist Billy Jones. Well he, Tat, is an old friend of mine. He plays at the Savoy. That's where the leader of the band, Nick la Rocca, heard him. Billy has offered me a fistful of tickets for their next concert at the Palladium on Saturday. Do you want to go?"

"Oh yes, please," Tat said eagerly, "I'd love to."

"Marvellous, apparently the seats are in pairs, dotted around the theatre. Do you think John and Chris would like to come along?"

"Oh, I'm sure they would. We thought your recordings were terrific."

"Right you are. Look I'll give you four tickets; give a couple to them and you can find another chum to accompany you, I'm sure."

Jack rummaged through a drawer in his desk and gave Tat the tickets. "Crikey I've got more than I thought. Take another couple."

"It's so generous of you. Are you sure you can spare them?"

"Oh yes, I've got twenty here. Billy told me he wants to get as many enthusiasts planted in the audience as possible. Keep your eyes peeled on the night and we'll have a drink afterwards."

John and Chris were thrilled at the prospect. Tat found Olly at the next opportunity, who jumped at the chance. He said he would bring his latest girlfriend along, a waitress at the Lyons Corner house in Oxford Street.

Tat left a note for Jane with the Beadle at the front entrance to the Slade, asking her to meet him in the quadrangle at four the same day. He was going to ask her to accompany him to the concert. As he waited for Jane his stomach growled with nerves. Was he doing the right thing? He got on well with her, always had done, but was he going to spoil it by presuming too much? He paced back and forth gripped by ever-mounting panic. He glanced across at the clock on the Beadle's lodge and saw it was nearly ten past four. Oh no, Tat thought, she hasn't got my note or even worse, can't be bothered to turn up.

"Hello, Tat," Jane said cheerily. "You look a bit serious. Sorry I'm late; I had to clean up a bit. Oil paint you know."

"Jane," Tat said, cursing himself for being caught off guard. "Oh, don't worry it's only..."

"Quarter past four," Jane said. "Do forgive me, Tat. Come on, let's sit down over there." She indicated one of the many benches flanking the gravel paths.

"So," Jane said once they were settled, "I got your note, obviously. To what do I owe the pleasure?"

Despite her customary bravado, Tat saw that Jane looked pale and rather drawn. Please don't let her be sickening with something, Tat thought. He took a deep breath and explained about the tickets Jack Douthwaite had given to him. He steeled himself and asked, "Would you like to come with me?"

Jane looked at Tat for a second or two. Tears flooded her eyes and she lent forward and embraced him. In a slightly choking voice she whispered in his ear, "Oh Tat, thank you so much, I'd love to."

JAZZ AT THE PALLADIUM

They met outside the Palladium in Argyle Street half an hour before the concert was due to begin. A huge, excitable crowd jostled about on the steps of the theatre, spilling across the narrow street. Jane tapped Tat on the shoulder and kissed his cheek. "Crikey," she said loudly, "what a crush, isn't it exciting?"

"It certainly is," Tat said, delighted at seeing her. "I didn't expect this, I must say. Let's fight our way in and find our seats." Jane revelled in the hustle and bustle of it all. She realised how cut off she had become. She had never set foot outside the studio in Neale Street with Giles. She was exhilarated by the sudden sense of being out and about. The excitement of the crowd was infectious. She linked arms with Tat and grinned broadly at him.

It turned out that their seats were dead centre in the front row of the lower circle, with a perfect view. Huge, crimson curtains edged with gold embroidery hung across the front of the stage; the orchestra pit was almost empty. Tat's only other theatrical experience so far had been La Traviata at Covent Garden. This couldn't have been more different. The audience was decidedly rowdy and reluctant to sit down in an orderly fashion. Tat noticed that the average age of the audience was mostly under thirty-five and, by the look of them, many were students from the various London colleges.

The first half of the bill consisted of jugglers, acrobats and a couple of dreadful comedians. The audience gave them a hard time and showed their impatience by stamping and jeering. Tat and Jane laughed more at this display of irreverence than anything happening on the stage.

"Would you say this lot have spent a significant period of time in the local pubs?" Jane shouted, leaning close to Tat.

"It rather looks that way, doesn't it? What a riot."

"Well, not to be outdone..." Jane said pulling her flask from her handbag, "have a swig."

"Oh, that lovely Navy rum again," Tat said after taking a good mouthful.

"Yes, cheap, but decidedly cheerful."

During the interval there was a continuous procession to the lavatories. Once the audience was more or less settled again, a huge roar went up as the curtains parted to reveal a grand piano and a complicated drum kit with three empty chairs set alongside. Suddenly, five young men dressed in immaculate dinner suits with stiff fronted white shirts and black bow ties strolled out onto the stage. Each wore a different kind of hat. The cornet, trombone and clarinet players carried their instruments. The cheering and clapping continued for well over a minute, despite the best efforts of the man holding the cornet to subdue the crowd. Eventually, he gave up and grinning broadly, signalled to the band to sit down. He stamped his foot four times and off they went.

The crowd gradually came to order as the music filled the auditorium. The tune was unbelievably fast and complicated with unexpected breaks when one or other of the players stood up and executed a short, flashy solo. Before long the trombone player executed a series of moaning phrases with a sort of hiccup effect within them. Somehow whilst all this was going on, they managed to swap all their hats around so that by the end of the tune they each wore someone else's. The band stopped playing abruptly and the crowd stood and yelled their heads off, Tat and Jane included. The band members exchanged slightly bewildered glances and arose to take a bow. They jostled about whilst they piled their hats onto the piano, before resuming their places. The cornet player picked up a loud hailer and yelled through it, "Hiya folks."

After more unruly yelling and clapping from the audience, he succeeded in making himself heard. "Well now," he boomed, "You're quite an audience. It's great to be so appreciated. That tune was called 'Tiger Rag' and that's the fastest we can play. Anyway, here's a slower tune called 'Livery Stable Blues'."

The band came in together to play the slow haunting tune which silenced the audience. Tat felt the hairs prickle on the back of his neck. He was amazed as to how loud and crystal clear the band sounded compared to the fuzzy hollow recordings Jack had played to them. As he craned forward leaning on the balustrade he could hear the breath pushing through the instruments, especially the cornet. The percussion from the drums vibrated in his chest. As he looked down at the audience in the stalls below he saw hundreds of heads nodding in time to the rhythm.

When the tune ended and the applause swelled up once more, Jane leant close to Tat and said, "Isn't it wonderful, Tat? I don't get it though; they don't have any music to play from. How on earth do they know what they're doing?"

"I know, amazing isn't it? Apparently they keep it all in their heads and more or less make the solos up as they go along."

The band got better and better as the concert proceeded; more than likely the enthusiastic audience urged them on to greater heights. They continued to swig from the flask. Jane had begun to draw in her sketchbook which she rested on the edge of the circle in front of her. Several times whilst playing solos the cornet player held a bowler hat over the bell of the instrument. He moved it back and forth creating louder and softer notes with a sort of sliding sound between them. He tossed the hat to the trombonist who did the same, occasionally operating the trombone slide with his foot.

The band was never still for long, continuously joking with each other. The clarinetist managed to tap dance whilst playing particularly complicated solo passages. Without warning, they would get up and march around the stage playing in a military manner for a while before breaking back into their usual style. Once the drummer, who was wildly energetic, created a machine gun effect on his snare drum and the cornet, clarinetist and trombonist fell down as though they had been shot. The crowd loved it all.

After an hour of growing pandemonium the cornet player announced the last number. "Let me tell ya," he yelled through the loud hailer, "we ain't never had a better audience, ever! We gonna sign off with another fast one called High Society. Oh yeah, listen out for Larry here on the clarinet, he gets to show off."

"Oh no, what a shame," Jane shouted above the applause, "I could listen to them all night."

"Me too, I can't believe it's really happening."

Half way through the tune, which they played at breakneck speed, the clarinetist stood up and walked to the front of the stage and played an amazingly complicated solo. It was difficult to believe that he could move his fingers so quickly or find time to take a breath. He waved his instrument above his head to acknowledge the thunderous applause before tap dancing back to his chair.

As Tat and Jane made their way through the good natured crush in the foyer, Tat saw Jack Douthwaite and his two flat mates descending the main stair case. "There's Jack," Tat said. "Let's wait and have a word with him; he saw the band at the Hippodrome last Saturday."

"Tat, my boy," Jack said beaming, "Well, what did you make of that then?"

"Terrific, just terrific! What a bunch of characters they are, absolutely hilarious."

"I know, they're outrageous. Come on then, Tat, introduce us," Jack said nodding towards Jane.

"Oh sorry, this is Jane; meet Jack Douthwaite, he's one of our lecturers."

"Hello Jane," Jack said shaking her hand briefly. "These two reprobates are Ben and Charles, my flat mates. More lawyers, I'm afraid. I've seen you knocking about the college in paint-covered togs. You must be at the Slade, am I right?"

"Yes I am," Jane said, "How observant of you."

"Ah, we legal types are trained to notice things. Comes with the territory. Anyway, we are going to join my chum, Billy Jones, the pianist, remember, for a quick one before closing time. Care to join us?"

Tat looked enquiringly at Jane and asked, "What do you think?"

"Oh yes, please, I could murder a pint and I'm dying for a fag." They struggled through the noisy crowd into Argyle Street and made their way towards the Carnaby Arms behind Liberty's. The pub was filling up with young people keen to slake their thirst after the show. Jack pushed through to the bar calling back over his shoulder, "Did you mean it about the pint, young lady?" Jane nodded enthusiastically.

"Let's grab that table," Charles said and led the way towards the back of the bar. They waited for Jane to make her roll-up before lighting their cigarettes.

"Well, I've never seen that before," Charles said.

"Proves what a sheltered life you've led then doesn't it?" Jane said cheekily.

"Touché" Charles said. He glanced over towards the bar to see how Jack was getting on. Turning back to the others, he said, "I say, isn't that the cornet player with Billy? Look, talking to Jack?"

Ben sat up straight and said, "Goodness you're right. It looks like we are about to meet the great Nick La Rocca no less. Well I never."

Tat's jaw dropped and he stared wide-eyed at Jane. She reached across and pushed his jaw back into place and said, "Now Tat, behave yourself," much to the amusement of Ben and Charles. They were still laughing when Jack joined them with a heavily loaded tray accompanied by the two musicians.

"Well, I imagine you lot recognize Mr La Rocca from the band and Billy Jones, the pianist," Jack said excitedly. The men folk stood up and introduced themselves to the newcomers. Jane remained seated, grinning from ear to ear.

"Hiya folks," La Rocca said taking off his trilby hat. "Nice to meet you." He turned towards Jane and said, "Hello, little lady."

Jane immediately stood and pulled herself up to her full height and said, "Oh I'm not that little Mr La Rocca; in fact I'm a bit taller than you." This broke the ice and they all laughed heartily and sat down. Jane was rather light-headed from the rum she and Tat had drunk at the theatre. She leaned forward and said, "Can I say Mr La Rocca, how much we enjoyed your performance. It was such a thrill really."

"Well, miss, thank you kindly," La Rocca replied. "I gotta say the reception we're getting here in London is amazing."

"Well, I can think of two good reasons for that," Jack said. "One is that very few of us have heard anything like it and the other is that your band is so good."

La Rocca nodded and smiled, "Billy tells me you have quite a jazz record collection, including some of ours. I didn't even know you could get them over here."

Whilst Jack explained about his uncle George, Tat took a good look at the cornet player. He was indeed rather short and thick set. His hair was combed straight back from his forehead and was shiny with oil. A reddish circular mark on the centre of his top lip was, Tat thought, caused by the pressure of the cornet mouthpiece. He wondered what on earth a lad from the Eden Valley was doing in the presence of an American bandleader who played jazz, of all things.

"So you guys are all attorneys, huh?" La Rocca asked. "Hey Billy you didn't tell me we would be drinking with a bunch of lawmen."

"Relax, Nick," Billy said grinning, "They're not exactly cops are you boys?"

"Certainly not," Jack said. "Anyway, young Tat is a student of mine and Jane is studying art."

"You don't say," La Rocca said, eager to return his attention back to Jane.

"It is completely accurate Mr La Rocca; in fact I'm going to draw you right now, if you don't mind?" Jane replied taking her sketchbook and pencil out of her shoulder bag. Then added, "Just ignore me, pretend I'm not here."

"A doll like you is kinda difficult to ignore," La Rocca said smiling.

"Honestly, you don't mind do you, it's too good a chance to miss?" Jane said persuasively.

La Rocca hesitated and said, "Oh I ain't so sure, young lady." Tat was having a hard time suppressing a fit of giggles. The spectacle of Jane gradually getting her way, as he had so often seen before, was rather like watching a mongoose tackle a snake.

"Look," she said, "I've already done half a dozen of the band." She pushed the sketchbook across the table. La Rocca leafed through the drawings, after a moment or two his eyebrows shot up and he whistled in surprise.

"Hey now, these are great. Have a look, you guys." The sketchbook was passed around and the drawings genuinely admired. Jane had captured the energy of the performance, emphasizing the comical antics particularly the tap dancing clarinetist.

"I tell you what, let me have one of these and you can do your sketch," La Rocca said, chuckling.

"Done," Jane said triumphantly. She removed the drawing la Rocca liked most and presented it to him. "Now just go on chatting."

"Okay it's a deal," La Rocca said good-naturedly.

"So," Jack said, "What's the real story about the Hippodrome concerts? Surely you were booked for more than one performance there?"

La Rocca drained a very large whisky Jack had bought him and said, "It was all down to that son of a bitch, George Robey, ain't that right, Billy?"

"Well, yes, there's no way round that I suppose," Billy Jones replied.

"There was an awful bust up straight after the opening show. Robey blew his top and told the management that either we went or he would."

"What on earth for?" Jack asked.

"He beefed about the applause we got. You were there, weren't you? We brought the house down, just like tonight. Robey couldn't take the heat," La Rocca said lighting a cheroot.

Billy Jones went off to the bar to get a last round in before closing time. La Rocca had given him a fiver to cover it. "Anyways, this Robey guy is some kind of big star over here, right? We, I think he's baloney," La Rocca said.

"Yes, he is popular; that's true." said Jack.

"So we get the bum's rush, no questions asked. Anyhow, a couple of guys from the Palladium saw the show and booked us the next day to do ten gigs for twice the dough."

"So everything has turned out for the best then," Jack said.

"Yeah I guess you could say that. It was a sticky moment though. You gotta remember we're a long way from home."

The drinks arrived and Billy Jones settled himself once more. Tat noticed that La Rocca had been supplied with another large whisky. La Rocca continued, "Then Russell gets sick. I'm telling you we would have been sunk good if your pal Billy hadn't crawled out of the woodwork. Boy, is he a quick learner." He clapped Billy Jones on the shoulder and added, "Thanks a million, buddy."

"My pleasure absolutely," Billy said, "I haven't done anything so exciting for years."

"There now," Jane said suddenly, "What do you think?"

"That's swell, int that something? How do you do that so quick?" La Rocca asked.

Billy craned across to look at the drawing and said, "My that's terrific, Nick, it's you alright. You're ever so good, miss."

For the next ten minutes Jane became the centre of attention. La Rocca persuaded her to swap the drawing she had already given him for the portrait sketch. Tat had a suspicion this might happen. Jane drove a hard bargain, however. "Only on the condition that you will sit for me on another occasion," Jane said firmly, then added, "Oh go on, have both drawings; thank you for being so patient."

"Okay, it's a deal. I know when I'm beat. You got real talent, young lady." Jane blew out a plume of smoke from her roll-up and smiled in satisfaction. Tat thought about what Jane had said in the theatre and said, "Mr La Rocca, Jane and I are mystified as to how the band can play such complicated tunes without any sheet music."

"Heck son, none of us can hardly read a note. It's all in here," he tapped his temple. "We're self taught, just kind of picked it up. That's how jazz is, kid. Mind you, we practice like crazy."

"How extraordinary," said Tat. "I mean I wouldn't have thought it was possible."

"Well, that's how it is. Believe me, if you think we're good you should hear some of the black guys back home. Now they are hot."

"What about the youngster with King Oliver," Jack asked. "Louis Armstrong, how do you rate him?"

"Oh Louis, he'll show us all the way, give him a few years, mark my words."

"It's his tone I like so much," Jack added.

"Yeah, he's great," and then looking at Tat, he said, "and he don't read a note of music."

AT LAST

Just then the landlord shouted time and rang the bell above the bar. They bustled out into Regent Street, saying their farewells, looking for taxis. Jane took Tat's arm and whispered in his ear, "Come home with me."

Tat tried not to show the panic that suddenly lurched up within him. He knew he was rather drunk and Jane must be as well. She sensed his anxiety, stood close in front of him and slid his arms around her waist. In a quiet voice she said, "Tat we've had a wonderful time; let's keep it going. It's Sunday tomorrow. Nicola's away, perfect timing, please, Tat." She kissed him softly on the lips.

Tat was surprised at the comfort and elegance of Jane's flat in Fawcettt Street. Most students he mixed with at UCL lived in rather run-down accommodation, up in the steeper parts of the city to the north of the college. Their taxi ride had taken them through south Kensington and on into Fulham, past elegant tree-lined squares. He supposed the absence of hills was due to the influence of the Thames, which he guessed was only a few streets away to the south. Jane had insisted on paying the taxi fare.

She hung their coats in the hallway and ushered Tat through to the sitting room, which she explained doubled as the dining room when she and Nicola gave a supper party.

"This is Nicola," she said, indicating a highly finished pencil drawing that hung amongst numerous examples of her work distributed around the walls. Meanwhile, she lit the gas wall lights and a couple of elegant oil lamps.

"Pretty girl, don't you think?" she added, pouring them both a generous shot of Navy rum from a walnut side table, covered with various bottles and glasses.

"Yes, she's lovely," Tat said. In truth he was rather taken aback, as the drawing depicted Jane's flat-mate dressed in nothing other than a black choker around her very long slender neck. Tat took his glass and vowed to make it his last drink of the night. He already felt light-headed and knew how fragile the dividing line was between euphoria and nausea.

Jane showed no such caution as she gulped down a generous mouthful. "Lovely! You know Tat I can't remember when I enjoyed myself so much. It was so sweet of you to include me." She leaned forward and kissed him again on the lips. Tat inhaled her perfume and he didn't quite know what to do next.

"You dear, sweet boy... Right, I'm starving, fancy an omelette?" She took Tat by the hand and led him through to the large, modern kitchen. "Sit there, Tat, and watch me cook." Jane chatted animatedly while she bustled about with an unlit roll-up in the corner of her mouth.

Tat told her how funny she had been in the pub. "You played Nick La Rocca like a fish. Talk about eating out of your hand. The drawings were fantastic, by the way."

"I was a bit cheeky, I suppose. I just couldn't help myself. Anyway, I was quite serious about doing more drawings of him. I might get a painting out of it; what do you think?"

"Well, why not? Mind you, I'm not sure how much he can be trusted. I think he took quite a shine to you."

"Oh don't worry. I'm perfectly capable of looking after myself. Do you think your chum, Jack Douthwaite, would fix up another chance to draw our Mr La Rocca?" She paused while she cracked six eggs into the frying pan.

"Give me a light will you?" Then, after blowing out a large quantity of smoke, Jane tilted her head to one side and asked, "What about you, Tat, have you taken a shine to me?"

Tat braced himself and said, "I think you are lovely; you must know that."

"You are right, I do know it, but I just wanted you to say it."

Tat had never tasted anything like the omelette Jane had made. She explained the trick was in the olive oil and herbs. Jane poured more rum, despite Tat's attempts to abstain.

"Nonsense, Tat. It's almost midnight so who cares. I think we both deserve to get a bit tiddly, don't you? Now then be a love and dump the dishes in the sink, I'm just going to pop to the bathroom."

Jane applied more perfume and freshened her lipstick. Whilst looking in the mirror she quickly removed the pins and grips from her hair and let it tumble free, smiling a slow smile. She was sure Tat was inexperienced; his shy innocence was one of the most appealing things about him. She knew exactly how to take care of herself and was confident in her recently acquired powers of seduction.

She found Tat in the sitting room looking at her pictures and smoking a cigarette. Jane walked slowly towards him, took the cigarette from his fingers and inhaled deeply on it before stubbing it out in an ashtray on the drinks table. Turning to face him, she put her hands behind his head, pulling him gently towards her and kissed him deeply. Drawing back slightly, she smiled and said,

"Come with me, Tat my darling." She led the way to her bedroom, which was softly lit by a single oil lamp.

When they awoke at almost midday their sleep-warmed bodies were quickly aroused and they revelled in their newfound intimacy. They ate toast and marmalade washed down with strong coffee, chatting easily, their naked legs entwined underneath the kitchen table. Jane prepared a hot bath and insisted that they share it together. Gazing lazily at Jane through the curling steam, Tat wondered whether some strange warping of time and space might have occurred and that he had died and gone to heaven.

CALM AFTER THE STORM

It was a sparkling, breezy day and Jane suggested that they take a walk down to the river. Along the way, she showed Tat where various painters lived; pointing out the tall windows they had incorporated into their houses to provide them with natural light. As they strolled arm in arm through Chelsea, Tat was somewhat overawed by the grandeur of many of the houses and the contrast with the humble mews associated with them. Jane explained that these were where the servants lived, more often than not.

As they entered Tite Street they could sense the river just ahead. The sun sparkled on the ruffled water, causing them to shade their eyes as they emerged onto the embankment. Tat hadn't seen the Thames that often since he had been in London. He was always thrilled by the sheer size of it and the amount of vessels ploughing up and down in both directions, belching out smoke and continuously sounding hooters and bells. On a Sunday, however, the water was relatively empty of traffic. They sat on one of the many benches on the pavement facing the water. Jane giggled with frustration as she tried to make a roll-up in the tugging breeze. Eventually, she succeeded and they both smoked, Jane resting her head against Tat's shoulder.

Suddenly, she looked up and said, "Tat, You never did tell me about the gypsy woman. You know, the one who smoked a pipe."

"Oh Hannah you mean; it all seems light years ago now. We were just little lads when it all happened."

"When what happened? Do tell please." Jane said squeezing his arm. Tat put his arm around Jane; she snuggled closer to him. He quickly warmed to the role of storyteller. When he recounted how he and the Machin boys had gauged the height of Bill Fletcher, Jane sat up straight and stared at Tat.

"Honestly, seven feet nine inches! Gosh, he was a giant. Are you teasing me Tat?"

"No, I'm not, believe me, Bill was a real giant. We were scared stiff of him," When Tat finally described the race into Pod Gill to save Hannah's baby, Jane couldn't contain her anxiety. "Oh no, Tat, don't say the baby died; I couldn't bear it," she said with tears in her eyes.

Tat found that his heart was thumping in his chest as the memories came flooding back. He lit another cigarette and continued, "No, thank the Lord, my mate Dick grabbed the baby, and saved her life. It was Bill who died."

He went on to describe the final moments of Bill Fletcher's life as the two trains thundered towards him on the viaduct. When he had finished he felt a tear slide down his unshaven cheek. Jane hugged him and gently kissed his cheek, saying, "You poor boys, how awful for you." Her lovely face was full of concern as Tat let out a deep breath and said, "Aye well, it was all a long time ago. Mostly if I ever think of it I see it as an adventure, but it was a tragedy I suppose; poor old Bill, sometimes I feel we were to blame."

They walked slowly back to Fawcettt Street with their arms around each other. As they approached the King's Road Jane stopped and held Tat's face between her hands and said, "I've never met anyone like you, Tat; you're adorable and if you don't watch out I'm going to fall in love with you. Would you mind terribly?"

Tat smiled softly and said, "I might be one step ahead of you, lass." They kissed and hugged each other tight, only separating when a passing cab driver tooted his horn at them and wolf whistled before speeding on his way. Back at the flat Jane set out cups and plates and made a pot of strong tea. She produced a beautiful fruit cake and cut them a huge chunk each.

"Our cook supplies these at various intervals for me to bring back from home. She thinks I'll waste away otherwise," Jane explained and then added, "while I've got you all to myself young man, I'm going to draw you."

"Oh alright," Tat replied, knowing that he couldn't reasonably refuse. By now he recognized that Jane was truly gifted and he admired her talent and sincerity. "Come on then, tell me what you want me to do, as if I could stop you," he added chuckling.

Jane dug out a light-weight folding easel from behind her wardrobe and pinned a sheet of paper to her drawing-board. When she was ready, she called Tat through from the kitchen, saying, "Right, my lad, let's have those clothes off, every stitch." She wanted him standing with most of the light from the window falling down his left side, casting deep shadows.

"Put your weight on your right leg, tilting your pelvis, put your hands on your hips like this." She struck the pose herself and got him to imitate it. "Right now, hold it steady."

Jane began work and was soon fully absorbed. She made three drawings of the same pose, one in pencil and the other two in charcoal. She got Tat to move so that she had a three-quarter view and finally drew him facing away from her.

"Hey, come on, Jane," Tat said eventually. "I'll have to move around a bit, I'm seizing up."

"Oh sorry of course you will, poor you, I quite forgot." She rummaged around in the wardrobe and handed him her silk dressing gown. "Look throw this on and I'll get us a tot of rum each. What do you think?"

"Well I'm not too keen on the floral pattern," Tat said, dismayed at the sheer femininity of Jane's dressing gown. "But I would love a drink."

"Oh, I think it rather suits you," Jane said, as she came back from the sitting room with two large slugs of rum. "Quite the pretty boy." She kissed him and patted his backside. They laughed and drank, moving across together to look at the drawings. As ever, Tat was amazed by how much she could achieve in such a short time. The images were so firmly established with an almost three-dimensional solidity. Jane slipped her arm around his waist and gave him a squeeze.

EXPLORING LONDON

After the next modelling session for Olly, Jane made her excuses, explaining that she was meeting her friend, Nicola, to go to the cinema. Tat and Olly went to the Wellington as usual for a couple of pints. Olly had noticed a change of atmosphere in the studio as he began to tighten and refine his portrait. The prospect of stripping to the waist in front of Jane didn't seem to cause any of the usual anxiety in Tat. He caught Jane and Tat exchanging sly glances at each other with knowing, secretive smiles. When Jane left them at the college gate she had kissed Tat and whispered something in his ear.

"Well, Tat," Olly said after they had settled down at a free table with their pints. "Are you going to tell me what's going on?"

"Going on? What on earth do you mean?" Tat replied, lighting a cigarette.

"Oh come on, Tat, don't make me drag it out of you. You and Jane, what's going on?"

Tat blushed and grinned from ear to ear. He was dying to share his secret with Olly. "Well promise you won't make a fuss, or tell anyone."

"Just get on with it... alright I promise, now come on."

Tat explained how he and Jane had ended up having a drink with Jack Douthwaite and his friends after the concert at the Palladium. Olly was goggle eyed when he learned that they had met Nick La Rocca and that Jane had ended up drawing him in the pub. Olly had loved the band and declared himself a jazz fan to all and sundry in the intervening week.

"Anyway," Tat said, leaning forward and lowering his voice. "Jane asked me to go on to her place in Fulham and well, we spent the weekend together; it was wonderful."

Olly took a puff on his cigarette and cocking his head on one side said, "You sly dog, or to put it another way, you lucky dog. Let's have another pint to celebrate."

When he returned from the bar with their drinks, he said, "You and Jane! You must be as pleased as punch. She's only the tastiest girl in the college and the most talented. What can she see in you, you bloody mountain man?" Olly drained almost half his pint in two huge gulps and added, "Everybody, including me in the past, has lusted after Jane but nobody has had any luck. I've always assumed she must have a serious boyfriend tucked away down in Kent somewhere. My God, she's a real beauty and no mistake, and what a figure!"

Olly tried his hardest to get the intimate details out of Tat. What Jane looked like naked and had they slept in the same bed? All Tat would tell him was that the weekend had been beyond his wildest dreams and that Jane had said that she loved him.

"What about you then? By the look of the silly grin on your face I needn't ask whether you return her sentiments."

"You're right there, Olly," Tat replied.

Gradually, Tat and Jane became relaxed about being seen together around the college. Whenever they could they ate together in the refectory or one of the many cafés dotted around the area. Tat withstood a certain amount of teasing, especially from his rugger pals. Ken Morland, the biggest forward in the team, suggested that Tat's new situation could only result in sapping his strength and slowing him down. It didn't last for long, however, and Tat took it all in good part.

One afternoon whilst finishing off tea and buns in a little place they frequented regularly on Tottenham Court Road, Jane told Tat she had some good news to share with him. After their first heady weekend together in Fulham it quickly became obvious that they didn't have anywhere to be alone together. Tat's hostel rules didn't allow female visitors after six in the evening and Jane was anxious not to jeopardize her relationship with Nicola by having Tat stay at the Fawcett Street flat overnight. They had tried to be together in Tat's room during the afternoon now and again, but it wasn't easy to relax with rowdy male students thumping up and down stairs and calling to each other along the corridors.

Jane took Tat's hand across the table and gave it a squeeze, then said, "Nicola had a long chat with me last night. She's been seeing one of the young doctors at the hospital for some time. Anyway, until recently, he's been living with his parents in Highgate, but now he's got a little flat in Warren Street."

Jane had begun making a roll-up, meanwhile; eventually she completed the job and asked Tat for a light, then went on, "She knows about you and me, I told her you came to stay for a couple of nights whilst she was away. Anyway, she's going to be spending most weekends with her boyfriend and suggests that you come to Fawcett Street to be with me at the weekends. Isn't that wonderful?"

Tat leant across the table, kissed Jane and said, "Wonderful? It's bloody marvellous!"

"This Saturday and Sunday will do nicely for a start, don't you think?"

"Oh yes please, I can't wait," Tat said.

On their way back to college Tat decided it was time to put his complete trust in Jane. Even so he had to screw up his courage and choose what he hoped was the right moment.

"Listen Jane," he said, "I'm rather worried that you might get pregnant. Shouldn't I get some French letters? I mean you know…"

Jane smiled tenderly at Tat and kissed him. "Trust you, Tat, always so considerate. Come on and sit here for a minute or two." She indicated one of the heavy benches in the quadrangle. Taking both his hands in hers she said, "Two days before we went to the Palladium I went to our college doctor. Helen Groves is a wonderful woman, ever so open and helpful and she gave me something to stop me getting pregnant."

"You mean you won't..." Tat blushed deeply, "you won't get pregnant?"

"Yes, my darling, that's exactly what I mean."

Later Jane began to block in the structure of the painting she had decided to make from the sketches she'd done of Tat and Olly in the sculpture studio. She struggled with herself, attempting to ease her conscience at having deceived Tat. He had accepted her explanation with relief and gratitude. She knew that because of his sweet and trusting nature, Tat would never suspect that she had lied to him. She found herself thinking back over the months of the illicit affair she had shared with Giles. She stopped working and made a roll-up. Whilst smoking it she shook her head, telling herself she was glad to be rid of her secret double life. She had Tat now with whom she could go anywhere she pleased and do anything she wanted. No more hiding away and lying to cover her tracks. She smiled ruefully to herself, recalling that she had lied to him only an hour previously. She wondered whether it would be the only lie she would have to tell her lovely, trusting Tat.

When the rugger season ended Tat had the Saturdays free and was relieved at being spared the aches and pains which followed most matches. As the weather warmed up, they took to exploring the city together. At first they walked though every central London park, taking picnics with them, often lying full length on the grass in the sun chatting or dozing. Then they went further afield, catching the bus up to Hampstead and spending whole days on the Heath. They discovered the ladies' bathing pool where, on the hottest days, Jane would swim whilst Tat studied his law books with his shirt off, flat out on the grass some distance away. There was an understanding that men were not allowed near the pool. As spring turned into summer they were both developing glowing suntans. Jane was jealous of Tat being able to strip to the waist and change into his rugger shorts whenever he wanted. She would sweet-talk him into standing guard after bathing in the pool so that she could sunbathe naked in the long grass without anyone seeing her. Her olive skin tanned quickly.

Eventually, they ventured onto the river, taking pleasure-boat rides to Greenwich through the bustling docks. Tat could never quite believe his eyes; the sheer scale and variety of the ships, from all quarters of the globe, loading and unloading their cargos was incredible. The clamouring noise and profusion of exotic smells outdid anything he had ever imagined. Jane drew frantically in her sketchbooks. She, like Tat, had never seen the docks before and found the whole thing so stimulating as the subject for future paintings she might undertake.

Greenwich, by contrast, was positively sedate. They would climb the hill above the Naval College and Observatory and gaze back at the loops of the river curving towards the Tower of London and St. Pauls. Occasionally, the glittering water was almost invisible so great was the volume of shipping upon it. The pleasure steamers went up-stream as well, where the river traffic was much lighter, on an almost domestic scale. They would catch a steamer from the wharf near Vauxhall Bridge and take it all the way to Hampton Court or Kew Gardens.

It turned out that Jane's parents were members of the Friends of Covent Garden Association. They acquired tickets for Tat and Jane to attend Rigoletto, La Bohème and Don Giovanni that summer. They sat midway back in the stalls with an excellent view of the enormous stage, rather than boiling in the heat, up in the Gods.

Jane took Tat to all the major museums; she told him everything she knew about the different schools of painting. He had only ever visited the National Gallery up to this point and told Jane how he had been introduced to the Vermeers on the day of his interview at UCL by his friend John from Canterbury. Jane was delighted as Vermeer was her favourite painter. She explained how he and many other painters in the past used various technical aids to facilitate their work.

"You see the chandelier in this wedding scene by Van Eyck," she said on one occasion. "How complicated it is, all those different angles and foreshortenings. Well, my tutor, Jack Seabury, brought a group of us here to study the Van Eycks and explained that it had probably been sketched in very quickly, using something called a Camera Obscura."

Tat looked puzzled and said, "You mean he didn't do it like you? You know, just looking at it and drawing it free hand?"

"No, he was able to project the reflection of it onto the canvas using lenses. It's quite complicated actually, but once the technique was understood nearly all the painters took it up. I tell you what, I'll show you how it works next week. Jack Seabury has made a replica of a Camera Obscura. It's tucked away in a store cupboard at the college. I'm sure he'll let me show you."

"So, does anybody use these things now, I mean do any living artists? What about you for instance?" Tat asked, frowning slightly.

"Oh no it was all given up some time ago really. Artists want a more real experience these days. Although some use photographs as a short cut, I believe. Olly tells me that Rodin, the great French sculptor, used photographs occasionally and he only died in 1917, I think."

"I had no idea it was all so complicated," Tat said, then added, "Olly showed me a thing called a Pointing Machine at the Slade and explained how it took most of the slog out of stone carving. I think I understood it. He said he'd give me a demonstration one day. I must remind him."

Olly joined them occasionally on their museum and gallery expeditions. Now and again he would bring his latest girlfriend along, much to Jane's amusement; it was rarely the same girl twice. Olly introduced them to the great sculpture collections at the British Museum and the Victoria and Albert in South Kensington. Tat grew to recognize sculpture in stone and marble in particular, which had been 'pointed', as Olly called it, or carved directly. Tat's horizons were opening up and he loved every minute of it.

In the early mornings at the weekends, Tat would run a few miles along the embankment. He knew that in order to keep up his speed and agility on the rugger pitch, he had to exercise all the year round. As Jane got used to this régime, she would wander down to the river to meet Tat at a pre-arranged point. This, as often as not, was the bench opposite the end of Tite Street. On the way back to the flat they frequently took tea and toast at a street stall on the Kings Road.

Jane always made time for her drawing and painting. Tat knew how important this was to her and brought his books and writing materials to the flat so that he could pursue his studies. Sometimes, Jane insisted that he pose for her, which he was always glad to do.

Tat wrote to Mary Hollis to tell her about the way things had turned out. He explained that she had been right; Jane had taken the initiative, after all. Tat hoped that he was able to convey to Mary how happy he was. He described the way he and Jane were exploring the city and what fun it was. Tat was careful to stress that he was continuing to do well in the law faculty and had been assured by his tutors that if he kept up his present standard, he would get a very good degree the following year. He wrote to his mother and said little more than he had met a very nice girl and they were going out together. Somehow he suspected his family would fail to comprehend how he and Jane felt about each other. He even suspected that his mother might resent Jane, especially if she ever met her. Without doubt, she would never be able to accept the intimacy of their relationship.

Tat had known from the first time he had met her that Jane came from a privileged background. In a very natural way, when she talked about her family life in Kent, it was clear that her parents employed several servants. The gardener, who had taught her to make roll-ups, seemingly had two lads working under him. The cook, who provided the delicious cakes, ran the kitchen with at least three maids. There was a chauffeur and a housekeeper with her own staff. For all Tat knew there might be half a dozen others whom Jane had simply overlooked.

When she asked him about his family and the farm back home, Tat was increasingly aware of the contrast. Despite this, Jane was full of curiosity and wanted to know every detail of Tat's home life. He was as honest as he could be, but felt almost ashamed to admit that he still shared a bedroom with his brother. Jane thought this was charming, however, but did find it difficult to envisage a household without a bathroom or inside toilet. When Tat explained how unusual it was for someone like him to get a university place, especially to study law, Jane said, "Oh, but Tat you are obviously so clever. They must be very proud of you. I'd love to meet your family one day. Could I come to stay?"

Tat smiled and replied, "I don't know; it takes eight hours on the train and somehow I can't see you using the outside toilet, wiping that pretty backside of yours with bits of newspaper and taking a bath in the kitchen in front of my brothers and our dad."

"Oh you, you're outrageous," Jane said, launching herself at him. They rolled around on the bedroom floor in mock battle, gradually subsiding into each other's arms.

Tat knew that, despite the idyllic picture Jane seemed to be developing about his family, the reality would be a different matter. Her only experience of farm life was probably based upon a handful of neighbouring gentleman farmers, working the rolling fields of Kent with hordes of labourers and the latest equipment. She remained blissfully unaware that life at Fell End was hard, involving his father and brothers in a seven-day-a-week struggle against what often seemed like insuperable odds. As time went on, it seemed she had set her heart upon visiting Fell End during the long summer vacation. Tat tried his best to reconcile himself to the idea, but failed to shift his misgivings. For one thing, there wasn't even a spare bedroom for her to sleep in. What would his mother and father make of her posh voice, never mind his cheeky older brothers? Tat's heart sank.

One evening after a delicious supper of Italian sausages Jane had got from Harrods, washed down with a bottle of good red wine, Jane asked Tat about his singing.

"Ever since Olly spilled the beans about your voice I've been longing to hear you. He told me once that he thought you ought to drop the law and study to be a professional singer."

"Oh Olly, he's got a bee in his bonnet that's all. He's a complete romantic, you know that as well as I do."

"Well, yes, but he's not a fool either. I reckon he'd be as good a judge of a singing voice as anybody."

"Well, actually my primary school teacher used to go on at me to take up singing seriously. She actually tried to persuade my parents to let me study music, without success obviously."

"Anyway, Tat, do sing for me now, please."

"Oh Jane, don't be daft. I mean I can't just sing on my own, I'd feel such a fool. Anyway, what about your neighbours?"

Jane stood up and approached him, taking his head in her hands and looking directly at him. "Listen, Tat, sing me a song and I'll take my top off. Now then, how can you refuse? Sing me one of your favourites."

"Oh well, if that's the way you're going, I'll sing as many songs as you like!"

"It's a deal, as you know who would say."

Tat got up and cleared his throat. He sang 'My Love Is Like A Red, Red Rose' as softly as he could. As he did so Jane undid her thin silk blouse and dropped it to the floor.

"Wonderful Tat, just wonderful, do sing another please."

"How can I refuse?"

Tat decided upon 'Era La Notte', a soft, keening aria from Verdi's Otello. His rich baritone, so beautifully pitched brought tears to her eyes. "Oh Tat, my love, you're breaking my heart, you sound like an angel." Her breasts were covered with tiny goose pimples of pure pleasure.

As Tat finished the aria she stepped across and kissed him whispering in his ear, "Thank you so much, you sweet boy. I love you more than I can say." As they embraced Tat wondered whether anyone else had been rewarded in such a way for singing a couple of songs.

DRAWING THE BAND LEADER

After negotiating with Jack Douthwaite, it was decided that Nick La Rocca would sit for Jane at his flat in Museum Street. Despite what she had said about being able to take care of herself, Tat had thought it best that the portrait be undertaken on neutral territory. Jack had suggested that Tat should be present, staying in the background, assisting him in filing his notes for a book on criminal law he was writing. Jane and La Rocca would be left to get on with the portrait in the sitting room where the light was particularly good.

Jane decided to make a series of drawings during the day and develop her oil painting from them in her own time. It was a method she had grown used to. Nick La Rocca arrived in a taxi in time for coffee. He was extremely dapper in a rather loud checked suit. As requested, he had brought his cornet with him.

"What do ya think? I only collected it from Saville Row yesterday. Prince of Wales check, that's what they call it."

"Very nice too," Jack remarked. "That must have set you back a pretty penny."

"Well, yeah I guess you're right," La Rocca replied. "But we've been doing OK. Anyway, I couldn't spend time in London and not get a suit made in Saville Row, could I?"

Jack and his friends had attended four different performances by the band since the Palladium concert. Two of these had been in small venues, the Morton Club in Bond Street and the Rectors Club in Soho and the other two at the Palais de Danse in Hammersmith.

"So Nick," Jack said as he served the coffee, "which do you boys like best, the small clubs or the big dance halls."

"Oh, we get off best in the little joints, that's for sure. The sound is nice and closed in and you're right next to the folks who've come to listen," La Rocca replied, offering cigarettes to everyone from a chunky silver case.

"No thanks," Jane said, "I'll roll my own if you don't object."

"Oh yeah, I'd forgotten about that little habit of yours. I told the guys in the band about it; they couldn't believe it."

When they had finished their coffee Jane took the initiative and suggested that work should begin without delay.

"OK, little lady, you're the boss," La Rocca said good naturedly. "I'm kinda looking forward to it."

"Right then," Jack said. "We'll leave you to it. Help me clear the pots away, will you Tat, then we'll get down to our work, filing notes, rather less interesting than having your portrait done, eh?"

Jane had arranged a ladder-back chair close to one of the tall windows which overlooked the street. She had brought her portable easel and drawing equipment and put everything in place so as not to waste time.

"Now Mr La Rocca, come over here and sit in this chair facing me. Oh yes, and could you hold your cornet across your knees?"

Nick La Rocca took his cornet out of its shiny leather case and sat down opposite Jane, then said, "Hey you got to call me Nick from now on OK?"

Jane made a number of quick sketches to get herself going and asked La Rocca to hold his cornet in several different positions. The light from the window was excellent, emphasizing the folds in the Prince of Wales check. She drew him looking first one way then another and finally decided to have him look at a point just over her right shoulder. Once she was satisfied with the set-up, Jane began a detailed study in pencil which took almost an hour to complete. She made notes on the edges of the drawing to remind her of the colours she would mix for the painting.

After ten minutes of silence, La Rocca said, "Say, Jane is it OK to talk or what?"

"Oh yes, absolutely, I should have said before, sorry."

"That's alright. We got some more gigs coming up at the Morton Club and in Hammersmith, why don't you and your boyfriend come along to see us again?"

"We'd love to, thanks, but you see, we are only students, Tat and I, and to be honest we can't afford it," Jane said ruefully.

"Hey, that ain't no problem. I'll arrange for tickets to be left for you at the door."

"Oh gosh, would you really? That would be lovely," Jane said, genuinely thrilled at the prospect. They chatted easily as Jane started a new study with La Rocca looking over his right shoulder at the street below.

"This is a great town once you get to know it. I'm gonna miss it when we head back to the States," La Rocca said.

"When will that be?" Jane asked.

"Well, we're doing some recordings. Colombia Records have a setup in Soho. We're starting work on them next month, all being well. Then I guess we'll head for home."

Jack tapped at the door and opened it cautiously. "I hope this is as good a time as any to break for lunch. I thought we would go to a nice little restaurant I know in Russell Square.

"Hey, now you're talking," La Rocca said. "I could eat a horse. What about you, Jane?"

"Oh yes I'm famished," Jane replied, then added, "Come and have a look Jack; tell me what you think."

"My goodness, these are wonderful," Jack said as Jane showed him the drawings, four quick charcoal sketches and two detailed pencil drawings. "Just look at these, Nick. I don't know how she does it."

La Rocca turned as Tat entered the room and said, "Hey kid come and look at these. I swear she's a genius. She's gonna be rich and famous."

By the end of the day Jane had done eleven drawings in all. She was satisfied that she could develop a good oil painting from them. La Rocca had found a sample of the Prince of Wales check in the inside pocket of his jacket and had given it to Jane saying, "Hey now, you won't have any excuse for getting the suit wrong. After what it cost me I want it just right. Is that a deal?"

"Oh yes, it's a deal."

Later as Tat helped carry Jane's equipment back to the Slade he said, "Well that seemed to go very well. Are you pleased?"

"Oh yes, I really am. Sometimes everything just falls into place and this was one of them," Jane said taking his arm.

"I notice you have got onto first name terms. How does that suit you then?" Tat teased.

"Oh, it's much better," Jane said, then added, "Actually, he's rather sweet. After lunch he told me how much he misses his wife and baby boy. I thought he might cry at one point."

"So he's not quite the hard man after all," Tat said relieved. He had been slightly anxious that La Rocca might spend the day flirting with Jane.

"No, he's tough on the outside but soft as candy floss inside. Anyway, listen he's offered to give us tickets to see the band again. He said he would fix it up with Jack as to when and where. Isn't that exciting?"

CASTING THE PORTRAIT

Olly instructed: " Right Tat, the bowl is half full, cold water remember, and then you mix the blue powder colour into it. Take a handful of plaster and sprinkle it evenly into the water, sifting through your fingers. Carry on adding plaster until you see it settling just below the surface of the water. Then mix it together with your hand until it's like smooth cream. Just keep supplying it to me bowl by bowl. Wash out the bowl each time in the big sink over there. Now let's get cracking."

The finished clay bust of Tat stood on a turntable in the casting room. It was divided up into sections with thin brass walls about an inch deep. Tat was impressed by the finished model; it was a remarkable likeness. Everybody who had seen it agreed on that, especially Jane. Beyond this, however, it had a pent up energy which seemed to come from within it. Olly said that it was his best portrait so far, by a long way. Jacob Epstein, the American sculptor who had lived in London since before the war, had done the odd day at the Slade, holding tutorials with the sculpture students. He had been particularly impressed with Olly's portrait of Tat and had said it should be cast into bronze. He had invited Olly to act as his assistant over the summer vacation. Olly was determined to save enough of his wages from working for Epstein to pay for a bronze cast of the portrait. Olly had told Tat that if he helped him with the initial plaster cast he would make an extra copy of it for him to keep.

Olly flicked the blue plaster onto the clay model with his fingers and frequently blew the smooth mixture into the various nooks and crannies where it set hard. Tat kept the supply of plaster coming, mixing bowl after bowl as Olly had instructed him. Eventually, the portrait was completely covered with a half-inch thick layer, evenly distributed all over it. Olly had scraped the top edge of the brass walls clear of plaster, explaining that these were the seams which would enable the mould to be opened when it was thickened up by further layers of white plaster.

As Tat mixed neat plaster, without pigment, the whole process speeded up. The negative impression of the portrait was safely captured beneath the blue coat so Olly no longer had to be so careful. Within a couple of hours of hectic, messy work the mould was complete. The top edge of the brass walls now showed as fine lines dividing the mould into its various parts.

Olly had loaned Tat a spare boiler suit knowing what a state they would both end up in. They were liberally spattered with blue and white plaster. Tat had several lumps of it tangled in his hair; Olly wisely wore an old cap.

"Right then, let's have a smoke whilst that lot hardens up. Look at the state of you, Tat."

"I know, thank the lord for your overalls eh? Do you know, Olly, I could get used to this. I can't remember when I had as much fun."

"Well, that is one way of looking at it I suppose. I know what you mean, though. It's all rather like magic isn't it?"

"You can say that again. Honestly, I had no idea about any of this. What happens next then?" "Well, in about half an hour we'll dribble water over the mould to open it up," Olly said. "You insert a knife into the seams here and there and the water seeps in by capillary action. Then the different sections can be prised away from the clay."

"So the impression is retained in the blue layer, is that right?"

"Right in one, my friend," Olly replied, stubbing out his cigarette on the plaster covered floor.

"So why do you colour the first layer blue? I mean why isn't it just white like the rest of the mould?" Tat asked, perplexed.

"It's all to do with what happens later on, when you chip the mould off. Best wait and see till then. Believe me, it will make sense, you'll see."

Olly had tipped the caretaker so that they could stay and work into the night. He'd given Olly a key to a back door which was hardly ever used. To Tat's surprise, Olly rummaged in a locker at the back of the casting room and retrieved two pint bottles of extra strong ale for them.

"I've got two more of these tucked away. Good health, Tat my lad, you've been damned good about this." Olly prised the tops off the beer with a pair of pliers and they both drank. Olly burped loudly, "Oh yes, just the job. Now let's open it up."

Things got even messier than they were already as they poured water over the mould and began to prise the individual sections away. Clay stuck to the blue plaster making the individual sections awkward to handle. Eventually, each part of the mould was laid out on the studio floor. The clay model, now exposed once more, was a ruin, battered and distorted with lumps of it missing altogether.

"My goodness, all that lovely modelling, ruined."

"Oh don't worry, that was always going to be the temporary bit. We're going to end up with a plaster version, perfect in every detail and permanent."

They worked away, removing every trace of clay from the inside of each section of the mould using cold water and paint brushes. Finally, when it was spotless, Olly showed Tat how to apply soft soap to the inside of the mould. Once this was done, they reassembled it again and Olly fixed it together with strips of hessian, called scrim, soaked in white plaster. The mould lay horizontally on the turntable.

"There now, Tat, take a look inside."

Tat bent forward and peered through the open end of the mould into its surprisingly cavernous interior.

"That's you in negative my boy, rather creepy isn't it?"

"How clever it all is, so what do we do now, fill it up with plaster?"

"Yes. Help me to stand the mould on its head end, we'll prop it up with bricks over there, see, a pile of them in the corner." Once the upended mould was stabilised they both mixed large black rubber buckets of neat plaster. It was a harder setting type Olly had explained.

"It's dental plaster actually, used in the moulding of false teeth, believe it or not, and in the ceramic industry."

They had to work together to lift the buckets high enough. The liquid plaster gushed noisily into the mould. It took two more to fill it to the brim. "Thank goodness that bit's over," Olly said gasping. "Come on, let's sit down for a bit. I'll fetch the other two bottles. Get your fags out, there's a good lad."

When they had settled down on the floor, leaning against the wall, they smoked and swigged from the bottles.

"We'll leave it for half an hour then I'll chip the face part out to show you how it works. After that it's all down to me to do the rest tomorrow."

Olly found a wooden mallet and two or three old carpenter's chisels in his locker and said, "Just feel how warm it is, Tat."

Tat laid his hands on the upended base of the cast and said, "My goodness, it's hot as an oven; what's that all about?"

"I know. Weird isn't it? I don't understand the exact science but I believe it's the chemical reaction within the plaster as it hardens. Look at the steam coming off. It'll cool down soon." After a struggle they heaved the now very heavy mould back onto the turntable the right way up.

Olly said, "Thank goodness there are two of us - it's so heavy. Really, I should wait till tomorrow, but I'm dying to chip out the face, then I'll leave it alone." He raised his mallet and chisel and began to chip away at the mould covering the facial area of the portrait. After a minute or so a blue area of plaster was uncovered.

"There, now you will understand all about the blue coat."

"Of course," Tat said in amazement, "it's to warn you that you're near to the plaster inside. You know, the sculpture itself."

"Spot on. You've picked it all up really quickly. Believe me, not everybody does."

Olly had uncovered the face of the portrait within the next five minutes. "See the soft soap is a separation. It stops the plaster fusing together, comes away like magic."

A few bits of blue plaster lay trapped in the tiny hollows of the now uncovered face.

"I'll pick those out with a sharpened stick later on," Olly said, dusting the plaster off his hands. "I'll finish the rest of the chipping out tomorrow. Come down after your lectures and it should be done, I reckon."

Before Olly turned the gas lights off, Tat paused in the doorway and looked back. The hair on his neck bristled slightly as he saw his own likeness peering across at him framed by the lumpy mould around it.

Olly slept in the armchair in Tat's room at the Gower Place hostel that night, or at least what was left of it. As they both drifted off, Tat said softly, "Thanks for letting me take part in it all, Olly. I've so enjoyed myself."

"Don't be daft. I should be thanking you; I couldn't have done it alone. Oh yes, many happy returns. Jane says it's your birthday today."

The next morning before lectures Tat wrote to his mother trying his best to describe the part he'd played in casting Olly's portrait of him. He dropped a couple of hints about Jane showing an interest in visiting Fell End some time later on in the long summer vacation. Tat was as uneasy as ever about the prospect but felt he was obliged to at least raise the subject.

Tat and Jane had lunch together in the college refectory. He told her all about helping Olly through the previous night in the casting of the portrait.

"Apparently, he's completing the rest of the chipping out today," Tat said. "He has asked me to go round to the Slade after lectures, about five thirty and inspect the finished statue. Why don't you come along? I'm sure he won't mind."

Jane gave him a little smile.

"Oh, he won't mind. I'd love to," she said giving his hand a reassuring pat. Tat realised later that she hadn't mentioned his birthday.

DAVID THOMPSON

THE UNVEILING

Tat was excited about seeing the finished portrait. It would no longer need wrapping up in wet cloths and he'd be able to run his hands over it, something he had longed to do on more than one occasion. He hummed 'Do ye ken John Peel' to himself as he made his way down to the Sculpture Department. Olly had told him that he would have taken the portrait back to his own studio space away from the mess and clutter of the casting room.

As he opened the studio door a loud cheer went up. About twenty people, most of them holding bottles of beer or wine, jostled towards him as he entered the studio, led by Olly and Jane. An open bottle was pressed into his hand amidst the hubbub.

"There he is, the man of the moment," Olly yelled. "Welcome to the unveiling ceremony, arranged by the lovely Jane, just for you, my lad. Oh yes, happy birthday again."

Jane kissed Tat on the cheek and smiling broadly said, "That's not entirely true, actually, Olly and I thought it appropriate between us."

Tat was blushing scarlet. "You could have warned me, Jane. I'd have at least put a jacket on."

"Well, if you had you'd have been the only one wearing one," Olly teased.

Most of the first fifteen were present as well as Jack Douthwaite and several law students, including John and Chris. They were all in a high old mood. Tat guessed that they had probably consumed a fair amount of booze before his arrival. In the middle of the studio a bulky shape stood on a wooden turntable covered with an old velvet curtain.

"Can you possibly guess what that is, Tat my boy?" Olly said slyly.

"I think I probably have a bit of an idea."

Jack stepped forward with a fresh bottle of beer for Tat. "Here you are, dear boy. You know I've never been down here before; isn't it fascinating. Anyway, Jane has asked me to unveil this statue of you I've heard about. You're simply requested to stand here and take your shirt off."

"Oh no! This is too much, Olly. I simply refuse." Jane took Tat's hand and led him to the designated spot next to the shrouded sculpture.

"Don't be a spoilsport, Tat," she said bossily. "Almost everybody here has seen you without a stitch on." He saw that he had little choice in the matter and allowed Jane to unbutton his shirt and slip it off his shoulders. He knew he was tanned and fit and that Jane was right; most of those present had seen him naked.

Olly bustled forward and manoeuvred Tat onto a low turntable a few feet to the left of the shrouded cast.

"Right, Tat, adopt the pose if you please; face me, arms folded; you ought to know the routine by now."

Jack stepped forward and, at a signal from Olly, carefully pulled the cover aside. "No, don't move Tat, you will get your turn in a minute," Olly said as Tat tried to steal a glance at the portrait. He could sense that Olly had prepared the way so that he stood at exactly the same height and angle as the sculpture.

There was a brief silence followed by a loud burst of spontaneous applause. The real Tat standing next to the sculpted version striking the same pose, presented an awesome spectacle. Olly's hand was shaken and his back thumped many times. Extracting himself from the scrum, he called to Tat, "Alright birthday boy, take a look."

Tat turned his head and almost fell off the turntable with surprise. Surely the portrait had somehow or other been cast into bronze. He stepped down to the floor and slowly walked around the sculpture. It was a rich metallic brown, impeccably finished and highly polished. It had a kind of majesty about it and seemed to pulse with energy.

He was speechless and shook his head in disbelief. "It's wonderful, Olly, just wonderful. But how..." He trailed off, unable to finish his sentence.

"Ah, dear boy," Olly said lighting a cigarette, "tricks of the trade that's all."

"Yes, but I still don't get it. Is it a bronze or what? Surely there hasn't been time."

"No, no it isn't. Your girlfriend and I have been working on it all day. It's a special concoction. Jacob Epstein told me about it. Shellac, bronze powder, boot polish and goodness knows what else. Convincing isn't it?"

Jack and Jane joined them. "Tat you must be thrilled to bits. I mean, imagine having a portrait like this made of you at your age," Jack said, genuinely impressed. "It's fabulous." He shook Tat's hand. Turning to Olly he said, "Congratulations, Olly, you are going to be very successful one day, mark my words. Don't you think, Jane?"

"Yes, I'm madly jealous," Jane replied, screwing up her face.

Somebody yelled out that they should move off to the Wellington. As people left in dribs and drabs, Olly and Tat were showered with more congratulations. Eventually, Tat, Olly and Jane were left alone with the portrait.

They looked at it from various points in the studio. Tat thought it was so full of life that it might move at any moment. He struggled to stop tears gathering in his eyes; he was so thrilled and impressed.

He looked at Olly and said in a low, trembling voice, "Thanks, Olly, you're a genius."

"Silly sod, come here," Olly said and trapped Tat in a bear hug. Jane embraced them both and said, "You lovely, lovely boys."

Later in the Wellington, Jane drew Tat to one side and gave him a small neatly wrapped package. She kissed him lightly on the lips and said, "Happy birthday, Tat."

"Oh Jane, you shouldn't have really," Tat said feeling more than a little overwhelmed.

"Of course I should. Go on then, open it."

It was an antique silver cigarette case with the words 'To my lovely Tat' engraved on it.

"It's Georgian," she said. "I found it in a junk shop in the Fulham Road. They do the engraving there too. Do you like it?"

"Oh, I'll say, it's beautiful, just like you," Tat said hugging her warmly. "Thank you so much. My goodness, what a cracking day it's been."

Jane leant close and whispered, "Nicola's at her boyfriend's place, so we can have a cracking night too."

After a couple of days Tat received a reply from his mother. He was so unsure as to what she would think about his suggestion that Jane might visit them at Fell End, that he delayed opening the letter for a couple of hours. He could tell by the weight of the envelope that the letter was longer than usual. His heart sank.

Indeed, it was a long letter. His mother did her best to unravel the complicated procedures Tat had described regarding the casting of Olly's portrait. The bulkiness of the envelope was partly due to the inclusion of a birthday card which had a five-pound note folded inside it from his parents and a ten-pound note from his Gran. The whole family had signed the card. His mother apologised for these arriving a day or two late.

She explained the delay as a result of 'running herself ragged' as she put it to find a way of accommodating Jane if she still wished to visit Fell End later in the summer.

"You see, Tat," she had written. "We just don't have anywhere for the lass to sleep, never mind the matter of no bathroom or inside toilet. You know yourself lad that we've never had a guest stop overnight at Fell End. I dare say your Jane will be used to all mod cons and such like."

Tat put the letter aside and lit a cigarette. So he had upset the applecart after all. He was angry with himself for ever having raised the subject. Jane's innocent assumption that a visit to Tat's family home would be a straightforward affair had pushed him to a point where he had distressed his mother. The last thing he wanted to do - he read on.

"Anyway, Tat, I had a bright idea and went to see Mary Hollis. She'll do owt for you, Tat, as you know. I put my cards on the table and asked if she could help us out. The long and the short of it is that she will be delighted to have your Jane stop with her. She said she'd love to have the company. Jane could come up to Fell End as often as she wanted and you and Mary could show her around, maybe take her to Appleby and such like.

"I hope this idea is alright. I've been that worried about it. I've been at my wits end. Anyway, try to explain it all to your lass and see what she thinks. Mary's that easy to get along with and her cottage is lovely, as you know. We are all looking forward to meeting Jane, so I've got my fingers crossed that she will fall in with these arrangements."

Tat almost wept with relief. Trust his mother to find a solution. He felt guilty at ever having thought she might be difficult. Mary Hollis was the perfect choice; she would adore Jane and probably spoil her to pieces. The next job was to explain it all to Jane so that she would be comfortable with the plan and not feel as though she was being given short shrift by his parents.

Jane thought the idea was wonderful. It turned out that secretly she had been worrying about putting Tat's mother to such inconvenience. She had taken Tat's descriptions of the lack of a spare room to heart, never mind the absence of bathroom and inside toilet. Despite having been brought up in such a privileged way, Jane was not blind to the sensitivity of others, by any means.

"I suppose it might have been rather difficult for me to take a bath in your kitchen in front of your father and brothers," she joked. Then added, "Mind you, they might have enjoyed it!"

So it was fixed, the second week in July. "You'll be able to help with the haymaking," Tat said chuckling.

"I certainly will. I'm much tougher than you think, my lad."

AN UNEXPECTED DRAMA

The weather was getting hot, especially in the centre of the city. Tat and Jane spent as much time as they could spare in the London parks. They swam in the Serpentine, accompanied, as often as not, by Olly and his girlfriend. Jane was due to spend a weekend with her family in Kent. Her mother, who by now knew about Tat, had asked her to invite him down for lunch on the Sunday. Jane felt this would place too much of a strain on Tat and had suggested that Olly should come as well. Safety in numbers she had thought.

The idea was for Tat and Olly to take a train from Victoria to Groombridge, where they would be picked up by car. The boys were anxious about how to dress for the occasion. "Oh nothing special, blazer and flannels, that kind of thing." Jane had suggested.

"Do we wear ties?" Tat asked anxiously. "I mean I've got my first fifteen blazer and cream linen trousers; will they do?"

"Yes, absolutely. As for ties I suppose you should really. Tell you what, bring ties with you and put them on when you arrive at Groombridge, you'll be half strangled otherwise."

Olly was a keen cricketer and had a lovely first eleven blazer from his days at Sedburgh, sky blue edged with braid. Between them they looked the part; two well-groomed, sporty students off on a summer jaunt to leafy Kent for the day. Neither of them had ventured to the south of London before. They were excited at the prospect of exploring different territory, albeit through the windows of a train. Once they left the suburbs of Bromley, they were soon speeding through the rolling fields of Kent. Orchards groaning with fruit and hop gardens with their attendant oast houses spread away on all sides. They stopped at Tonbridge, then Tonbridge Wells which was surprisingly hilly. "Bloody hell," Olly said showing a surprising spasm of nerves. "Groombridge is the next stop Tat, better get our ties and blazers on."

"I suppose this is going to be rather like entering a different universe," Tat said anxiously. "I'm not even sure I'll know which knife and fork to use. Olly, I'm terrified."

"Don't worry, old son," Olly said with a weak grin. "Just start at the outside and work inwards."

"Yes, I suppose so. My God, they're bound to be so posh, don't you think? I mean the way Jane speaks for a start."

"Listen Tat, just be yourself; don't try to put on airs and graces, it never works. They'll love you for your rustic northern charm, you'll see. Here have a smoke to calm your nerves."

The station was on its own out in the country. Presumably the village of Groombridge was somewhere in the vicinity. There was a pub on the roadside adjacent to the station entrance. Parked outside it was a gleaming black Rolls Royce.

"Oh my goodness, just look at that," Olly said. Jane jumped out of the front passenger door and ran towards them. She was dressed in a beautiful flowered frock which floated around her. She looked as cool as a cucumber. A tall, grey haired man got out of the driver's seat dressed in a linen suit and slowly walked towards them.

"Hello you two, my, don't you look nice," Jane said, grinning broadly as she embraced them both. "Come and meet my father." "Daddy, this is Tat and Olly."

The drive to Jane's home only took ten minutes or so through narrow lanes which the overhanging trees transformed into leafy tunnels. Jane's father, who was amused at the friends' excitement at experiencing their first ride in a Rolls, pointed out several huge rocky promontories on either side of the lane. He slowed down and said, "Look over there, rock climbers. They come from all over the place to practice. There are several notorious overhangs. I used to do it myself when I was your age."

"They're just like Brimham Rocks near where I come from in Yorkshire," Olly said. "I had no idea such things existed in the south."

"Oh Kent is full of surprises," Jane's father replied, just as he took a left turn through a rather grand gateway with a lodge alongside it. They drove slowly along a gravel drive for at least five minutes. They passed several handsome houses set back in large well kept gardens. Sweeping views of the surrounding countryside shimmered in the heat stretching for miles in all directions.

"Oh there's that man with his awful dogs," Jane said suddenly. Two straw coloured dogs bounded around the car, barking furiously. They both had a ridge of stiff hair down the middle of their backs. A man in shirtsleeves, wearing a panama, called to the dogs from a grassy knoll a hundred yards away to the left of the drive. Eventually, the dogs gave up the chase and ran back to their owner at breakneck speed.

"Foul creatures," Jane's father said grimly. "One of our neighbours has rented his house out to that chap for the summer. He is a coffee planter in Kenya."

"Yes, and those dogs," Jane said, "are called Rhodesian Ridgebacks, apparently. They are bred for lion hunting. I can't bear them."

"Well, I suppose you have to live and let live. They'll only be here another month or so," Mr Cranshaw said with a sigh.

"Here we are, boys," Jane said as the car rounded a bend. A huge house with conical towers at each corner loomed ahead of them through a profusion of cedar trees. Immaculate lawns interspaced with shrubs and flowerbeds swept back on either side of the drive. Tat spotted several more eroded outcrops of rock with ferns tumbling over them where the garden bordered the surrounding woodland. As the car pulled up alongside the wide curving steps in front of the main entrance, two Springer spaniels erupted from the nearby shrubbery.

"Oh here they come," Jane said. "This is Anno and Domini who will lick you to death if you let them." The dogs gambled around them as they got out of the car. Tat and Olly were both used to farm dogs and allowed them to sniff their shoes and hands in order to put them at their ease.

"Oh well done, boys," said Mr Cranshaw. "Quite a lot of visitors stay in their cars until these two are shut away. They are complete softies as you can see."

"Oh I knew Tat and Olly could cope," Jane said. "They are both country boys aren't you?"

"Oh yes, we're just simple bumpkins aren't we, Tat?" Olly said with a smirk.

Mr Cranshaw smiled and said, "Well, actually, Jane has spent a considerable time telling my wife and me how clever you both are."

"Oh she's absolutely right there," Tat said. Amidst the general laughter the dogs scampered up the steps to greet a tall beautiful woman and two young men who had emerged from the cavernous front entrance. "Ah so there you all are, darling," Mr Cranshaw said. "Come and meet our visitors."

Jane ran up the steps and took her mother's arm. "Oh mummy darling, don't they look sweet. Tat and Olly this is my mother and my two terrible brothers." As they all shook hands, Tat's head began to reel with the confusion of it all. He took a couple of deep breaths in an attempt to calm himself. Jane's mother was a stunning beauty, calm and statuesque with an easy smile. It was obvious where Jane got her looks from. "Well," she said. "It is so nice to meet you. Jane never stops talking about you so you've got a lot to live up to."

Tat groaned inwardly wondering what on earth Jane had been saying. He didn't really know whether she had made it clear as to whether it was himself or Olly she was particularly attached to. He didn't have long to wait on that score, however. Jane put her arm around his waist and said, "Now you can see how lucky I am, Mummy. Isn't he the most handsome man you have ever seen?"

Tat felt the inevitable blush spreading across his neck and cheeks. "Oh Jane, you will embarrass the boy, do behave yourself. Don't take any notice of her, Tat, she's been ridiculously excited all morning."

"Oh I still am, even more so," Jane said and kissed Tat on the cheek. Jane's brothers, Jack and Marcus, wore white open necked shirts and cricket flannels. Jack, the older of the two said, "Look, you chaps must be boiled. Let me take your blazers and ties. I'll hang them in the hall."

The enormous hallway was several degrees cooler than the garden where the temperature was steadily rising. A wide staircase curved up and away at the far end of the hall. Tat noticed that the walls had numerous stuffed animal heads mounted upon them. Most of them were various types of antelope, but Tat stopped in his tracks when he spotted several lion and tiger heads grimacing down at him with bared teeth.

"Don't worry, my boy," Mr Cranshaw said standing next to him. "They are rather an acquired taste. My father was a bit of a hunter in his day. I promise you none of these were dispatched by me."

They made their way through to the drawing room. It was quite simply the biggest room in a domestic setting Tat had ever seen. It had at least six luxurious sofas in it and numerous wing-backed armchairs. The windows, which reached almost from the floor to the moulded ceiling, looked out onto yet more beautifully tended gardens. Ornate flower arrangements stood in huge vases on various tables and pedestals. The walls were hung with oil paintings in heavy gold leafed frames. It was so impressive that Tat felt his heart thudding.

A maid in a neat black dress and white apron brought in a tray with delicate china cups and saucers on it. A second, dressed identically followed with two silver coffee pots with a matching milk jug and sugar bowl. These were set down on a low antique table which Tat thought might be Chinese. As the maids poured the coffee, Tat realised that the whole ground plan of Fell End would quite probably fit into this one room, with a bit to spare.

Jane took Tat's hand and led him over to the big central window. As they looked out at the garden she whispered, "I'm so glad you came, Tat. I know it's all a bit much, but Mummy and Daddy are such sweeties; I know they like you already." She led him back onto the room to chat to her brothers. It turned out that Jack and Marcus had both been to the Kings School in Canterbury. Tat asked them if they knew his friend ,John Lumley, even though he would have been a year or two above them.

"Oh yes, he was ever so clever, and a very good cricketer," said Jack.

"Yes, he plays for the UCL first eleven," Tat replied.

"And you two are in the first fifteen Jane tells us," Marcus said.

"Yes, I think it would be fair to say we are their star players, wouldn't you agree Tat?" smiled Olly.

Tat, despite everything, was beginning to relax. "Oh yes," he said. "They don't come much better than Olly and me." Marcus explained that he was due to go to Kings College, Cambridge, the following September. "I have serious hopes of getting into the college first team. I'm usually at scrum half but I can play hooker as well. I enjoy both positions actually."

"Oh well," Olly said. "Young Tat here is your man, he's our hooker. There's nothing he doesn't know about the job."

Jack was already studying at Wye Agricultural College and would eventually take over the management of the various family farms scattered around Kent. "Yes, that will be a huge relief to me," Mr Cranshaw said. "I have no time at all for that side of things and it's a nightmare relying on managers."

Tat thought of Dick at Newton Rigg and couldn't help comparing his small wiry friend with the beautifully spoken, languid youth seated opposite. He almost surrendered to a fit of giggles as he recalled Dick's description of his plans for the bar maid in Penrith.

Eventually, Jane's mother suggested that they go through for lunch. As they followed her back across the hall to the dining room Marcus said to Tat, "I say I do like your blazer; is it UCL's rugger club?"

"Yes, it's nice isn't it? My parents gave it to me last Christmas." Tat liked Jane's brothers. They were easy to talk to and carried the family good looks. He wondered if wealth and privilege had some sort of effect upon the way people looked.

The dining room was only marginally smaller than the sitting room. It was panelled throughout with dark, ancient timber edged with linen fold patterns. The ceiling had huge exposed beams, whilst the floor was made up of irregularly sized speckled flagstones.

"Gosh," Olly said, "What a room eh, Tat?"

"It's ancient," Tat replied. "I don't quite understand why it's so different to the room where we had coffee."

"Yes, indeed," Jane's father said. "This is the old side of the house. It's Jacobean and hasn't really changed for hundreds of years."

"You must have done that painting, Jane," Tat said indicating a large family portrait hanging at the far end of the room. "I'd recognize your style anywhere."

"I did it last year," Jane said. "It took ages."

"Yes," Mrs Cranshaw said, "we were all obliged to sit for hours at a time, not necessarily all at once, mind you."

"You even put yourself in it, that must have been difficult. How on earth did you manage?"

"Oh the tricks of the trade, my boy," Jane said smiling at Tat. "Do you like it?"

"Oh yes," Tat replied. "It's wonderful."

"You had better steel yourself, Tat," Mr Cranshaw said. "She's bound to get you to sit for her sooner or later."

"Oh she already has," Tat said and began to blush when the memory of Jane drawing him naked flashed into his mind.

"Olly has made a portrait of Tat," Jane said quickly. "They were kind enough to let me draw them whilst they worked on it."

Mr Cranshaw indicated where they should all sit. Tat glanced at the copious amount of cutlery set neatly either side of each place mat on the big antique table. He resolved to keep a close watch on the order in which they were selected before chancing his arm. He was surprised when Jane's brothers tucked their sparkling white napkins into their open neck shirts, whilst the two maids who had brought the coffee began to serve the soup.

"This is lobster," Mrs Cranshaw said. "Fresh from Whitstable; I hope you like it." It was quite simply the most delicious soup Tat had ever tasted and it was pink into the bargain. He understood why Jack and Marcus had worn their napkins in such a bizarre fashion. He took extra care not to spill a drop. The soup was followed by Dover sole. Then a huge joint of roast beef was placed in front of Jane's father who carved it expertly. The maids served the vegetables and side salads. Tat felt happier as the supply of cutlery gradually lessened with each course.

Mr Cranshaw took charge of the wine himself which had been put into cut glass decanters previously. They had dry white wine with the fish and rich fruity claret with the beef. Then when the sweet was served Tat had his first taste of pudding wine. He almost pinched himself to see whether he was dreaming. He thought of his own family tucking into the roast turkey last Christmas at the Black Bull. My goodness, how the other half live. He wondered if he would ever be able to tell his parents and brothers just how luxurious this lunch was.

They had coffee in the drawing room again. Mr Cranshaw said, "Do smoke if you want to boys. I'm going to have a cigar." He offered one to Tat and Olly who wisely declined after such rich food. Jane began to make a roll-up.

"Oh, Jane, when are you going to stop that disgusting habit?" Mrs Cranshaw said fixing her own cigarette into a long holder.

"Well, you can blame dear, old Jackson," Jane said blowing out a plume of smoke.

"Jackson's our gardener. Jane insists it was him who taught her to do it," Mrs Cranshaw explained.

"I know," Tat replied. "She's told me that story herself. I never knew whether it was true or not."

"It most certainly is, Tat," Jane said. "Anyway, I won't have a word said against Jackson; I adore him."

"Have you told your parents about Nick La Rocca's reaction to you rolling your own?" Tat said.

"Oh, he was horrified wasn't he?" Jane said with a squeak. "You remember me telling you about Mr La Rocca don't you, Mummy?"

"Oh the American band leader; aren't you doing a portrait of him?"

"Yes, actually I've already done the drawings for it. Don't worry I was chaperoned by Tat and one of his tutors."

"I keep reading about this La Rocca fellow and his band in the papers," Jane's father said. "They seem to be taking London by storm."

"So, you've met him have you, Tat?" Mrs Cranshaw asked. "What do you make of him? I imagine you will have a slightly more balanced view, compared to my excitable daughter, that is."

"Oh he's a real character. He talks like I imagine American gangsters talk. I'm sure Jane will make a terrific portrait of him."

Jane took Tat and Olly around the gardens which turned out to be much more extensive than it first seemed. Some distance off, behind the house, there was a considerable lake with a boathouse.

"We swim in here. Wouldn't it be lovely to go in now, it's so very hot." For a moment Tat thought she was going to suggest that they all take a dip naked, there and then. To his relief, she didn't. However, they rowed a boat across the lake and back again to feel the cool air rising off the water. When they approached the house they saw Jane's brothers playing croquet on a well-tended stretch of lawn.

"Come on, boys," they called out. "Let's make up a four, us against you two. Jane's useless anyway."

"He's right there, you go ahead. I'll sit in the shade over here."

"Actually, I've never played before," Tat said.

"Oh don't worry," Marcus said. "It's mindlessly simple. Not that I'm suggesting you're mindless, of course."

Much to his surprise, Tat was rather good once he got the hang of the game. The four of them generated a lot of noise, howling with laughter at each other's mistakes. Tat noticed that, despite the racket they were making, Jane was dozing off in her deck chair. They had all drunk more wine than they were used to at lunch. Tat and Olly managed to beat the brothers three games to one. They were determined to have their revenge when Mrs Cranshaw called to them from beneath a particularly large cedar of Lebanon to come across for tea.

Marcus shook Jane roughly to wake her. "Come on, sleepy head. It's time for tiffin."

The tea things were set out on an elaborate wrought iron table surrounded by matching chairs. One of the maids was pouring tea. Tat noticed that she was adding the milk last and wondered if it was yet another habit adopted by the wealthy. Jane suddenly squealed with delight. "Oh hello, Dorkins. I wondered where you'd got to."

She bent down and picked up a sleek black cat which had appeared from the nearby shrubbery and cuddled it against her bosom. "Oh you are the most beautiful cat in all the world, yes you are," Jane cooed.

"Come on now, Jane," Mrs Cranshaw said. "You can cut that wonderful looking coffee cake."

"Bye for now Dorkins. We'll have another cuddle in a minute."

Jane dropped the cat down on the grass where it stretched and yawned. A movement caught Tat's eye some way off across the lawn. He shaded his eyes with his hand and saw the two straw-coloured dogs trotting in their direction, apparently following a scent. They stopped, raised their heads and stared intently towards them. Tat stood up and said, "I don't want to worry you but..." that was as far as he got. The dogs ran snarling into their midst before he finished his sentence; the stiff ridge of hair bristling spikily down their backs.

Before anyone so much as uttered a sound, the dogs ripped the black cat in two. The head end with one leg attached was tossed high into the air before landing noisily amongst the tea things. Jane screamed as gobbets of blood spattered into her face. Mrs Cranshaw choked on her coffee cake and suddenly vomited as a tangle of squirming intestines landed in her lap. Jane's father struggled to his feet shouting,

"Oh my God!" and staggered across to his wife who was falling sideways being sick across her silk dress. Alerted by the sudden movement, one of the dogs turned and raised its head snarling through bared teeth. Olly, acting more on instinct than anything else, stood up and landed a mighty kick to the creature's lower jaw. It let out a single yelp as its head snapped backwards then sank to the ground, its legs twitching.

The two springer spaniels, attracted by the commotion came

tearing across the lawn. The other ridgeback was fully occupied tearing the remains of the cat into shreds. Jane became completely hysterical, screaming repeatedly and banging her fists against her head. Marcus tried to subdue her but she fought him off and attempted to run away. Jack and Jane's father were trying to lift Mrs Cranshaw from the ground where she had finally fainted. The spaniels, barking furiously, began to attack the remaining ridgeback which whirled around on them, fragments of black fur sticking to its bloodied jaws. It lunged at the nearest spaniel and sank its teeth into its neck just behind its head. Then it ran off clumsily, holding the squealing spaniel clear of the ground.

Mr Cranshaw yelled, "Tat and Olly go after Jane and try to calm her. Marcus get my shot gun and shoot that monster. Right now." He and Jack were obliged to lay Mrs Cranshaw on the grass again. Mr Cranshaw shouted, "Jack, go and phone Dr Clayton, tell him to come here immediately."

The ridgeback had stopped under a cedar tree where it began to toss the now dead spaniel into the air above its head. Jane was crawling back towards the house on her hands and knees, her hunched body wracked with continuous sobbing. Tat and Olly knelt beside her but their attempts to comfort her seemed only to make her more agitated. Tat looked up and saw Marcus running towards them with a shotgun. Tears were pouring down his face. "I can't do it," he sobbed. "I'm shaking too much."

Tat stood up, "Is it loaded?"

"Yes, yes it is," Marcus replied hanging his head miserably.

"Give it to me," Tat said through gritted teeth. He turned and walked quickly towards the ridgeback which he could hear growling, even though it was at least fifty yards away. "Marcus," he shouted over his shoulder. "Get hold of the other spaniel."

The ridgeback looked up from its bloody work and without hesitating ran straight at Tat, snarling deep in its throat. Tat stopped, removed the safety on the shotgun and took aim at the ridgeback's head. When the dog was about ten feet away he fired. The ridgeback's snarling face disappeared in a welter of gore. The dog's momentum carried it forward so that it rolled to a stop at his feet.

Tat and Olly were driven to Groombridge station by the chauffeur. The London trains ran on the hour until ten o'clock. The family doctor had sedated Jane and her mother and stayed until they were both in bed. Mr Cranshaw had called the police. After they had taken stock of the carnage in the garden, the sergeant, accompanied by two constables, had gone to question the owner of the ridgebacks. Jackson, the gardener, was given the grisly job of removing the three dead dogs from the scene and the scattered remains of Dorkins, the black cat.

Olly suggested that rather than catch the next train, they should go to the pub on the roadside. "I don't know about you, Tat, but I am in need of a large whisky."

As they walked towards the pub Tat noticed for the first time that Olly was limping. "Well, I gave that dog everything I'd got," he explained. "Trouble is, unlike a rugger ball, its head was as solid as a rock. It hurts like hell," he added.

They were the first customers of the evening. When they settled at a table in a bay window with large whiskeys apiece and two pints of the local bitter, they sat in silence for a while. Tat was the first to speak.

"How on earth is it possible? A completely idyllic day in that wonderful place, to end in such horror. I can't believe it really happened."

"I know, you end up wondering if you are having your worst nightmare and that you'll wake up soon. Do you think the bloke who owns those bloody dogs will be arrested?"

"I shouldn't think so, but he'll face a hefty fine. Jane's father will certainly take it to court. I've never seen a man so angry."

"With good reason... my foot is killing me. Let's have another round. My shout."

Jane didn't return to the Slade until the last week of term. Tat had telephoned a couple of times to see how she and her mother were recovering. The first time Mr Cranshaw answered the phone. He said that Jane and her mother were up and about but still having to rest. When Tat asked about the results of the police inquiry he confirmed that there would be a court hearing in Tunbridge Wells the following month. Mr Cranshaw concluded by saying, "My boy, I want you to know how grateful we all are to you and Olly. We would have been in deep trouble without the intervention of the pair of you." His voice shook slightly. He suggested that Tat should telephone again towards the end of the following week.

JAZZ AT THE MORTON CLUB

Jack Douthwaite asked Tat to call at his study. "Our friend, Nick La Rocca, and the band are playing at a place called the Morton Club in Old Bond Street this Saturday. He has invited you and Jane to come along as his guests. Can you make it?"

Tat told Jack about the dreadful events at Jane's home and explained that she was still struggling to get over it all. "Her father says she is on the mend but she won't be up to it I'm afraid."

"Oh, how dreadful. Poor girl, she must be shattered. So that's why Olly is limping. I saw him hobbling across the quad yesterday."

"Yes, apparently he broke a toe. Mind you, not many people can claim to have killed a Rhodesian Ridgeback with a single kick."

"I suppose that's true. You shot the other one, then. What a stroke of luck that you two were on hand. You're heroes… both of you." It was decided that Tat and Olly would take up La Rocca's invitation.

"Nick will be disappointed. He has a soft spot for Jane. Oh yes, you will have to wear black ties. We'll work something out I'm sure."

It turned out that Ben and Charles, Jack's flat mates, were unable to go to the club. They suggested that Tat and Olly should borrow their evening suits. When they had called at Jack's flat on the Friday evening to try the suits on, Tat came off best as he and Ben were about the same size and shape. Olly was obliged to show rather more wrist and ankle than he would have wished as he was a good four inches taller than Charles and two stones lighter.

"Oh don't worry," Jack said laughing. "The lighting is very subdued in the Morton Club. Nobody will take the slightest notice."

They were to collect their tickets at the door of the club at 9pm. Olly suggested that they should have a few pints at the Goat, only five minutes walk from the Morton Club. Leon Kussoff had come to his rescue when he had heard about the less than satisfactory fit of Charles' evening suit and had offered Olly his own. His father, a diplomat at the Russian Embassy, had insisted his three sons be equipped suitably for formal occasions. He was almost exactly the same size as Olly. So it turned out that Olly was the immaculate one. Tat was sure that Olly would not have suggested going anywhere near the Goat or any other pub if he had been wearing Charles' dinner suit. After four pints and a couple of whisky chasers, they made their way to the Morton Club in a decidedly mellow mood.

"That was perfect," Olly said lighting a cigarette. "You can bet your boots the drink will cost a fortune at this Morton place."

Following Jack Douthwaite's directions, they found the Morton Club two doors to the north of Agnew's Art Gallery. Tat had, even at this stage, a nagging doubt that some failure in communication would end in them having to argue the toss with the doorman. He needn't have worried, after consulting a list pinned to the wall by his desk, he handed them their tickets and said, "Just show these to one of the waiters down there and they'll take you to your table. There is a lady and gentleman already seated, I believe."

They made their way down the steep staircase and entered a surprisingly large space with tables covering most of the floor. Many of these were occupied by well-dressed couples drinking and talking animatedly. A waiter approached them and after glancing at their tickets led them to a table close to the stage. They spotted Jack Douthwaite filling a champagne glass held by an exceptionally beautiful woman.

"Blimey," said Olly, "she's a bit of a corker isn't she?"

"I'll say. She must be the fiancée I've heard him mention, they're getting married this autumn, apparently."

"Lucky Jack, I say."

"Hello you two," Jack said. "Come and sit down. This is Christine, meet Tat and Olly."

Jack waved to a waiter and ordered another bottle of champagne and two extra glasses. "Now then, this is my treat boys. I won a rather lucrative case last week so I'm unusually flush. Olly you look very smart. What's the explanation? That most definitely is not Charles' suit."

"Oh one of my chums took pity on me," Olly said grinning. "He actually has his own dinner suit and is the same size as me. Don't tell Charles though, will you Jack?"

"Your secret is safe with me, dear boy," Jack said. Then, turning to Christine, explained how he had expected Olly to turn up with his trouser bottoms half way up his shins. Christine laughed showing her perfect, even white teeth.

"Well you look very smart, you both do," she said fitting a cigarette into a short, mother of pearl holder.

"Have you heard the band before?" Tat asked her.

"Oh yes, Jack has made sure of that. Aren't they wonderful? I shall miss them when they leave us."

"Tat's girlfriend, who can't be with us tonight, is painting a portrait of Nick La Rocca," Jack said. "She's a student at the Slade."

"Oh really," Christine said, raising her eyebrows, "I'd love to see it one day."

"Well actually, I've had a thought about that," Jack said. "Tat, do you think Jane would let me buy the portrait when it's finished? I really am serious."

"I should think she'd be thrilled to bits."

"Well, I thought the drawings were terrific. I happen to know that Nick would like to buy one of the finished pencil drawings when Jane has finished work on the picture," Jack said.

"Blimey," Olly said. "That'll cheer her up, eh Tat?"

"Yes I should say so. I'll tell her all about it next time I telephone."

"Well," Jack went on, "I happen to know that Nick was going to put the proposition to her tonight. He'll be ever so disappointed that she's not here. You're a handsome lad, Olly, but you don't quite have the ethereal beauty of our Jane."

"That's true," Tat said laughing. "Actually she told me that Mr La Rocca is quite a softie underneath. Jane likes him. I'm sure she'll agree." Jack poured more champagne and looked at his watch.

"They're late as usual," he said. "Have you noticed the double bass on the stage. A friend of Bobby's is playing with the band tonight. It will probably sound quite different."

Suddenly, the crowd burst into applause as the band emerged from a side door and mounted the stage. Tat looked around and thought how different this audience was from the unruly lot at the Palladium. Jane would have loved it.

The band began with a very fast 'Tiger Rag'. Jack was right; the double bass did make a difference. At such close quarters, with all those bodies to absorb the volume, the band had a tight, compact sound. The snarl of the wind instruments took Tat by surprise and he could feel the percussive drumbeats resonate in his chest.

Wild applause erupted after each tune. Nick La Rocca didn't bother with any announcements, choosing instead to count the band in by stamping his foot when the clapping and cheering faded slightly. This added a kind of break neck momentum to their performance. Several couples got up to dance in the small space in front of the stage. Some of the younger ones did 'The Charleston' which was the latest dancing fashion. It was a jerky affair which involved complicated sideways kicks and hand movements. The couples rarely touched but executed the intricate routines facing each other with fixed grins. To Tat and Olly's surprise, Jack and Christine joined the dancers and proved to be very agile. Olly leaned over to Tat and shouted, "What a night this is turning out to be!"

After a dozen tunes, most of which were fast ones, La Rocca rose from his chair and yelled, "Ok folks, we're gonna take a half hour break. We got some drinking to catch up on."

He made his way towards their table accompanied by Bobby Jones. Every few feet or so members of the audience rose to greet him, shaking his hand and slapping him on the back. Jack beckoned to him and held up a large whisky which he'd ordered in advance from the waiter.

"Hey Jack," La Rocca said rather breathlessly when he finally reached them. "Let me have a slug of that." He and Bobby sat down and shook hands with everybody. La Rocca looked across at Christine and said, "Well, you're looking even more gorgeous than ever, Chris. You're one lucky guy, Jack." After gulping another mouthful of whisky he looked at Olly and Tat with raised eyebrows and said, "Hey wait a minute, where's my good friend Jane? I been looking forward to seeing her again all week."

"I'm afraid she's not very well," Tat said. "She's spending a few days at her parents' place. She sends her love."

"No kidding, that's too bad. I got a present for her backstage, some of the records we been making at Colombia. Will you give them to her for me, kid?"

"Of course, she'll be thrilled."

"Great, mind you I'm broken hearted not to see her," La Rocca said.

"Nick," Jack said, "I've mentioned that you are very interested in having one of her pencil drawings when she's finished with it."

"You bet your life. I was gonna ask her about it tonight. What do you think, kid?" he asked looking at Tat.

"Oh I'm sure you won't be disappointed. I'll tell her when she's back at college."

It turned out that the band were due to sail from Liverpool the following week. They had been in London a full eighteen months and had become the talk of the town.

"I tell you," La Rocca said after demolishing a second large whisky, "Me and the boys have had a ball over here. But all good things gotta come to an end, I guess."

It was two in the morning when Tat and Olly made their way back to the Gower Street hostel. They were euphorically drunk and none too steady on their feet. They took great pains to put their borrowed suits neatly on coat hangers. Olly slept on Tat's armchair, realizing wisely, that he was too far gone to make it back to his digs. Tat slid the packaged gramophone records under his bed and noticed that La Rocca had written on the brown paper,

'To my beautiful friend, Jane, a great artist and true English rose, Love Nick."

Jane had been more or less like her old self when Tat telephoned the second time. Not unnaturally, she did not want to talk about any of the details which had taken place in the garden that terrible Sunday afternoon. She did say that they had buried Dorkins and Anno in the garden near the lake and her father had ordered headstones from a local stonemason which she had designed.

"Dear Daddy has been a pillar of strength. He has been so patient and kind to Mummy and me, bless him." Tat was relieved to have the good news about Jack Douthwaite and Nick La Rocca to tell her.

"Gosh how exciting. I must make sure the painting is up to scratch; I can't wait to get back to work. I've been drawing of course, but I need to be back in town to pick up the pieces again. I can't wait to see you."

Jane was driven up to Fulham by her father on the Saturday afternoon, so that she would have the weekend to find her feet before facing college for the final week of term. It was agreed that Tat would call at Fawcett Street at six the same evening.

"Oh Tat how lovely to see you, let me give you a hug."

They embraced tenderly on the doorstep; Tat could feel that she had lost weight. When he pulled back to look at her he noticed that her cheek-bones were more prominent. If anything she looked even more beautiful than ever.

"I know, I've lost weight, just over a stone actually. I couldn't eat for ages. Daddy says you have to fatten me up."

"I was just thinking how lovely you look," Tat said, stroking her hair.

"Poor Mummy said the same. She says it's the fashion to be thin."

"Well, I wouldn't call you thin, just a bit thinner."

UNPREDICTED LARGESSE

"Oh Tat, I'm so worried, I don't know what else I can do with the place," Tat's mother said, the anxiety showing clearly on her face.

The big kitchen had been freshly painted with creamy coloured distemper. There wasn't a cobweb to be seen amongst the oak beams which straddled the ceiling and the flagstone floor was spotless. The parlour had been re-papered with an attractive floral design, whilst the piano and dark heavy furniture gleamed, not a speck of dust was to be seen. The whole place smelled attractively of wax polish.

"Listen, Mam," Tat said laying his hand on his mother's arm. "It all looks beautiful; I can see what an effort you've put in. Stop worrying. Jane will love it I promise you. She's only a young lass after all, not a duchess."

"Aye I know lad, but when you described what her home is like, all them servants and such," Tat's mother replied. "Well, I can't help but think this old house will be a let down."

Tat had been shocked to discover how much work his mother had put in when he had arrived two weeks previously. Admittedly, his Gran had loaned her Clarrie and her handyman-cum-chauffeur from the Black Bull to help her out. The biggest surprise of all was the conversion of the outside lavatory in the yard. Mrs Watson's handyman took care of all the plumbing and electrical jobs at the pub.

"Now you won't want this lass of our Tat's sitting down on a rough old plank with a hole in it, now will you?" Mrs Watson had said. "I'll get George to have a look at the job."

The outcome involved a good deal of fetching and carrying from Kirkby Stephen. After three days of hard work George had replaced the old earth closet with a shiny white flushing pedestal and smooth mahogany seat which lifted up and down on hinges. High on the wall behind it was a water cistern with a chain hanging down which activated the flushing mechanism. Higher up still in the eaves he had secured a water tank which had to be refilled every two days with a hosepipe attached to the yard tap. The building had been newly painted inside and out and even had a toilet paper holder attached to the wall. A roll of white toilet paper, divided up into equally sized segments by perforated seams hung upon it. Two spares stood to one side upon a shelf, beside a vase of freshly cut roses, whose perfume pervaded the place.

Tat and his brothers had spent hours digging a trench across the yard which ended up in the orchard. There they dug out a huge hole in the ground which was to be the cess-pool. They fitted ceramic drainage pipes end to end all the way from underneath the new toilet pedestal back to the cess-pool, making sure the trajectory of these was inclined downwards to ensure effective drainage. The cess-pool had a three-foot layer of broken limestone in the base, heavy planks were fitted over it, topped off with earth and sods of grass.

"By God, our Tat," Michael had said, perspiring profusely, whilst easing his aching back. "She'd better be something special this Jane lass."

"Aye, don't you worry lad. She's that alright, you'll see." Tat assured him.

Despite all the sweaty dirty work, the new flushing toilet turned out to be a revelation to the Taylors. 'Going across the yard' as they called it, became a quick, easy, almost pleasurable experience. No more foul smells and especially no more emptying of the noisome bucket every two or three days. Ivy, in particular, was delighted; it was something she had longed for but never thought she would have.

"Mind you, she'll still get wet if it's raining and she might lose her way in the dark," she said, unable to stop worrying.

"Never mind, Mam," John had said, "Our Tat'll build a covered walkway from the back door with fairy lights on it tomorrow, won't you, Tat?"

Tat cuffed him lightly on the shoulder and said, "You cheeky beggar, I might just do that. I can't thank you enough for what you've done, all of you. I know Jane will love it and I know you'll all think the world of her."

Tat collected the mail from the letterbox mounted on the gatepost where the farm track met the lane to Winton. He was surprised to find a letter addressed to himself. It was an expensive envelope and his name and the address were typed, as though it might have been sent from an office of some sort. It turned out to be from Jane's father. Tat sat down on a boulder in the bright sunshine and lit a cigarette. As he unfolded the letter several separate pieces of paper fell out and fluttered between his feet. He picked them up and was staggered to find that they were five white fifty pound notes. He stared at them whilst finishing his cigarette, then folded the notes and put them in his shirt pocket. Shaking his head in disbelief, he read the letter.

My dear Tat,

I have thought long and hard about how best to show my gratitude for what you did for us on that ghastly Sunday afternoon. Our family owes you and Olly a huge debt. My wife and Jane are much better, but of course you have seen Jane since the tragedy and will see her again next week when she visits your family in Westmorland. She is so looking forward to this and I'm sure it will do her the world of good. I know you will look after her.

I want you to accept the enclosed from me without reservation. My idea is Tat, that you will use the money to buy something you consider to be useful to you in your future life. It might be a suitable car, or the down payment on a house of your own, wherever you choose to start your legal career. Take your time to think it over. Can I ask you to keep this confidential, particularly from Jane? I know I can trust you.

In addition, on a lighter note, I have dispatched a package from my wine merchant in St James' to be collected at Kirkby Stephen railway station. It could well be there already. I suggest you telephone the stationmaster there to check up on it. It contains some rather palatable vintages which I want you and your family to enjoy this summer. Jane will be bringing some of her art materials with her. I feel I should warn you. Alert your family to the inevitable scrutiny she will subject them to. No doubt your wonderful landscape will also inspire her.

I gather that Olly is very keen to have the portrait he has made of you cast into bronze. I intend to contact him in the very near future and inform him that I wish to cover the cost of this for him. It doesn't surprise me that he is the goal kicker in your first fifteen at UCL. Thank God we had somebody who could kick straight and somebody who could shoot straight amongst us when it all happened. I will always be in your debt.

Kind Regards,

Charles Cranshaw.

Tat remained seated on the boulder for several minutes trying to come to terms with what had happened. Having met Jane's father, he had no doubt about the sincerity of this act of generosity; however, it was the very last thing that he expected. As he saw it, he and Olly had simply done what had to be done. He took out the five fifty pound notes and smoothing them across his knee, stared at them. He had never even vaguely thought about owning a car, never mind a house of his own. Perhaps the best thing to do, he thought, would be to put it into a bank account and forget about it until he had graduated in a year's time.

He decided to walk over to Kirkby Stephen and phone the railway station from his Gran's at the Black Bull. "Aye lad," the stationmaster told him, "there's a big basket up here for you lot. It's damned heavy an' all; takes two good men to lift it."

When Tat got back to Fell End he told his mother about Mr Cranshaw's letter. He explained that he had sent them a gift of wine which was waiting to be collected at the station. He kept silent regarding the £250. "Apparently, it's in a great big basket," Tat said. "The station master says it takes two men to lift it."

That same evening Tat and his father took the pony and trap over to the station. When he saw the size of the basket, his father said, "There must be enough of it to float a ship on in there! Your Jane's dad must be made of money." With the help of one of the station trolleys and a couple of porters, they eventually got the basket, which was indeed extremely heavy, loaded into the trap. When they reached the farm track they both dismounted and walked the pony the rest of the way avoiding the deepest ruts where possible.

Tat and his brothers were given the job of unloading the bottles before supper. Each one was expertly wrapped in corrugated brown paper. When they had finished, the kitchen table was filled from end to end with twenty-four bottles of red wine and the same number of white, plus twelve bottles of champagne. All the labels were in French.

"My goodness," Tat's mother said. "I've never seen owt like it, not even at the Black Bull. It must have cost a fortune."

"I tell you what, though," Michael said grinning from ear to ear. "It makes digging that cess-pool seem almost worth it."

Tat had, of course, told his family about the dreadful incident with the ridgebacks at Jane's home. They had been genuinely shocked and impressed by Olly's quick wittedness and Tat's shooting prowess.

"Well, Tat," his father said, "I dare say you never thought your heroics would result in this lot eh?"

"No I didn't, I feel almost guilty," Tat said shaking his head.

"Well, I dare say a few bottles of this stuff will cure you of that," John said smirking, then added, "can we have a drop with our supper, Mam?"

Ivy said sternly, "We'll wait until Jane gets here; there's an end to it."

"No, Mam," Tat said, "Jane's father says he wants us to enjoy it in his letter so I say let's have a couple of bottles of champagne right now."

Ivy knew when to capitulate, surrounded as she was by four grown men. "Oh well, go on then, but I'll open it. My mother taught me years ago how to do it without it flying all over the place."

"Thanks, Mam," Tat said hugging her. "After all we're not exactly going to run out whilst Jane's here are we?"

Tat and his brothers stowed the white wine in the pantry and the red under the stairs. He had gleaned enough knowledge from Jane to know that the white should be kept cold, whilst the red needed to remain at room temperature.

The bubbling, golden liquid quickly worked its magic. They drank out of plain half pint beer glasses. Tat's brothers had never tasted it before and screwed up their faces as the champagne fizzed in their throats and noses. Despite this, they quickly recognized how potent it was, asking for refills as their spirits rose. As Tat's mother served the supper the noisy banter between the brothers grew louder. Tat, without consulting anybody, retrieved two bottles of white wine from the pantry and after rummaging in the kitchen table drawer, found a corkscrew and opened them. Ivy caught him pouring everybody a generous measure as she placed a dish of salad on the table. Tat's father put his hand on her arm and grinning broadly shook his head before she could object. He stood up, raised his glass and called for silence.

"I give you a toast," he boomed. "To our Tat, whose sharp shooting brought us this good fortune."

"To our Tat," they all shouted before gulping white wine and cheering raucously.

JANE VISITS FELL END

Amidst the swirling steam and smoke, whilst the train doors banged, Tat spotted Jane hauling her luggage onto the platform. She looked up as he called to her and, leaving her bags in a heap, ran towards him shouting, "Oh Tat, how lovely to see you." She fell into his open arms, hugged him tightly and they kissed tenderly. "Gosh Tat," Jane said, as they piled her two cases, plus her portfolio and portable easel onto a trolley, "you're right about the journey, I thought I'd never get here."

"Well, I did warn you, just under eight hours."

"I did sleep a bit actually. But the last bit, when you reach the mountains, well honestly I thought I was in Switzerland. It is so beautiful. Oh Tat, I've missed you terribly." She stopped him pushing the trolley and said, "Oh you lovely boy, let me hug you again."

Mrs Watson had insisted that George accompany Tat to the station with the Rover so that he could drive them to Mary Hollis' cottage in Winton. He got out as Tat and Jane approached the car and began to open the boot.

"Jane, this is George; he works for my Gran. He's going to drive us to Mary's place."

"How do you do, George," Jane said shaking hands. "I'm pleased to meet you. Gosh what a lovely shiny car; oh super the top is down."

"Yes," Tat said, "It's been ever so hot so we thought you'd appreciate the fresh air after your journey."

As they drove down the main street towards the market square Jane snuggled close to Tat. She had pulled on a soft cloche hat to stop her hair from becoming too dishevelled as the car gained speed.

"We're going to make a very short stop at my Gran's pub on the way through town. Is that alright? She insists on being the first member of the family to meet you."

"Of course, I'd love to meet her," Jane said. Tat had already asked George to drive round to the rear of the Black Bull and park in the stable yard. He wanted to avoid having Jane run the gauntlet of the inevitable crowd of drinkers who spilled out onto the street on summer evenings. Mrs Watson must have been keeping an eye out for their arrival as she was standing at the back door when they pulled into the yard. She walked across as Tat helped Jane down from the Rover, grinning broadly.

"Gran, this is Jane," Tat said. Jane stepped forward and taking both Mrs Watson's hands bent down and kissed her on the cheek. She was at least six inches taller than the old lady.

"I'm so glad to meet you, Mrs Watson. Tat has told me so much about you."

"And I'm glad to meet you, lass. Come away in and have a sherry; you'll need it after that train ride." She linked arms with Jane and led her into her sitting room. Tat followed, smiling to himself, confident that his Gran was already smitten with Jane.

"Sit down lass, make yourself comfortable. Tat can you pour us all a sherry? It's on the sideboard over there." Jane removed her hat and shook her hair loose about her shoulders. "I must look an awful fright. I hope you'll forgive me."

"Well, if you're a fright lass, you're the bonniest one I've ever seen." Then turning to Tat she said, "Eh our Tat, what a beauty she is and no mistake."

"Now Gran," Tat said, bringing three large schooners of amontillado over to the table on a tray. "You'll embarrass the lass."

"Oh no," Jane said, grinning broadly. "I can take any number of compliments, honestly."

"There now," Mrs Watson said, handing Jane her sherry, "welcome to Kirkby Stephen."

It was dark when Tat made his way back to Fell End across the fields. There was just sufficient moonlight to see by although he could have easily made his way blindfold. Mary Hollis and Jane had taken to each other instantly as Tat had thought they would. The cottage, overlooking the village green in Winton couldn't have been more welcoming. Tat had taken Jane's luggage up to Mary's spare bedroom. He had never been up the stairs before and was impressed with how cosy and comfortable it was. Just off the landing he discovered a very attractive bathroom with a toilet and fluffy cream towels hanging on a brass rail. Jane would like that, he thought.

Mary had poured them all a dry sherry by the time Tat came downstairs to the sitting room. Tat noticed that even though the cottage had been recently supplied with electricity, Mary still preferred to use oil lamps in the evening.

"Now Jane, would you like a bath, my dear? There's plenty of hot water. I'm sure it would refresh you after all that travelling."

"Oh gosh, that would be heaven," Jane replied.

"Come on then," Mary said, ushering Jane up the stairs, "I'll show you where everything is. We'll have something to eat when you are done." Tat had helped Mary set out the supper things in the tiny oak beamed dining room; cold ham and salad with new potatoes. Tat had brought two bottles of white wine from Mr Cranshaw's consignment which Mary had stood in cold water to chill.

"What a charming creature she is," Mary had confided to Tat in a low voice, whilst they bustled about in the kitchen. "I don't think I've ever seen such a beauty before, you're a lucky lad, Tat."

Jane had changed into a flimsy, cream cotton dress which showed off her tan to perfection. "I'm sorry this is a bit creased. I've hung everything else up in the wardrobe. Oh, that bath was just the ticket, I feel wonderful."

"You look wonderful my dear, doesn't she, Tat?"

"I've never seen her look anything else," Tat said.

"Blimey," Jane said blushing slightly. "I've never had so many compliments before."

Tat made his way across the farm yard on tip toe so as not to disturb the dogs and set them barking. So far, so good, he thought. Of course, he knew that what had taken place up to now was always going to be the easy bit. Even so it had gone well; his Gran had been on her best behaviour. When he had taken his leave, Mary and Jane, with half a bottle still to drink, were talking animatedly about art. Tomorrow would be the real test.

Tat arrived at Mary's cottage just after nine the following morning. "Come in Tat we've just washed up the breakfast things," Mary said. "Jane's ironing some of her clothes as they got crushed a bit in her suitcases. Will you have a coffee?"

"I won't if you don't mind. Mam will have it ready when we get up to Fell End."

Jane emerged from the kitchen with several freshly ironed dresses draped over her arm. "Oh hello Tat, darling," she said kissing him on the cheek. "I'll just hang these up; I won't be a minute."

"Did you sleep well?" Tat asked smiling.

"Like a top," she called back as she set off up the stairs.

"Oh Tat," Mary said, resting her hand on his arm. "She's such a darling, your family will love her."

"I'm sure they will; thank you Mary for helping us out. I really appreciate it so much."

"Well, she's a joy to be with Tat, I'll miss her when she's gone."

Tat and Jane slid their arms around each other's waists as they left the village behind them. It was hot already and would get even hotter later in the day. Curlews wheeled and dipped overhead calling continuously. Now and again they caught glimpses of their fluffy, long-legged, flightless young running for cover amongst the grass in the fields bordering the lane. As they climbed the hill, the fells rose up before them, outcrops of limestone sparkling in the bright sunshine. When they reached the Scots pine at the summit Tat said, "Now my girl, turn around and look at the Eden Valley."

"Oh my goodness," Jane gasped, "How magnificent. You can see for miles, those mountains and the huge sky. Tat it's paradise."

"Do you think you could paint it?"

"Well, it would be a challenge for sure, but I'd give it a good shot."

"You see there about half way along the valley bottom?" Tat asked, pointing into the distance. "Some wisps of smoke rising up, well that's Appleby, where I went to school."

"Gosh it makes you feel so small don't you think? All that space with the mountains on either side soaring up. It's positively biblical."

"Well, I've never heard it called that before - now this tree, or that branch to be more accurate." Tat put his hand on the warm trunk of the Scots pine. "That's where Bill Fletcher ducked to pass under it. Do you remember me telling you about it?"

"You mean he was that tall, surely not?" Jane said incredulously, gazing up at the branch.

"Seven feet, nine inches. I've still got the piece of string we measured the height with come to think of it. I'll show you it later."

"This I must see."

They climbed the stile and set off across the fields. They joined the track leading to Fell End and soon the farm came into view, half hidden by summer foliage on the wooded knoll. The Hartley Fells rose steeply beyond it less than a mile away. Jane stopped for a moment to take it all in and said, "It's so lovely Tat, come here, let me kiss you."

"Jane, let's sit down for a moment I want to talk to you." When they were settled on a fallen log by the side of the track he took her hand and said, "I don't quite know how to say this, but well, my mother, bless her, has got herself into a real old state about meeting you. She's not used to visitors, I suppose and, well, she's nervous."

Jane put her hand up to his cheek and smiling said, "Tat, my darling, I'm nervous too. I've been trying to find a way of telling you but I didn't want to worry you. I'm scared stiff. I mean what if your family don't like me, what then?"

Tat drew her to him and gathered her in his arms. Jane snuggled close and held him tight. When she looked up tears swam in her eyes. She wiped them away impatiently, "Oh blast, I mustn't cry or I'll have puffy eyes, that simply won't do."

"I had no idea you were nervous as well. You always seem so full of confidence. Look how you dealt with Nick La Rocca. Now he is scary, to me, at least."

"I know, I know," Jane said shaking her head and frowning. "The thing is Tat, my famous confidence has deserted me rather since that awful business with the dogs."

"Oh I see, well that's hardly surprising really."

"That's not all though," Jane said, and then taking Tat's face in both hands she looked deeply into his eyes and added, "Do you love me, truly love me?"

"You know I do. I adore you."

"I love you too, my darling, and that might cause trouble."

"How on earth could it?" Tat said, genuinely surprised.

"Listen, Mummy and I talked a lot when we were at home together. She asked me whether you and I loved each other. Of course I said I loved you to bits and that I was sure you felt the same."

Jane rummaged in her shoulder bag and found her tobacco tin. "Come on, let's have a fag." When they had both lit up, Jane went on. "She told me that some mothers, particularly with sons, could feel threatened when one of her boys brings a serious girlfriend onto the scene. Especially the youngest son, her baby."

"Good Lord, really? I don't think…" Tat said raising his eyebrows.

"No sweetheart let me try to explain. Mummy experienced this first hand when she and Daddy were courting. He is the youngest of three brothers, like you. His mother was very frosty towards Mummy and took quite some time to accept her and you know yourself how lovely Mummy is."

"She certainly is, I don't see how anyone could think otherwise."

"Exactly, neither do I. But that is how it was and Mummy says such a reaction is quite common and that I should be prepared."

"Well look, just stay close to me, I'm sure nothing like that will happen. Our Mam is just nervous, she's shy I suppose."

"Mummy said that the way she won her future mother-in-law over was to spend time alone with her, just the two of them. So that they could get to know each other properly. What do you think?"

"Well, I don't know, Mam might be even more jittery with just you alone I mean."

"What do you think she'll be doing after we get there? I mean what's her routine?"

"Well, she'll be preparing the sandwiches and such like for my brothers and Dad. She takes it out to whichever hayfield they're working in. It's a picnic really, I suppose."

"Oh good, when I was a Girl Guide I could make sandwiches for England. I'll help her and you can keep in the background. I'm sure it'll break the ice."

"Well, I don't see why not, then we can all go to the field together. You'll love our Dad, but be prepared for a bit of cheek from John and Michael. They're a bit of a handful."

"Come on, then," Jane stood up and straightened her linen skirt. "As long as you are within reach, I'm sure I can cope."

"Oh you'll cope alright," Tat said kissing her on both cheeks. "I just hope Mam can."

As they approached Fell End Jane said, "Now that will make a lovely painting, the stone farmstead on the wooded hill, perfection." The dogs gambolled around them as Tat and Jane crossed the yard, barking excitedly.

Ivy looked out of the window over the sink and patted her hair with shaking fingers. As she watched the beautiful girl fussing the dogs, a spasm of nerves churned through her stomach. She grimaced as the bow on her apron converted itself into a tight knot. As the back door opened down the passage she gave up trying to unravel it and cut the strings with the kitchen scissors. She thrust the apron into the cutlery drawer as Tat called out, "Hello, I've got a visitor for you." Tat led Jane into the kitchen, holding her hand.

"Mam, this is Jane," Tat said, wondering whether he wasn't the most anxious out of the three of them.

Ivy held out her hand formally and said, "How do you do." Jane shook hands and lent forward kissing Ivy on both cheeks.

"Oh Mrs Taylor," she said grinning broadly. "I'm so glad to meet you." Then looking around her, "My what a lovely big kitchen you have."

Ivy had submitted to the kisses stiffly and couldn't help noticing Jane's perfect white teeth and the whiff of expensive perfume which drifted around her.

"Aye well it'll be a bit old fashioned from what you're used to, I dare say but we manage well enough," Ivy said as the kettle began to whistle on the hob.

"Well, I think it's beautiful; will you let me paint it?"

"She means paint a picture of it Mam," Tat explained.

"Aye I know that much our Tat. I can't think why you'd want to lass, it's such a jumble of a place."

"Well, it's just so atmospheric; do say you'll let me draw it at least?" Jane said glancing anxiously in Tat's direction. Without answering, Ivy crossed over to pour hot water over the coffee grounds. She had borrowed a Victorian pewter pot from her mother, as she would have been ashamed of the old chipped enamel jug she normally brewed morning coffee in. Then she said, "Take the lass through to the parlour, our Tat. I've set out the coffee cups in there." Tat's heart sank, he had asked his mother not to take coffee in the parlour. He knew from past experience what a stultifying effect the room had upon people. It was too small to accommodate the over stuffed furniture and the piano, a black lacquered affair, which seemed to suck the light out of the room. He knew he was powerless to change the situation, however. Jane gave him a quick kiss on the cheek as Tat led her down the flagstone passage. Ivy caught a fleeting glimpse of this as she followed with the steaming coffee pot and pursed her lips.

Tat and Jane stood awkwardly whilst Ivy poured the coffee.

"Sit down, lass. Do you want milk and sugar?" Ivy said rather brusquely.

"Er, no thanks, I'll take it black, please," Jane said. She had been about to say what a pretty room the parlour was, but something told her not to. Instead she said, "Do you play the piano, Mrs Taylor?"

"Oh not really, I can knock out the odd tune. What about you?"

"Oh yes, I was put through the mill at school. I used to play a lot, mind you I have to have the music in front of me. I'm no good without it." Tat cringed as he realised just how beautifully spoken Jane was. He loved her perfect Home Counties accent but knew that in his mother's eyes it would mark Jane out as a posh southerner, an altogether alien species.

"Oh I didn't know you played," Tat said. "Maybe we can persuade you to play for us whilst you're here."

"Well, there's not much sheet music here," Ivy said unsmilingly.

"Never mind, we can borrow some of Mary's. I'm sure she won't mind, she's got reams of it."

"Well, I can't see that there'll be enough room for us all in here," Ivy continued, unable to shake off the negative sensation she'd felt ever since she had seen Jane plant a furtive kiss on Tat's cheek.

"Oh never mind Tat, really it doesn't matter," Jane said anxious to change the subject. She was beginning to feel the tension in the air.

"I'll tell you what, we'll move the piano into the kitchen one night; there's bags of room in there," Tat said eagerly.

Ivy Taylor glanced up at the grandfather clock and stood up, again without responding. "Well, I'd best get started on the sandwiches and such like; they'll be starving as usual."

"Oh do let me help," Jane said. She reached out to pick up the tray but Ivy beat her to it and left the parlour abruptly, the coffee cups rattling against each other. Tat looked helplessly at Jane and shrugged his shoulders in bewilderment. Jane took a deep breath and in a low voice said, "Tat leave this to me, why don't you go and find this piece of string you told me about?"

"But listen, I can't just..."

Jane stepped across and gently placed her hand over his lips, cutting him short. "My darling, trust me; I think I know what your mother is going through. Please leave me with her for a bit."

When Tat and Jane entered the kitchen Ivy was placing a large loaf of bread, baked that morning on a much-used board in the middle of the table.

"Have you got a spare apron I could borrow?" Jane asked.

"Nay lass, you don't want to be mucking about making sandwiches," Ivy said bringing a huge chunk of cheese and a slab of butter from the pantry. Then added, "Tat show her around the farm while I get stuck in."

"Oh don't worry he's going to find something he wants to show me, a piece of string he never stops talking about it."

Tat hovered in the kitchen doorway unsure what to do for the best.

"Now then how many slices do you want me to cut? I was telling Tat that I was regarded as the top sandwich maker in the troop when I was a Girl Guide," she looked across at Tat and added, "Go on Tat, we'll be finished in here before you've even started your search."

Tat made his way up the passage to the outside door with a heavy heart. Jane picked up the bread knife which lay alongside the loaf and began to cut it into neat slices with surprising dexterity. Ivy watched her for a second or two struggling to overcome the mixed emotions surging through her. She shook her head and crossed over to the big dresser and opening a drawer selected a clean apron. Ivy unfolded it and stood by Jane's side. After a pause she said,

"Here lass, put this on or you'll muck up that bonnie outfit. I'll say one thing you can cut bread and no mistake."

Jane lay the knife aside and put the apron on. The two of them looked at each other in silence. Jane reached across and took both Ivy's hands in hers, she felt tears prickling against her eyelids and a lump was forming in her throat. "Do try to like me," she said falteringly, "I so want you to."

Ivy was shocked to see the distress in the girl's face. She had made up her mind that with her fancy posh accent and gushing manner that they could never get along. How could they when they were so different? Her father, with his lavish gift of wine, obviously had more money than sense. The beautiful hazel eyes swimming with unshed tears and the lower lip quivering, were suddenly all that mattered. She was a guest in her home; invited there by her favourite son and she, through her own stubborn, jealous behaviour, had almost made her cry. As Tat had said, she was only a lass, not a duchess.

Ivy melted and said, "Nay lass come here to me," she enveloped Jane in her arms. "There, there, never mind me love, I'm that nervous I don't know what I'm saying."

Ivy stepped back a pace and held Jane at arm's length. Two big fat tears slid over those sculpted cheekbones, Ivy reached up and wiped them away with her thumbs. Cupping Jane's face gently in her hands, Ivy said, "By Jove, but you're a beauty, lass, I've never seen the like before and that's the truth." Then she added, "Now then butter the bread while I slice the cheese."

Jane, to Ivy's surprise, did prove to be an expert sandwich maker. So much so that she left Jane to apply the homemade chutney and arrange the sandwiches into neatly ordered stacks. She brought an earthenware jug from the pantry and filled it with home made lemonade.

"Now then," Ivy said at last, "we'll wrap everything up in these cloths to keep the sun off."

Jane sensed that the worst was past and as she helped Ivy load everything into two large wicker baskets she asked, "Mrs Taylor, what can I call you? Apart from Mrs Taylor of course, I mean it seems so formal don't you think?"

As Ivy spread the red and white checked cloths over the contents of each basket she paused for a moment then said, "Aye you're right it does sound a bit stuffy, call me Ivy that'll do the trick."

Tat sneaked an anxious glance through the side window of the kitchen before entering the passage door. He saw Jane and his mother chatting easily enough and noticed that the picnic was all packed up and ready to go.

Ivy looked up as he came into the kitchen and said, "Just in time our Tat, we're going to need your brawn to carry this lot over to the meadow, aren't we lass?"

"I should say so. It all weighs a ton." She gave Tat a furtive wink of reassurance without his mother noticing.

"Look," Tat said relieved, "Just let me lay this out along the passage before we go."

"What on earth have you got there, lad?" Ivy asked.

As Tat stretched the length of string over the flagstones he said, "Well, I don't think you've ever seen this Mam. It's the bit of string we measured Bill Fletcher's height with when we were little kids. You see the blue chalk mark, well from there to the stone tied at the end is seven feet nine inches."

"Surely that's impossible, Tat? Nobody could be so enormous could they Ivy?"

Tat's spirits lifted as he heard Jane use his mother's Christian name. They must have reached some sort of accord after all.

"Nay lass, Bill Fletcher was a real giant. A freak of nature I suppose. Poor devil, he never had any real harm in him. He just didn't know what he was doing, did he Tat?"

"I suppose not. I've told Jane the story, but I'm not sure she believes it."

"Well I must say it takes some swallowing," Jane said.

"Oh it's all true. I'll never forget it till the day I die."

"Oh well I must stand corrected," Jane smiled.

"I should think so too," Tat said, retrieving the string and stuffing it into his pocket. "After all, I could hardly make it up now could I?"

"Oh I wouldn't put it past you," Jane said giving him a playful poke in the ribs.

Tat took the bigger of the two baskets whilst his mother and Jane carried the other between them. As they made their way across the yard, Ivy said, "As it happens Patrick Kenny and his oldest lad are helping with the hay, Jane might get his side of the story."

Tat explained to Jane that Patrick Kenny was the father of the baby Bill had carried off.

"Aye," Ivy continued, "he often helps with the haymaking does Patrick. He and Hannah went on to have three more bairns, all lads. His eldest, Liam, is the spitting image of his Mam."

"Ah now I remember," Jane said. "Hannah, she's the beautiful gipsy lady who smoked a pipe."

"Aye lass, she still does," Ivy said laughing. They entered a wood and followed a well-worn path through the dappled shade, rabbits scuttled away amongst the brambles on all sides. Three of the farm dogs had accompanied them and gave chase barking noisily. When they emerged into the sunlight once more the fell sides were noticeably closer, dotted with outcrops of boulders and criss-crossed with ancient sheep tracks. Below them were several hay fields flanked by dry stonewalls. The grass in the nearest of these had been cut and turned two days previously, taking advantage of the hot dry weather.

Tat was surprised to see that the hay had already been raked into dozens of stooks. John and Michael were forking these up onto the big cart where Patrick Kenny and his eldest boy, Liam, were distributing it evenly to make a sound load, which wouldn't shift. Tat's father was leading the big Clydesdale between the rows, pausing briefly as fresh fork loads of hay were passed aloft. Tat opened the field gate and set his basket down. He put two fingers lightly on the tip of his tongue and whistled loudly. The sound echoed around the fell sides as the haymakers looked up and waved.

"We'll set up shop over yonder," Ivy said, pointing along the wall to a generous patch of shade under a big sycamore. The dogs rushed off to greet the men who by now had stacked their rakes and pitch forks on the ground. Tat's father led the horse and half loaded cart to another patch of shade in the nearest corner of the field where a stone water trough was set in the wall. Meanwhile, John had thrown Michael's cap amongst the dogs; they scampered off tossing it between them. The brothers gave chase pushing and shoving each other. John howled with laughter as the dogs almost let Michael retrieve his cap before rushing off with it once more.

"They don't get any better do they?" Jack Taylor said as he drew near, then added, "So this will be Jane, I presume."

Jane, who had been helping Ivy lay out the food on the checked cloths, stood up and smiling broadly said, "And I presume that you are Tat's dad. I'm very pleased to meet you."

Tat stood by quietly, reassured that Jane had regained some of her confidence. She held out her hand which his father shook warmly. Tat winced slightly when she bent forward to kiss his father on either sunburnt cheek but was relieved to notice how delighted he was by the gesture.

"Pleased to meet you, lass," Jack said, touching his cheek with his fingers. "It's a good job I found time to shave this morning."

"Do I get a kiss an' all then?" John gasped wiping the sweat from his forehead with a grubby spotted handkerchief. He had trotted across to join them, leaving Michael to retrieve his cap on his own account.

"This terrible article is our John," Tat said, grinning.

"How do lass," John said, shaking Jane's outstretched hand. Then, quick as a flash he planted a kiss on each of her cheeks taking her completely by surprise. "There you are," John said grinning cheekily. "I've saved you the bother." They all laughed while Jane pretended to be more astonished than she really was. Tat thought she might be blushing slightly.

"Pleased to meet you, John. Tat warned me that you were a bit of a scallywag," Jane said.

"Who me? Never in this world," John said flopping down in the shade. "Now then, our Mam, what have you got for us? I'm starving."

"Just you hold on till Michael gets his cap back. Goodness only knows what a state it'll be in. Here have a drink of lemonade to be going on with."

Meanwhile, Patrick Kenny and Liam had joined them, having splashed their faces with cold water from the trough where the horse was tethered.

"Now then lads," Jack said, "This here is Jane, our Tat's friend from down south."

"Glad to meet you Miss." Patrick muttered; Liam was too shy to speak but managed to smile briefly and nod his head. Tat couldn't imagine how the gypsies would have reacted if Jane had gone across and shaken their hands, let alone kiss their cheeks. Luckily she did neither, but smiled warmly instead, and said, "Hello, pleased to meet you."

By teatime the effects of the eight-hour train journey from Kings Cross caught up with Jane. Tat walked her back to Winton before the family gathered for supper in the kitchen. She was so tired that she went straight to bed without anything to eat.

The next morning, after Tat had collected Jane from Mary's cottage and they joined the farm track leading to Fell End, Tat asked Jane what she would like to do with the day.

"There's plenty of choice. We could help with the hay, water the stock and collect the eggs, or take a hike onto the fell tops, or you could do some drawing."

"How clever of you," Jane said, tapping her shoulder bag. "I've got my sketch book and drawing stuff in here. I want to draw you lot in the hay field. I know you'll be expected to help out, so it will kill two birds with one stone, won't it?"

"Fair enough. We'll just pop in to say hello to Mam, then get straight over there."

"I'll sketch for a couple of hours, then go back to help your mum with the picnic. I think she trusts me enough now, don't you?" Jane said, then squealed with delight as she saw the farm dogs racing towards them barking madly.

The big cart was filling up fast with the remaining stooks. One haystack had been completed in the furthest corner of the field and a second was well on the way. Jane waved over to the haymakers as Tat joined them. She positioned herself in the patch of shade under the sycamore and began to draw the scene.

Later, Jane called down the passage as she let herself in at the side door and found Ivy brewing coffee in the kitchen. Ivy looked over her shoulder and smiled.

"Hello, lass, I've just made some coffee, sit yourself down."

"Gosh, what a lovely day it is. They finished that field; Michael and John say they'll have the one next door cut by the time we take the picnic over. They say they'll press-gang me into turning it or something, after lunch."

Ivy poured the coffee and said, "Aye, it's not as easy as it looks lass; you'll get blisters for a start off."

Jane, who had put her sketchbook on the table, began to make a roll-up. Ivy watched, still unsure as to whether it was appropriate for a well brought up young woman to be doing such a thing.

"What's that then?" she asked, nodding towards the sketchbook.

"Oh, I've been doing some drawing; have a look. I've done quite a lot actually. I'm rather pleased with them," Jane said, lighting her cigarette.

Ivy opened the sketchbook. It was a new one which Jane had started that very morning.

"Good lord, these are marvellous," Ivy said, shaking her head. "I had no idea you could do owt like this; they're so life-like."

"Oh I'm glad you approve. It's a super subject, especially in that setting, you know, with the stone walls and the fells beyond."

"You've done so many. There's eight all together in what, two hours? I never knew that was possible. Wait till Jack and the lads see these; they'll be thrilled."

"Well, I've got quite fired up by it all. Sometimes it just comes out right, I'd really like to develop them into a painting or two, perhaps later."

"Well, our Tat has always said how gifted you are, in his letters like, I see what he means now."

They were soon stuck into making the sandwiches. When the bulk of it was done, Jane retrieved her sketchbook and said, "You know I asked you if I could draw in here? Would you mind if I did a quick study now, before we go across to the field?"

"Well, I still think it's a funny old set up lass, but you do as you like." She spread the gingham cloths over the contents of the baskets.

After a few minutes, Jane said, "Look Ivy, they won't miss us for ten minutes, sit down opposite me. I'd like to put you in the drawing."

"Nay lass, you don't want to be wasting your paper on me, whatever next." She had already seen what Jane was capable of, however, and rather surprised herself by sitting at the opposite side of the table. "I'd better get rid of this apron. I must look an awful fright."

"No please, just as you are, trust me."

Ivy settled back with a slight shake of her head. "Well what do you want me to do, lass? I can't just sit here like a pudding."

"Fold your hands on the table and look towards the window. That's it, lovely, now leave the rest to me." Jane began to draw using a soft conte crayon.

Once she had established the basic composition, Jane drained her coffee cup and poured them both a refill. "No, don't you move," she said firmly, "I'll do it. Do talk if you like."

"How are you settled at Mary's cottage then?" Ivy asked after a pause.

"Oh very well, thanks," Jane said, choosing a finer crayon from the pencil box. "She's a lovely person, and obviously thinks the world of you all."

"Aye she's a grand lass and she's been that good to Tat. In a way, she's the one that set him on his road." She had begun to relax, as she realized that sitting still doing nothing for a while was actually rather enjoyable. Ivy hesitated for a moment or two and said, "It was ever so kind of your father to send us all that wine. Will you thank him for us?"

"Well, I was surprised as well, I can tell you," Jane said, rubbing at the paper with her thumb. "Daddy was so grateful to Tat and Olly for being so brave. They saved our bacon you know. Goodness knows what would have happened otherwise."

Beyond This Horizon

"How's your mother coping now and yourself for that matter?" Ivy asked gently.

Jane swallowed hard and her face puckered. She put her hand up to her forehead. "Oh Ivy, it was just so horrible; I don't think we'll ever forget it."

"Oh there, there lass, don't upset yourself." She got up and put her arms around Jane's shoulders. Jane leaned her head against Ivy as a few tears slid down her cheeks.

"Nay love, I shouldn't have asked. I'm sorry here, use my apron."

"No, no, I'm too sensitive," she dabbed her eyes.

"Well, I never," Ivy said suddenly. "Just look at what you've done; how on earth do you do it so fast? That's me alright, in my own kitchen. By Jove, you're so clever."

Jane had found her handkerchief and blew her nose, then smiling broadly, she asked, "Oh do you approve? I'm so glad."

"I think it's grand. Fancy me having my portrait done, whatever next?"

"Would you like to have it, Ivy? It would please me so much."

"Oh thank you, lass," Ivy said excitedly. "I'll treasure it forever." She hugged Jane and kissed her warmly on the cheek. She held both Jane's hands. "I'm sorry I made such a mess when you arrived yesterday, lass. I was so nervous I didn't know what I was doing."

"I bet you weren't half as nervous as I was," said Jane. They both laughed and hugged each other again.

During the picnic under the sycamore Ivy asked Jane to show the men the drawings she had done that morning. As the sketchbook was passed around Jane quickly became the centre of attention.

"I tell you what, you'll be making a fortune before too long if this lot is owt to go by," Jack said.

"You should see her paintings; they really are something," said Tat.

"She does them so fast," Michael said, scratching his head. "I always thought it took ages to get detail like this. I wouldn't care, but we're all on the move all the time."

Tat could see that Jane was thrilled to gain the approval of them all. Just then, John said, "Have you seen this one of our Mam at the back here? She got you to the life, Mam." John held the sketchbook up, opened at the crayon drawing of Ivy in the kitchen. They all crowded together, stooping forward, to get a good look.

"It's a real cracker, Jane," Tat said, "You've made it so life-like, it's wonderful."

"Aye and she's giving it to me to keep as well," Ivy said, beaming. Any residual anxiety Tat still had drifted away as he watched his mother smiling. It was going to be alright, with a bit of luck.

A CHANCE MEETING AT THE R.A.

After spending four days with her family in Kent, Jane returned to London. She was keen to start the portrait of Nick La Rocca and needed the peace and quiet of the flat in Fawcett Street to concentrate wholly on the project. All her drawings of La Rocca were there, along with her materials and equipment. As she spread dustsheets over the carpet to protect it from spillages, she remembered that the Royal Academy Summer Exhibition was in full swing. She decided to go to the show there and then, it might help to sharpen her vision to look at a cross section of paintings before starting the portrait.

The forecourt of Burlington House was thronged with well-dressed people in summer clothes. Many of the women carried parasols to protect them from the bright sunlight. Jane wore a loose cotton frock that showed off her tan, which had become quite pronounced during her stay in Westmorland. Jane knew that a suntan was regarded as unfashionable, but she felt that her glowing brown skin suited her and made her feel healthy and relaxed. As she picked her way through the crowd she wondered what reaction some of these elegant women might have if they knew that her tan covered her body from head to toe.

On several occasions she had undressed when Tat had taken her off on expeditions up the fells. He would find a secluded spot and keep watch while she sunbathed naked in the unlikely possibility that a shepherd or hiker might pass by. He had convinced her that nobody would be about in such high, deserted places. She would never forget the excitement of feeling the hot sun and the light breeze on her skin. It had been so special to be alone with Tat on the high fells where they could talk about anything they liked and make love on the springy turf.

She had so enjoyed getting to know Tat's family. After the first awkward period with Tat's mother, she had got on with her like a house on fire. They prepared the daily picnics together as well as the evening meals, chatting and joking easily as if they had known each other for years. Jane had been genuinely surprised to discover that her father had sent the generous gift of wine to the Taylors. Supper times were noisy and cheerful affairs with the three brothers constantly teasing each other. The piano had eventually been moved into the kitchen. Mary Hollis was only too glad to let Jane select examples of sheet music from her considerable collection, so that she could entertain the family when the supper things were cleared away. Mary had cycled up to Fell End on two occasions to join them all for supper. She had insisted that Tat sing for them, knowing as she did what pieces to select to show off his voice at its best.

The lobby of the Royal Academy was cool after the heat of the forecourt. Jane showed her Slade student card at the desk after queuing for several minutes and was delighted to gain entry to the exhibition for half the normal price. She bought a catalogue and climbed the wide staircase which was crowded with visitors talking animatedly. This was only her third visit to the summer exhibition and as ever she was stunned by the spacious elegance of the place. Owing to the sheer size of the galleries there seemed to be less of a crush and most conversations were carried out in hushed tones.

Jane found plenty of portraits to study, most of which were far too rigid and stuffy for her liking. She took her time concentrating on examples in which the paint was used loosely and the pose of the sitter less conventional. After about an hour she entered the round gallery at the centre of the exhibition and there it was. Jane stopped dead in her tracks, her heart thudding against her ribs. On the opposite wall some twenty feet away from where she stood was the life-size portrait of Efua. She approached the picture with faltering steps and stood gazing at it, transfixed by its smouldering sensuality. She had forgotten what a marvellous piece of painting it was, the lustrous brown skin seemed to possess an inner glow. As she looked into the beautiful, deep-set eyes she recognised the hint of secret knowledge there, which had so unnerved her during the previous winter.

"Well, now you and Efua are not far off the same colour. The summer suits you." Jane almost jumped out of her skin. Giles Clinton was standing only a couple of feet behind her and when he saw how shaken she was he placed a hand under her elbow and said, "I'm sorry I didn't mean to alarm you, my dear. Here, come and sit down for a minute." He led her over to one of the green leather benches in the middle of the gallery.

"Gosh, you took me completely by surprise, Giles. I didn't expect to see you here."

"Well, I don't know why not, I am a member of the place after all," Giles said, smiling broadly. "I'm sorry I made you jump, forgive me."

"No, no, I'm just being silly. How are you, Giles?" without waiting for an answer she added, "The painting looks fantastic; it's by far the best thing here."

"Why thank you, Jane. That is praise indeed coming from such a talented painter. You'll notice it has a red dot next to it."

Jane looked back at the picture. "Why so it has, congratulations. Do you know who has bought it?"

"Well actually I've just met him in the member's bar, that's why I'm here today. He's a Swiss collector, nice fellow and filthy rich of course." He looked at Jane for moment, and then said, "Let me show you my other pieces."

Giles led Jane into the adjoining gallery where his other five exhibits were grouped together on one wall. There were four spectacular landscapes painted in Italy and Corsica and, to Jane's amazement, one of the charcoal drawings he had made of her in his studio all those months ago. All the pictures, except the drawing, had red dots stuck to their frames.

They stood in silence. Jane was trying to reconcile conflicting emotions. She gazed at the image of herself with her bare shoulders and cleavage emphasised by the dramatic lighting, her face, seen in profile, half hidden by tousled hair tumbling free.

"I hope you don't mind my exhibiting the drawing, but it means a lot to me." Giles said. Jane was still trying to adjust to the image of herself in such an intimate condition being on display in a very public place.

After a pause she said, "Gosh no, of course not, it's a wonderful drawing. I see it's still unsold."

"That's because it's not for sale. I don't want to part with it."

"Oh I see, well I'm very flattered," Jane said, not entirely sure of herself.

"I chose this one because with your hair falling across your face, no one would necessarily know that it was you. I suppose only you and I know that it is."

"Yes, I suppose so. It's just as well, because my mother and father will visit the exhibition over the next few weeks." They both laughed, which lightened the atmosphere.

"You look well, my dear, with that wonderful tan you look positively Mediterranean."

"Why thank you, I love the sun, always have."

"Look, do you fancy a drink; we could go to the members' bar? It was almost deserted when I left there ten minutes ago."

"Why yes I'd love to. I can tell my friends that I've been, they'll be ever so impressed."

Giles ordered two Pimms from the waiter as they settled themselves at a table next to a window, which overlooked the forecourt. The room stretched the full width of the building's façade and was lined with dark oak panelling. Portraits of past presidents of the Academy hung at five-foot intervals around the walls.

"Do you know there's not one decent portrait amongst the lot of them?" Giles said in a stage whisper.

"That's a pity, especially if you consider where we are."

"Well, I've been approached to do the next one, as it happens. I'm damned sure I can knock one out that's better than this lot." Giles said, lighting a cheroot, and then added, "Tell me, do you still roll your own smokes?"

"Yes I do. Can I get away with it in here do you think?"

"Of course you can. Do you know, I got to learn how to roll my own in Morocco back in the spring? They smoke hashish there;

makes you as high as a kite, lasts for hours, absolute heaven. I brought a bag of it back with me."

Giles lit Jane's roll up with his lighter, and said, "Drink up, let's have another; they do make a lovely Pimms here, don't you agree?"

"Absolutely, they're delicious," Jane said, draining her glass.

Whilst the waiter fetched the drinks, Giles leaned forward and placed his hand over hers across the table, "I've never stop thinking about you, not for one moment."

Jane surprised herself by leaving her hand under his, enjoying the sudden warmth and weight of it. Despite herself, the sound of his husky Irish voice had the same almost hypnotic effect on her as it always had, especially at close quarters. She glanced around the room and realised they were its only occupants apart from the waiter and barman. As Giles lent further forward his knee came into contact with one of her own. She saw that Giles noticed what had happened, but didn't move her leg away.

"I'm crazy about you, you know that don't you?"

"Giles you shouldn't talk to me this way," Jane said.

"Why not, it happens to be true."

Jane felt light headed and took a deep gulp of her Pimms, fighting to restore her composure, she said, "Giles this is impossible, you're a married man with children, remember."

"I've left them. I couldn't carry on with it. As I said Jane, I've never stopped thinking about you."

"You've left them! When for goodness sake?"

"Soon after you walked out on me. Don't worry; they're very well catered for. They live in Ireland now and want for nothing. I'm not a cruel man Jane, you of all people ought to know that."

"No of course not, I didn't mean to imply that, not ever. Anyway, things have changed."

"Not for me they haven't. I've got a thirst on me like the very Devil," Giles said, draining his glass. He signalled to the waiter to bring two more Pimms. He lit another cheroot and sat back in his chair, stretching out his long legs under the table. The waiter brought their third Pimms. Giles picked up his glass greedily and after clinking it against Jane's, took a big gulp and wiped his mouth with the back of his hand.

"Christ!" he said. "Just look at you, I could eat you, you look so good." He glanced over his shoulder to check on the whereabouts of the waiter and barman. Satisfied that, with his back to them, they would not be able to guess what was happening, he leaned forward and placed his right hand upon her knee, slowly sliding it half way up her inner thigh, caressing her silky tanned skin. She didn't resist and felt her heart begin to pound.

"I know you want me Jane, just by the look of you. Go on say it."

Jane felt lightheaded and feared she might faint clean away. The power of the man's lust was irresistible.

"Damn you, Giles, you know me too well," Jane said, taking a long slow breath. "Alright I'll say it, I want you, the sooner the better." Her voice was decidedly hoarse.

"Come on then," he said. "Let's get out of here and find a cab."

During the afternoon and into the evening, back at 23 Neale Street they ravaged each other in a frenzy of passion neither of them thought possible. Giles rolled cigarettes filled with the hashish he had brought back from Morocco. Jane revelled in the dreamy sensations the drug induced in her; everything was more intense and seemed to last forever. Eventually, utterly exhausted, they slept, sprawling naked together on the bed.

A substantial living area had been constructed in a far corner of the studio. Over coffee the next morning Giles explained that he had had it installed after he had moved out of the family home in Highgate. He'd lived in the studio since then and explained what a pleasure it was to be so close to his work.

"I know you've got a boyfriend," Giles said, pouring more strong black coffee. "I've seen you out and about with him. He's a fine looking lad."

Jane raised her eyebrows in surprise, "I hope you haven't been spying on me?"

"Well, perhaps a little bit. I just wanted to catch a glimpse of you before I set off on my travels and I saw you two or three times around Gower Street with the boy, arm in arm."

Jane blushed. "It just happened I suppose; I wanted a relationship I could be open about, with someone my own age. Something I didn't feel guilty about."

"I don't blame you; it can't have been easy for you coming here in secret like a thief in the night and me being married and all."

"No it wasn't. I mean I couldn't talk to anyone about you, I felt trapped by it all."

Giles lit a cheroot and looked at Jane though the curling blue smoke, then said, "Now listen to me, my girl. I had no idea what we did yesterday was going to happen. But I have no regrets, I loved every minute of it."

Jane was wearing one of the silk dressing gowns which Efua had used. She pulled it aside and displayed her tanned legs.

"That's the trouble, Giles" she said ruefully, "Neither do I."

On her return to Fawcett Street she had been overwhelmed by guilt. How could she have allowed herself to do such things with the very man she had escaped from all those months ago? She groaned with mortification at the memory of the orgy back at his studio. Was she a fundamentally flawed person?

On the third day after beginning the portrait of Nick LaRocca in her bedroom, Jane admitted to herself that she would not be able to stay away from Giles. The intensity of her desire for him was simply overpowering and with every passing hour proving impossible to resist.

She had been so relieved to find that Tat wanted her and that she had become so close to him so quickly. She had taken it for granted that she loved Tat and had even begun to consider that one day they might get married and have children. Her family liked him, especially after he had been so calm and brave that dreadful day with the dogs. Her visit to Fell End had been wonderful. The Taylors had welcomed her with open arms. Tears slid down her cheeks at the memories of her sunbathing, way up on the fells with Tat patiently keeping watch. He had proved to be a kind and considerate lover, never selfish or over demanding. She had become used to his ways as time went on, and perhaps had even grown complacent, subduing her darker side, which had now been stirred again. Thinking back to the ease with which she had surrendered to the thrusting overture at the Royal Academy, she put her brushes aside and stood them in turpentine, before rolling herself a cigarette. Despite herself, she bathed and dressed with provocative care, before catching the 14 bus to Bloomsbury.

ASSISTING EPSTEIN

Olly had spent most of the summer working for Jacob Epstein in his studio at 23 Guildford Street. Epstein was engaged in a substantial carving in Portland stone to be sited in Hyde Park. It was a memorial to the author and naturalist W. H. Hudson, and depicted a powerful female figure set amongst stylized birds and foliage. Olly was engaged in making plaster casts of numerous portraits which Epstein had been commissioned to carry out. He was good at the job and in the main Epstein left him alone to carry on, with just the odd suggestion as to how to proceed now and again. He was responsible for keeping the various clay models in exactly the right state of malleability. At the end of each day he cleared up the studio, coping especially with the large amounts of stone chippings resulting from Epstein's vigorous carving technique.

Occasionally, Olly took selected plaster-cast portraits to the Art Bronze Foundry at the far end of the Kings Road in Chelsea. He would pack the casts into tea chests surrounded by layers of screwed up newspaper and when he was fully prepared, go out into the street and hail a cab. The people at the foundry treated him respectfully, as he was clearly a trusted employee of Epstein, who was becoming very well known throughout the art world. Epstein himself, however, often complained about how badly he was treated by the London establishment. Not only was his sculpture seen as being too radical and confrontational, but his being an American and Jewish seemed to cause problems as well.

Olly liked him enormously; he was funny and spoke plainly with a wonderful New York accent, and above all he was terrifically hard working, something Olly considered himself to be. Epstein was the ultimate direct carver in stone, utterly contemptuous of those sculptors who still used pointing-machines and employed masons to knock out their carvings for them. Epstein made drawings and maquettes to work out his ideas and then tackled the stone, head on, doing all the work himself.

When Olly delivered casts to the foundry it gave him an opportunity to check up on the progress of the bronze cast of Tat's portrait. He had been amazed to receive 250 pounds from Jane's father during the early weeks of the summer. In the letter which accompanied the money, Mr Cranshaw had explained how grateful the family were for the part he and Tat had played in saving them from the Ridgebacks. He added that he knew from Jane how keen he was to have his portrait of Tat cast into bronze and that he hoped the money would cover the costs at the foundry of his choice. Olly had been staggered at this act of generosity; it was the answer to his dreams.

He had expected to scrimp and save throughout the summer, in an attempt to amass enough money to approach a London foundry. Now he had seen the wax version of the portrait and applied the finishing touches to it at the Art Bronze Foundry. In another two weeks it would join the next batch of moulds to be filled with top quality moulten bronze. Another two weeks after that the portrait would be finished and ready for patinating. He had been asked to be present during this final process to ensure that he got the exact colour he wanted. He wrote to Jane's father thanking him profusely and promising to keep him informed about the progress being made at the foundry.

In her letters to Tat, Jane found, to her surprise and shame, that she could cover her tracks with relative ease. She was able to keep her letters light and chatty. Initially, she described the progress of her oil painting of Nick La Rocca, explaining how she had constructed the painting from the drawings she had made in Jack Douthewaite's flat. The project was going well, she wrote, and was occupying most of her time. Although she had only spent a few days with her family on her return from Westmorland, she told Tat that she spent the weekends in Kent. Her family were all well, she wrote, and sent him their love. Jane found that she could express her love and affection for Tat in ways that seemed natural and sincere. Indeed, they were sincere; she did love him and missed him. At the heart of it all, however, she was only too conscious of her treachery with Giles.

As the weeks went by, Jane was ever more aware of the summer vacation drawing to a close. She was committed to joining her family during the last two weeks of August for their annual cruise. Her father kept a sea-going yacht at Folkestone and at the same time every year the whole family spent two weeks sailing down the French coast. He and his sons were experienced sailors but usually hired the same local crew every summer. Jane, up until now, regarded it as the high point of the year.

She dreaded the return of Tat at the start of the new term. Try as she might, she just didn't know how she was going to deal with it. Should she simply tell Tat that she was sorry but she was no longer able to be his girlfriend? Should she tell Tat the truth of what had occurred since her return to London? What if she took the most deceitful route of all and tricked Tat into believing everything was as before? Was she capable of doing such a thing? Could she have two men in her life? One young and honourable, the other old enough to be her father. The trouble was, she couldn't discuss any of this or seek advice of one sort or another. Certainly she couldn't approach the subject with her mother, and not even with Nicola; it was just too shameful, all of it. Somehow she had to find her own way out of the mess she had created.

It was Giles who insisted that they go out for a walk one evening. They had drunk champagne and the weather was hot and sultry. He said that they both needed some fresh air and suggested that they stroll down to Soho. Jane was hesitant at first but she was rather drunk and Giles wouldn't take no for an answer. She had always assumed that they shouldn't venture out together in case they were seen by somebody who would recognize them.

David Thompson

A SHOCK FOR OLLY

Epstein decided to accompany Olly to the bronze foundry. They took a taxi and loaded two boxed plaster portraits on board in the boot. By now Olly was assured that Epstein was the Art Bronze Foundry's best client. He had a more or less continuous run of bronzes all at various stages of the casting process going through the place. Olly was looking forward to viewing his portrait of Tat which he had been told was completely finished, apart from being patinated.

Epstein was treated with a great deal of respect. Mr Gaskin, the owner, shook hands with him and several of the workers took off their caps whilst talking to him. Four of Epstein's portraits were ready to patinate and stood in a row on turntables. Olly's piece was placed a few feet to the left, glowing brassily and fully fettled. Whilst Epstein discussed his bronzes Olly inspected Tat's portrait at close quarters. He was thrilled by the high quality of the workmanship. Every nuance of his modelling technique was faithfully captured in the metal. He even traced several of his finger prints amongst the textured surface. He picked the sculpture up and was surprised as to how light it was. It was a very good, thin casting.

"So what colour have your decided on, Olly?" Epstein asked joining him, "I must say it's a beautiful, clean job."

"I know, I'm so pleased with it. Oh, I thought I'd have a classic brown patination; you know like an old penny."

"Well yes, it would be a safe solution. But why not be a bit more adventurous and try a mottled green over brown?"

"Well," Olly said doubtfully, "I don't know if I dare risk it. I thought of trying to enter it at the Royal Academy Summer Show next year. They might not approve of anything too radical."

Epstein laughed out loud at this. He made a point of making his sculpture as radical as possible. He was a modernist and saw it as his duty to push the barriers of the subject.

"Well, it's up to you my lad, but remember you're young, right at the start of your career, be willing to chance your arm and take a risk."

Epstein turned to Mr Gaskin and asked, "Have we time to patinate these now, before your boys go home?"

"Oh yes, we'll work a bit late if necessary." Then, turning to Bill Gaunt, his top metal worker he said, "Come on then Bill, get this lot heated up and let's get cracking."

Bill got two of his lads to play blowtorches over Epstein's portraits whilst he sorted out his bottles of chemicals. When the bronzes were hot enough he brushed various combinations onto the hot metal. The liquid spat and steamed as it bit into the hot casts and filled the place with acrid, eye watering fumes.

Epstein got visibly excited as the bronzes darkened, pointing out areas which Bill had missed, especially in the undercuts. Gradually, Olly saw the green emerge over the dark brown as if by magic. There was even a hint of dark blue amongst the mottling by the time the process was completed.

"So what do you think, Olly?" Epstein said beaming broadly. "They look like some of those Greek sculptures that have been under the sea for centuries, don't you think?"

"They look terrific. You've convinced me. I'll have mine done the same way please."

Within half an hour, Tat's portrait was still steaming, with the same mottled green patination, whilst Epstein's casts were being waxed before polishing. The wax had a similar effect upon the patination as varnish does on oil paint. It enriched the colours and brought out the texture to a remarkable degree. When the bronzes were cool enough to be buffed up with a soft shoe brush they were positively lustrous.

Epstein was so pleased that he gave one of the lads a fiver and said, "Pop out and get a bottle of whisky, kid. We need to celebrate."

The whisky had gone down a treat. The foundry men had jostled their teacups together on a grimy workbench and Epstein had poured everyone a generous measure. Cigarettes were lit up, as they tasted the first round. There was enough in the bottle to supply them all with a second shot apiece. A lighthearted atmosphere quickly developed which was heightened still further when Epstein gave each worker a gold sovereign. Not Mr Gaskin however; as the foundry owner, he was regarded as above such largesse. Arrangements were made to have the bronzes delivered to the studio, including Tat's portrait.

To Olly's surprise when they were settled in a taxi for their return journey Epstein said, "Let's go for a drink or two. What do you say? Maybe have a bite of supper?"

They were dropped off at the Queen's Elm in the Fulham Road. The pub was already crowded, despite the fact that it had only been open half an hour. The Queen's Elm was a favourite watering hole for artists, literary folk and actors. As Epstein led the way to the bar he was greeted effusively on all sides. "Let's have beer," he said. "That scotch has made me as dry as a cactus."

"Oh thanks," Olly said. "That will do nicely."

"Jacob, my boy, we don't see you in here very often, how are you?"

A tall, thin man with tousled, shoulder length hair and wild eyes had thrown his arm around Epstein's shoulders. "Augustus," Epstein said grinning, "I might have known you'd be in here at this early hour."

"Well, I couldn't stand another minute in the studio; it's like an oven in there," the tall man replied.

"Oh yes, any excuse, eh," Epstein replied, then added, "Oh Olly, this reprobate is Augustus John, the painter."

"How do you do," Olly said and shook hands. "I've seen you before actually; you came to one of our sketch clubs at the Slade last year."

"Oh yes, so I did," John replied. "It was rather good fun as I recall. So are you a student at the old place?"

"Yes I'm in the sculpture department, one more year to go."

"Actually, Olly is an outstanding sculptor; he's working for me this summer," Epstein said wiping beer froth from his mouth.

"Oh I see, well you have my deepest sympathy," John said to Olly, "Jacob has a fully deserved reputation as a slave driver."

"Absolute rubbish," Epstein said, "take no notice of him, Olly."

"Oh I like hard work," Olly said, "I suppose I sort of thrive on it."

"Actually, we've just left the Art Bronze Foundry. We've been watching them patinate a clutch of bronzes, one of which was Olly's. It really is outstanding; you should see it."

"Well, well, how impressive, not many young chaps of your age manage to get their work into bronze," John said. He had lit a hand rolled cigarette which looked in danger of falling to bits.

"They're all being delivered to the studio tomorrow. Why don't you call round and see them sometime?"

"Oh I will," John said, "I must finish that drawing I started of you Jacob. I could find the time next week."

"Fine, make it early evening," Epstein said glancing up at the wall clock above the bar. "Now Olly, drink up and let's have some food, I'm starving."

After a very tasty meal at a little Italian restaurant in Frith Street, Epstein suggested a nightcap in the King's Head, before they went their separate ways. They made it ten minutes before time was called. Epstein ordered two large brandies and once he and Olly were settled at an empty table, he lit a very large cigar. Both of them were decidedly mellow.

"Olly, I've noticed that you don't seem to know what to call me. In fact I don't think you use my name at all."

"Oh really?" Olly said, slightly embarrassed. "I suppose Mr Epstein sounds a bit sort of pompous and to use your Christian name seems sort of..."

"Too familiar? Well, that's just not so." He took several huge puffs on his cigar surrounding them in clouds of blue smoke. "From now on Olly, my boy, you will call me Jacob and that's an order, shake on it." They shook hands and grinned at each other. They drained their glasses and stood up rather unsteadily to take their leave as last orders were called.

"Right then," Jacob said. "I'm going to find a cab; I take it you'll walk to your digs from here?"

"Yes, but first I must find the lavatory. See you tomorrow then. Thanks for supper."

"Yes, bright and early. Goodnight Olly," Jacob called over his shoulder as he left the bar.

Olly found his way to the gents at the back of the pub. He passed through several different rooms before he found it. One had booths with leather seats separated from each other by panelled screens. He noticed several couples occupying these, some of whom were taking advantage of the intimate spaces to have a kiss and a cuddle.

As he left the gents and set off back to the main bar at the front of the pub, something about the embracing couple in the darkest corner caught his attention. Olly stood back in the shadows. The woman rolled her head back briefly before kissing the man again. It was Jane Cranshaw. Olly pulled his cap low over his face and hurried past the couple. He glanced at them once more before entering the main bar room in an attempt to identify the man. Olly had a trained artist's eye and he saw enough of the man's face to recognise him as Giles Clinton.

Once Olly was well away from the pub he leaned against a wall and lit a cigarette with shaking fingers. Jane in a Soho pub kissing a man at least twice her age, what the hell was it all about? What would Tat think about it, if he ever found out? Olly gulped smoke into his lungs tying to calm himself. Before he realised it Jane and Giles Clinton passed by where he stood on the opposite pavement heading along Frith Street towards Soho Square. Olly decided to follow them to see where they were going. Maybe that would offer some kind of explanation. There were very few people about.

Jane and Giles Clinton had their arms around each other and stopped every now and again to embrace. The heavy foliage on the plane trees and lack of adequate lighting in the square, created impenetrable shadows. The couple were soon swallowed up in the gloom. Olly followed anxiously, afraid of blundering into them if they had happened to stop for some reason.

Indeed, they had stopped; Olly spotted them about twenty feet away next to one of the wrought iron benches dotted around the square. He slipped behind a tree and watched in shear amazement as Jane hitched up her skirt and leaned over the back of the bench. The black silhouette of Giles Clinton loomed over her momentarily obscuring Jane from sight. Olly simply couldn't believe his eyes; he felt his gorge rise and knew exactly what was going to happen next. Too horrified to watch, he blundered away and as he reached the far side of the square lost his lovely Italian supper down a drain.

The clear memory of what he had seen that night gnawed at him continuously over the following week. Epstein had his latest batch of bronzes photographed and had suggested that Olly's portrait of Tat should be included. It was his responsibility to clear a space for the photographer to set up his equipment, free of clutter and dust. Epstein worked with the photographer to get the lighting and angle of each exposure just right. He explained to Olly how to get the best results. Olly did his best to concentrate but, try as he might, he couldn't shake off the feeling of disgust at what he had seen in Soho Square.

Jane, of all people, behaving like a bitch on heat with Giles Clinton in a public place. How would he ever face her again and what on earth was he to do about Tat? The new term would begin in ten days or so. Would he find enough courage to tell his best friend about Jane's deceit? If so, how on earth would he go about it? As each day passed he became more miserable and nervous.

The photographer delivered the prints to the studio sooner that expected. Olly was thrilled with the photographs of Tat's portrait. They were glossy ten by eights which gave the sculpture an added drama due to the expert way in which the lighting had been deployed. He decided to send a print to Mr Cranshaw to let him see for himself how well the bronze he had paid for had turned out. As he posted the package he couldn't help thinking how horrified Mr Cranshaw would be if he knew what his darling daughter was up to.

On the final Saturday of the long summer vacation, Olly received a letter in an official looking envelope with the name of a legal practice in Tunbridge Wells embossed upon it. Mystified somewhat, he opened the envelope whilst preparing a couple of slices of toast for his breakfast. As he read the typed letter his stomach lurched and he had to steady himself against the kitchen table. It was from the Cranshaw's family solicitor and read as follows:

Dear Mr Sinclair,

I have taken over the correspondence of the Cranshaw family for the time being. I enclose the photograph of your impressive bronze sculpture you sent to Mr Cranshaw.

It is with the greatest regret, that I must inform you that the Cranshaw family have perished at sea. Their yacht was overwhelmed during a freak storm off the Brittany coast and sadly no one survived.

I have sent a letter explaining this tragedy to the Registrar at the Slade. I am very sorry to be the one to convey this sad news to you, as I gather you were a particularly close friend of Jane's. Perhaps you will be kind enough to inform any of her college friends you may know. I am sure she will be sadly missed.

Yours faithfully,

George Henderson.

Olly's face drained of colour as tears poured down his unshaven cheeks and splashed onto his now trembling, clenched fists.

GRIEF

Tat had dug Olly out of his lodgings on his first evening back in London after the long summer vacation. Jane was not due back until two days later. They went for a few pints at Olly's local. Tat sensed his friend was pre-occupied, not his usual outgoing self. Later, back in Olly's digs they intended to consume a half a bottle of whisky Olly had insisted on buying before leaving the pub. Eventually, he took both Tat's hands in his, after they had drunk a couple of glasses of the cheap liquor. His voice shaking and with tears swimming in his eyes, Olly told Tat the dreadful news of Jane's death at sea. Then Tat understood why Olly needed those extra shots of whisky. The poor chap had been building up Dutch courage in an attempt to steel himself before breaking his best friend's heart.

Olly insisted that Tat stay with him. He explained that he needed Tat to be there, as Jane had been so close to them both for so long. The week of grief he had suffered prior to Tat's return to London had taken its toll on him. He had almost gone out of his mind with worry as to how on earth he could break the news to Tat. Now that he had, it was difficult to assess which of the friends needed the other most.

They wept together, drank a lot and neglected to eat adequately, or even keep themselves particularly clean. Eventually, Jacob Epstein gave Olly the biggest dressing down he had ever had. Olly had been missing from Epstein's studio for three days. The loud knocking at the door of Olly's digs late one night had raised the young men from yet another boozy session of self-pity. Epstein expressed his disgust at the state of Olly's lodgings. He told them both to shape up and gave Olly one last chance to retain his position as his assistant. When he left he shouted, "Bring your useless friend with you; he can sweep the floor and clean the windows. Don't either of you turn up filthy and smelling of cheap booze."

Somehow it did the trick, or went half way towards doing so. They both turned up at the sculptor's studio at 8 a.m. the following morning. Olly had explained that only a complete fool would sacrifice a position of trust with Jacob Epstein. He dragged Tat along, not only because Jacob had told him to, but because he was afraid to leave Tat on his own.

Epstein had three portrait-heads in clay he required Olly to cast into plaster. The mess and clutter in the studio, which consisted of several large rooms and an outside yard, was formidable. Epstein instructed Olly to tell Tat how to go about cleaning it all up and show him where the numerous rubbish bins were stacked outside.

"When he's done all that he can clean the windows," Epstein snapped, before closing the door on the room he used for stone carving. Tat carried out the jobs in a kind of daze. He was thankful to be occupied doing straightforward, physical work. Later in the afternoon Tat was cleaning the windows in a room which was used for storing finished work. Several impressive bronze portraits were placed on wooden plinths and spare modelling stands. He was taken aback when he recognized Olly's portrait of himself amongst them. To see it in these surroundings, now cast into bronze so beautifully, moved Tat to the verge of tears. Memories of Jane inevitably flooded in and overwhelmed him. He sat down on a nearby stool, buried his face in his hands and wept silently, his shoulders shaking. As he gradually regained his composure and was wiping his eyes on the cloths he had been using to clean the windows, he started, as he realized a bulky figure stood framed in the doorway.

"I owe you an apology, young man." Epstein said softly. He approached Tat, pulled up a chair and sat opposite him.

"Olly has told me what has happened, and how upset you both are, especially you." He pulled out a blue paper packet of cigarettes.

"Try one of these. They're French and rather strong compared to most English brands." He fumbled about for his lighter and they both lit up. The rich blue smoke billowed around them as they sat in silence for a while.

I'm sorry I insulted you when I burst in on you both last night. I was angry with Olly for neglecting his work here. You got lumped in with it, I'm afraid. I have a bad temper, I'm told. Anyway, I'm sorry."

Tat could only manage a nod. His eyes were puffy and red-rimmed from weeping and his throat ached.

"Of course, I realise you are the subject of Olly's wonderful bronze over there. He tells me you are studying Law at U.C.L.. So for me to call you stupid was not only insulting but also completely inaccurate. Please, shake my hand."

Tat shook hands with the sculptor and recognized the pressure of a hand toughened by continuous physical work.

"You have hands like my father and my brothers," Tat said, with an effort he controlled his voice.

"Oh yes, they are rather like blunt instruments I'm afraid. So what do they do, your father and brothers?" Epstein asked.

"They're farmers, way up in the north."

"Do you know?" Epstein said, "I've never been to the North of England, and I don't know any farmers, at least not in this country. They must be proud of you, studying law and all."

"I suppose so."

After a brief pause Epstein leaned closer and said, "I know how grief feels, my boy. Two years ago both my parents died within a few months of each other." He paused whilst he took out his French cigarettes once more.

"I lost so many close friends in the War. I think about them every day. But I know that grief can be kept under some sort of control by hard work and effort. It takes guts, that's for sure, but believe me, it helps. Olly tells me you are due back at college this Monday. I want you to promise me that you both will be there. I know it will be hard, but I want you to promise me, nonetheless."

Tat looked into the sculptor's big tough face, and saw the sincerity in his eyes. He gathered all his strength and said, "Yes, sir, I promise."

For Tat, signing in for the new academic year was indeed hard. Somehow, giving his word to Jacob Epstein, after he had taken the time to talk to him so considerately, made it possible for the two friends to walk through the college gates together. Tat knew that the awful news about Jane would take some time to filter through the college community. He would have to steel himself to receive the sympathy of his friends as they learnt about the tragedy. Some might be too embarrassed to approach him. He found a note from Jack Douthwaite in his cubby-hole, asking him to call in at his study after the introductory lecture given by Professor Lewis at ten thirty.

"Tat, my boy, come in. I've just made a fresh pot of tea." Jack Douthwaite said, shaking hands enthusiastically. Tat was genuinely pleased to see Jack, although he knew that within a few minutes the jolly welcome would inevitably be clouded by sadness. How right he was.

"Look, Tat," Jack said anxiously. "I've heard the shocking news about poor Jane and her family. I can't tell you how sorry I am."

Tat was determined to control himself but nevertheless he felt the strange lump in his throat begin to throb and tears prickle beneath his eyelids.

"Thank you, Jack," he managed to say rather shakily. "How on earth did you find out?"

"Oh I ran into the registrar from the Slade at a drinks party last night. All faculties are expected to turn up for these things at the start of each academic year. I've known the chap quite well for ages. Anyway, he told me about it. Shocking, absolutely shocking."

"Honestly, Jack," he said, as a few tears broke free and slid down his cheeks. "I can hardly believe it's happened. I only found out myself a few days ago. Olly told me."

Jack poured some tea and offered Tat a cigarette from the silver box on his desk. When they had both lit up, he said, "I know, it's shattering." After a pause, he sighed and added, "Look, Tat, you know I can arrange for you to have some time off, on compassionate grounds. Give you a chance to recover a bit. What do you think?"

Tat clenched his fists inside his jacket pockets and waited a few seconds, to be sure he could speak firmly.

"Thank you, Jack, but I made a promise to someone that I would try my best to be strong. I intend to keep it."

After a few more days roughing it at Olly's lodgings, Tat moved back into his room at the hostel in Gower Place. They had spent a couple of hours cleaning up the unholy mess they had made and gone for a pint at Olly's local.

"You impressed Jacob, you know. He told me he'd had a chat with you. Even said he'd felt he should apologize to you. He doesn't do that very often, believe me."

"You know Olly, it's because of the chat I had with him that I was able to walk through those gates with you last Monday." Tat drained his pint and added, "Somehow we've got to be strong enough to get through this, and come out the other side in one piece."

Tat forced himself to take Epstein's advice and engage in as much activity as possible. A full list of U.C.L.'s rugby fixtures for the term had already been posted on the appropriate notice boards, with details of training schedules. The first of these was on the Wednesday of the opening week, followed by the first fixture against Loughborough on the following Saturday. This suited him perfectly.

He threw himself into the training session with an energy which even surprised himself, never mind his teammates. Setting his alarm clock early, Tat ran each morning, usually in Regent's Park or along the deserted streets of Bloomsbury, pushing himself harder and harder. Loughborough was a teacher training college in the Midlands, with a fine reputation in all sports. Their rugby team was regarded as one of the best in the country. Throughout the game, Tat played faster and harder than he had ever done before, dominating the scrums and line-outs. Frequent glances of surprise and even bewilderment were exchanged between his teammates, as Tat went from strength to strength, with what seemed like an inexhaustible supply of energy. He managed to drop a goal late in the second half, giving his team a three point lead, which Loughborough could not overcome, try as they might.

Later, in the back bar of the Wellington, Tat was congratulated profusely by one and all. He managed to accept only a couple of pints out of the many he was offered. He tried to be sociable and hide the deep heartache which threatened to overwhelm him.

Just moving around the college, Tat experienced difficulties he hadn't anticipated. He was obliged to cross the main quadrangle several times each day. He had met Jane there so often that there was not one inch of it that failed to remind him of her. He couldn't linger near their favourite bench, where they had sat, holding hands, deciding how to spend the longed for weekends. Frequently, he crossed to the opposite side of Gower Street to avoid passing close to the No. 14 bus stop. In fact, in his final year at U.C.L. he never travelled on a No. 14 bus again.

The most difficult part of the college for him was the Slade itself, occupying, as it did, the whole left hand flank of the quadrangle. There were two seats on either side of the imposing entrance, where he had sat and waited for Jane dozens of times. The idea of entering the building to call on Olly in his studio space in the evening was out of the question. He just couldn't do it. He haltingly explained this to Olly, who to his credit was very understanding. Eventually, Tat took to using the back entrances to U.C.L. in order to avoid the quadrangle as much as possible.

He worked like a demon at his studies. The problem was, that apart from lectures and tutorials, studying law was a mostly cerebral experience, carried out shut away in isolation. Tat gritted his teeth and forced himself to stay in his room, endlessly reading, taking notes and writing essays. Sometimes it would be too much to bear, and he would go to the college library to continue. There, at least, there were others at work which he found comforting.

THE VOICE FINDS IT'S PLACE

Determined to occupy himself as much as possible, he finally did what so many people had advised him to do. He joined the University College Choral Society. Tat was required to give an audition to the choir master, an extremely friendly man called James Hurren. He was in charge of all the musical aspects of the college. These included not only the choral society itself, but also all the various services and public events, such as the degree ceremonies, concerts and recitals.

James Hurren's study was a rather beautiful, panelled room, a good deal bigger than those of his own tutors. He greeted Tat warmly and once they were settled on two comfortable armchairs, asked Tat about his singing ambitions. Off to one side Tat spotted a large, very shiny, grand piano.

"Well, I suppose I've always sung, one way or another. I was in the choir at school, of course. Some of my teachers tried to persuade me to study music, but my parents weren't too keen."

"I see, and how would you categorize your voice?"

"Oh, it's a baritone, no doubt about that."

" How fortunate, we can never get enough good baritones and basses." James Hurren stood up and said, "Well, Mr. Taylor, will you sing something for me now?"

Turning to the back of the room, he indicated rows of shelves with slim volumes stacked vertically in alphabetical order, hundreds and hundreds of them.

"Now then," he said leading Tat towards them, "just about every worthwhile musical score is up here on these shelves. Tell me what you would like to sing and I'm sure I'll find the sheet music quickly enough."

Tat had already made his mind up and without hesitation said, "'The Skye Boat Song' and 'My Love is Like a Red, Red Rose'."

"Ah, Scottish ballads, they are over here, in one volume. Do you know the songs well, Mr. Taylor?"

"Yes, I've sung them often."

"Good, so you won't have to look over my shoulder to see the lyrics. Could you stand facing me, over there?"

Tat moved across so that he was about ten feet away as James Hurren sat down on the piano stool and placed the score of 'The Skye Boat Song' in front of him.

"Now then, I will play the short introduction. Do you know when to commence or should I nod you in, so to speak?"

"Oh, it's all right, I know when to come in."

On his last run in Regent's Park Tat had rested for ten minutes to steady his breathing. He knew the place was deserted at such an early hour and had gone through both songs a couple of times, so as to prepare himself for the audition. He was sure his voice was richer and more powerful than ever.

After the short introduction Tat sang out full and strong; he felt completely in control, even a little light-headed. He saw James Hurren glance up at him and raise his eyebrows. Tat remembered how Mary Hollis had loved how he sang the Scottish ballads. She had encouraged him to express the emotion in them, by subtle modulations of tone. Light and shade she had called it.

When he had finished, James Hurren stared at Tat for several seconds without saying anything.

"Well, Mr. Taylor, I've rarely heard the song sung better. You have a truly remarkable voice. I welcome you into the Choral Society without hesitation, on the strength of that single performance alone."

Tat felt a blush coming on; he was so pleased and relieved that he grinned broadly and said, "Why thank you, sir."

"You are studying law, is that right?"

"Yes. This is my last year."

"Why on earth didn't you come to us before now? You would have been singing lead parts and solos long ago."

"I don't know really," Tat said rather hesitantly. "I play rugger for the first fifteen and, well, there's always so much work to do."

"We'll have to make up for lost time then won't we?" James Hurren said, full of enthusiasm, then added, "Look, why don't you sing some more of your favourite songs for me? That is, if you don't have something else to go to."

"No, I'd be glad to."

Tat stayed for an hour. He sang two or three more ballads, some Verdi and Puccini arias and a couple of hymns. He and James Hurren got on like a house on fire, so much so that they polished off well over half of his bottle of Bristol Cream between them.

"You know," James Hurren said after their third glass of sherry, "I honestly think you are a bass-baritone, rather than a standard baritone."

"Oh, really? I have noticed that my voice is getting deeper and possibly louder."

"Absolutely, you have no problems at all in the upper register, but I do sense that considerably lower and deeper notes are within your range. Are you familiar with Verdi's Requiem at all?"

"Yes, I think it's one of the finest choral pieces I've heard. My housemaster used to play gramophone records to some of us at school. I heard it several times, in fact. He even gave me the score to study."

James Hurren leaned forwards and said, "So, therefore, you will know that one of the four soloists is a bass-baritone."

"I do. I remember a particularly stunning solo about half way through." Tat felt relaxed and uninhibited, thanks to the sherry. "It goes like this." Before he knew it he was humming the solo. When he had finished, James Hurren stood up and said,

"Well, I'm blowed," before approaching the shelves again and quickly selecting a score.

"Right, come and sing it for me. You can follow the libretto over my shoulder. Sing full out." James Hurren counted Tat in and he sang as if possessed. He surprised himself with how well he remembered the solo and felt he made a good stab at pronouncing the Italian libretto. James Hurren sat in silence for a few moments when they had completed the piece. Tat's voice seemed to linger in the darkening room.

"My goodness, Mr. Taylor, you surely were born to sing the part."

"Well, I don't know about that." Tat said, feeling another blush warm his neck.

"Ah, but I do. Come and sit down; I've a proposition to put to you."

After pouring them both a generous tot of sherry, he continued, "I intend to start rehearsals for Verdi's Requiem after Christmas. I want you to sing the bass-baritone part."

"But I don't have any experience." Tat said falteringly. "I rather fancied hiding away back in the chorus, keeping my head down."

"You have the perfect voice for Verdi, young man, especially the Requiem. I want you for the part and I am used to getting my own way in these matters."

It was decided that James Hurren would coach him over the following months, for at least one or two evenings each week.

"I know you can do it, Mr Taylor, and I will take great pleasure in proving it to you. Now, one last sherry don't you think?"

"What is the Choral Society rehearsing at the moment?" Tat asked eventually.

"We are about half-way through Handel's Messiah."

"Oh gosh. I know it, of course. I love it, but all those short notes running up and down the scales. How on earth is that done? I've often wondered."

"It takes practice and tuition. You are right, of course. Trilling, as it is called, is notoriously difficult. We've already had four rehearsals concentrating upon that alone. But that is what most Baroque music is all about."

" Anyway, it's one type of singing I know I could never tackle." Tat said, shaking his head.

"Well, it doesn't apply to Verdi, Mr Taylor, as I'm sure you know.

But let me make a suggestion. Come to next week's rehearsal and see what you make of it."

"But honestly, sir, I simply don't have the ability. I'd spoil it all, I really would."

"You know, as far as the chorus is concerned, trilling only occurs about fifty per cent of the time. The rest is quite simple melodic choral stuff, well within your grasp."

"I don't see how I could fit in though." Tat said, genuinely puzzled.

"Look, call round here on Friday evening, around six, and I'll have a score ready for you. I'll underline all the sections suitable for you to sing in green ink, alright?"

When he left he felt as close to contentment as was possible, under the circumstances. He had discovered something else to occupy him, and found a place for his singing at last.

THE LETTER

Sooner rather than later Tat knew that a dreadful task had to be carried out. As the days went by he knew he could postpone it no longer. He would have to write to his family to let them know about the tragedy which had engulfed him. The thought that Olly, who was as devastated as himself, might help him was eventually dismissed.

Tat had successfully cut down on his drinking since the first few days of boozy oblivion he'd spent with Olly. The furious outburst from Jacob Epstein, when he had come to Olly's lodgings, had shaken him. He knew that trying to drink his grief away was no answer. However, after screwing up half a dozen false starts when he had summoned up enough courage to attempt the letter, Tat went to the Wellington and bought a couple of bottles of strong ale. He drank the first of these, running phrases through his head.

The painful lump in his throat ached and he knew he would weep before the task was completed. Having opened the second bottle, Tat gritted his teeth and started again. For the first time he wrote to his father, knowing that he would stand the shock much more stoically than his mother. Tat knew his father would then pick the best circumstances in which to tell her, and then John and Michael. The alcohol steadied him a little.

Dear Dad,

I am writing this letter to you because I know that what I have to tell you will be too much for Mam to take.

When I got back to London my friend, Olly Sinclair, had terrible news for me. My lovely Jane has been drowned, along with the rest of her family. Heavy seas overwhelmed their yacht whilst they were sailing off the Brittany Coast.

I know you all liked Jane when she visited us in the summer, Mary Hollis included, of course. Dad, please break the news to Mam and Mary as gently as possible, and to John and Michael.

Be sure that broken-hearted though I am, somehow I will find the strength to get through this terrible time. I am trying my best to keep as busy as possible. The sculptor Olly works for gave me good advice about that.

Please excuse me for the briefness of this letter. I'm sure you can understand how difficult it is to write about it.

Love from Tat

Tears were flowing freely down Tat's cheeks. Some inevitably landed on the notepaper and made the ink smudge. He simply couldn't write it out again, so he blotted and folded it into an envelope with trembling fingers. Tat printed his father's name and their address, so his mother would not recognise his handwriting. He wept, his throat aching dreadfully, and finished the rest of the beer.

THE FIRST REHEARSAL

The next rehearsal of the Choral Society was on Wednesday evening the following week. It was the best thing that could possibly have happened to Tat in his present condition. The rehearsals always took place in the Great Hall, situated below the library. Tat had looked through the huge double doors out of curiosity on a couple of occasions. It was big and very grand, with a high, moulded ceiling and a spacious stage at the far end.

Slightly nervous, he was surprised by the number of students milling around in the hall, and the sheer volume of their excitable chatter. He recognized a player from the second fifteen and nodded to him, and two first year students from the law faculty. He reckoned there were just about the same number of males and females. Before Tat spoke to anyone, James Hurren broke away from a group of students who seemed to be discussing the score and approached him, smiling broadly.

"Mr Taylor, how nice to see you again. Let me have a quiet word before we start. I've been thinking things over. Do you mind if I ask you to pull back a bit initially on the volume? You have such a big voice that the other singers might feel a bit inadequate by comparison."

"Oh, really?" Tat said genuinely surprised, "Of course sir, anything you say."

"Your voice has a genuine operatic quality you see and very few choral singers have that, in my experience."

"I'll try my best to fit in, I promise." He felt flattered and slightly confused by what the choirmaster had said.

"Ah, you've remembered your customized score, I see. Just take it steady until you find your feet. I'm sure you are going to settle in quickly." He looked around at the rather chaotic and noisy scene and added, "I'll be calling everyone to order very soon. I hope you enjoy yourself Mr Taylor."

"Hello Tat, I didn't know you were joining us." It was Joe Atkinson, the second fifteen full-back.

"No, I only made my mind up recently."

"Well, I've heard you sing in the pub a few times so I'm not surprised you've ended up here eventually."

"I didn't know you were a singer at all, Joe."

"Hidden talent you see," Joe said, narrowing his eyes, "I'm a tenor and you, of course, are a baritone."

"Well, I've been told by James Hurren that I am a bass-baritone; you live and learn, I suppose." Tat had noticed a group of four students, two males and two females, near one of the two grand pianos on either side of the stage. They looked like they were having a serious discussion over their scores.

"Who are they then? They look a bit different from everyone else."

Joe glanced across and said, "Oh, they are the soloists. They are from the Guild Hall, I think. The solo parts are so tricky that James felt they ought to go to trained singers, not like us lot. It's all the trilling, you see."

"Between you and me Joe, Mr. Hurren has let me off the hook over the trilling stuff." Tat showed Joe his specially annotated score briefly.

"You jammy sod, Tat," Joe said indignantly. "I can only just hang on to it myself by the skin of my teeth, despite all the rehearsing."

"Well, I couldn't even offer to tackle it," Tat said, laughing. Just then James Hurren shouted above the din, "May I have your attention please, ladies and gentlemen."

A SUBDUED CHRISTMAS

Tat was both looking forward to Christmas at Fell End and dreading it in equal measure. Seeing his family again after the heartbreak he had suffered wasn't going to be easy. After all, the last time they had been together Jane had only just left to join her own family prior to their doomed yachting holiday.

It was as though he carried a scent of grief about him. Everyone was very cautious, unconsciously treating him as though he had suffered an illness, from which he was still recuperating. Jane was never mentioned. Tat didn't know whether to be grateful for this or not. He wondered whether he should attempt to raise the subject, perhaps after supper one night when they were together. He could tell them that after ten weeks or so of facing up to the tragedy, he had gradually gained strength and knew in his heart that he would get over it. Not that he would ever forget it, but that he would find a way through it. Tat never did summon up the courage, however.

Instead, he had joined John, Michael and his father at dawn each frosty morning to work on the farm. There were the sheep and cattle to tend to. The latter were indoors in the long byre beneath the hayloft, whilst the sheep had been brought in off the high tops and secured in small pastures close to the farm. There they were fed hay every day.

The stone walls gave the sheep some protection from the icy winds blowing in from the north and east. He kept the advice Jacob Epstein had given him alive in his mind and impressed his father and brothers with his resilience and determination.

Tat had a certain amount of studying to do. He usually spread his books out on the kitchen table, in order to make notes before tackling his essay on criminal law, which Jack Douthwaite had set. His mother busied herself elsewhere while he concentrated on this, usually joining him for coffee around mid-morning. She kept the conversation light, or tried to. Tat sensed on a couple of occasions that she was about to raise the subject of Jane's death, but thankfully she kept her thoughts to herself. Alone together in the warm kitchen, Tat knew they would both have broken down, which was the last thing he wanted.

After supper one particularly cold and stormy night, just before the table was cleared, Tat lit a cigarette and said, "I've got some news you might be interested in."

His mother paused whilst carrying the steaming kettle over to the sink to start the washing up.

"Come and sit down a minute, our Mam; it's good news, believe me." Tat said, smiling reassuringly. When his mother had settled herself, he went on. "Well, you remember I wrote to you about joining the College Choral Society and singing a bit with the chorus in Handel's Messiah?"

"Aye our Tat, we were that proud of you, weren't we Jack?"

Tat's father had his pipe charged up and nodded eagerly through the blue smoke drifting up towards the beams.

"Well," Tat continued, "James Hurren, the choir master, offered me a leading part in a big choral work. He's been coaching me a bit and we start full rehearsals after Christmas. The concerts are during the last week of next term, just before Easter."

Tears of pride swam in his mother's eyes. For a few moments she was unable to speak. Sensing this, Jack Taylor put his hand on her arm and gently patted it.

"By jove lad," Jack said. "That's a bit of a step up from singing round the piano at the Black Bull and no mistake."

"It certainly is. You remember that Italian song I sometimes sing? You know, it goes like this." Tat sang the opening bars of 'De Provenca'.

"Oh, that one. I've always loved that one," his mother said, smiling. "We all do."

Tat's father and his brothers nodded in agreement.

"Well, it's from an Opera called La Traviata, written by Guiseppi Verdi. This big choral job is by him too. It's called Verdi's Requiem. I've got the big bass-baritone part. I can't tell you how thrilled I am about it"

"Well, what a feather in your cap." Tat's mother beamed. "I tell you who'll be thrilled, and that's Mary Hollis, never mind your Gran."

"I thought I'd pop over to Winton tomorrow to see Mary. Do you think you could do without me tomorrow afternoon, Dad?"

"Aye, Tat lad, you get off and see Mary. Anyway, you've done enough graft these last few days to earn your keep and more. You can always change tack you know, and come back into the fold." Looking toward Ivy he added, "He's worked like a dog, you know, hasn't he lads?"

"Aye," Michael said. "He's tougher than he looks, is our lad."

As Tat made his way across the fields towards the lane to Winton, he knew in his bones that Mary Hollis was the one person who would want to talk about the tragedy. Mary had become very fond of Jane while she had stayed at her cottage during the summer. They had so much in common, music, art and literature. Tat recalled how often he had left them in the evening deep in conversation or playing duets on Mary's piano.

"Oh Tat, how lovely to see you." Mary said. She embraced Tat warmly and kissed him on the cheek. "Come away in, it's cold, real Eden Valley weather."

She settled Tat by the fire in the sitting room and bustled about in the kitchen making a pot of tea. After a few minutes Mary joined him, carrying a tray, which she set down on a small table. Tat noticed two slices of very rich fruit cake.

Mary settled herself in the armchair opposite him. "We'll just let that mash for a minute or two. Do smoke if you want Tat." she said, reaching up for an ash-tray on the mantle-piece.

"Oh thanks, Mary. Are you sure you don't mind?"

"No, not at all. I rather enjoy the smell now and again."

Tat lit up, settled back in the armchair and said, "I love this cottage you know. I wouldn't mind ending up with a home just like it one day."

"Well thank you Tat, what a lovely thing to say," Mary said, before turning to pour the tea. "Try my fruit cake, this one is almost up to the same standard as your mother's, even though I say it myself."

Tat took the slice Mary passed him, taking a bite and chewing it slowly. "Well now Mary, it's a cracker and no mistake, simply delicious."

After a pause Mary put her hand on Tat's arm and said, "Tat I know it must be difficult to speak about, but I must say how terribly sorry I was about what happened to poor Jane and her family."

Tat stared into the fire and steeled himself. He had to keep control; above all, he must not break down. Very carefully he said, "I know how fond you became of her Mary; it's been a hard time and no mistake. I'm gradually coming to terms with it, somehow or other."

"I've been so worried about you, Tat. I've started several letters to you, but somehow I couldn't complete any of them."

"Thank you, Mary. I knew it would upset you in particular. You and Jane had so much in common. She thought the world of you."

"Bless the child," Mary said, with tears swimming in her eyes.

"Actually, I was helped a lot by the sculptor my friend Olly Sinclair works for. He talked to me soon after I heard the news. I was in an awful state." Tat pulled out his cigarettes and lit up again with quivering fingers. "He advised me to fill up my time with hard work and to find as many things as possible to occupy me. Anyway, he was right; keeping busy has definitely helped me."

"Well, he sounds like a sensible man. I'm so glad you are finding your feet gradually. Remember how long I've known you, Tat. I know you have inner strength. Time will heal the wound as well as hard work."

After an awkward pause, Tat said, "One of the things I've been filling my time with is singing."

"Oh yes, do tell me about it."

"Well, I finally joined the Choral Society and I sang a bit with the choir. One of your favourites Mary, Handel's Messiah."

"Oh, how exciting," Mary said, clapping her hands together. "I want to hear all about it."

"Well, I did an audition with a very nice man called James Hurren, who's the choir master. You'll be glad to know that he accepted me after I sang 'The Skye Boat Song' for him."

"You mean one song and that was it? How wonderful," Mary said, smiling broadly. "You've always sung the ballads beautifully, mind you."

"Anyway, he asked me to sing some more songs, just for fun really. I stayed over an hour and we drank a bottle of his sherry between us."

"Now that's a good idea." Mary said, getting up. "Let's have a glass each to celebrate your success."

As they sipped the delicious liquor, Tat told Mary how James Hurren had invited him to join the rehearsals for Handel's Messiah.

"He suggested I only sang the most straight forward bits. I told him I wasn't up to all that trilling. He even gave me a score marked with green ink so I wouldn't get confused."

"How very understanding of him."

"Eventually, he told me that they were planning to begin rehearsing Verdi's Requiem when we get back after Christmas. I told him I knew the big bass-baritone solo 'Confutatis Maledictis', and blow me down, if he didn't find the score and have me sing it to him there and then."

"I didn't know you knew it Tat."

"Yes, Philip Mott played the records of The Requiem at Appleby. He even had the score and taught me to follow it."

"So how did you get on?"

"He offered me the part and told me I was born to sing it."

Mary sprang up out of her armchair with delight, and gave Tat a hug and kissed the top of his head. "Oh Tat, how thrilling! I knew that voice of yours would be recognized eventually. How wonderful! Have you told your parents?"

"Yes, I told them last night after supper. They were thrilled to bits."

"I should think so. It's such an achievement. I'm so proud of you, Tat." Mary said with tears shimmering in her eyes once more.

As Tat made his way back to Fell End, head bent down against the ferocious wind, he thought over the conversation he'd had with Mary. He came to the conclusion that discussing Jane's death, no matter how briefly, had been of help to him. After all, he had not broken down and wept. Perhaps he would be able to raise the subject at home, with his mother at least, after Christmas, that might be best.

As usual, the whole family spent Christmas Day at the Black Bull. It was jolly enough, although Tat could still detect an air of restraint in the atmosphere from time to time. Eventually, enough beer had been consumed by the men to lighten their spirits. Tat was more or less obliged to rally himself and sing a dozen songs or so, with Mary Hollis at the piano. She had become a regular guest for Christmas Dinner at the Black Bull. Mary had acquired the sheet music for Verdi's Requiem from the library in Appleby and insisted upon Tat rounding off his performance with 'Confutatis Maledictis'. He gave it all he'd got and rather stunned his audience with the drama and force of his singing; he even surprised himself. He explained how the solo fitted into the Requiem as a whole and occurred just after the big tenor solo. He made them laugh when he explained that he was determined to out-do the tenor. "They always get the glory," he'd said. "But not this time!"

Tat was rather thankful that he was spared meeting Dick Machin for their usual Christmas booze-up. Dick had completed his two-year course at Newton Rigg and got a job as under manager on a big farm beyond Penrith. He would not be around for any of the time whilst Tat was at Fell End.

Tat felt guilty about this, but he had been dreading seeing Dick, who knew nothing about what had happened. He would inevitably have asked Tat how things were going with that "bonny, posh lass of yours," and this would have obliged him to tell Dick the whole sad story. It would have been impossible for Tat to attempt this without cracking up. Sooner or later it would have to be faced, but thankfully not yet. Tat thought that eventually he might write to

Dick about it.

Jack Taylor took Tat to the station in the trap, both of them muffled up against the keen wind. In the event, it was his father who broke the family silence regarding the tragedy as they sat close to the fire in the station waiting room. "Your Mam asked me to speak to you, lad. I don't know if it will be on the cards or not, just say if you want me to shut up and I will do."

"No, it's alright, Dad. Go ahead." Tat replied, masking his surprise.

"Well then, you remember all them drawings Jane did of us haymaking last summer?"

"Aye, I do. They were terrific, weren't they?"

"Your Mam was wondering if maybe you could get hold of them somehow. We'd both love to have them as something to keep. In memory of the lass."

After a pause, Tat said, "It's a grand idea, Dad, I'll see what I can do. Leave it to me."

DISCOVERING TREACHERY

Tat had plenty of time to think about this unexpected proposition on the chilly journey to King's Cross. Occasionally he had wondered what had happened to Jane's paintings and drawings and the sketchbooks she always carried around with her. He had kept the drawing she had given him of Olly modelling his portrait, flattened between two law books. Olly had suggested that he should press it flat so it would be easier to mount and frame eventually. He had been anxious about looking at it as time passed, in case it stirred up poignant memories of happier times.

She had, of course, made numerous drawings of him. Then there were the studies she had made of Nick La Rocca. The bandleader had hoped to acquire some of these and Jack Douthwaite had expressed a desire to buy the oil painting which Jane intended to develop on her return to London from Westmorland.

He decided to get in touch with Nicola at University College Hospital, to see if she had any information. After all, she had shared the lease on the flat at 12 Fawcett Street and would probably have had some hand in dealing with Jane's belongings. He would leave a note for her at the porter's office at the main door.

A few days after taking up his studies once more and continuing his coaching sessions for the Requiem with James Hurren, Tat found an answer from Nicola in his pigeonhole. She apologized for not having contacted him sooner, but explained that she had been just too upset to do so. Jane's folders, paintings and sketchbooks had all been taken to the Slade, as there was no family left to accept them. She suggested that he contact Jack Seabury, Jane's former tutor, as he had arranged the whole thing.

Tat approached Olly eventually to ask if he could help. He was unaware of the work having been taken to the Slade, as well, and offered to ask Jack Seabury if Tat could have access to it. He was sure he would be able to achieve this once he had explained the connections. A few days later, Tat steeled himself for the encounter, having arranged to meet Olly at the main doorway of the Slade, a location he had avoided for so long. He tactfully turned down Olly's offer to help him sort through Jane's work and was soon introduced to Jack Seabury in a very cluttered office upstairs. Most of the communal painting studios were located here and the smell of oil-paint, turpentine and linseed oil were all-pervasive. After a few pleasantries Olly took his leave, arranging to meet Tat for a drink later that evening in the Wellington.

Jack Seabury was a small, wiry man in his forties, dressed in a Harris Tweed jacket and baggy corduroy trousers. He explained that Olly had told him that Jane had been his girlfriend.

"I'm truly sorry for your loss, Mr Taylor. Needless to say, we are all shattered here at the Slade. Jane was so popular and talented. I, of course, was her personal tutor. I miss her terribly."

Tat fought hard to steady himself. This was more difficult than he had bargained for.

"Anyway," Jack Seabury said at last, "Let me show you where Jane's work is stored. I should tell you that selected pieces will be kept in the College Archive of past student's work. It will be my job to choose those."

"Well, all I am looking for is the sketch-book she worked in last summer. It's full of drawings of the haymaking on our farm in Westmorland. My parents would so like to have it, in memory of poor Jane and so would I," Tat tailed off rather, recognizing the familiar ache in his throat.

"Of course," Jack Seabury replied, sensing his discomfort. "Naturally, you must have it if you can find it and anything else of a personal nature."

They passed along a corridor before Jack Seabury stopped and unlocked a black painted door with a set of keys he took from his jacket pocket.

"Here we are. Over there against the far wall, that's all her stuff, folders, paintings and the sketch- books stacked on the left. Are you sure you're up to this, Mr. Taylor?"

"It's something I've promised to do," was all Tat could manage to say.

"Yes, of course, I understand. Look you carry on, come and find me in my office. Back down the corridor, last door on the right, when you're finished. I'm writing reports all afternoon."

Tat stood still staring at the sum total of what remained of Jane: her effort, her talent, her short life. Taking a deep breath he approached the stack of sketch- books. The haymaking book was second from the top. They were dated on the front cover, typical Jane, Tat thought, brushing away a tear. He leafed through the sketch- book, his heart hammering, as the images leapt off each page. What a joy it had all been and how hard it was to look at it again. He suddenly found he was gulping for air; staggering slightly, he made it to the nearest wall and leaned heavily against it.

Slowly his head cleared, he gathered the sketch-book to his chest and prepared to leave, when he suddenly thought about the Nick La Rocca drawings. Perhaps he should look for them and give them to Jack Douthwaite. It was possible that he could send one of these to Nick La Rocca and keep the others for himself.

Jane had attached labels to each folder with dates printed on them. Tat set the haymaking sketch book aside and after steadying his breathing, selected the folder most likely to contain the drawings of the band leader. He found them quickly enough and arranged them on the floor side by side. Some were highly finished and the others were more like quick sketches. She had La Rocca to the life; wearing the Prince of Wales checked suit he was so proud of, holding his cornet across his knees.

He glanced inside the folder once more to see if he had overlooked any further studies of La Rocca, when he noticed a small portfolio tucked away at the bottom. It was bound in black leather and looked expensive, not the kind of thing a Slade painting student would normally own. Tat lifted it out and saw that it had a name and address embossed on the top, left-hand corner of the front cover. He tilted it slightly so that the raised lettering caught the light. It read as follows:

Giles Clinton R.A., 23 Neale Street, Covent Garden, London.

Tat sat cross-legged on the floor holding the portfolio tightly in both hands. It was roughly the same size as one of Jane's sketchbooks and held secure with small clasps. As he undid these he began to sweat.

It contained about twenty drawings of a beautiful young woman striking erotic poses. In some she wore scanty underwear whilst in others she was completely naked. It was Jane. Each drawing was neatly signed in the bottom left-hand corner in black ink, Giles Clinton R.A., with the date alongside. The drawings had been done in the few weeks after Jane had returned to London from Westmorland and just before she had died.

Tat sat shaking with the drawings scattered around him, as the enormity of what he had discovered sank in. Over the next few hours Tat was never quite sure how he functioned or how he retained his self-control. He was increasingly gripped by cold, seething rage and the need to take action.

Tat gathered up the drawings and stuffed them into the portfolio along with the sketches of Nick La Rocca. He slid it down his shirtfront and fastened his sports jacket, using all three buttons. With the hay-making sketch-book under his arm, Tat made his way to Jack Seabury's office. He stood up and said,

"Ah, you found the sketch book I see. I hope it's in good condition?"

"Oh yes, very good. Thanks for helping me out, Mr Seabury, it's very kind of you."

Tat went round to the back of the college where he knew the main boiler room was situated. It was run by two old Cockney labourers who Tat had seen often enough shovelling coke into barrows. He found one of them sitting on the coke heap, rolling a cigarette. Tat gave him two shillings and asked if he could burn a few items on the boiler fire. The old boy held the furnace door open whilst Tat thrust the portfolio and sketchbook into the flames. They caught immediately and were gone forever.

REVENGE

Tat was waiting for Olly in the Wellington a few minutes after opening time. After gulping greedily at his pint, Olly asked, "So how did you get on Tat, find what you were looking for?"

"You'd be surprised Olly, believe me," Tat said coldly.

"Are you alright, old son?" Olly asked, suddenly aware of a strained atmosphere.

"Olly," Tat said, looking straight into his friend's eyes. "Exactly who is Giles Clinton R.A?"

"What on earth do you want to know that for?" Olly asked, the colour draining from his face.

"I need to, that's all. You know about the art world in London, so who is he?"

Olly drained his pint, and playing for time, ordered two more.

"Well R.A," he said at last, "that means he's a member of the Royal Academy."

"Come on, Olly, even I know that. What do you know about him?"

"He judged one of our sketch clubs about a year and a half ago. Irish bloke if I remember correctly." Olly sensed that he was about to be cornered and dreaded it. Then added, "Tat what is this all about?"

"Now listen, this must never go any further, but somehow this Giles Clinton got his hooks into Jane, towards the end of the summer vacation."

He explained about discovering the shocking drawings, all signed and dated by Giles Clinton.

"Olly, I have taken all I can, this is the bitter end and I intend to do something about it. When I asked you who Giles Clinton was you looked like you were going to pass out. If you know something, for goodness sake tell me."

Olly knew the game was up. He ordered a couple of whiskies and offered Tat a cigarette, taking one for himself. He blew the smoke downwards onto the bar top, where it seemed to splash, like liquid, in all directions.

"Come on Tat, let's sit down over there." He indicated an empty table, well away from the bar. Once they were seated Olly gulped his whisky down in one and took a draught of his beer. Tat noticed that his hands were shaking.

"Listen Tat," Olly said, after taking a deep breath. "I hoped I'd never have to tell you this, or anybody else for that matter."

"Go on, Olly," Tat said grimly. "Just tell me, whatever it is."

"Well," Olly said in a low voice, "about a week before I got that terrible letter telling me that Jane and her family were all lost at sea, I saw something. It's been gnawing away at me ever since."

"How do you mean, you saw something?"

"I'd been to the bronze foundry with Jacob. Apart from looking at his casts, I saw my portrait of you in bronze for the first time. It looked marvellous, we even saw them all being patinated." Olly was looking more miserable than ever.

"We had supper at an Italian café in Soho and finished up having a couple of shorts in the King's Head, next door. After Jacob left to get a taxi, I went to the gent's at the back of the pub. On my way back I saw a couple kissing and cuddling in one of those partitioned booth things. It was pretty dark, but I easily recognised Jane and then I saw that the bloke was Giles Clinton."

"Oh no, I will..." Tat said through clenched teeth.

"Tat, I swear on my honour, that I never thought I'd have to tell you. I figured with poor Jane dead I would take it to my grave with me. The whole bloody thing has just about cracked me up. I feel awful." A few tears ran down Olly's cheeks, which he dashed away impatiently with a closed fist. He hung his head in silence.

"Oh Olly, look, you've had a worse time than even me." He went to the bar to get two more pints with whisky chasers, leaving Olly to compose himself. He never knew that Olly was struggling with the memories of what he had seen when he had followed Jane and Giles Clinton into Soho Square. Mercifully, Tat never would know.

After they had knocked back the whiskies and lit cigarettes, Tat asked, "Olly, do you know where Neale Street is?"

Olly shook his head in an effort to concentrate. "Well, yes I do, actually. It's only about ten minutes walk away. Why do you want to know?"

"I'm pretty sure that this Giles Clinton lives there, or works there." He explained that the portfolio, in which he had discovered the drawings, had Giles Clinton's name and Neale Street address embossed on the leather.

"Listen Olly, I know you are shaken up by all this. We both are, for goodness sake. But I want you to take me there right now."

They finished their pints and walked straight down Gower Street until they joined Shaftesbury Avenue. They hardly spoke until Olly indicated a side street leading off at right angles.

"This is it," Olly said. "It leads straight across to Covent Garden, more or less."

"Right then, let's find number 23," Tat said grimly.

Olly laid a restraining hand on Tat's shoulder. "Look Tat, you've got to tell me what you have in mind. You don't want to make things worse than they already are."

"I don't rightly know what I'm going to do Olly. But you can't expect me to do nothing."

"I suppose not, but you've got to give it some thought surely. Hold on, across the street, the blue door, that's it, number 23."

They stared at the five-storey building. Several lights showed at various levels without blinds or curtains. Suddenly, pointing up at the top floor, Olly said, "That's got to be it. See the windows are twice the size of the others. Those blinds set at different heights; that's the way painters control the daylight when they're working. I'd put money on it, Tat."

"I reckon you're right Olly. Anyway it's all dark up there now. Listen, I'm going to hang around and see who comes and goes.

Why don't you leave me to it?"

"Don't be daft, I'm staying with you. Look, there's a pub a few doors back, we can watch from there."

The place was practically deserted. They took their pints to an empty table next to the window overlooking the street. Most of the small shops and businesses were closed and in darkness. They saw several people let themselves into number 23, although most were leaving. The lights were being turned off. Eventually, the whole building was in darkness apart from a gas light illuminating the front door. Olly pointed out that the last remaining place still open for business was a brightly lit Italian Restaurant, five doors to the right of number 23. It looked busy.

"I bet the grub is terrific over there, Tat. I could eat a horse."

As he spoke a tall man on his own left the restaurant. Olly sat up straight and stared hard as the man strolled towards number 23. Once there he inserted a key in the lock, fully illuminated by the gaslight.

"Tat," Olly said urgently. "That's Giles Clinton."

They both looked up at the top floor. After a few tense minutes the lights were turned on and a shadowy figure lowered the blinds one by one. Eventually, Tat managed to persuade Olly to give him time on his own, for a couple of days, to sort out what he was going to do. Olly didn't like this much. He knew how angry Tat was and was fearful that he would do something rash in the heat of the moment.

Tat wrote a brief letter to his father saying that he had been unable to locate the haymaking sketch-book. He hated lying to his father of all people, but the thought of seeing those drawings at Fell End in the future was too much for him to bear.

For the next three evenings he returned to Neale Street and kept a watch on number 23. Tat decided that there were several businesses located on the four floors below Giles Clinton's studio. He watched people coming and going until the place appeared to be deserted and in darkness by around six thirty in the evening, except for the top floor, which remained fully illuminated for a further hour or so. Giles Clinton proved to be a creature of regular habits. Sitting at the table by the window in the gloomy little pub, Tat saw him stroll along to the Italian restaurant at around seven thirty three nights running. He exercised all the will power he had to stop himself from confronting the painter on the street. He needed privacy to carry out his intentions.

At six o'clock on the fourth evening Tat loitered on the pavement outside number 23, guessing there were still a handful of people on the point of leaving. Within minutes, a couple of young men in overalls came out into the street. Before they shut the door Tat stepped forward and said, "Oh, that's a stroke of luck. I've got a message for a bloke upstairs. Could you let me in please?"

"Yeah, go ahead mate." The taller of the two said pleasantly, an unlit cigarette bobbing up and down between his lips. Without hesitating, Tat began climbing the dingy staircase until he reached the fifth floor. A strip of light showed at the bottom of the door at the far end of the landing. In the gloom Tat saw that there were smears of paint around the door handle. He paused to steady his breathing, acutely aware of the hammering of his heart, and then knocked three times.

After a short pause Tat heard footsteps approaching and the door opened wide. Giles Clinton stood in the threshold wearing a paint-flecked smock. The enquiring look on his face was wiped clean away as Tat drove his right fist into it with all his might. The force of the blow sent the painter staggering backwards into the cluttered studio. He crashed against an easel supporting a large canvas and took it with him to the floor, where he lay in a crumpled heap, blood pumping from his shattered nose.

"You lousy, cheating bastard," Tat growled, before slamming the door shut and clattering back down the stairs. As he walked down Neale Street towards Shaftesbury Avenue he breathed deeply and looked at the knuckles on his right hand. They were red and throbbing in a deeply satisfying way.

Tat called in at the Wellington, hoping to find Olly there. Sure enough he was in the back bar with a couple of his friends from the Slade. Tat ordered a pint of bitter with a whisky chaser and gestured for Olly to join him at an empty table.

After a minute or two, Olly brought his pint over, sat down and said, "Well now Tat, are you going to tell me what you've been up to for the last four days? I haven't seen hide or hair of you."

"I've been exacting a bit of old-fashioned Biblical revenge, Olly, that's what I've been doing." Tat said, before gulping back his whisky. After he finished telling his story, Olly sat in stunned silence before lighting a cigarette with trembling fingers.

"Crikey Tat, what if he goes to the cops?" he said eventually.

"Oh don't worry, he won't. He knows that if the gutter press find out about his private life, he'll be done for. I doubt whether he'll even dare to be seen in public for a week or two. Even then he'll have to explain how he got his face re-arranged."

WELCOME ENCOURAGEMENT

There were two more coaching sessions to come with James Hurren and four rehearsals with the full choir. The orchestra from the Guildhall School of Music had accompanied them for some time now. Up to then James Hurren and one of his assistants had done the job on two pianos. The orchestra and choir together created a power and range far beyond anything Tat could have imagined. The tenor and two soprano solo singers were also studying at the Guildhall. At first they had been rather distant with Tat but once they had heard him sing that quickly changed. They knew he was at least as good as them, if not better.

Tat was surprised to find a stranger in James Hurren's study when he turned up for his final lesson with the choirmaster.

"Ah Tat, how nice to see you," James Hurren said, ushering Tat through. "Let me introduce you to my good friend, Dick Lambert." Tat shook hands, with a large, bearded man wearing well-cut tweeds.

"I've taken the liberty of inviting Dick along to hear you. He's in charge of the singing activities at the Guildhall."

Despite having gained a considerable amount of confidence in his singing ability since joining the Choral Society, Tat felt a flurry of alarm at the prospect of singing to a complete stranger. Especially to one who held such a prestigious position. Sensing Tat's discomfort, James Hurren patted his shoulder and said, "Don't worry my boy, Dick listens to young singers on a daily basis. Anyway, I've told him what a treat is in store for him."

"Blimey, I hope I'm up to it. I don't want to let you down."

"I doubt that will happen. I've never come across anybody who's developed as quickly as you have. I've suggested that you sing your favourite Scottish ballads before we concentrate on The Requiem."

Tat was relieved; he felt he would be on safe, familiar ground with the ballads. As he waited for James Hurren to collect his music from the shelf Dick Lambert said, "Forget I'm here Mr Taylor.

I'll just sit over here and help myself to another glass of James' delicious sherry."

As James Hurren settled himself at the piano, Tat decided that now would be the opportunity to try out the falsetto technique James had taught him. He knew that the ballads were the perfect compositions in which to vary the tone of his voice. Mary Hollis would be proud of his newfound ability to make the top notes so soft and mellifluous.

"Now then Tat," James Hurren said, smiling reassuringly, "let's do our old favourites 'The Skye Boat Song' and 'My Love is Like a Red, Red Rose'. These are the first songs young Tat sang for me Dick. I warn you, old boy, prepare to have your heart broken."

Tat had never sung with such emotional intensity before, it just seemed the right thing to do on this particular occasion. As the last few notes hung in the still air of the softly lit room, tears swam in his eyes. He glanced at James Hurren and saw how moved he was too. After a moment of charged silence, Dick Lambert rose to his feet and applauded. He walked over to Tat and shook his hand. Looking at James Hurren he said, "Well James, you said there was a treat in store for me, but that was outstanding. Mr Taylor you have the voice of an angel, congratulations to you."

Tat struggled to retain his composure and was only able to say, "Thank you, sir." As he did so a tear slid down his cheek. To mask this he turned away, pretending to clear his throat, and swiftly wiped his eyes.

"Right, what we all need is a sherry to help us calm ourselves," James Hurren said, moving across to the low table near the hearth. The cut glass decanter with its amber contents seemed to glow in the firelight. The three of them settled in armchairs.

James Hurren was the first to speak, "Tat, you must have been practicing that falsetto technique; you have it off to perfection. Don't you agree, Dick?"

"I most certainly do. It often takes our basses and baritones two terms or more to become half as proficient as Mr Taylor here. From what you tell me James, you have only spent a few weeks tackling it."

"Absolutely, young Tat here obviously is a natural, nothing seems too much for him."

"So he is," Dick Lambert said enthusiastically. "Would you let me hear what you've been doing with The Requiem? I presume you won't be using much falsetto in that part?"

Tat had regained his equilibrium and answered confidently, "Hardly at all sir, James has encouraged me to sing out loud and clear."

"Well, let's give Dick our version of' Confutatis Maledictis', eh Tat?" James Hurren said, making his way back to the piano.

Tat gave the solo everything he had. He knew that with all that James had taught him his voice was bigger, richer and more resonant than ever. Half way through the aria Dick Lambert got up and stood opposite him, behind James Hurren. He stared wide-eyed, his mouth shaping the phrases as Tat sang. James Hurren's study seemed scarcely capable of containing the sheer volume of Tat's voice.

As the silence settled through the turbulence once more, Dick Lambert shook his head and seemed lost for words. At last he said, "Listen, Mr Taylor, I've worked with singers for years, but I've seldom heard 'Confutatis' sung as well as that. Amazing, truly amazing."

"I know," James Hurren said, grinning broadly, "and he only joined us a couple of months ago."

"Well believe me, if you had auditioned at the Guildhall you would have been accepted immediately. Come to think of it, why not join us when you've completed your degree? I'm sure I could get you a generous bursary. What do you say?"

They resumed their seats and James Hurren poured more sherry. Tat tried not to show how proud and excited he was and rather brought the atmosphere back to earth by explaining that, as soon after graduating as possible, he would be obliged to earn a living.

"Well, remember the offer is there, should you change your mind,"

Dick Lambert said. After a short pause he added, "What ever else happens, promise me that you will keep singing."

Even though Dick Lambert had only intended to stay a short while to hear Tat sing a couple of songs, he stayed for the whole of Tat's lesson with James Hurren. Indeed, he contributed to it, generously suggesting subtle ways for Tat to raise his game even further. It was an evening Tat would never forget.

THE FINAL REHEARSAL

James Hurren used the final two rehearsals to run through the complete Requiem without any interruptions. He conducted from the front of the stage using a baton and flung himself into the role with great enthusiasm. The stage hands had erected a scaffold structure with sturdy planks fitted to it, which created four raised tiers, each one a couple of feet higher than the one in front. The choir stood in rows upon these, grouped according to their category of voice. The sopranos and tenors made up the central group, with the basses and baritones on either side. The orchestra was seated at stage level with the four soloists standing centrally between them and James Hurren. All the singers held their scores at just above waist height using both hands.

To enhance the theatrically of the last rehearsal James Hurren had sent word around each department to invite any students who wanted to attend to make up an audience. As the singers and orchestra took up their positions the students milled around trying to find seats with the best viewpoint. The general hubbub threatened to develop into chaos.

Tat chatted to his three fellow soloists and watched it all from the stage. He had been relieved when he'd heard that an audience would attend this last rehearsal; he felt sure that all those taking part would benefit from it. The swelling crowd was a rowdy bunch, however, and seemed reluctant to sit down in an orderly fashion. Tat found it uproariously funny, especially when he spotted a decidedly scruffy Olly waving at him with both hands from the back of the hall. He'd obviously come straight from the sculpture studios, without bothering to change. He actually held up a bottle of some sort of liquor, and gestured to Tat to join him. Tat recognized several of the U.C.L. rugger crowd, jostling around, choosing seats close to Olly.

It was at least ten more minutes before the audience were settled enough for James Hurren to raise his baton to signal that the performance was about to begin. Tat had always enjoyed the way the very quiet opening passages of The Requiem masked the emotional barrage that would soon develop. By now he knew it inside out, not only his own part, but also everybody else's as well. Nevertheless, it was a comfort to have the score to hand with James Hurren's green ink marking his lines.

After about five minutes of the orchestra and choir setting the scene, gradually increasing the volume, the four soloists began their first ensemble. Singing an introductory phrase each, then merging together as a quartet, Tat felt instinctively that they were all on top form. He was determined to watch for the reaction of the audience when the next passage began.

He smiled when most of the students visibly jumped in shock as the percussionist pounded his base drum, underpinning the soaring phrases from all sections of the choir singing in unison. The drumming resembled cannon fire and those not familiar with the piece were invariably taken completely by surprise.

Although The Requiem seems to flow onwards in a seamless succession of majestic passages, it is subtly made up of fifteen movements. Tat sang several base lines alone, which were relatively short in length, before joining his fellow soloists in complex surging harmonies. His big moment came after the tenor solo, however, about half an hour into the performance. 'Confutatis Maledictis' represents Verdi's showpiece for the bass-baritone. Tat had grown to love the aria; it required a big voice which could fill a concert hall. He now knew he had this in abundance. As James Hurren had said, he might have been born to sing the part.

He felt in complete control as he moulded the slow soaring phrases, building up the power to fill the place with ever-higher top notes. The audience were completely still, seemingly transfixed by the sheer intensity of his performance. Then, as the final note faded, to his astonishment, they erupted into thunderous applause. It started in the back three or four rows where the rugger club were situated and quickly spread forwards towards the stage. Soon the rugger boys were on their feet cheering and waving college scarves above their heads. The students from the law faculty soon followed suit, Jack Douthwaite included.

Tat looked around him and was amazed to see that the choir, the players in the orchestra and his fellow soloists were all grinning with what looked like genuine pleasure and surprise. Ben Morgan, the Welsh tenor from the Guildhall, even patted him heartily on the back and said, "Go on Tat boy, and take a bow; that was bloody marvellous."

James Hurren stepped forward and shook Tat's hand. Beaming from ear to ear, he leant close to him and said, "Well Tat, it looks like this is your moment. Go on, do as Ben says, and take a bow. Then we'll have to stick the whole thing back together. You were magnificent."

Tat walked to the front of the stage, spread his right hand on his chest and executed one simple bow. The applause welled up again, and Tat found himself wondering just how much Olly, who no doubt had polished off the contents of his bottle, had to do with it all. As the atmosphere settled back to something resembling normality, James Hurren raised his hands high, still smiling, he called for silence. At last he was able to make himself heard.

"Well, ladies and gentlemen, that was not exactly what our friends on the railway would call a scheduled stop." He paused whilst a wave of good-natured laughter rippled through the hall, then continued, "Our wonderful bass-baritone, Mr Taylor, seems to have met with your approval." Another burst of applause and laughter broke out.

"I get the feeling that his colleagues in our esteemed rugby club, sitting I believe at the back of the hall, may have initiated that wonderful response. I must say I don't blame you."

Tat saw Olly, still standing, stick both his thumbs in the air. He waved briefly and held a finger vertically up to his lips, appealing to Olly to sit down and behave himself.

"Anyway," James Hurren continued, "We, up here, have worked long and hard to get this performance ready for you. Believe me, we appreciate your enthusiasm, but can I ask you please to allow us to complete the remainder of The Requiem without interruption."

After a polite and respectful round of applause James Hurren raised his baton to, as he had put it, stick the whole thing back together.

The four soloists and the leading violinist from the orchestra were ushered into James Hurren's study after the performance. It had taken some time for the choir to find their belongings and even longer for the orchestra to pack away their instruments and scores. James had made a brief speech congratulating everybody concerned, emphasising that for a student cast to achieve such a high standard of performance was quite exceptional.

He reminded everyone that the public performances were scheduled for Friday and Saturday of the following week, to commence at six o'clock sharp. Ladies were to wear white blouses, while the men were to make sure they had a clean white shirt and dark neck-tie. He insisted that all performers should arrive an hour early and that their families would have free tickets.

After James made sure his guests had a generous glass of sherry and were seated comfortably around the fire-place, he remained standing and obviously had something to say. "When young Tat stopped the show with his 'Confutatis,' I must confess to you that my heart sank. Restarting anything efficiently is hard enough, but a piece on the scale of The Requiem represents a nightmare."

He turned to Joe Forest, the leading violinist from the orchestra and said, "Joe, it was mostly down to the sheer discipline and nerve of you and your musicians that we pulled it off. I want to thank all of you for being so cool, calm and collected."

They all murmured their thanks and covered their embarrassment by draining their glasses. James weaved his way between the armchairs with the decanter and topped them up again. Tat took advantage of the pause. He was still excited at the response to his solo but only too aware of the problems it had caused. Taking a breath, he said, "James, all of you in fact, can I say how sorry I am that my rugby mates got out of hand this evening. They're a smashing lot, but as you now know only too well, a bit rowdy. Honestly, I was mortified."

"Oh come now, Tat," James said urgently. "You weren't responsible for it. You sang beautifully, that's what lit the blue touch paper, no more, no less."

Ben Morgan drained his glass, and shaking his head from side to side said, "I only wish my rugger club from Swansea had been here, I didn't get a peep."

"Now listen," James said as the laughter died down, "You sang your hearts out and even though it was tricky getting a clean start again, you all managed it. The work you did on the second half was outstanding. Anyway, let's face it, did you expect to have so much fun this evening?"

Tat relaxed after this and joined in the general chitchat. He and Ben Morgan exchanged a few rugby stories while James filled their glasses for the last time.

"Now then," he said eventually. "I have one last thing to pass on to you singers. I want you all to go to 'Moss Bros', the outfitters at the top of St Martin's Lane, this Saturday morning. I have arranged for you to be fitted up with evening clothes for the performances next week. Dinner suits and black ties for you two chaps and evening gowns for the ladies. Here, in these envelopes you will find a five-pound note, courtesy of U.C.L., to cover the costs. I should add that Joe and his musicians all have their own evening clothes for their numerous concert performances. Bless you for your hard work, talent and good humour."

Throughout the next day Tat found, to his surprise, that he was the centre of attention. Almost everywhere he went students who had attended the rehearsal told him how much they had enjoyed The Requiem, especially his solo. Frequently, they referred to the spontaneous outburst of applause and what fun it had been. As the day went on any thoughts he had about finding Olly and giving him a dressing down faded. Finally, his singing had been recognized as outstanding and he felt proud of himself. It was just what he needed after the turmoil he had suffered.

DAVID THOMPSON

GOOD NEWS FROM FELL END

He had found a letter from his mother in his pigeon-hole at the hostel next morning. In a gap between lectures he finally had an opportunity to read it, while having a coffee in the refectory.

Dear Tat,

We all hope that you are fit and well. I've got some good news, which might come as a bit of a surprise.

Your Gran has decided that she wants to attend this concert you are singing at. She has brought it up a few times since she first heard about it at Christmas. Anyway you know what she's like when she's made up her mind and gets the bit between her teeth.

She wants Mary and I to come with her on Saturday next, in good time for your performance, stop the night, and then travel back on the Sunday. Can you arrange tickets, and book a couple of rooms in a hotel close by? Your Gran will pay for everything, bless her.

I hope you like the idea. Needless to say I am so nervous that I haven't been able to settle since. Kendal is the furthest I've been and that was only once!

Mary is over the moon about it. I believe she has been to London a couple of times when she was younger. She has offered to make all the arrangements, but would like to talk to you first. She wants you to telephone her and says she's always at home of an evening.

Once Mary has got the go-ahead from you she'll tell your Gran and me what's what. I hope you like the idea Tat. Just being there will be like a dream come true.

All my love, Mam.

Tat read the letter a couple of times and experienced some difficulty taking it all in. It was typical of his Gran to boss everyone around until she got what she wanted. But the idea of his mother plucking up the courage to travel to London when, as she had said, she had only been as far as Kendal, once, in her life, took his breath away. How on earth would she, and his Gran for that matter, cope with it all. He felt humbled to think that they would take on such a challenge just to hear him sing. Mary, of course, would be a Godsend. He would telephone her that evening.

After his last lecture of the day, Tat knocked at Jack Douthwaite's study door. Jack greeted him effusively, "Ah, the conquering hero. Tat my boy come in. I've just made some tea."

"Oh thanks Jack, I'd love some."

"Well Tat, that was quite a performance last night," Jack said, pouring tea for them both. "I've heard about your singing now and again of course, but I had no idea you were so accomplished. It was spectacular."

"Thanks Jack, it did seem to go well."

"I should think so. To my shame, I've never attended any of James Hurren's shindigs before. I had no idea the Choral Society could take on anything on that scale. I was totally flabbergasted, and you, Tat, were the star turn."

"Oh I don't know about that," Tat mumbled, blushing.

"Come on Tat, you brought the house down with that big booming solo of yours. I ought to know, I was right in the middle of it."

"Well yes, that's true, I suppose. I saw you sitting with our lot, just in front of the rugger club."

"Now you can't tell me you weren't pleased with the reception Tat. You must be thrilled to bits by it all."

Tat went on to describe how difficult it was to get a performance like The Requiem started up again after an unplanned interruption. He explained how James Hurren had pulled them through it and how relieved he was that he had taken it all with good grace.

"Well that's James for you, Tat. He's an eccentric sort of a chap, but obviously knows his stuff. Anyway, I was so impressed by it all that I've got tickets for the performance next Saturday."

"That's wonderful Jack. Look, I wonder if you could help me out?" Tat told Jack about the letter he'd received and asked if he could use his telephone to call Mary Hollis.

"Of course you can. I'll slope off to the common room and have a drink. There are a couple of blokes I need to see anyway. I'll be back in half an hour or so." Jack took his leave.

As usual, the telephone connection to the remoter parts of the Eden Valley was hit and miss, to say the least. Eventually the operator at the Penrith exchange announced that she had got through.

"Oh hello Tat, you're quick off the mark. I imagine you've got your mother's letter?"

"Yes, I got it this morning. To tell you the truth, Mary, I can't really believe it's going to happen."

"Well, you know what your Grandma is like, Tat. Your mother told me she first got the idea a few weeks ago and is determined that we get our skates on. Anyway, are you pleased?"

"Oh yes, thrilled to bits. Look, I know you will cope, Mary; I'm just a bit worried about our Mam and Gran. All that travelling and then London, never mind the concert." Tat said anxiously.

"Well, I know your mother's nervous about it, but your Gran doesn't know the meaning of the word. As for me, well I'm so looking forward to it, I can't tell you. Anyway, don't worry Tat, I'll do my best to see that your mother enjoys herself and your grandmother, of course."

"Mam says that you are making the arrangements Mary, but you wanted to speak to me first."

"What we need to know is what time does the concert begin and where exactly is it being held?"

"It's in the main hall here in the college and starts at six, although all of us taking part have to be there at five."

"I've telephoned the station at Kirkby and we can get the seven o'clock train next Saturday morning and be in London at two in the afternoon. Will you be able to meet us at King's Cross, Tat?"

"I certainly will. Our Mam has asked me to book rooms at a hotel close to the college; there are lots near by. We'll get a taxi from King's Cross; it's only a short distance. I'll show you the concert hall and reserve three seats near the front. You'll be able to walk from the hotel to the college for the performance."

"Well, that sounds grand, Tat. Your mother suggests that she and your grandmother share a double room with twin beds and I'll have a single."

"I'll sort it out, Mary. The hotels along Gower Street are small but nice. Lots of people visiting the college and the hospital use them. What time do you start your return journey on the Sunday?"

"Two o'clock, so if we got up early we could go to see Trafalgar Square or the Houses of Parliament perhaps. Your mother and grandmother would love that."

"What a good idea. Look Mary, have you spoken to them about it yet?"

"No, I've only just thought of it."

"I'll tell you what Mary, let's keep it as a surprise. There's hardly any traffic about on a Sunday, especially early on. We could take a horse-drawn cab if the weather's good. There are still some around."

THE FINISHING TOUCHES

Ben Morgan and Tat went to get kitted out at Moss Bros. together. On the few occasions he had been obliged to wear a dinner suit Tat had always borrowed one.

He was looking forward to being measured up professionally and achieving the perfect fit. As he and Ben made their way up St. Martin's Lane, Tat glanced at the headlines on the various newspapers being sold from street kiosks and tobacconists along the way. Even though he was confident that Giles Clinton would have continued to keep his head down over the last few weeks, he still felt slightly anxious in case anything leaked out. As ever, no alarm bells rang out, and he felt sure they never would after so long.

They were shown the various styles of formal evening wear on offer at Moss Bros. and were surprised by the variety of choice. The assistant who dealt with them expressed the opinion that the new double-breasted dinner suit was what most customers required. However, Ben and Tat preferred the classic single-breasted jacket worn with low cut matching waistcoats and stiff-fronted shirts. They chose wing collars and ready made up black bow ties fixed with a small clasp at the back. Neither of them wanted to bother learning the notoriously troublesome discipline of tying the bow themselves.

"Tat," Ben said, "Take my advice and get a collar one size bigger than you normally wear. Your neck swells quite a bit while you're singing. You'll thank me for it, believe me."

Tat asked Jack Douthwaite to help him choose a suitable local hotel for the Westmorland visitors. He knew Jack would have an opinion as he was used to finding accommodation for visiting lecturers and barristers from out of town.

"Oh, I would choose the Bloomsbury Hotel, just down Gower Street, about a hundred and fifty yards over the road, opposite the Anatomy Faculty. Very cosy and welcoming." Jack said, without hesitation.

"I know where it is. I've passed it countless times on the way to the pub."

"Anyway, I've recommended it to scores of folk visiting the college over the years. They all speak well of the place. Oh, yes and the rates are very reasonable."

Tat made the booking that same evening. He was shown the rooms on the first floor overlooking the mews at the back. Jack was right; it was very cosy and welcoming, run by a middle-aged couple who had been there for years apparently. Following his Gran's instructions, passed on through Mary, he ordered afternoon tea, followed by supper to be taken in the dining room after the performance.

THE VISITORS ARRIVE

Tat felt both nervous and excited as he waited by the ticket barrier at King's Cross. Glancing up, yet again, at the huge clock suspended above the platforms, he saw that he still had ten minutes to wait. The place was busy enough but nowhere near as crowded as it was during the morning rush hour. A pall of smutty fumes hung stubbornly below the massive curving glass roof, cutting out most of the natural light.

As he paced to and fro Tat thought back to the performance of The Requiem the previous evening. He still found it hard to believe it had really happened and that he had been part of it. The whole thing had gone like clockwork. All the hard work and effort, the seemingly endless rehearsals and study had resulted in a flawless performance. He felt sure that the look of it all added an extra ingredient which up to then had been missing.

James Hurren had a plan for the public performances, which he had pretty much kept to himself until the full cast of the choir, orchestra and soloists had turned up one hour before the concert was to begin. He decided that as the audience arrived and found their seats, the heavy stage curtains would be fully closed.

At six o'clock, after checking that the audience was fully settled, the curtains would be drawn apart by two of the student volunteers who were involved in various ways behind the scenes. This would reveal the choir and orchestra already established in their positions. After a brief pause, the soloists were to enter simultaneously, the soprano and mezzo-soprano from the left and the tenor and bass-baritone from the right. As they lined up together in the centre of the stage in front of the orchestra, James Hurren was to make his entrance, also from the right and stand facing the audience in front of the soloists. After a second or two James and the male soloists executed a single bow whilst the sopranos curtsied. James had many years of experience in organising musical events within the university and knew that this procedure would stimulate a round of applause.

James Hurren, resplendent in white tie and tails, stepped forward as the clapping subsided and made a short speech of welcome, ending with a subtle reminder that, for the sake of continuity, all applause should be kept on hold until the end of the performance.

Tat had been astonished as to what a huge difference these elements of stage management had made. The whole event seemed to assume a shape and form into which they all fitted. The fact that they were wearing formal evening clothes was the icing on the cake as far as Tat was concerned. James had arranged for the lighting to be dimmed in the auditorium as he raised his baton to cue in the first hushed whispering chords from the violins. You could have heard a pin drop. Tat decided to keep all this to himself so that the full impact would be a complete surprise to his grandmother, his mother and Mary. They would love it all.

Tat saw the Carlisle train edging its way into the cavernous building through gushing clouds of steam and smoke. He fished in his pockets to find his platform ticket just as the grimy hissing engine nosed into the buffers. The first class carriages were always coupled-up immediately behind the engine. Tat walked quickly past these towards the second-class section as the doors began to open and passengers stepped down onto the platform with their luggage. Mary had said they would travel second class. Then, among the confusion of banging doors, porters loading luggage onto trolleys and hissing steam valves, he saw them. How small they looked, or at least his mother and grandmother did; Mary was a good deal taller than both of them.

He reached them before they spotted him. "Hello you lot," he said grinning broadly, "welcome to London."

"Oh, our Tat," his mother said. "Thank goodness you're here, lad. I've never seen such a crush." He took her in his arms whilst she buried her face against his chest then dabbed a few tears away with her handkerchief.

"Now then Gran, what do you make of all this then?"

"Well our Tat, it's a bit bigger than Kirkby station and no mistake, aye, muckier as well."

Turning to Mary, he kissed her on both cheeks and shook her hand.

"What was the journey like, Mary?"

"Oh, we've had sunshine all the way," Mary said, smiling. "There's so much to see."

"Aye, she's given us quite a geography lesson has Mary," his Gran said. "We've been through how many counties, Mary?"

"Oh at least nine, all looking wonderful in the sunshine."

"Come on then," Tat said, "let me carry your bags and we'll find a taxi outside."

"Nay Tat, we'll get a porter to do that," Tat's Gran insisted. "Then me and your Mam can hang on to you in case we get lost."

As they approached the main exit with the porter following close behind, Tat thought he should warn them about the congestion of traffic they would encounter on Euston Road. He knew what a shock it had been to him the first time he had experienced it.

"Listen, the traffic outside will probably strike you as a bit chaotic, but don't worry, they all know what they're doing, we won't come to any harm."

As they joined the short queue at the taxi rank Tat felt his grandmother and his mother grip his arms tightly. They looked in all directions, open-mouthed with shock, even Mary looked concerned.

"Surely we're not getting amongst that lot, Tat? We'll get squashed flat surely," his mother shouted, trying to make herself heard above the snarling roar of the traffic.

"Don't worry, Mam," Tat shouted back. "It looks worse than it is. I've made the trip many a time. Look upon it as an adventure."

The taxi edged its way into the jostling stream of traffic, amidst a cacophony of blaring horns and revving engines. His mother and grandmother kept hold of his hands whilst staring anxiously at the crush of traffic crawling along with them, literally only inches away. Mary seemed quiet as well. London had obviously become a good deal busier since her last visit.

Tat began to point out some of the more impressive landmarks in an attempt to ease the tension.

"Now then, Gran," he said, pointing across the road. "That's St. Pancras Hotel, it has over a thousand rooms, so I'm told."

His grandmother craned across as the enormous building slid by.

"Well, I'm blowed, it looks more like a palace than a hotel; just look at it Ivy. We're not stopping there are we Tat?"

"No don't worry, Gran, I've booked you into something a little smaller than that," Tat said with a chuckle. "There's another railway station behind it, and this, just coming up on the same side, is Euston Station."

"Three stations all on the same street. Well I never," his mother said. It was the first time she had spoken since getting into the taxi. Tat noticed that she was no longer holding his hand quite so tightly.

"Not far to go now, Mam," he said, leaning over to kiss her cheek. A few minutes later they turned left into Gower Street, where the traffic was significantly lighter.

"You know when I was last in London the traffic was all horse-drawn. Just look at it now," Mary said, as a couple of buses came alongside.

"Now then, look to your left, through the gates with the lodges on either side. That's University College, where the concert is tonight. Could you slow down a bit, driver?"

In fact, the driver pulled into the kerb and stopped opposite the college entrance, with the engine running. They all looked across the quadrangle, where students strolled to and fro, or stood chatting in groups, towards the portico with its twelve fluted pillars supporting the triangular pediment and dome.

"My, what a beautiful place it is, Tat. Don't you think so, Ivy?" Mary Hollis said.

"Aye, I do, to think our Tat comes here every day to do his studying. I just can't believe it"

"Somehow I thought it might look a bit like the grammar school at Appleby," Tat's grandmother said. "I'd no idea it would be as grand as this." Just then an imposing figure emerged from the right-hand lodge, dressed in his maroon livery, complete with top hat and gloves. It was 'The Boss', curious to see why the taxi had pulled up outside the gateway.

Tat leaned across and lowered the window, "Afternoon, Boss," he called out cheerfully.

"Ah, Mr. Taylor," the Beadle said in his deep voice. "I didn't see you tucked away amongst these lovely ladies."

"I'm just showing them the College. This is my grandmother, my mother and my former primary school teacher. This is Mr Steadman, known to everyone as the Boss."

The Beadle tipped his hat and said, "I bet I know why you're here ladies, you'll be attending the concert tonight, no doubt."

"Aye, you're right there," Tat's grandmother said, smiling broadly. "We're so much looking forward to it."

"Well, you've got a treat in store, I can tell you," the Boss replied. "I was there last night and this young man is the king pin of the show, believe me."

The taxi drew away and edged through the oncoming traffic in order to pull up outside the Bloomsbury Hotel. Tat helped everybody onto the pavement, then retrieved the bags from the luggage boot and paid the driver.

"Bye, but he's a grand looking chap is that," Tat's grandmother said, gazing back down the way they had come.

"Yes, and he rules the college with a rod of iron, I can tell you," Tat said. "Come on then, let's get you inside."

After the visitors were shown to their rooms, Tat sat in the reception area and smoked a couple of cigarettes whilst flipping through the assortment of magazines scattered across a low table. There was a fire crackling cheerfully in the hearth nearby. He was relieved that the first, and probably the most challenging, hurdle had been tackled successfully. They were here at last, safe and sound.

Half an hour later afternoon tea was served in the sitting room. It turned out to be delicious, with triangular shaped egg and cress sandwiches, scones and fruit cake. His mother seemed to relax as the ordeal of the journey and the taxi ride faded away.

"It's a grand little place is this, Tat," his grandmother commented approvingly. "The rooms are very comfy. Next time we'll stop a bit longer. What do you think, our Ivy? Aye, and it's so quiet, you'd never think all that hustle and bustle was going on outside."

"I can see you've got a taste for London already, Mrs Watson," Mary said, helping herself to a second slice of cake.

Tat glanced at the grandfather clock near the door; it was almost four. Time to get organized. "Now then," he said, "we should make a move shortly. I'm going to take you back to the college, on foot our Mam, so don't worry, to show you where the performance will take place. But first let me tell you about what I've sorted out for tomorrow."

"What's all this then, Tat?" his grandmother asked.

"Well, if we get an early start tomorrow morning, I've got a treat in store for you."

"Could this be a spot of sight-seeing, I wonder?" Mary asked, raising an eye-brow.

"Spot on Mary. It was you who got me thinking about it when we spoke on the phone. Let's have another cup of tea while I tell you about it." Tat lit a cigarette as his mother poured the tea.

"Anyway, one of the other beadles at the college has a brother who runs a horse-drawn cab; you remember seeing the odd one among the traffic today?"

"Aye, goodness knows how they manage among all them motors," his grandmother said, shaking her head.

"Oh, they've been at it for hundreds of years, Gran," Tat replied. "Well, I've booked his cab for seven o'clock tomorrow morning. He'll pick us up here and take us on a grand tour of the sights, finishing up at Lyons Corner House, just down the road for Sunday lunch, before you catch the train back at King's Cross." Tat glanced at his mother, who was looking anxious again, and said, "Don't worry Mam, we'll have the roads to ourselves on a Sunday morning and the weather's going to be fine."

"Go on then," Mary said, obviously thrilled at the prospect. "Tell us what we're going to see."

"Oh we'll have enough time to see everything: Piccadilly Circus, Trafalgar Square, down Whitehall to the Houses of Parliament, then round by Buckingham Palace. Of course there's the Tower of London and St Paul's Cathedral as well as the docks where all the ships are. It'll be grand."

"Somebody pinch me," his mother said, her eyes wide with anticipation. "I must be dreaming."

The Boss tipped his hat to them once more as they passed between the lodges and crossed the quadrangle. The place was more or less deserted by now. The main entrance to the left of the portico led straight into the wide, airy corridor which connected the whole of the central flank of University College. Turning right it was only a short walk until they reached the curving twin staircases, which converged together on the first floor in front of the entrance to the college library. Between them the double doors to the main hall stood open. Tat gave them a moment or two to take in the grandeur of the huge space, with its moulded ceiling and row upon row of identical seats, all facing the stage. The stage curtains were drawn, as Tat knew they would be. He led the way down the central aisle and stopped at the third row from the front.

"There you are," Tat said, indicating the three end seats to their right. They each had a card with 'RESERVED' printed upon it, resting on the seat. "This is where you will sit. I know for a fact that the view is excellent from here."

"Eh, our Tat lad," his grandmother said. "You've come a long way from Fell End and no mistake." With that she hugged him tightly.

He accompanied them to the hotel, making sure they would remember the way back, "We don't want to send the beadles out in a search party, now do we?"

"Mind you, I'm glad it's only a short walk away," Tat's mother said. Lastly he took out his wallet and found the three tickets for the performance.

"Who's going to take charge of these then? Just give them to the lass on the door."

"Oh it had better be Mary," his grandmother said. "She's the one with the brains."

"I suggest you take your seats at about five thirty or so, then you can watch everybody turning up and get comfortable," Tat said, as they stopped on the pavement outside the hotel.

"What sort of supper do you think they'll give us later on then?" his grandmother asked.

"Well Gran, everybody speaks very highly of the place. Why don't you have a look at the menu in the mean time?"

"Good idea, I'll get some wine sorted out as well, after all we'll be celebrating won't we?"

Tat gave them all a hug and hurried off, realizing he was ten minutes late. As he went backstage to the dressing room he shared with Ben Morgan, he could hear the orchestra tuning up. He was amazed at how the discordant caterwauling gradually melted away until every instrument settled accurately on the note 'A'. Not for the first time he felt admiration for Joe Forest who made it happen with such consummate ease.

As he left the dressing room in his beautifully fitted evening suit, he almost collided with Ben Morgan as he bustled in, looking flustered and out of breath.

"Hello mate, the traffic jams are murder out there I honestly thought I was going to miss the boat".

Tat continued on his way to the stage where the choir was climbing carefully onto the scaffolding tiers. James Hurren was trying to be everywhere at once, as usual.

Tat approached the curtains so that he could look through the peephole. The auditorium was filling up with ever more people making their way forward to find their seats. To his great relief, he saw his grandmother, his mother and Mary already established next to the central aisle in the third row. They were wearing their best frocks and had tidied their hair. His mother, in particular, looked around frequently at the gathering crowd. He could already picture her describing it all to his father and brothers. Bless them, he thought; if it hadn't been for the determination and affection of these three women, he wouldn't be here at all.

He felt a tap on his shoulder and there was James holding a finger up to his lips and gesturing towards the wings on the right of the stage. Once there, James whispered close to his ear, "Pop back to your dressing room and hurry Ben up, Tat, there's a good chap. We've got less than five minutes."

He entered the dressing room to find Ben struggling with the clasp of his bow tie.

"Thank goodness, Tat, do this blessed thing up for me, will you?"

Then they looked in the mirror together, "Not bad for a couple of out of towners, eh?" Ben said smiling broadly. Then, rummaging in his jacket pocket, he added, "Have a sip of this."

He unscrewed the cap from a battered hip flask and they quickly drained its fiery contents between them, before hurrying to re-join James, who immediately signalled for the curtains to be drawn back.

As he and Ben walked towards the centre of the stage to join the female soloists he muttered, "Come on then Ben, let's give it to them with both barrels."

THE END

Acknowledgements

I would like to express my gratitude to the following people for their encouragement, patience and practical help:

My brother Peter Thompson;

My wife Rebecca and our son Ben;

My grown up son Oliver;

Brian Campbell, Glenys Lumley, Gill Prett, the late John Douthwaite, Stephen Walker, Sandra Hemstock, Lucy Hemstock, Erik and Barbara Thompson, John Calvett, Robert Bryan, Alison Fairhurst and Sue Skelton.

Especial thanks to:

George and Carolyn Hill, Adrian Dawson and Jo Sayer: for their time, enthusiasm and expertise.